FIRE AND ADJUST

Daniel N. Brockington

ORANGE DOOR BOOKS

To the men and women in uniform, whose sacrifices go beyond the battle-field, and whose struggles are often unseen but never forgotten. This book is for those fighting to heal, to rebuild, and to find peace. May you always know that you are not alone in your journey.

To the ones who carried me when I couldn't carry myself, who stood by me when I needed strength the most, and whose wisdom shaped me into the man I am today —I owe you more than words can express.

To my beloved Wife, whose unwavering love and support carried me through every dark moment and showed me the light in the midst of the storm.

Contents

[PREFACE]

THE HÜRTGEN FOREST IS a place that holds the weight of history. Its ancient trees and thick fog have borne witness to one of the longest and bloodiest battles of World War II. Between September and December 1944, American and German forces clashed relentlessly within its dense woods. The Battle of Hürtgen Forest was brutal, lasting 88 days, and leaving behind scars that time cannot fully erase. For the soldiers who fought there, it was a fight not only against the enemy but against the forest itself. A place so unforgiving it became as much an adversary as any soldier in a uniform.

Over the course of this grueling battle, the U.S. First Army suffered staggering losses, with up to 55,000 casualties. The Allies sought to clear the Germans from this vital terrain, hoping to secure their advance toward the Rur River. But the cost was steep. So many lives were lost the forest seemed to swallow them whole. It was a battle that would ultimately fade from the public consciousness, overshadowed by the more widely known Battle of the Bulge.

Somehow the ghosts of this battle remain. The forest has never truly forgotten what happened there. Even today, unexploded ordinance from that time still lurks beneath the earth, a silent menace that occasionally claims the lives of those who live in or visit the area. Tank tracks, helmets, weapons, and uniforms, all relics of a war long past, can still be found among the trees. They serve as stark reminders of the violence that once unfolded there.

In this book, I have woven together the echoes of history with a tale of those who still bear the weight of the past. The ghosts of the Hürtgen

Forest are not just in the land or in the metal remnants scattered across the ground; they are in the minds of those who were there, and those who have come after. The trauma, the guilt, and the haunting are not confined to history. They endure, sometimes in ways we cannot explain, and they continue to shape us, even when we think we've moved beyond them.

Though the battle ended over 75 years ago, the forest still remembers. Time may heal some wounds, but others only grow deeper, twisting into something far darker than we could ever imagine. As you step into this story, know that the forest still watches, and the past is never as far behind us as we might hope.

"We're all ghosts. We all carry, inside us, people who came before us."

— Liam Callanan in "The Cloud Atlas"

[PROLOGUE]

WAR DEPARTMENT
UNITED STATES ARMY
OFFICE OF THE ASSISTANT CHIEF OF STAFF, G-2
SECURITY AND INTELLIGENCE DIVISION
WASHINGTON, D.C.
December 27, 1944
MEMORANDUM FOR RECORD
SUBJECT: CLASSIFICATION AND REDACTION ORDER

Following a formal investigation into the events occurring between December 16, 1944, and December 20, 1944, in the vicinity of Hürtgen Forest, Germany, it is the determination of this office that all references, reports, and records concerning the M4A3E8 'Easy Eight' Sherman tank, designation **Calculated Vengeance**, assigned to **Bravo Company, 3rd Battalion, 8th Armored Regiment, 3rd Armored Division**, are to be immediately classified under War Department Directive 210-44.

The crew of Calculated Vengeance is hereby listed as follows:

Tank Commander: Staff Sergeant James Casey

Gunner: Sergeant Vince Harris

Driver: Private First Class Richard "Rich" Thompson

Loader: Private Anthony "Fitz" Fitzsimmons

Assistant Driver: Private Thomas "Tommy" Reynolds

Any mention of this vehicle, its crew, or its last known operational status shall be redacted from all official reports, records, and archives. Existing documentation, including field reports, radio transcripts, and eyewitness statements, will be transferred to restricted archives under Section IV, "Classified Intelligence Files," and sealed indefinitely.

Personnel directly involved in the incident are hereby ordered to cease all discussion regarding this matter under penalty of court-martial pursuant to Army Regulations 380-5 and WPB 12-13. Any inquiries into the status or fate of the aforementioned tank and crew are to be met with the standard response of "**No Records Exist.**"

This directive is effective immediately and shall remain in force until further notice. Any unauthorized attempt to access, distribute, or disclose classified material related to this case will be met with maximum punitive measures under the Articles of War.

Maurice Rose

Major General

3rd Armored Division, Commanding General

NORTH ATLANTIC TREATY ORGANIZATION

SUPREME HEADQUARTERS ALLIED POWERS EUROPE

OFFICIAL NATO ORDERS

Classification: NATO RESTRICTED

Reference No.: NATO/SHAPE/OPORD 2024-17-1889

Date: 10 December 2024

SUBJECT: Deployment Orders – U.S. Army M1A2 SEP V3 Abrams Main Battle Tank "Controlled Violence"

Pursuant to NATO Directive 404/24 and in accordance with the established framework of the NATO International Armored Competition, the following tank crew of the United States Army is hereby ordered to participate in all scheduled exercises, trials, and live-fire events conducted under NATO supervision in the Federal Republic of Germany, effective immediately.

Unit Designation – Order of Battle

Vehicle: M1A2 SEP V3 Abrams, call sign "Controlled Violence"

Assigned Unit: Bravo Company, 3rd Battalion, 8th Cavalry Regiment, 3rd Armored Brigade Combat Team, 1st Cavalry Division, United States Army

Crew Manifest – M1A2 SEP V3 Abrams "Controlled Violence"

Tank Commander (SSG): Staff Sergeant Jack Michael Carson

Gunner (SGT): Sergeant Ryan Turner

Driver (SPC): Specialist Victor "Vic" Hayes

Loader (PVT2): Private Two Aaron "Fitz" Fitzgerald

This crew is designated **Team Eagle** (United States of America - Army) and will serve as the sole representative armored element of the United States Army for the duration of the competition. All results, observations, and records pertaining to their performance are to be compiled for review by the Allied Armored Systems Evaluation Board.

By Order of:

General Philippe Lavigne

Supreme Allied Commander Europe (SACEUR)

[ANNOTATION – ADDED 27 DECEMBER 2024]

Per NATO Classification Directive 28/52-A4 Section 3b, all data and documentation related to the previously mentioned Team Eagle's activities, including, but not limited to, any operational reports, communications logs, and after-action reviews, shall remain classified at the **NATO SECRET** level pending the outcome of ongoing the investigation into anomalous incidents reported during the course of NATO operations. Unauthorized discussion or disclosure of said activities is strictly prohibited under NATO Security Protocol, Section IX.

[CHAPTER ONE:
THE TANKER'S
PLAYGROUND]

"Halfway down the trail to Hell,"

14 DECEMBER 2024

"Dismissed."

The Bundeswehr officer's voice cracks like a gavel. He's been reading the briefing like it offends him personally, and the second he is done, he bolts from the tent without so much as a nod.

Cold air slams into me the moment I step outside. Not the dry kind, either, this is that damp, bone-sinking chill that laughs at jackets. My breath fogs in the stillness, curling into the wind before vanishing. Engines idle somewhere behind the treeline, a low, distant growl, as if the forest is trying to mimic us.

I pivot toward my crew and our tank. Even with jet lag chewing at the corners of my brain, adrenaline surges. We've trained for this. We live for this. This isn't just another competition. This is **the** international event. NATO's finest, one team per country. And we're it. The only American crew.

The flags lining the garrison grounds snap in the breeze—Britain, Germany, Canada, Norway, Sweden, and a dozen more. Ours stands dead center, defiant in the icy gusts.

I catch sight of the other tank crews speaking a dozen languages as I make my way down the line. Soldiers move between the vehicles, their voices mixing with the sharp scent of diesel and the distant clatter of maintenance crews making final checks. Most huddle near their tanks, sipping coffee and pretending they aren't freezing. The others are looking over their shoulders and sizing each other up without trying to look like they are.

The lineup of tanks looks like a war museum with an ego problem. German-made Leopard variants everywhere. Unfortunate, but no surprise there. Next to the line of Leopards, the Brits park their Challenger like it deserves a parade. Sleek, massive, smug. The French hang around their Leclerc. It's boxy, overdesigned, and still somehow still acting as if it's superior. Our Abrams squats at the end like it owns the place. Heavy, loud, unapologetic. Just how I like it. The tanks are lined up like a photo from a military history textbook. But, I'm not here for trivia—I'm here to prove that our Abrams, our crew, our flag, can go toe-to-toe with any of them.

Each team competing mirrors its machine in some way. The Brits are all business, barely speaking. The French crew is laughing, like they've already won. The Germans? Rigid. Like their tanks. Norway and Denmark mingle freely, throwing in quiet jokes.

And at the very end of the tank line, the new blood.

Finland and Sweden—brand new NATO members, yet standing like they've been here all along. Calm, cool, confident. They aren't here to prove that they're better. Just to show it. I respect that.

My eyes finally settle ahead on my tank, *Controlled Violence*. It looks mean, even parked. As I approach, I see the rest of my crew lounging around the tank, sipping lukewarm coffee and eating their cold breakfasts.

Vic's on the back deck already, checking oil levels like it's Sunday morning and this thing is a Harley. He never stops working. Can't. Vic used to be a mechanic before he joined us in the turret. Still acts like one most of the time. His hands are always in the guts of the tank, and frankly? I'm glad. He makes sure she runs like a dream.

"Mount up, boys," I call, stepping onto the freezing slope of the tank.

Turner flicks the last of his cigarette onto the ground and grinds it out with his boot. "Bet the new guy's still dreaming about boot camp. You don't even have a combat patch, isn't that right, little slick-sleeve?"

Fitz looks up from his MRE bar, unamused. "Hey, I've seen some stuff, alright? I grew up in Chicago!"

Fitz squares up to Turner attempting to look as if he's preparing for a fight, but he somehow manages to look like a young puppy squaring up to a bear. "Back in high school, this kid pulled a knife in the cafeteria while brawling with someone that he was bullying. Cops had to come and everything. I'm pretty sure the kid he pulled the knife on went to the hospital even."

Turner snorts. "Aw, look at that! Our little war pup got his first scar story."

Turner stretches, cracking his back against the turret. "Tell me when you've seen so much 'stuff' you start forgetting which parts actually happened."

Fitz frowns. "I'm just saying. I've been in it."

Turner grins. "Kid, I believe you. But let me tell you something. When you've really been in it, you stop trying to convince people you have."

Vic leans over the side of the tank, oil rag in hand. "Can we all just agree none of us joined for the food?"

I laugh. "Or the pay."

Turner nods. "Or lifelong back problems."

Fitz mutters, "Still better than working retail."

I grin. "Glad we all survived our traumatic pasts. Now how about we act like professionals for five minutes?"

Turner, lounging like he has nowhere to be, raises an eyebrow. "You were at that briefing long enough, Sergeant. Get lost on the way to meeting your ego?"

Fitz, from his perch on the front slope, jumps in with a smirk. "Or maybe he was rereading the manual on how **not** to throw track on the first obstacle."

Vic groans and rubs his face. "*One* time—and it wasn't my fault. That ditch came out of nowhere." He shoots a look at Turner. "And **someone** was too busy running his mouth on the radio to call out the obstacle."

Turner chuckles. "I called it. You just ignored it. It's not my fault you learned how to go deaf to my gorgeous voice."

Vic points a finger at him. "The maintenance guys had to tow us out in front of Red Platoon. I'll never live that down."

Turner shrugs. "You're lucky all I had to bribe them with was beer. I was this close to throwing in Fitz."

Fitz grins. "Joke's on you. I would've helped push."

I let their banter roll over me. It's a familiar rhythm that grounds everything we do. Same crew, same energy. Exactly how I like it.

After the chuckles die down, I pull out my notes from the earlier briefing and get down to business.

"Alright, boys and girls of all ages, here's the deal," I say, thumbing through my notes. "The first stage of the competition is something they call 'The Playground.' It's basically a driving course. Obstacles. Mud. Stuff to crush."

I glance around, noticing the only one actually paying attention and heading to his station is Vic.

"And we get to blow stuff up," I add with a grin, raising my voice enough to hopefully catch their attention.

This finally earns the spark between the last two brain cells of my unashamed favorite amongst the crew. Sergeant Ryan Turner, our gunner. He's a Samoan, built like a boulder at 5'7" and 250 pounds of pure muscle. He shoots like a man who's seen a thousand firefights and walked away from all of them. If someone told me he had over a hundred confirmed kills, I'd believe it—hell, the real number is probably more. At least, that's what the Bronze Star on his dress uniform convinces me of.

His skill is not luck—it's calculation. Around the Battalion footprint, he's a myth in uniform. Some say he was born with a rifle in hand. And honestly? They might be right. Physics tends to lose when Turner takes the shot.

I flash him a grin. "Relax, I'm messing with you. It's just a driving course. But now that I've got your attention, you can start cleaning up this mess." I gesture to the assortment of energy drink cans, protein bar wrappers, and dip cans scattered across the front of the tank.

The crew grumbles but gets to work, clambering onto the tank to gather the litter and shove it into a bag. They toss it into the spare road wheel we keep on top of the turret. Not only is it our spare but it's also our little makeshift trash can. It doesn't take long before the front of the tank is cleared, and everyone is in position. The snow begins to fall softly, large flakes drifting down in the gray morning light. I glance at my notes and read off the radio frequency we were briefed on earlier.

Fitz dials it into the radio that sits within the Loader's station. He's eager and works hard, but he's still green and his inexperience is obvious at times, but he makes up for it in enthusiasm and the occasional comedic relief.

After loading the radio with its fill he fights with the back of the loader's seat trying to get it to lay flat and, after many swear words were shouted, eventually he's able to get it to work. By flattening it to use as a makeshift stool, the loader is able to stand up, and help the commander with spotting obstacles and navigation. It also means he'll be with me in being half-exposed to the frigid German winter.

Without prompting, Vic hits the starter. The turbine whines—the jet engine is clearly having a bad day—then it coughs out a cloud thick enough to choke a moose. The EPA would have a stroke watching this thing breathe. I guess the engineers who designed it didn't have the environment on their minds when they drew up the plans.

The plume of exhaust curls into the trees, disappearing just as fast as it was produced. I pause for a moment, squinting at the treeline.

No birds. No wind. Just a weird, breathless silence. The whole damn place is holding its breath.

For a second, I think I see something move between the trunks. Just a flicker. A shape of some sort. But it's gone before I can blink. I shake it off. Probably jet lag. Or some afternoon shadows.

But what sticks with me is the silence. The kind that makes you feel that ***you're the thing out of place***.

I quickly get out of my head and run a comms check, making sure everyone's plugged in and the radio's on the right frequency.

"Alright, crew, can you hear me loud and clear?"

Turner's voice crackles in my ear. "Loud and clear, Sarge. Just like your morning breath."

"Good to know you're still alive. What about my other two knuckleheads?"

Vic very audibly settles into his station, "Yeah, yeah. I'm here. And I'm *not* putting us in a ditch this time—promise."

"And Fitz?"

"Just along for the ride, Sergeant."

"Good to hear. Let's have a nice, easy ride, folks."

Turner grins and aims his next comment low. "That's what your sister said. You know, the last time I visited."

"Yeah, keep it up, and I'll make you all walk back to the barracks," I shoot back into the comms.

The first tank from the left rumbles to life, kicking up a cloud of snow as it rolls toward the "Playground".

After about an hour of driving through the picturesque, snow-covered German countryside, we finally reach the track. Everyone pulls into a small parking area where the tanks will stage while waiting for their turn to tackle the course.

The lot is a simple concrete pad just big enough for each tank to have its own space. At one end of the pad, a narrow two-lane road leads into the assembly area, while a small, dirt tank trail exits at the other end, winding its way toward the driving course. Beside the mouth of the trail, a table is set up with a few senior officers and event planners hurriedly assembling a large stopwatch for the course. The table is cluttered with maps, radios, and notepads, all strewn about in a disorganized frenzy as the start of the event approaches. Everything is held down by steaming thermoses and fluttering in the icy wind.

After what feels like only minutes of being in the area, the first tank pulls up to the starting line and comes to a stop. It's the British crew in their white-painted Challenger 2 sitting heavy at 69 tons, the engine humming as it prepares to take on the course. At the sound of the starter pistol, the tank lurches forward, charging down the trail and quickly vanishing behind the trees.

Since our tank is last on the roster, we have plenty of time to shut down the engine and either chat with the other crews or relax while we wait our turn.

"Give it two, Vic," I say calmly.

The Abrams needs time to spin down—like a pissed-off turbine winding itself to sleep. We **could** double-tap the kill switch, but then the engine throws a tantrum and someone ends up writing a maintenance report.

I hop off the side to stretch my legs and hopefully get the opportunity to get into one of our competitors' vehicles. You know, for science.

The Leopard next to us idles and begins judging everything in sight. Its body is covered in sharp lines, and an ice-cold posture. Even parked, it looks ready to break ribs.

"Staff Sergeant Carson," I introduce myself to the tank's commander, offering a hand.

"Oberfeldwebel Vogel." He grips my hand with confidence and a smile that doesn't quite reach his eyes. "How are you finding our lovely countryside? I grew up around here," he says, gesturing to the rolling hills and trees that surround the assembly area.

"Nice country," I reply. "Looking forward to getting a hike in, maybe check out trails in the Hürtgen Forest."

Vogel's body language instantly shifts. He folds his arms and eyes me uneasily.

"Be careful in the Hürtgenwald," his voice is harsh. Cold. Flat. "We don't go there. Not unless we have to."

Before I can muster any sort of questions, one of his crew members speaks to him in their native language. His gaze returns to me, and he offers a sad attempt at a smile before abruptly climbing back onto his tank, speaking to his crew.

I return to my tank and settle onto my favorite spot on the turret. What is it about that forest that makes it so disliked by Vogel? Is it a painful memory from his past? A local myth or superstition? The possibilities swirl in my mind.

I lean back against the tarp-wrapped duffle bags resting in the bustle rack and stare at the treeline. His warning hangs in the air like a fog. Something about it is stuck in my mind and is impossible to shake.

"Sergeant," Fitz begins, shaking me a bit hard. "Sergeant."

I sit up slowly, groaning. "What, Fitz?" I hadn't realized I had fallen asleep. I guess the jet lag and exhaustion from lack of sleep finally got to me.

Fitz crouches low beside me, helmet in hand. "Sergeant. We're up."

He hands me my CVC helmet, and I begrudgingly pull it on. I faintly hear radio chatter in the background. It takes a moment for my tired brain to register the words.

I press the button on the mic. "This is Team Eagle Actual. Was I being called? Over." My voice is thick, barely more than a groggy mumble.

"Finally. It's your turn, chaps. Line up and prepare to tackle the Playground. Out." The voice crackles over the radio, dripping with the unmistakable tone of an aristocratic British Officer who was born with a silver spoon.

I glance over at the table, where one of the officers holds a starting pistol and a clipboard, his eyes fixed directly on us. His body language is clear. We're behind schedule. Not the impression I want to make, especially on the first event.

"Vic, get her running! Everyone mount up!" I bark, rushing to the commander's hatch. I climb in quickly, settling into my station as I prepare for the driving course ahead. If we're late, then they could deduct points from our overall score, which could cost us the competition.

No matter how prepared I feel, a slick of sweat creeps down my spine. I still feel the need to perform—excel, even. The tank lurches into motion toward the starting line. It's too late to worry now. We're in it. No turning back.

We line up, the engine rumbling under us as we come to a stop just behind the starting line. I look at the table and I give them a quick thumbs-up. The officer with the starting pistol acknowledges with a nod, and raises the starting pistol high into the air. There's a sharp crack as the shot pierces the cold air.

The tank lurches forward with a force that throws me back as we begin to surge down the trail, the vibrations of the tank reverberating through every inch of my body. The ground beneath us seems to disappear and reappear with every bump and jolt as we pick up speed, the cold wind whipping around the turret.

The first turn comes quickly, a gradual S-curve just fifty meters ahead. The path narrows, and I can see the dirt winding around like a serpent, scarred with tracks from other tanks. As we navigate the bend, the track opens up again, and ahead of us looms a massive mound of dirt. It's worn down from the dozens of crews that have gone before us. It's the kind of obstacle that you expect in a course like this, designed to challenge the suspension and test the tank's agility.

We hit the berm at full speed. No hesitation. The engine screams, the front of the tank lifts, and suddenly, we're airborne. My stomach lurches. Vic was supposed to slow down. Ease over it. What the hell is he doing?

Then, with a violent crash, the tank slams back down. The impact sends a jolt through my knees, my spine so harsh I feel it in my teeth. Pain flashes up my back like a warning shot. For a second, I can't even breathe. Not from fear, but from the sharp, white-hot certainty that something important just shifted.

The first thought that breaches the haze isn't to scold Vic for driving like a lunatic—it's the inevitable letter I'll get from the VA in five to ten years: "*Your injuries are not service-connected.*"

"I know it's your time to shine, Vic, but just please don't break anything you can't fix!" I shout into the microphone, trying to shake it off.

We rumble forward, the terrain shifting with every turn. The path narrows into twisting trails that snake for miles, each bend another chance for disaster. Trenches, narrow bridges, boulders. Vic handles them with a kind of chaotic grace. Fitz calls out now and then, giving Vic updates on the loader's side, while I stay locked in on the commander's.

The course opens up into a long, straight stretch of trail, the terrain firming up beneath the tank as we hurtle toward a low water crossing nestled at the bottom of a small ravine. Vic doesn't slow down. We hit the water in our freight train of death. Cold spray blasts up over the hull and slaps me in the face. Fitz yells something that sounds a shout of joy mixed with the sound of a squealing hog.

Once we're clear of the ravine, my eyes snap to the sharp left-hand turn carved into the hillside above. It's tighter than I expected. It's sharper, steeper, no margin for error. If Vic overshoots even a little, we're rolling.

I brace hard, white-knuckling the seat as the tank lurches into the turn. The treads bite into the dirt, suspension groaning under the weight.

But we hold. We power through. The tank claws its way up the slope, cresting the bank on the other side.

I start to lean forward to call out the next turn.

And then I see it.

At first, it looks like an old, rusted army jeep. Half-sunk in mud and debris, its frame barely visible through the overgrowth. But as we close the distance, a cold unease settles in. What the hell is it doing out here? Why is no one stopping us? Why hasn't Range Control flagged it?

The sight sharpens, and there's no denying it now—it's real. Battle-worn. Battered. Abandoned right in the middle of the course.

We're barreling toward it at full speed. And no one's saying a damn thing.

The Jeep sits in the middle of the tank trail like a forgotten corpse, half-sunk into the damp earth, its frame skeletal under a layer of moss and rot. I begin to think that it's a part of the course as an obstacle for us to avoid. But then I notice that it isn't rusted like it should be if it had been sitting on this course for years. At least not fully. The olive drab paint clings stubbornly to the metal, faded but eerily intact, as if time had considered claiming it but changed its mind. It looks *hollow*, like a shell of something that should have mattered, but doesn't anymore. The air around seems as if it's still, voiceless. The forest itself is holding its breath, waiting to see who will dare get closer.

"Drive around it," My voice is calm and commanding.

Vic reacts expertly and begins maneuvering the tank to avoid the large, shadowy shape blocking the middle of the trail. We power around it, Vic's hands steady on the controls as we skirt the obstruction, but my mind is racing.

But when I turn to look back—

Nothing.

Just the trail. Empty.

Tracks in the mud show where we'swerved. But the jeep? Gone.

I rub my eyes.

Maybe I'm tired. Maybe it's nothing.

But my gut says otherwise.

We finish the course in a blur. 46:14 on the clock. Fifth overall.

I climb down, still emotionally shaken. Vogel stands nearby, clipboard in hand.

"You guys ran clean," he said. "No penalties."

"We swerved for a jeep halfway through," I said. "Didn't want to hit it. Looked abandoned."

Vogel frowned. "There's no jeep on the course."

"It was there. We dodged it. Vic saw it. I saw it."

He glanced at the forest.

"Sometimes kids sneak in from the villages. Old parts get dragged around. Maybe it was that."

But his voice lacks conviction. His eyes linger too long on the trees.

"Be careful where you look out here, Carson," he says, turning away.

I chuckle and quickly try to change the subject. "You're lucky. You must've done this course hundreds of times."

He looks up and feigns a grin. "Not hundreds... maybe thousands," he tries to say as friendly as he's able to muster. "Either way, you guys finished fifth overall. First in the Abrams category." He flips open his notebook to show me the rankings. It's not the best start, but at least we aren't last.

I raise an eyebrow, still confused. "Uh, we're the only Abrams here," I remind him, the puzzlement creeping into my voice.

Vogel's lips curl into a thin, almost mischievous smile. "Ah, *ja*, I know," he says, his accent thickening just a touch for effect. "You see, we like to win... but we also like to make sure you don't *feel* like you lost too badly."

He turns to walk away, his chuckle trailing behind him like a low rumble. "Is it not funny?"

After a few moments, the order is given over the radio for all the crews to mount up and begin to form a single-file line, and make their way back to the garrison where the barracks are located. The drive back feels long, the weight of the day's events hanging heavy.

Once we finally return, I head straight for the barracks. I strip off my gear and jump into a hot shower, hoping it'll wash away the tension in my muscles.

Afterward, I collapse onto my bed and pull out my laptop. As I flip it open, the black screen stares back at me. The image of the jeep hovers in my mind. Its hollow frame. The way it seemed to exist outside of time, untouched by rust yet heavy with decay. Like something pulled forward from the past that didn't want to be seen.

I blink, rubbing my temples. I should be thinking about scores. About the next course. But that thing is lodged in my brain like shrapnel.

I need to know.

I open a new tab.

Hürtgen Forest history

I'm not sure what I expect to find. But I have a feeling whatever was out there—

It isn't finished with us yet.

[CHAPTER TWO: FROZEN LACES AND BROKEN BOOTS]

"In a shady meadow green"

14 December 1944

"Sergeant?" The voice, though far off, reaches me.

"Sergeant?" Again, requesting my attention from afar.

Returning to reality, I feel the heavy weight of exhaustion. My eyes settle on a young soldier standing in front of me, stewing in nervousness. He doesn't look a day older than eighteen, hell maybe not even that. His face is fresh, untouched by the grime and stubble that marks the rest of us. There's not a single shadow of a beard on his chin, just smooth, unblemished skin. His helmet sits awkwardly on his head, a bit oversized, like a kid playing dress-up in his father's uniform.

I study him closer, the way he grips his duffle bag tight against his chest, knuckles white. The way his lips press together, like he's trying to keep them from quivering. He hasn't been here long. Probably just arrived as a recent replacement. A week? Maybe less. I'd bet my last dollar he hasn't even fired a rifle outside of basic training, that is if he even went to basic. Christ, he likely lied about his age just to get here, desperate to prove himself in a war that doesn't care how old he is. I sigh, rubbing the bridge of my nose. I've seen boys like him before, too many times. I know how this ends.

"Sorry, what?" The response comes after a few moments.

"Your new assistant driver… PFC Tommy Reynolds." He speaks softly enough that I can't fully hear him over the distant sound of artillery fire and the constant ringing in my ears. He clutches his spotless duffle like it's a lifeline—fresh off the boat, no doubt.

I eventually register what the young man is saying. I am whole-heartedly exhausted from constant fighting for the last day and a half. We've had under an hour's rest since the relentless assault and freezing temperatures began.

Together, we make our way towards the group of M4A3E8 "Easy Eight" Sherman tanks.

"That's home." I say, talking towards the kid without realizing he probably doesn't realize which tank I'm speaking about. I follow up with the name of our metal coffin. "*Calculated Vengeance.*"

The M4 Sherman isn't a bad tank, not by any means. It's reliable, easy to fix, and fast enough to get us where we need to go. But against the Germans' newer armor, it's showing its age. A regular Sherman, especially the older models with their thin armor, doesn't stand a chance against a Panther or a Tiger front-on. The new German armor usually causes 75mm shells to harmlessly bounce off. Then the German 88mm from a Tiger bites back and tears through a Sherman like it's made of tin. Plenty of good crews have been lost that way.

That's why the M4A3E8, the Easy Eight, is a godsend. When they gave us *Calculated Vengeance*, it was the best shot we had at coming out of this war in one piece. It's heavier, standing at over forty-two tons. But with that extra weight comes armor that can actually take a hit. The frontal plate is nearly double that of a regular Sherman, and it sports a massively improved turret with even more steel, making it damn near impervious to anything short of a direct, close-range hit from an 88. They also added a high-velocity 76mm gun. It isn't perfect, but it gives us a fighting chance. At the right range, with the right shot, we can punch through a Panther or even a Tiger before they do the same to us. It's still not an unstoppable juggernaut—in fact, it's far from it. But it's tougher, deadlier, and just durable enough to keep us in the fight. And in this war, that's the best we can hope for.

Once we arrive at the Easy Eight that we call home, it's obvious that the rest of the crew is lying about on top of the tank struggling to stay awake. The gunner, Vince Harris, is the most weary looking of them all. Understandably so. The last 24 hours had him shooting the co-ax machine gun and the main gun nearly constantly. He's been hosing down the enemy troop positions and foxholes just to provide covering fire for the accompanying infantry while they attempt to make some sort of push through this horrific white hellscape.

Calculated Vengeance sits where I left her, a battered but unbroken beast of steel and grime. Her thick, sloped armor is scarred with the day's violence. It's covered in shiny streaks where enemy rounds had kissed the armor but failed to bite. Its wide, heavy tracks are caked in mud and torn-up earth, a testament to the hell we had pushed her through. The long 76mm gun juts forward, soot-streaked from the countless shells she had thrown towards the enemy. The added weight of her reinforced hull makes her squat lower than the standard Shermans, giving her a defiant, immovable presence. She is ugly in the way only a mother could love. There's only a little original paint that is barely visible under the mud. Matching scorch marks and mud cake the outside. On the scuffed edges is her name painted in white bold letters. There's a faint scent of burnt oil and cordite that clings to her like a second skin. Despite her shortcomings, she's our pride and joy. And as exhausted as I am, as soon as my boots hit the hull, I feel a litt le safer.

I climb onto the front of the tank, glancing over at our new hull gunner, Tommy. He stands there, staring at the vehicle in awe. Without a word, I motion for him to climb up. He slings his bag toward me, and I catch it, setting it on the turret. When I look back, he's scrambling up the front of the tank, trying, and failing, to keep his uniform clean from the mud. Once on top, he pauses, taking in the scene: spent shell casings litter every inch of the vehicle. Like turret lizards, the rest of the crew sprawls out, soaking up the small amount of sun that peaks through the clouds.

"Where's my... spot? Is that what you call it?" he asks nervously.

I gesture toward the front right hull of the tank. The assistant driver's position. "That's your seat. Your job's simple: keep that bow machine gun singing when the enemy shows up." I tap the metal beside the hatch. "When you climb in, etch out the last guy's initials and scratch yours into the wall. Tradition."

"What happened to..." Tommy starts, but our driver, Rich, cuts him off.

"Shot in the face. Didn't get his hatch closed fast enough when we took contact," Rich says, his tone flat, matter-of-fact. He doesn't sit up, doesn't even look at the new guy.

Silence lingers, heavy and awkward. Then, after a beat, Rich finally adds, almost like an afterthought, "He was funny, too."

Before we can continue with the "introductions," our platoon's baby-faced Second Lieutenant rushes over to my tank, his boots squelching in the mud.

"Sergeant Casey!" he calls out, a little too eager. "Sergeant Casey!"

I sigh, biting back my first response. "What is it, sir?" I manage, keeping my tone just this side of respect. It's nearly impossible. His last bright idea got my bow gunner killed.

It was a reckless push through open ground with no recon, and no covering fire. The Lieutenant assured us there was no enemy ahead, just a simple field to cross. So we went, because that's what we do.

We were sitting ducks, and the enemy didn't waste the opportunity. A burst of MG fire cracked through the air, stitching across the front of the tank like a swarm of angry bees. Smith never even had a chance. He was still halfway through a joke when the rounds found the one exposed part of his body. His face.

He didn't scream. Didn't make a sound. One second, he was there, and the next, he slumped over, silent.

The Lieutenant, though? He barely even registered it. Just moved us along like losing a man wasn't anything different from losing a spare track link.

After several moments of being lost in thought, the Lieutenant shoves a folded piece of paper into my hands, snapping me out of my daze. "Your marching orders."

I glance at it. It looks similar to that of a telegraph printout. Odd, but not surprising. With the radios acting up and command swinging positions, written orders have been more reliable than garbled transmissions lately.

From: Commander, 3rd Battalion, 8th Armored Regiment, 3rd Armored Division

To: Commander, Tank, full-tracked, M4A3E8 "Easy Eight" Sherman "Calculated Vengeance"

Message: The tank and its crew are to reposition immediately to the assembly area located north of the current treeline. Upon arrival, proceed to on-load ammunition, fuel, and rations. Afterward, link up with Alpha Company, 4th Infantry, for further instructions. Execution of these orders is mandatory and to be carried out without delay.

The anger in me boils. Doesn't the Battalion Commander know that we've been fighting hard for the last 24 plus hours? My crew isn't capable of continuing on because of pure exhaustion. It feels like ants are crawling under my skin, rage twitching in every nerve. But then I realize that failing to follow the order would result in something far worse than what the lack of sleep will do to me.

"Mount up, boys. We got orders to move," I commanded with a groan. "I promise we'll get some rest when we get where we're going."

The entire crew groans in unison as if one organism. But eventually everyone starts out making their way towards their respective stations. The engine roars to life and Rich gets our steel beast moving out from where we had been attempting to get some rest.

The assembly area is just a concrete slab, surrounded by tall trees on all sides. The concrete's mostly hidden beneath layers of mud and snow, only revealing itself in spots where artillery craters have exposed chunks of it. I'm sure that normally, this place would have looked picturesque in the winter, but for those of us here, stuck in this frozen hell, it's anything but. The pad's barely big enough for an ammo truck, a fuel truck, and a tank to pull up side by side, so we can load up and refuel at the same time. Leading away from one end of the slab, there's a two-lane road. The other end is a treeline with a simple trail just wide enough for a tank to drive through. This trail leads towards the front line. The pad is busy with soldiers hustling around, handing out boxes of ammunition like it's their job. Which, I guess, it is.

Rich pulls our tank up to the side of the trucks and kills the engine, the deep rumble fading into the distance, leaving the cracks of gunfire and the voices of busy soldiers as the only sounds around. He doesn't even move after that, his hands still resting on the controls, head slumped forward. He's probably already asleep. Pure exhaustion likely overrode any thought of crawling out of the driver's hatch. I don't blame him.

Harris is out cold in the gunner's station, his head resting awkwardly against the turret ring, breaths slow and steady. Fitz, our loader, has sprawled himself across the turret like a discarded sack of gear, his arms hanging limp over the edge as he snores loud enough to make himself a target. Soot streaks his jacket; he suffered a fresh sleeve rip earlier when shells hammered against our tightly buttoned armor. None of it matters now. Sleep is the only thing stronger than fear, and for the moment, the war is silent inside our steel home.

"Alright, Tommy, time to get to work," I say, pulling my throat mic off and letting it hang around my neck. "And don't you dare wake up the others." My tone's sharp enough that I don't even need to glance at him to know he got the message.

"Work with the fuelers to get the fuel going. Then we'll load the shells," I continue to instruct.

The fuel truck stands amongst the snow and mud, its once-pristine steel cylinder now coated with a thick layer of grime, the red and white markings barely visible beneath the muck. Its engine hums steadily, puffing out clouds of vapor into the cold air as the men assigned to the truck are a buzz, filling dozens of jerry cans. The truck's tires, caked in snow and dirt, seem to sink deeper with each passing minute, leaving behind deep impressions in the frozen ground. There's the unmistakable sound of metal cans rattling with the weight of the fuel as they pass from hand to hand, their handles slick with cold moisture. The air smells of gasoline and wet earth, sharp and pungent. Workers carefully fill each can, ensuring that every ounce of the heavily rationed fuel gets accounted for and properly distributed.

Next to the fuel truck is the ammunition truck. Low on its suspension, the overburdened vehicle groans under the sheer weight of its deadly cargo. On top lie stacked wooden crates, each stenciled with bold black lettering: "CAL. 30 BALL, " "CAL. 50 AP, " "76MM M79 SHOT AP-T". The crates are lashed tightly under a worn canvas cover, bulging at the seams as if the vehicle itself is struggling to contain its load. Brass casings gleam in the dim light where some crates have split open, revealing belts of .50 caliber rounds coiled like serpents, waiting to be fed into the hungry Brownings.

The brass shell casings are still factory-clean, and neatly racked alongside one another in wax-sealed containers, their chemical scent mixing with the heavy stench of oil and canvas. The truck's tires are coated in a fine layer of mud, its sides peppered with dust and grime from endless supply runs through the war-torn roads. It's a rolling arsenal, a lifeline for the front lines—but also a deathtrap. One stray round, one well-placed artillery hit, and the entire thing would erupt into a fireball that could take an entire platoon with it.

I quickly glance over at Tommy and explain where the fuel cap is on the vehicle and how it opens. My voice feels worn down from pure exhaustion, which causes my throat to feel sore, but I push through the soreness and ensure that I'm clear about the steps so he doesn't waste any time fumbling around. He nods like he's heard it all before, and as if he already knows exactly where the cap is and how it works, and that everything will go smoothly.

I can't help but feel a small twinge of doubt. Little does he know that, in the best of times, the fuel cap is notoriously difficult to open. It's always been stiff and stubborn. But today, with the freezing cold seeping into every inch of our gear, every movement feels ten times more challenging. I know from experience that the metal of the cap is going to be frozen, stiff with the cold, and it's going to take more than a simple twist to get it open. There's no doubt that Tommy has yet to come to a similar conclusion.

Tommy curses under his breath, fumbling with the fuel cap like it's some kind of foreign puzzle box he's never seen before. His fingers, stiff with cold, slip against the metal as he pries at it, his frustration mounting. "Damn thing won't budge," he mutters, glancing back like one of us might have the magic touch. The battered Jerry cans rest on the engine deck of the tank, full of precious fuel, waiting.

After realizing that no one is coming to his aid, he tries again. This time he grits his teeth and struggles harder than before, and finally, with a stubborn twist and a metallic clunk, the cap gives way. A sharp stink of gasoline fills the air as it mixes with the fumes.

"Got it," he grumbles, after smearing a streak of splashed fuel across his already filthy sleeve. He stands up and begins using the fuel cans to fill up the tank with what little fuel we're allotted.

Once the tank has taken in the meager fuel rations, it's time to load up on ammunition. Fortunately, there are no such restrictions when it comes to arming the tanks. We're too valuable on the battlefield to be left needing ammunition.

I nod to Tommy, pointing him toward the ammunition truck. "Get to it," I say, watching as he hurries off. "The beast is hungry, and it's time to feed."

Tommy grabs a crate but severely underestimates the sheer weight of the box of main gun ammunition. He struggles and staggers under the weight of a wooden crate stamped "76MM M79 SHOT AP-T". He slogs his way towards the tank with the precious cargo, his boots kicking up mud and snow as he hauls it from the overloaded ammunition truck. It's clear that his arms are already aching from the few moments he's been carrying the crate. He pauses, grunts, and adjusts his grip, the rough wood biting into his palms as he trudges toward the tank.

"Christ, Sarge, you ever think about shooting less?" he huffs, setting the crate down on the ground next to the tank with a heavy thud. Sweat streaks through the grime on his face, and he rolls his shoulders, already eyeing the next load like a man facing a firing squad being forced to work.

This time, I step over and grab one end of the crate, helping him carry it. We move in silence, hauling the crates back and forth between the vehicles. After what feels like an eternity, I notice we've barely stacked a few.

"That should be enough," he says, panting. I glance down at the crates we've hauled, M79 AP-T rounds, all of them. Great for punching through armor, but useless for taking out infantry or blasting through fortified positions. I shake my head.

"We need HE too," I mutter, tapping the crate with my boot. Tommy exhales sharply, rolling his shoulders as he turns to trudge back to the pile. He knows I'm right, but that doesn't make the load any lighter.

I wipe my hands off and turn back toward the dwindling stack of crates. Together we haul over a box marked with a faded stencil: "M89 HE." High-explosive. In unison, we set it down, exhaling and rubbing the cold from our fingers.

I keep helping him stack crates, moving in a rhythm now, both of us working without a word. The stack slowly grows as the minutes tick by. Finally, Tommy pauses, wiping his brow, and looks down at the pile.

"That enough for you?" he mutters, half-joking, half-exhausted.

I crouch down to double check the markings, tapping the crate. "This'll do." I glance up at him, giving a small nod. "Can't just punch holes in things, Tommy. Sometimes you gotta make 'em disappear."

He lets out a short laugh, shaking his head before hopping on the front of the tank and preparing for me to hand him individual rounds for the ready rack.

I pry the crate open with the knife I keep on my belt; fresh brass gleams even in the dimming light. The scent of oil and gunpowder mixes with the stale air.

"Ain't about shooting more, it's about making 'em count," I say, lifting a shell and passing it up to Tommy. He takes it, sets it by the loader's hatch, and gets it ready to load inside. The clink of metal as it settles into place is familiar, comforting, even. "The war will end... eventually." I glance at Tommy as he works, his face shadowed by exhaustion. "But before that, a lot more people gotta die."

We continue loading the ammunition onto the turret until we run out of main gun ammunition. But before we load it into the vehicle, I look back at the ammunition handlers. They have already started laying out the linked machine gun ammo. There's still plenty of work to do, and the war sure as hell isn't waiting for us to finish.

Once the last crate gets cracked open and discarded, and its contents secured within the tank, our shelter and home is now fully loaded and ready for whatever hell comes next. The turret's ready racks are stuffed tight with fresh 76mm shells, their brass casings catching the faint glow of whatever residual light bounces around the inside of the tank. HE, AP smoke—every round packed tight, ready to scream downrange at whoever's next. Even the wet storage hull racks get packed to max capacity, every available space stuffed with as much ordnance as we can manage.

The machine gun belts are draped in neat, deadly rows, feeding into both the co-axial .30 cal, bow .30 cal, and the commander's .50 up top. Spare ammo cans are wedged into every crevice we can find, some cans are even strapped down on the outside with whatever we have on hand. It's a comforting sight, knowing we won't be caught short if things go bad. And in this place, they always do.

The tank is heavier now, weighted down with enough firepower to tear through whatever poor Nazi gets in our way. But in the pit of my stomach, I know that no matter how much ammo we load, it'll never feel like enough.

Once we finish loading the ammunition, I reluctantly wake Rich, reminding him it's time to move. He begins throwing a fit like a child, but I promise him that once we're there, I'll leave him alone long enough to get some rest. Grumbling, he turns the key, and the engine roars to life again.

The ride over to the infantry company is quiet, just the low rumble of the tank as we move through the muddy terrain. By the time we arrive, the engine hums to a stop, and Rich sinks back into his seat, finally allowing himself the rest he desperately needs.

Ahead of us stands the Infantry Captain. He's hunched against the cold, standing near the edge of the muddy road with a tattered map in his hands. His uniform is a mess, wrinkled, streaked with mud and blood, the fabric frayed at the elbows. Dark circles hang beneath his eyes, telling the story of sleepless nights spent planning and waiting. His fingers, smudged with grime and gunpowder, trace over the creases in the map, muttering under his breath as he tries to make sense of the shifting front lines. A cigarette dangles from his lips, barely flickering as the wind steals the warmth. Every few moments, his gaze lifts toward the road, frustration mixing with the expectation in his eyes. He had clearly expected more than just one tank to arrive, but out here, the brutal reality of supply and demand leaves no room for expectations.

The rest of the infantry company sits huddled in groups scattered throughout the edge of the treeline beside the muddy road, their forms blending into the gloom of the late winter afternoon. Eighty men give or take about a dozen; they don't look so much like men but more like ghosts. They sit silent, exhausted, and caked in filth. Their uniforms, once olive drab, are now a patchwork of mud, sweat, and dried blood, stiff from the freezing temperatures. Some men crouch in shallow foxholes they had carved into the frozen earth, their rifles resting across their knees, while others lean against the skeletal remains of trees, too weary to even speak. Their breath curls in the frigid air, misting like smoke from a dying fire.

The mud is merciless, swallowing their boots with each sluggish step. The cold has cracked the leather of their boots, leaving deep, jagged lines across the surface, and in places, some have tried to patch them with scraps of cloth or tape. Their socks, if they even have them, are soaked through or frozen, and their feet are a numb, aching mess inside boots that offer little protection. Some have wrapped rags around their ankles, desperately attempting to fight off trench foot, but it does little against the biting chill. The snow, mixed with mud, has turned to a slushy, brown paste that clings to everything from coats to weapons, and eventually faces.

A few men mutter to each other, their voices hoarse from cold and exhaustion, but most simply stare at the road, waiting. Waiting for orders. Waiting for relief. Waiting for the tanks that might just be the difference between holding the line and being overrun.

"We're going to hunker down here for the night." He begins addressing me before I'm even able to haul myself out of the turret. "Get some rest. In the morning, we need you to scout this treeline here." He points to a treeline on the other side of the massive field before us, standing about 600 yards away from where the infantry hunkers down. "I'd introduce myself... but I'm not wasting my breath. If we make it out of here alive, then I'll care to learn your name." His words are short and to the point. You can tell just from his tone that he's no-nonsense and simply wants to get out of this place. All of us do.

I decide it's time for some rest for myself. I close my hatch and find myself a nice attempt at a comfortable spot inside of the tank and settle in, letting the sleep rush over me like a waterfall.

I wake up the next morning feeling like I never truly slept. My head is heavy, like it's stuffed with damp wool, and there's a dull ache sitting behind my eyes, throbbing in time with my sluggish heartbeat. My mouth is dry and stale, like I've been chewing on old pennies in my sleep. I try to take a deep breath, but my chest feels tight, my lungs unwilling to expand fully. The air in the tank is thick, stale, carrying a faint, acrid scent that lingers in the back of my throat.

I blink hard, trying to shake the fog clinging to my brain, but everything feels slow and off. My limbs are sluggish, like I'm wading through molasses just to sit up. Around me, the others are stirring alongside me, groaning, rubbing their faces like they're trying to wake up from a nightmare that won't let go. The dim light filtering through the vision slits feels too bright, stabbing into my skull. I swallow hard, my stomach churning uneasily, and exhale a breath that feels heavier than it should. Something's not right.

I notice that the tank is running and immediately realize the issue. The thing about these Shermans is that they roll off the production lines with blistering speed. Over two thousand a month, or so they say. Because of the breakneck speed of assembly, corners will be cut and sometimes not enough attention gets paid when assembled. This can manifest in a myriad of ways. I've learned to accept it... mostly. But every so often, you get a little reminder that these steel coffins weren't built with luxury in mind.

Ours has a habit of leaking exhaust back into the fighting compartment. It's not much, just a faint wisp creeping in through the engine bay seals, but after a long day inside, you feel it. A dull headache, and a little sluggishness. As if the tank itself is sucking the air right out of you. We usually prop the hatches open most of the time, but sometimes it's not practical because of either the enemy or the cold air that bites at our faces. When we button up for a fight, that's when it gets bad. The air turns heavy, tinged with the bitter tang of burning fuel. It sits in your lungs, seeps into your bones. You wind up feeling like you've been drinking bad whiskey all night, head pounding, stomach twisted. Just another minor price to pay for keeping this war machine moving.

Once I finally haul myself out of the tank, the biting cold greets me like a sharp slap, shocking the last remnants of drowsiness from my fogged-up mind. I realize that the Captain stands at the front of my tank, waiting, his posture stiff with exhaustion. I drop down from the top of the tank, my boots crunching against the frozen ground. That's when I notice his laces. Both are snapped clean through, ruined by the relentless cold. His boots are barely holding together, each step a miracle.

With a sigh, I crouch down and tug at my own bootlaces, my fingers stiff and clumsy from the cold. The knots are tight, frozen nearly solid, but after some struggle, I eventually manage to work them loose and remove them. I stand and hand them to the Captain, who hesitates before taking them, his chapped lips parting like he's about to protest. But he doesn't. We both know he needs them more than I do.

Without saying a word, I unbuckle my belt, pulling it free with a sharp snap. I wind it tight around my left boot, cinching it down hard to keep the leather from flapping open. It's not perfect, but it'll hold until I can scrounge another pair. It'll have to do for now. The Captain gives me a nod, quiet but full of gratitude, as he bends down to thread the laces through his battered boots.

He finishes lacing up his boots without a word. When he finally looks up, his expression is cold and grim.

There's no need for a briefing. We already know the plan. We've done this before. It's reckless even with a full platoon of five tanks.

With just one?

Suicide.

With an exhausted breath, the nameless Captain addresses me. "Your crew ready to finally earn your place in this war?"

[CHAPTER THREE: LIVE ROUNDS AND GREYHOUNDS]

"Are the Souls of all dead Troopers camped,"

15 December 2024

The morning air is crisp, carrying the distant rumble of engines as crews prep their tanks for the one of the many live-fires. Our tank, *Controlled Violence*, sits ready. Our crew is already in position, checking over gear and running last-minute inspections. Everyone in the crew... Except for one.

Then comes Turner.

He jogs toward us, looking like hell. His eyes are sunken, hair a mess, unshaven and a uniform screwed up like he's slept in it, if he slept at all. He's out of breath, rubbing his face as he slows to a stop.

"Rough night?" I ask, already knowing the answer.

He lets out a dry chuckle. "Didn't sleep. Not even a little."

I frown. "Nerves?"

Turner shakes his head, scanning the area like he isn't sure if he wants to say more. "I... I kept hearing things. Thought I was losing my mind." Turner leans in close. "You know **what** I'm talking about, **when** I'm talking about, and **where** I'm talking about."

I nod knowingly. I remember distinctly. Though, I try not to.

There's a reason Turner is the gunner he is today. A reason he's as fast and precise as he is. Why he double-checks every target, why he trusts me without hesitation when I give a correction. It wasn't always like that. There was a moment, the one we don't talk about, when everything nearly went wrong. A single heartbeat where instinct had to override training, where hesitation could have meant disaster. His crosshairs weren't where they should have been. People could have died. Yet I caught it. And from that day on, he's been different. More focused. Sharper. I don't think he's ever forgiven himself for it, even though nothing actually happened. But I know one thing for sure. Turner will never make that mistake again.

A tank crew is like a living machine in which every member has their role, their responsibilities, their expertise. But the relationship between the commander and the gunner is the most critical of all. A well-trained crew is essential, but a commander and gunner who are truly in sync can turn a tank into something far deadlier than just steel and firepower.

Once a gunner and tank commander qualify together during a gunnery, they become a "qualified crew." That designation means they're locked in together, working as a team until either one of them gets reassigned. The Army doesn't like splitting up crews unless they have to. The reasoning is simple. There's too much muscle memory, too much instinct built between two people who have spent hours upon hours hunting targets together. In a fight, that kind of connection can mean the difference between hitting first or being hit.

Turner and I have been a qualified crew for what feels like forever. We've sat through hours of dull classroom briefs together, spent sleepless nights in the field hating life together, and drilled the same gunnery exercises so many times that we could probably do them in our sleep. There have been moments of victory. There have been those rare times when we cleaned house on a gunnery range, making every shot count. And there have been moments we wish we could forget like stupid mistakes, bad calls, and the kind of miserable experiences that only seem funny years later when you're swapping war stories over beers. We've been to combat together and even shared countless moments of vulnerability with each other.

At this point, I don't need to tell Turner what I'm thinking when we're in the turret. I can see it in the way he adjusts his sights, I can hear it in the tone of his voice when he calls out a target. He knows how I command, and I know how he shoots. And today, in this live-fire round, I need him at his best, because if he's not, we're going to have a problem.

A quiet beat passes between us, the distant echoes of other tanks firing downrange filling the silence. I know what he dreamed. What he heard, and I know it had rattled him.

"Think you can still shoot straight?" I finally ask, breaking the tension.

He smirks, but it doesn't reach his eyes. "Wouldn't miss this for the world."

"Good, mount up. We've got ammo to upload this morning." I haul myself up on the tank as I've done thousands of times.

The turbine engine roars to life—first a low, guttural whine, then a steady scream as Vic eases us forward. *Controlled Violence* rumbles onto the dirt path and begins kicking up a thin mist of mud in its wake.

Unlike the busy staging area—where tanks crowd together in organized chaos, swarmed by maintenance crews and tank crews working on their vehicles—the ammunition pad is spread out, deliberate, and isolated for good reason. One mistake here, one dropped shell or mishandled warhead, and the whole place could go up in flames.

Each nation has its own section, separated by wide margins and marked with flags or name boards. Rows of stacked ordinance sit ready for loading, arranged with careful precision. Ahead of us, several Leopard crews are already hard at work, their blue-tipped shells hoisted into turrets with smooth, practiced movements.

Vic slows to a stop, and I hop fully out of the hatch and then slide down the front of the tank. The cold air hits me as I climb out, scanning for our assigned spot. Turner steps up beside me, rubbing sleep from his eyes, while Fitz clambers out behind us, eyes wide, taking it all in.

We walk the line for a few minutes, boots crunching against gravel and packed snow, past pads bearing Union Jacks, Tricolors, and Bundeswehr crests. Finally, we spot the banner fluttering above an empty loading zone—stars and stripes, faded but proud.

Our pad.

"Uh... Sarn't?" Turner mutters. "Tell me we didn't forget to arrange our own ammo."

I exhale slowly, jaw tightening. "Nope. I sent the request directly to the event coordinators. Our allocation should be here. There's supposed to be a pad with our flag on it."

But after several minutes of walking the perimeter, frustration sets in. We circle the area again and again, boots scraping the concrete, eyes scanning for something—anything—that might have been missed.

The other ammunition pads around us are a model of efficiency. Crates stacked high. Pallets lined in perfect rows. Trucks rumble back and forth, unloading round after round. Every national section is clearly marked: crisp flags flutter in the breeze, names printed in bold on large signs, nothing left to chance. The Germans have a proud black-red-gold banner hanging above their ammunition stacks. The Brits have neatly labeled crates under a taut Union Jack. Even the French have their section marked with military precision.

But our pad? Our designated space? It's empty. Completely barren. Just an open patch of concrete with faint tire tracks and not a single shell in sight. No crates. No sign. The only thing we have is our proud fl ag.

It doesn't make sense.

I stare at it longer than I should, trying to force something into existence. It feels wrong—not like a clerical error, but something intentional. Like we've been erased.

Turner stands beside me, arms crossed, his jaw working quietly. He scans the open pad like it might rearrange itself into answers if he looks hard enough. Fitz hovers behind us, clearly uneasy, his hands gripping the hatch edge tighter with each passing second.

The silence settles in thick and heavy. Not the normal quiet of a worksite between shouts and diesel engines—but something deeper. Emptier. Like the pad is holding its breath.

Something is off.

Way off.

"Can't we just use German rounds?" Fitz asks, his voice dropping through the silence like a pebble being tossed into still water. "I remember reading something about that in the tank manual... Plus they use 120mm like we do."

I glance at him. Surprisingly, he's not wrong. At least, not entirely.

I put a hand on the front slope like I'm trying to hold the tank down. "Here's the deal. On paper, yeah, we **should** be able to fire German rounds. Back in the day when I was a spring chicken like you, my mentor, Sergeant First Class Aguilar— our Battalion master gunner back then— taught me something about this gun. This gun, the M256 120mm smoothbore, isn't some homegrown American design we cooked up from scratch. It's a direct descendant of the German Rheinmetall Rh-120, the same cannon they bolt onto the Leopard 2. Ours got tweaked and built here, but the bones? Same exact pedigree.

"Back in the Cold War, when everyone was losing sleep over the Soviets rolling across the Fulda Gap, the brains figured that if the big war in Europe ever popped off, we might burn through our ammo faster than the supply ships could sail it over. So they designed the

Abrams' main gun to be able, **in theory**, to swallow NATO-standard shells from all our European buddies and keep right on fighting."

I glance toward the stack of German rounds, my stomach knotting. "But reality's never that clean. The devil's in the details—different propellant loads, slightly different casing lengths, fire control calibrations that don't match. It's all just enough to turn 'compatible' into 'maybe.' And here's the kicker. Our gunner's display doesn't even have a setting for German ammo. We'd have to pick whatever American flavor we think is closest, send the first round, and then Kentucky-windage the rest based on where it actually lands."

I let the silence hang for a moment. "And Fitz... I've never heard of a crew actually doing it. Not once. That doesn't mean it won't work, but if we try, we're betting the gun, the tank, and our asses that the theory lines up with reality."

As if on cue a Bundeswehr ordinance officer approaches with a clipboard in hand, his posture stiff and his expression unreadable. He's coming from the same direction as Oberfeldwebel Vogel and his crew. It looks like they were having a pretty intense conversation prior to my arrival. I already know we're about to have a problem.

"Ah, so unfortunate," he says with a clipped, practiced tone laced in ice-cold sarcasm. "It seems your nation's ammunition... didn't arrive in time." He flicks his eyes toward the massive stacks of German ordinance behind him, then back to me without so much as a blink. "It happens. Some shipments are just... delayed." There's a faint curl at the edge of his mouth—a smile that never reaches his eyes.

"You'll make do with what you can, I suppose," he adds, almost as an afterthought. "And don't be surprised if your resupply request doesn't show up anytime soon. Might want to upload what you'll need for the... **entire** competition."

I don't respond. I just stand there, jaw tight, heart drumming somewhere low in my chest. There's something unsettling about how casually he delivers the news—like it's not an inconvenience, but a decision. Deliberate. I can't tell if this is bureaucratic negligence or something colder, but either way, it feels intentional. Too clean. Too precise.

As he turns away, I catch a glimpse of Oberfeldwebel Vogel. He's watching us from a short distance, arms crossed, expression unreadable—until it isn't. His look hardens, shifting from idle disinterest to something close to hostility. That's not a man interested in cooperation. That's a man who'd rather see our tank dead on arrival than share a single round of ammunition.

I push the thought away, forcing myself back into the moment. The mission hasn't changed. We're still here, we still have a job to do—but the cold twist in my gut won't let go. We're being boxed in. No ammo. No support. Just a quiet, loaded smile and a suggestion to "make do".

Maybe I'm reading too much into it. Maybe it's just one of those logistical flukes that happens during big, international ops. But the longer I stand in that empty ammo pad, the more it feels like we weren't just forgotten.

We were left out on purpose.

And that thought? That thought stays with me long after the ordinance officer walks away.

After what feels like years we're finally shown which racks we're allowed to pull from, and we get to work. No one says much—we just fall into rhythm. Uploading ammunition is second nature by now, a practiced choreography of movement and muscle memory. Methodical. Precise. Every one of us knows our role.

Vic eases the tank into position as the turret swings toward the ammo stacks. Fitz takes the lead, climbing into his spot and flipping the knee switch. The thick armored door hisses open, revealing the ready rack tucked inside the turret bustle. It's the heart of the tank's firepower—each round is nearly sixty pounds of controlled destruction that has to be seated just right.

Fitz starts loading the rounds by hand, sweat already beading on his neck. He's deliberate, placing each shell in his preferred position—APFSDS for armor, HEAT for soft targets, and the occasional canister round in case things get personal. Every round has a home, locked into its own compartment within the rack. He might not have the raw speed of a seasoned loader yet, but what he lacks in pace, he makes up for in consistency. No wasted motion. Just focus.

The rest of us move in sync, handing the rounds down in a steady relay—from stowage, to hull, to turret, to Fitz. It's a heavy, physical process, but when it's done right, it's fluid—it can take about 20 minutes from crate to combat-ready. One motion feeds the next, a mechanical dance we've done more times than we can count. It's one of the few times we all move with total unity, no questions asked.

Once the last round is locked in, we climb back into our seats. The tank rumbles to life, and we roll out from the pad.

I glance over my shoulder as we pull away. The other nations' pads are still buzzing with activity—trucks backing in, forklifts unloading, crews shouting to each other over the din. Every section is cleanly marked, color-coded flags flapping in the breeze.

But where ours should be—where our ammo should've been from the start—there's only an empty patch of pavement. No crates. No signs. Just open space, like we were never meant to be here in the first place.

And somehow, that blank concrete says more than anything else ever could.

Something about it doesn't sit right. The absence of any recognition for the American crew isn't just a clerical oversight—it feels too clean, too exact. Like it was meant to be missing. I turn it over in my mind, again and again, and the more I do, the more it smells of intent. Not a mistake. Not a mix-up. Something else.

I shake my head, trying to push the thought away before it festers. Paranoia doesn't help anyone, especially not now. Maybe it *is* just a supply error—some lazy quartermaster or a misrouted manifest. No point in chasing ghosts. We've got bigger things to focus on.

The gunnery course is up next. That's what we came here for.

The tank rolls forward, treads grinding against the frozen mud, and eventually pulls up to the firing line. The vehicle settles into a heavy, collective quiet. No banter. No music. Just each of us locked into our own thoughts, prepping for the range. To the left, the firing line stretches out, dotted with tanks from every flag, each crew waiting for their run. Sunlight glints off metal, long shadows stretching across the snow-packed field like teeth.

There's always a flicker of nerves before gunnery—no matter how many times you do it. Each run is a test of focus, precision, and pressure. Hit the wrong target, lag a second too long, and the whole score tanks. Still, it's familiar ground. Predictable. For once, we're playing by rules we understand.

We're not up yet, as we're placed in the middle of the firing order, but that just gives us time to get locked in. No more wondering about ammo shortages or missing manifests. When it's our turn, it's just us and the gun. No excuses. No distractions.

Just the mission.

While the other crews move down the range, I take the opportunity to study every inch of it, my focus sharpening with each pass. In this kind of environment, details matter—every tank, every approach, every target. I need to know exactly what we're up against.

I scan the field, marking each target's position, gauging distances, and noting the placement of obstacles meant to test both timing and precision. I sketch quick layouts in my notebook, scribbling down anything that might throw off a shot—uneven terrain, stray glare from the snow, the way the wind cuts across the open field.

No surprises. That's the goal. When it's our turn, I want every shot to be calculated, every movement deliberate. This isn't just about hitting targets—it's about rhythm, about reaction. The way we move, the way we think. Timing is everything.

The crew needs to be locked in—no questions, no hesitation. By the time we're called forward, I'll know this range like the back of my hand. Whatever it throws at us, we'll be ready.

"Crew report," I say into the intercom after taking my seat. We're positioned at the top of the range, prepped and ready to go.

"Driver ready, tank in drive."

"Loader ready, Sabot loaded."

"Gunner ready, Sabot indexed."

Each crewmember checks in, crisp and confident. With that, we're green across the board.

I key up the radio and call the tower. "Team Eagle ready to tackle the range."

"Cleared hot. Enjoy, lads," comes the reply—delivered in a voice straining to sound polite. The kind of tone that tries to hide its contempt behind a thin layer of civility. Barely.

"Driver, move out. Gunner, scan right," I order.

The tank jolts forward with a mechanical grunt, treads chewing into the snowy mud of the trail. Turner pivots the turret, scanning the right flank. I bring up my Commander's Independent Thermal Viewer—CITV—and sweep to the left.

The CITV is our second set of eyes. Mounted on top of the turret, it feeds me high-res thermal imaging, day or night. It lets me pick up heat signatures and threats without waiting for the gunner to find them. If I need to, I can override the shot—either to pull the trigger myself or to make damn sure someone doesn't.

"Identified tank, range 1600!" Turner shouts.

I swing my gaze to the gunner's sight extension. Through it, I see the outline of a cardboard T-90 silhouette—one of the range targets. Right where I marked it earlier. It lines up with the sketch in my notebook. Perfect.

"Up!" Fitz yells.

He throws the arming handle into the armed position next to the breech.

"Fire and adjust!" I snap.

"On the way!" Turner replies, pulling the trigger.

The shot rocks the tank like a sledgehammer to the chest. The recoil slams through the hull, knocking the breath from your lungs, as if something massive just punched straight through your ribcage. The shockwave slaps against your face, instant and jarring. The air itself seems to snap backward. Inside, the roar of the main gun is absolute—deafening, punishing, like standing inside a pressure chamber at the moment of detonation. The sound doesn't just fill your ears. It crawls through your bones and buzzes in your spine.

Then, the aft cap ejects—spent casing from the round sliding out with a metallic clatter into the swing gate at the loader's feet.

Fitz lowers the arming handle. The breech slams open.

He hits the knee switch. The heavy ammo door swings wide.

Then he reaches for the next round, HEAT, his hand hesitating just for a second. He's still getting used to the rhythm, and this one fights him. The round resists like a cornered animal—unwieldy, dense, and eager to make his life hell. He wrestles it free from the rack and shoves it into position, finally slamming it into the breach.

We're back in business.

"HEAT loaded," he mutters, voice heavy with exhaustion.

"Target hit," the control tower crackles through the radio, signaling us to move on.

"Start scanning. My notes say this next one is far out there by that treeline. Should be a personnel carrier," I order, shifting to the CITV and beginning my own scan.

I'm glad I took the time to prepare. Hitting a soft target like a personnel carrier with Sabot would be ridiculous—pure overkill. HEAT's the better fit. Designed for this. Cleaner. Smarter.

But after several seconds of scanning, nothing shows. Just static treelines and shifting wind. The silence starts to stretch a little too long. Are the tower guys messing with us? Could it be a glitch in the range control system? Another "coincidence," like the ammo mix-up? It's hard to tell. Part of me wants to laugh it off. The other part isn't so sure.

Then I catch movement through the CITV—a shift of contrast, a flicker of motion. Finally, I swing the reticle to meet it, expecting the moving target I'd planned for. But something's off.

That target's not supposed to show up yet.

It's too early. We haven't reached the next phase of the course. I pause, unsure. The timing doesn't make sense. Are they really screwing with us? Or is this some kind of curveball?

"Designate tank! Moving right to left!" The call comes out of me on instinct.

I press the designation button with my thumb. Instantly, my reticle locks onto the moving figure and syncs the gunner's sight with mine. I release it, eyes still locked on the shape, waiting for Turner's call.

Nothing.

The seconds crawl by.

I expect him to reply—quick and confident, confirming the target and prepping the shot. But the radio stays silent. The turret doesn't shift. Nothing moves.

"Gunner, identify," I say, my voice tight, sharp.

I pull back from the optics and glance down. Turner's pressed against my knees, locked into his scope. Silent. Still. Staring.

And not saying a word.

I use my knee to give his back a little shove.

"Identified… but… it looks like a… Tiger?" Turner says, his voice laced with disbelief.

For a second, my mind blanks. A tiger? In Germany? Then it clicks—he means the *Tiger tank*. The legendary Panzer. WWII.

I switch from looking at the thermals on the CITV to the Gunners Extension which is currently set in daylight view, needing confirmation with my own eyes.

There it is—moving along the far side of the range like it's always belonged there. Like it never left.

It's unmistakable. That towering boxy hull, the thick armor, the deliberate crawl of treads chewing through earth like it's stuck in a slower time. It glides just beyond the treeline, maybe 1600 meters out. The silhouette is crisp and solid in the dimming light—too solid. Not some museum piece dragged out for a display. It moves with eerie purpose, like it knows the land better than we do. Like it's done this before.

It shouldn't be here. It should be dead. It should be long gone.

Yet there it is—steel flanks weathered and dulled, but not broken. Except for one glaring detail: a ragged, blackened hole just beneath the turret ring. Like something punched through it with brute, unrelenting force. The damage is fresh. Not rusted. Not faded. Like it happened yesterday.

And yet, it rolls on, untouched by the present, blind to the range flags, the control tower, the decades that separate us.

Then Vic's voice cuts through the intercom—sharp, urgent. "Troops, front left!"

I snap upright instinctively, popping out of the turret halfway, scanning our immediate front. Fitz has already seen them—cardboard silhouettes of infantry crouched behind a low berm, no more than thirty yards from our left tread.

"Light 'em up, Fitz!" I shout, jabbing a finger toward the loader's M240.

Fitz doesn't hesitate. He flips the traverse and elevation locks open and immediately swings the machine gun toward the targets. The weapon barks to life, spitting brass into the turret as he sends precise bursts downrange.

The 7.62mm crack echoes across the field, rhythmic and fast. One by one, the silhouettes shudder and drop, shredded by controlled, efficient fire. There's no panic in him. No wasted movement. Just focus

He keeps the bursts tight, short, disciplined. It's the cleanest I've ever seen him shoot. No flinch. No hesitation.

When the last silhouettes slumps forward, Fitz releases the trigger and sets the weapon to safe, his breath coming fast but steady.

"Targets down," he reports, voice firm.

I give him a nod, briefly catching him smiling to himself. I'm proud of his improvement over the short time he's been with us. He came to us shy and nervous. He's turning into a confident and proficient loader.

"Target destroyed. Nice job adapting to your... changing environment," the voice from the tower crackles over the radio.

There's laughter behind the transmission, muffled but unmistakable. They're joking—laughing at us. They're pulling tricks on us. But why?

I drop back into my seat, forcing my eye back to the reticle. The sight picture is clean. Empty. The ghost of a tank is gone.

I blink, hard. Then again. Shake my head like that'll rattle the weirdness loose. Maybe it was a trick of the light. Mirage from heat shimmer. Maybe I'm overtired. But I **know** what I saw. That hulking shadow gliding across the treeline—the glint of steel, the sluggish crawl, the dead eye of that ruined turret ring. It wasn't in my head.

Still, I rub at my eyes anyway, trying to reset something inside me that doesn't want to be reset. I got a full night's rest. Hydrated. Ate. There's no reason I should be hallucinating.

There's no time for debate now. Now it's time to prove ourselves on this range. We need to prove that we're the best team out here no matter what they throw at us.

The rest of the live-fire feels like it happens without me. My body moves, gives the right orders, reads off the firing solutions and confirms damage assessments. Turner calls targets with precision, Fitz is loading faster than ever, and Vic's driving like he's back in Fort Irwin during peak evals. We're good. We're dialed. But it all washes over me like background noise. Just another day of training, right?

Except it's not. Something's off.

It's not just the hallucination—or whatever that was. It's the tower. The order of the targets, the pacing, the types—they're off. Everything I wrote down this morning is useless now. The "script" we were supposed to follow? It's been rewritten on the fly.

And no one seems to care but me.

Between engagements, I keep swinging the CITV back toward that patch of trees where I saw the Tiger. Same grid. Same treeline. Nothing there. Just dirt, shrubs, and the fading edge of the forest.

But I can still *feel* it. That tank. That **presence**. Like the steel is still echoing out across time. Like something's waiting to be acknowledged.

And Turner saw it too. He said it. *"It looks like a Tiger."* That wasn't a joke. That wasn't confusion. And Vic saw the jeep yesterday. The one no one else did. The one that vanished.

So I start doing the math. I start connecting the dots I really don't want to connect.

What if we're not imagining these things? What if they're not mistakes, or tricks of light, or breakdowns in stress? What if these are glimpses of something bleeding through? Something old. Something violent. Something that doesn't want us here.

The more I think about it, the more I try to pin it down in my mind, the more it slips from certainty into something looser. Something less reliable.

But I have to believe it was real. I **have** to. Because if it wasn't—if I'm wrong—then something's wrong with **me**.

And I'd rather face a ghost with teeth than admit that.

I keep circling back to yesterday. To the moment I pulled Vogel aside.

We were standing between the tanks. I'd tried to be friendly. And I told him—quiet, careful—about the jeep. How it came out of nowhere, old as hell, no markings, then disappeared when we turned around. I made it sound casual, like I was just asking if maybe there was a historical vehicle unit nearby or if some civvie wandered onto the range by accident. I didn't say I was spooked. I didn't say I lost sleep over it. I didn't say it made my blood run cold.

But maybe I didn't **need** to say it.

Did he pick up on it anyway? Did he read between the lines? Hell, maybe I **wanted** him to. Maybe I was looking for someone to tell me I wasn't crazy. That there was a logical explanation and I could stop checking over my shoulder every five minutes.

But now I wonder if I miscalculated. If Vogel took my quiet little confession and turned it into something else. Something louder. Maybe not on purpose. Maybe it just slipped—over beers, in a debrief, or possibly around the card table last night. *"You hear Carson saw some old WWII jeep out on the trail? Vanished into thin air? Might be seeing ghosts, boys."* Something like that. A joke. A warning. A whisper.

And now today? The Tiger. The ghost tank. The control tower screwing with the target order. The laughter in the background. I'm starting to feel like we've been marked. Like the whole competition's eyes are drifting toward us, watching for signs. Waiting for the next crack.

Did I do this? Did I open a door that should've stayed shut?

The thought chews at me.

What if the guys start thinking **I'm** not right in the head? What if they start questioning my calls, hesitating when I give orders? You can't lead a crew if they think you're spiraling. And if Fitz and Vic and Turner start wondering if **I** can't tell real from unreal… this whole damn tank falls apart.

I should've kept my mouth shut.

[CHAPTER FOUR: IRON AND FIRE]

"Near a good old-time canteen."

15 December 1944

The Easy Eight rumbles to life, the engine's low growl settling into a steady rhythm. The crew is in position, each man at his station, ready. Outside, the infantry moves along the roadside, their silhouettes cutting against the dull morning light. Everything is set. We know our t ask.

On paper, the mission is straightforward. In reality, it's damn near suicidal. The infantry holds a small rise, overlooking a mile of open terrain stretching out to the east. Beyond that, a thick treeline marks the beginning of the forest. Under normal circumstances, this would be perfect ground for them to hold. If not for some high-ranking - officer, safe behind a desk, deciding they need to cross this barren kill zone and assault the trees head-on.

And that's where we come in. We're the only ones with armor, the only ones with the firepower to flush out whatever waits in the treeline. Our job is to roll out first, draw their fire, and find out if this open field is just another stretch of earth, or if it will become the graveyard these men will soon be swallowed by.

Moments go by, though they feel like lifetimes. My order is quiet, hesitant almost. "Driver, move out."

The tank lurches forward, its engine straining under the weight of armor and ice as it begins its slow, deliberate crawl into the open.

It feels hesitant, almost as if it shares the same unease settling over the crew. Inside, I know every man is gripping their stations a little tighter, their breaths shallow, their nerves wound like a coiled spring.

Harris, our gunner, keeps his eye pressed against his sight, steadily sweeping the treeline with the turret, searching for any sign of movement. I raise my binoculars, scanning the scattered patches of terrain dotting the vast, open expanse ahead of us. Any of them could be hiding a waiting threat, a perfect hunting ground for German anti-tank teams.

But for now, there's nothing.

The silence is unnatural. There are no birds, no rustling branches. Just the distant, rhythmic thunder of machine guns and artillery rolling across the battlefield like an unending storm. Even the wind seems to have vanished, as if it too is afraid to move. Besides the roar of our engine nothing dares to make a noise.

And then, without warning, the tank stops.

The engine sputters, then dies, swallowing its own growl and leaving us in an eerie, suffocating silence. We haven't even made it a hundred feet. Now, we're just sitting here... motionless, vulnerable. It's as if the tank itself has decided this is a terrible idea and simply refused to go any farther.

"Rich," I whisper, my voice barely carrying over the stillness. "What's the issue?"

There's a pause. A long one.

"I... I don't know," Rich finally stammers. "Maybe it stalled? I'm not sure." His voice is tight, uncertain. Fear laces his words, and I know he feels it too, that sinking, gnawing dread settling over all of us.

We're stranded now. No longer tucked safely within the treeline but perched on a slight ridge, fully exposed. The open field stretches ahead, empty but ominous, while the treeline in the distance watches like a predator waiting for its moment to strike. Whatever might be out there, whatever unseen force just cut our advance short, we're at its mercy now.

After what feels like an eternity of waiting in this frozen wasteland, my breath shallow and my pulse pounding in my ears, I realize I'm grateful for the silence of our dead engine. Because now, I can hear it.

Faint at first. A distant murmur beneath the ever-present rumble of distant artillery. But then, unmistakable. The deep, guttural purr of a German cat. The sound of over-engineered death rolling through the snow. My stomach tightens, every nerve in my body standing on end. No American tanker wants to hear that sound.

It's the whine of a predator, the mechanical growl of something deadly and patient, something built to hunt. Then comes the sharp squeal of its tracks grinding against the frozen earth, the heavy clatter of steel against ice as it moves.

And then, like a ghost emerging from the treeline, it appears.

Sliding into view from the right, broadside to us, its massive form illuminated in the dull winter light. The infamous Tiger.

It doesn't see us. Not yet. The monster prowls forward, oblivious to the eyes locked onto it. My hands tighten around the rim of the hatch, heart hammering against my ribs.

This is it.

We have one chance.

"Load AP," I whisper into the comms, my voice barely more than a breath. The Tiger is three quarters of a mile from our position, if I had to guess. Either way, there's no way it could hear me. I know that. But logic means nothing right now. My pulse is pounding in my ears, each thud a war drum inside my skull. It feels like the whole world can hear my heartbeat, like even the slightest noise might draw the beast's gaze.

Fitz doesn't say a word. He doesn't need to. As if reading my thoughts, he moves with painstaking slowness, treating each motion like a matter of life and death. With deliberate care, he slides the Armor Piercing round into the breach.

Clang.

The metallic snap of the breach slamming shut sends an ice-cold shock through my veins. My breath catches in my throat. My whole body tenses.

I know the Tiger can't hear us. I *know* that.

But I still feel like it just did.

"Harris..." I whisper, barely able to hear myself over the blood rushing in my ears.

"Boss?" His voice is steady, calm, cool as ice. You'd never know that the deadliest thing on the planet to us was sitting right in front of us, oblivious to our presence. It's almost comforting, how unaffected he sounds. Almost.

"Kill it."

Before I even finish the word, the world explodes.

The tank shudders violently as the high-velocity 76mm cannon roars to life, its fury unleashed in a deafening shockwave that threatens to rip the air from my lungs. My ears ring, my vision shakes, and for the briefest moment, I swear my soul leaves my body.

The inside of the tank is a swirling cloud of smoke and cordite, thick and suffocating, burning my throat as I suck in a breath. The pressure rebounds off the steel walls, crushing my chest like a vice. My skull throbs from the concussive force, and I barely have time to process it before the shell is already halfway to its target.

There's no turning back now. If they didn't know we were here before, there's no mistake—they know we're here now.

Time slows to a crawl as I track the glowing tracer, my breath caught in my throat. The round streaks through the icy air, cutting a path of fate straight toward the Tiger's exposed flank.

Impact.

A deafening *crack* reverberates across the battlefield as the shell slams into the Tiger's side, just beneath the turret ring. **The perfect shot.** The armor doesn't just break; it caves inward as if swallowing the round whole. For a heartbeat, nothing happens. That is until...

Hell erupts.

The shell punches deep into the Tiger's steel siding, finding its mark among the stacked ammunition racks. There's a flicker of orange within the vision slits, just a whisper of flame before it becomes an all-consuming inferno. The Tiger shudders violently, its insides turning into a furnace as the first round detonates, setting off a chain reaction.

A **boom** rips through the tank's hull, followed by another, and another. The hatches rattle, buckling under the force of each explosion. Then, a spear of fire erupts from the commander's hatch, an angry geyser of flame and shrapnel shooting skyward as the overpressured hull turns into a steel death trap.

The turret lifts, just slightly, before slamming back down with a sickening finality. Smoke, thick and black, billows out of every crevice, carrying the smell of scorched metal, gunpowder, and something far worse.

The crew inside never had a chance.

The Tiger is nothing more than a burning tomb now, its once-mighty presence reduced to a funeral pyre. And yet, even as I watch, heart hammering in my chest, I can't shake the fear coiled in my gut.

Because if there's one Tiger, there's bound to be more.

Almost as if on cue, the engine roars to life.

"I... I didn't start it..." Rich stammers, his voice laced with confusion and fear as he fumbles to make sense of the engine's sudden, almost unnatural return to life.

"Don't care! *PUSH!*" I bark, urgency overriding everything else. "Get us out of this damn field!"

Rich doesn't hesitate this time. With a grinding shift, he throws the tank into gear, and the Easy Eight lurches forward, its treads biting into the frozen earth. We need to close the distance to the treeline, *fast*.

Out here, we're sitting ducks. This entire area, this empty stretch of land, is more than just open terrain. It's a death trap. Part of Germany's "West Wall" defensive network, this region is littered with expertly hidden defenses, killing zones designed to annihilate any-thing foolish enough to cross.

And we're right in the middle of it.

The Germans have had years to prepare, to perfect their deadly art. Every treeline, every rise in the earth could be hiding something. Their Pak guns are devastatingly accurate and nearly invisible until it's too late. They're usually positioned in interlocking fields of fire, ready to turn any advancing force into scrap metal. Even now, I can't shake the feeling that we're already in someone's sights.

The tank rumbles forward, each second stretching unbearably thin. If there's a gun out there watching us, we'll know soon enough, because the first shot fired is usually the last thing a crew ever hears.

I know I don't want to be shot at, but deep down, I think it's inevitable. Every second feels impossibly long, my nerves wound so tight I can hear my own heartbeat pounding in my ears. I brace for the first crack of incoming fire, for the telltale flash of a muzzle in the distance.

But it never comes.

The silence gnaws at me as we press forward, the Easy Eight groaning under its own weight. My eyes dart across the terrain, searching.

Waiting.

And then, near the smoldering wreck of the Tiger, I see it. Flickers of movement. Shadows shifting.

No hesitation.

"Enemy contact, two o'clock, two hundred yards, hose it down boys!" I bark.

Before the words have fully left my mouth, the tank roars to life with the sharp, rhythmic chatter of the bow machine gun, followed by the co-axial spitting lead into the dark void of the trees. Muzzle flashes flicker in rapid bursts, the tracers cutting through the haze like lightning in a storm.

Something is out there. Something ***waiting***.

And we aren't about to give it the chance to strike first.

After several minutes of furious machine gun fire, I give the order to hold. I'm expecting some sort of return fire but nothing comes. It's again ***deathly*** silent.

We finally reach the treeline. It feels like a fleeting moment of relative safety, at least for now. The canopy of the trees stretches overhead, offering some shelter, a crude blanket of wood and leaves that feels as though it can shield us from the world outside. The low hum of the engine is drowned by the rustling leaves above.

I brace myself for the sight of all of the bodies from the Germans we'd surely just torn through with a hail of MG fire. I expect to see the remnants of our deadly work, a field littered with the twisted, lifeless forms of our enemies. But as we push deeper into the trees, I'm met with an eerie silence.

There's nothing.

The ground isn't covered in bodies. Instead, it's marked by the jagged remnants of craters, still smoking from artillery barrages that had rained down here for hours, perhaps even days. The stench of burned earth lingers in the air, the only evidence that we hadn't been the first to tear through this patch of ground.

What lays scattered across the forest floor are the remnants of the enemy's retreat. Discarded German uniforms, half-eaten rations, discarded weapons, and boxes of unused ammunition. But no sign of the men who had once worn them. No trace of life.

It's almost as if the whole area had been abandoned in a hurry, the soldiers vanishing into thin air. A ghostly, unsettling emptiness hangs over the place.

Again, the engine sputters and dies, the sound of its dying growl quickly fading into the thick, oppressive quiet. The cold creeps in, a biting chill that seems to seep through the metal skin of the tank, wrapping itself around my bones. Outside, the distant rumble of artillery fire is muffled, barely a whisper on the wind. At the moment, it almost feels like it doesn't exist at all, like the world beyond this cramped, steel box might be a distant dream.

If I closed my eyes, I could almost convince myself that this cold, desolate stretch of forest is nothing more than a strange kind of peace. The tension of battle seems to melt away, replaced by an eerie calm that settles into the pit of my stomach.

But just as the silence seems to swallow us whole, the radio crackles to life, shattering the fragile stillness like glass breaking. The radio crackles again, this time louder, as if something is pressing up against the speaker. The voice is distorted, raw, broken. My hand instinctively moves to the volume, but it's already at the highest setting.

"—*...need... to... get... out... they're... coming...*" The voice is faint, jagged, like it's caught between static and something worse, something deeper.

My pulse quickens, the blood rushing in my ears making it harder to hear through the crackling interference.

"Who's...?" I start, but the words catch in my throat. The voice isn't just broken; it's hollow. Almost... distant.

"—*they'll be... so... soon... you... can't... hide...*" The voice sputters, then fades again, only to return with a chilling certainty. "*They... know... where... you... are...*"

It isn't even the words that rattle me; it's the way they're spoken, like something or someone is right on the edge of the frequency, slipping in and out of clarity. It sounds almost... familiar. But it also isn't. A blend of something I can't place. Is the garbled mess an American warning? Could it be a German accent that's playing psychological games on us? Maybe both, bleeding together.

I can't breathe. My hands tighten around the radio knobs, as if trying to physically silence the voice. But it comes again, just as broken, just as relentless.

"—*you... think... it's... over...*"

I glance around at the crew, but no one says a word. Is anyone else hearing this? Or am I losing my mind, trapped in the same damn field we can't escape?

"*...you... know...*" The voice lingers on the last word, each syllable stretching into a grotesque echo that seems to rattle the very insides of the tank. The static cuts off abruptly, leaving only the thrum of my heartbeat and the oppressive silence.

For a moment, all I can do was stare at the radio, as if it might suddenly give me the answers I'm desperate for. But it just sits there, cold, silent.

Who... or what... was that?

The crew sits in pure silence, confirming to me that they'd heard the bizarre, chilling words over the radio.

I peek my head out of the top of the hatch, eyes darting across the shadows beneath the canopy. I'm looking for danger, looking for *anything*. Looking for whatever is coming for us. But something doesn't sit right.

I remember driving only **a few yards** into the treeline, stopping when the engine died. I can clearly remember the jolt in my chest as it sputtered to a stop, the eerie silence that followed. Yet as I glance behind us now, I freeze.

The tracks in the dirt stretch back... **hundreds of yards**. What the hell?

How is that possible? We came in, stopped, and then... What? We didn't move that far. Did we? My stomach tightens as I try to make sense of it. But there's no logic, no explanation. The tank's path is clear in the mud, but it's wrong, twisted somehow.

I force myself to look away, shake my head, and glance down at my watch. Almost 1630 in the afternoon.

Impossible.

I glance up again, trying to make sense of the creeping dread pooling in my chest. We started this mission at first light, barely an hour after sunrise. The sun had barely crested the horizon when we set out. How is it almost setting now? Where are all of the German uniforms, rations and ammunition we saw when we entered the forest? What happened to the knocked out Tiger tank that was right next to the treeline. It's all ***gone***.

It's been hours since we stopped. But the day... it feels like it's vanished. No memories of the time passing. No feeling of the sun crawling across the sky. It just... is.

The whole world seems off. The shadows seem to stretch just a little too long, the air just a little too heavy. I blink, trying to shake it off, but the feeling lingers, crawling along the back of my neck like something unseen is right behind me.

The treeline feels like it's closing in. And I don't know why, but I *feel* it. Whatever's coming for us is closer than we think.

I sink back into the seat, the weight of the situation settling on my shoulders again, heavy and unrelenting. The sounds of the forest are muffled, the engine a quiet hum now that it's running again, but my mind is anything but still. I glance across the turret at my crew. Fitz, is hunched over the ammunition that sits waiting for an enemy, eyes dull, as if he hasn't slept in years; Harris, his face a mask of calm determination, even with the shadows of fear flickering behind his gaze. His hands are white knuckled on the gunner's controls. Our near-perfect driver, Rich Thompson, is already snoring desperately trying to recharge his batteries. Lastly our newest addition to the crew, Tommy Reynolds, sits in the assistant driver's position while trying to come to grips with his new reality.

They look as if they are almost frozen to their stations.

I think about the role of the commander. The one who directs, who leads, who makes the tough decisions when the bullets start flying. That's the job, right? To push the crew forward, to guide them through chaos. But as I sit here, surrounded by my men, I realize there's something more, something deeper.

The commander is the one who protects.

I've trained for this—tactics, strategy, battle plans meant to give us the edge. But in the end, it always comes down to one thing: protecting the crew. The men who follow me into fire, trusting I'll bring them back.

Fitz sits across from me, hands steady in his lap, jaw clenched tight. Harris grips the controls like they might break apart in his hands, his foot hovering close to the gun trigger on the floor. He tries to look fearless, but I see it—the same fear I'm hiding under my own skin.

They trust me. And I trust them. Whatever's out there—German or otherwise—it doesn't matter. We're a team.

I'll fight to protect them, to my last breath, until there's nothing left of me but the will to keep them alive.

That's what I am now. Not just a commander, but a shield. They'll fight for me, and I'll fight for them. We'll hold this line together.

Or die trying.

The hum of the engine rumbles through the tank, snapping me out of the dark place my thoughts had wandered. We've lingered here long enough. The longer we stay, the higher the chances of a German ambush in the night. Darkness is their ally, and ours will be gone if we stay too long.

With a surge of determination, I push myself up, my body moving on instinct, half in the hatch, half out, my eyes scanning the area. The air feels thick with the weight of what's coming, but the tank is our steel shell, and right now, it's the only thing keeping us alive. I focus on the task at hand, forcing myself to take control again. The crew needs it. They need me to lead them out of this nightmare.

"Rich," I say, my voice carrying with a confidence I barely feel. I want to sound sure, like the commander they need me to be, but inside, I'm just as unsure as them. Still, I push it down. "Turn us around and get us out of this... *place*."

The words come out sharper than I expect, and for a brief moment, I feel the power of leadership, the weight of it pushing me forward. We can get through this. We have to.

The tank lurches to life as Rich swings the tank around, the metal groaning under the stress. With a violent, grinding shift, the tracks begin to spin in place, flinging clumps of wet earth and thick mud in all directions. The sound is deafening compared to the immense quiet that is the forest. It's similar to a massive beast thrashing in the undergrowth. The tank's carving up the forest floor as it completes its turn. The earth is lumped into a thick, uneven mound as the tank straightens out, completing the turn. This sends a huge splash of mud flying and packing the air with a foul, wet smell. The surrounding trees tremble, their leaves rattling in the storm of noise and force.

Once the tank is facing the way we came, the movement becomes smoother, but the ground beneath the treads remains uneven. We roll down the trail, and every second feels like an eternity. The tank shudders with each bump in the path, the engine whining in protest as we push through thick mud and matted undergrowth. Time feels warped, like we're moving through a long tunnel, the world around us stretching and contracting in some strange way.

And then, after what feels like an hour of endless travel of the same damp, endless trees passing by in a hauntingly familiar rhythm, the tank begins to slow. I glance around, studying the area, eyes narrowing. My stomach drops. The path ahead looks... wrong. This is where we made the turn. The disturbed earth, the churned-up mud. It's all exactly the same as it was when we turned around.

We've come back to the same spot.

My mind races, trying to make sense of it. There's no way we could've circled back. The trees are the same, the ground is the same. There's even a spot devoid of snow and ice where the tank had previously sat with the engine running. The heat from the engine melted the snow and ice on the ground. Somehow everything feels wrong. The silence around us is deafening now, even more oppressive than before. The only sound is the raw rumble of the engine.

"Rich, stop," I command, my voice a little too sharp. "What the hell is going on?"

The tank comes to a halt. The engine shuts off, and for a moment, all is still. The eerie quiet of the forest presses in, suffocating. My crew is silent, no one daring to speak, as if the words might shatter the fragile peace that hangs over us. I look at the disturbed earth again, unable to shake the feeling that we've been here before. Almost as if we're caught in a loop, the forest itself watching us, trapping us in its endless cycle. The trees seem to close in, leaning toward us as if trying to conceal the truth, whatever that may be.

The weight of it all presses down on me, the uncertainty, the danger, the nagging fear that we're not just lost in a physical sense, but something deeper, something far more sinister. A chill runs down my spine, not from the cold, but from the creeping realization that something is wrong, and I'm not sure we can escape it.

I exhale slowly, gripping the edge of the hatch tighter, my knuckles white. "We need to move. Now," I say, trying to force confidence into my voice. But even as the words leave my lips, I wonder. Where are we even going? And what happens if we never leave this place?

As Rich starts the engine and shifts the tank into gear again, I feel a heavy weight settle in my chest. We're moving again, but for how long? And what waits for us beyond the trees? The questions swirl in my mind, unanswered, as the tank roars back to life, pushing forward into the uncertain darkness ahead. The forest looms, and I can't shake the feeling that it's not just the trees watching us anymore. Something else is out there. It's waiting. It's **wanting**.

[CHAPTER FIVE: ECHOES OF SILENCE]

"And this eternal resting place."

The morning air is crisp, carrying the scent of damp earth and spent gunpowder. The kind of air that makes you feel alive. That is until you remember what you're out here to do.

I glance down at my gloves, already stained with mud and grease, and huff. This isn't the glamorous part of being a tanker. It's not about thundering gunfire, not about the rush of battle drills, not about the power of a 70-ton war machine rolling across the earth. No, today is about cleaning up after ourselves.

Scattered across the range, half-buried in churned-up dirt and mud, are the discarded petals of sabot rounds. These chunks of metal fragments once guided high-velocity tungsten darts toward their targets. Yesterday, they were instruments of destruction. Today, they're just trash, and it's our job to pick up every single one.

I crouch down, plucking an ice cold shard of steel from the ground. It's a reminder. For every shot fired, for every explosion that makes your blood pump harder, there's a quiet aftermath. The recruiter never mentioned that for every hour of cool guy stuff we did, we had to do several hours of boring admin or maintenance... or cleaning up spent sabot petals.

They've got every crew on the range out here today, boots in the mud, doing the same tedious cleanup. Every tank that fired yesterday, which is all of them, left behind a mess, and now it's our turn to make it disappear. A truck crawls along behind us, its trailer slowly filling with discarded sabot petals as crews toss them in, one by one.

My crew is working the far right end of the stretch, where luckily, the ground isn't too littered. It gives us more time to shoot the shit, crack jokes, and maybe even appreciate the crisp German winter—if it weren't for the churned-up mud from the tanks, the fresh snow that fell overnight, and the fact that it feels like my damn face is about to freeze off.

The lack of petals for us to grab earns us more than a few cold stares. Some of the other crews glance up from their own cluttered sections, eyes narrowing beneath wool caps and helmet liners. Their hands are full of twisted aluminum and steel, while ours remain mostly empty. They don't say anything at first—just watch. Judging.

Then the muttering starts.

Short bursts are spoken in Polish, French, or whatever that crew's native language is. Some of the words, however, are in fact in English. They are muffled beneath their hushed breath and with a heavy accent. Their intent carries loud and clear. We hear it anyway. "Lazy Americans." "Soft." "Tourists in uniform."

One of the French gunners even intentionally, and harshly, bumps my shoulder, not even trying to hide the scowl on his face. I catch him saying *fainéants* before turning back to his task. I don't need to speak fluent French to get the message—dead weight.

Even the Germans, the hosts of this whole thing, eye us with a kind of reluctant tolerance. Like they're wondering how we made it this far. Like we're not pulling our weight.

Vic stiffens beside me as a Norwegian loader walks past and mutters something sharp and fast in his native tongue. Whatever it is, it's not friendly—judging by the bitter laugh that follows from his buddy. Fitz starts to ask what he said, but I shake my head and keep walking. Doesn't matter. We know what they mean. We're not dumb. Just outnumbered.

It's not fair; we didn't choose this side of the field. Command divided up the cleanup zones, and ours just happens to be light. But fairness doesn't mean much when everyone's freezing, tired, and pissed about having to play janitor after a live-fire exercise. We look like slackers. Even if we're not.

And frankly, I think some of them were just waiting for a reason to hate us.

I move slowly down the range, my boots sinking into the half-frozen sludge with every step. Each sabot petal I pick up is cold and slick in my gloved hands, its sharp edges dulled by mud and frost. I toss them into the truck's trailer without a second thought, the clinking sound barely audible over the distant rumble of engines from the various trucks behind us. The rest of the crew is ahead of me, laughing about something, but I let their voices fade into background noise. My focus is on the ground, scanning for more petals, but also... something else. I don't know what.

As we near the end of our section, a strange feeling settles over me. It's slow at first, creeping in like the chill that seeps through my jacket. I pause, straightening up, my breath misting in the cold air. My eyes drift past the treeline ahead, and then it hits me. This spot. This exact spot.

The Tiger.

The wrecked tank I saw the other day, the one in pristine condition, save the large hole in the side. It was here. Just outside these trees. A dull pressure builds in my chest, like a weight pressing down, slow but insistent. The logical part of my brain tells me that even if the tank was *real* then it's just a tank. Just an old husk from a war long past. But another part of me, the part that still remembers the way it looked, waiting... that part isn't so sure.

Turner glances back at me, his expression shifting as he sees that I've stopped. He knows. Maybe he doesn't know exactly what I'm thinking, but he feels it too. That same pull. That same unease.

Without a single thought, without hesitation, my feet start moving. The crunch of frost and mud beneath my boots barely registers as I step off the range and toward the treeline. The cold air seems heavier here, thicker.

I need to see it. I need to see the ground, the untouched mud, the absence of tracks. I need to prove to myself that what I saw yesterday wasn't real. That the Tiger, moving, watching, was just a trick of the mind.

Because if I don't check, I don't **know**. If I don't **know**, I can't shake the feeling that maybe it was real. And that means something is very, very wrong.

I step carefully into the clearing, my boots sinking slightly into the cold, damp earth. The area in front of the trees is open, eerily still, as if the world itself is holding its breath. I scan the ground, my eyes catching on several deep divots in the soil just outside the treeline. Their shape is unnatural, too round, too violent, like scars left behind by something that was never meant to be unearthed.

I swallow hard and take another step forward stepping directly inside one of the smaller craters. It feels old, but not ancient. Time has softened them considerably but yet they are still deep and scarring. The ground should have settled more, the elements should have worn them down more. But instead, they remain deep, jagged, almost fresh, as if something had torn through the earth with unimaginable force and then simply... stopped.

And then I see it. Just beyond the first line of trees, draped over roots and half-buried in the frost-covered dirt. Uniforms.

At first I think they're just coats, discarded hunting gear maybe, but as I step closer, the shapes sharpen. Heavy wool, the kind nobody wears anymore. Dark field-gray, trimmed with faded insignia that mean nothing to me but look military all the same. The cut is old-fashioned, too rigid, like something out of a black and white photograph. They don't look rotted either. Aside from the frost clinging to the fabric, they look almost fresh, like someone laid them out yesterday and walked away.

They aren't tossed haphazardly like forgotten trash, nor do they bear the decay of time. They sit eerily intact, untouched by years of wind and rain. Their fabric should be rotting, discolored. Instead, they look as if they were left here **yesterday**. The colors remain sharp, the stitching firm. Even from here, I can see the crisp folds where the fabric bends unnaturally over unseen shapes beneath.

Next to them, scattered across the ground, are weapons. Ammunition. Rations. But they don't look abandoned, not in the way old battlefield relics should. The wood of the rifles isn't cracked, the metal isn't rusted. The cans of rations gleam faintly in the dim light, as if they've been waiting almost preserved in time, untouched by years of neglect.

I take another step, and a shiver crawls up my spine. And then another. Without realizing it, I'm walking towards the uniforms. Towards the frontlines.

This isn't right.

This isn't **possible**.

I shouldn't be seeing this.

My foot catches on something thick and unyielding. A gnarled root that snakes across the ground like a grasping hand. I barely have time to register it before I'm falling, the earth rushing up to meet me. My hands shoot out, but the ground is unforgiving, knocking the breath from my lungs as I slam into the cold dirt.

For a moment, I just lay there, dazed. The sting of the impact lingers, but there's something else. A creeping sensation in the back of my mind. That root... it hadn't just been in my way. It had *taken* me down. Like the tree itself had reached out, grabbed me, **wanted** me to fall.

I push myself up slowly, shaking off the dirt and snow clinging to my uniform. My pulse hammers in my ears as I glance toward the treeline, expecting, *needing*, to see the uniforms, the weapons, the untouched relics of war.

But they're gone.

The trees stand silent, empty. There's nothing but bare, frostbitten ground and the craters that remain etched into the earth. No fabric, no gleaming metal, no impossible remnants of another time. Just... nothing.

I swallow hard. My breath curls in the cold air as I take a shaky step back. Had I imagined it? Or had the forest simply changed its mind on showing the secrets it hides?

Boots crunch through the frostbitten dirt, and before I can fully gather myself, Turner's already on me.

"Jesus, are you planning on digging your own grave, or was that just a really aggressive way to kiss the ground?" His voice is laced with amusement, but there's a flicker of something else—concern, maybe. Not much, but enough.

I brush off the dirt clinging to my jacket, scowling. "Yeah, yeah, laugh it up, fuzzball." My voice comes out more irritated than I mean it to, but honestly, I don't mind the distraction. It's better than standing here, staring at nothing, questioning my own damn sanity.

Turner smirks, crossing his arms. "I mean, you went down **hard**. For a second, I thought the earth was reclaiming you." He pauses, tilting his head. "Or maybe the trees just don't like you." A deep laugh escapes his chest. He lands a solid punch on my shoulder.

I huff, rolling my shoulders. "Yeah, well, if that's the case, they can get in line."

Turner snorts. "Fair enough. You good?"

I nod, still unsettled but grateful for the shift in focus. "Yeah. Let's just get this over with."

He claps me on the shoulder, still grinning. "Try not to get tackled by any more tree roots on the way back, huh?"

I shake my head, forcing a small smirk. "No promises."

Turner starts walking, leading the way back toward the others, but I can't stop myself from looking over my shoulder. The treeline lingers in my vision, the craters standing like scars in the earth, the place where...

I don't even know. I don't even know **what** I saw. Or if I saw anything at all.

But I can *feel* it. Something pulling at me, just beneath the surface of my thoughts. A quiet, nagging sensation that I should go back. That if I step just a little further in, I might find *something*.

Proof I'm not going insane? Answers to questions I don't even know I need to ask?

Hell, why do I even feel like I need to *ask* anything? It's a damn forest. Trees don't have answers. Trees don't whisper, and roots don't reach out. I shake my head, feeling ridiculous.

"You coming, or do I need to hold your hand, baby girl?" Turner calls back, a smirk in his voice.

I force myself to turn away. "You're not my type, Turner."

He laughs. "Your loss."

I follow him, but the feeling lingers. A weight at the back of my mind. Like the forest is still **watching**. Waiting.

I walk in silence, my boots sinking slightly into the damp earth with every step. Turner's a few paces ahead, occasionally glancing back, probably making sure I haven't tripped over anything else.

I should tell him.

I mean, what if I **am** just seeing things? What if it's just my brain playing tricks on me, the way it does when you're running on too little sleep and too much caffeine? Or maybe I just **wanted** to see something weird, so my mind filled in the blanks.

But what if I didn't?

What if something is **actually** wrong here?

I slow my steps, my stomach twisting. Turner notices almost immediately, stopping and turning to face me, his smirk fading.

He deserves to know. For the sake of my crew.

"What's up?"

I hesitate for a second, then take a breath. Screw it. If anyone's gonna think I'm crazy, might as well be Turner.

"I saw… something." My voice comes out quieter than I expect. Almost scared.

Turner raises an eyebrow. "Yeah, you saw the ground real close a minute ago. Did you hit your head?"

I give him a flat look. "No, before that. When I was near the treeline."

That gets his attention. His amusement dims just a little, replaced by something closer to curiosity. "Alright," he says, folding his arms. "I'll bite. What'd you see?"

I glance back again, as if the forest is going to answer for me. It doesn't. The clearing is still.

"I saw uniforms," I say finally. "Right inside the trees. Like someone had just left them there. No bodies, no blood, just... uniforms. And weapons. Ammo. Rations. All of it looked like it was left behind **yesterday**."

Turner doesn't interrupt, just lets me talk. So I keep going.

"And then I tripped," I say, my voice growing quieter. "And when I got back up, it was gone. Just... gone. The only thing left was the craters."

Turner's expression doesn't change much, but I can see the gears turning in his head. He's thinking. Processing. Trying to decide if I finally lost all of my marbles.

Finally, he exhales and rubs the back of his neck. "Huh."

"Huh?" I echo. "That's all you got?"

"What do you *want* me to say?" He gives me a lopsided grin. "That sounds freaky as hell, man, but didn't you say this morning this place has a history? Maybe you just..."

"Imagined it?" I finish for him.

He shrugs. "I wasn't gonna say it like *that*, but..."

I sigh. I expected that, but somehow it still bugs me. "I know what I saw, Turner."

He looks at me for a long moment, then nods. "Alright."

"Alright?"

"Yeah. Look, I don't know what you saw, but I **do** know you're not the type to freak out over nothing. So whatever happened back there, it was **something**."

I study him, searching for any trace of sarcasm or dismissal, but there's none. Just Turner being Turner, an annoying and cocky soldier, but still one of the only guys I trust.

I nod. "Yeah. Something."

Turner claps me on the shoulder, his usual grin creeping back. "Well, let's make a deal. If a ghost Nazi tank crew jumps out of the woods tonight, I'll believe you a hundred percent. Sounds fair?"

I shake my head but can't help the faint smirk. "Yeah, sure, Turner. Sounds fair."

But even as we keep walking, I know I won't stop thinking about it.

We walk in silence for a little while, continuing to clean up the massive range inch by inch. Foot by foot. One sabot petal at a time. The tension starts to fade, and Turner, being Turner, can't help himself to entertain others at my expense.

"Man, I gotta say, that was one hell of a fall back there. You *fully committed* to eating dirt. I'll bet your ex would have been jealous."

I let out a short laugh, shaking my head. "Yeah, yeah, real funny. Glad I could entertain you."

Turner grins, walking backwards for a few steps and spreads his arms like a comedian finishing a set. "Hey, it's the little things that get me through the day."

We walk a little further, the humor lingering between us. But then Turner slows down. His grin fades, replaced with something more serious. He looks down for a moment, kicking at the mud with his boot before speaking.

"I, uh... I do remember seeing something yesterday," he says quietly hoping the others don't hear.

I glance over at him, my stomach tightening. "The Tiger?"

He nods. "Yeah. Glad you saw it too." His voice is steady, but there's something beneath it. "I didn't get a great look, but when you pointed it out, I saw something moving out there. And I remember thinking..." He trails off, shaking his head like he's trying to find the right words.

"What?" I press.

He exhales, rubbing his hands together like he's trying to warm them up, even though I know that's not why. "It just... didn't feel right, man." He looks at me, his expression unusually serious. "I mean, I know *some* of the history of this place. At least whatever you wouldn't shut up about this morning when I was half listening to you. But when I saw that thing, it was like..." He hesitates, then finally says, "...like it **shouldn't** have been there."

A cold chill runs down my spine.

Turner keeps going. "And now, hearing what you saw today? I don't know, man. Maybe you're not crazy. Or maybe we both are." He lets out a dry chuckle, but there's no real humor in it.

I nod slowly, swallowing the lump in my throat. "Yeah. Maybe."

For a moment, we just stand there, both of us staring out toward the treeline. The forest is quiet. Still.

Then Turner claps me on the shoulder again, a little firmer this time. "But hey, if we *are* going nuts, at least we've got company, right?"

I let out a breath and nod. "Yeah. Could be worse. I could be related to you."

He smirks. "Damn right. Now, let's get this crap over with before they make us stay out here all day."

I force myself to move, but my mind is still turning over everything. The uniforms. The Tiger. Turner's words.

Maybe I'm not crazy.

But if I'm not... What the hell *is* going on out here?

The cleanup had gone much smoother than we expected. My crew was relieved to get some good downtime in the chow hall around some very poorly made coffee and a sub-par card game of spades. The other crews seemed to share the same relief. Everyone knew the quicker we finished, the sooner we could settle down. With most of the spent petals picked up and the range cleared, the once chaotic stretch of dirt now looked almost serene. It felt like we'd been running non-stop since we'd gotten here, so the thought of a quiet night, even if it was spent on the tanks, was a welcome one.

Before we can even complete a game of cards, though, we're summoned for a quick briefing. We get instructed to take our tanks on the range and camp out in the vehicles tonight. Once we're set we'll begin preparing for the next day's event. The air has a sharp, biting chill to it now, but nothing that can't be handled by the warmth of a few tank engines running. It isn't a luxury, but it's enough for us to recharge before the next phase of the competition. We park our tank in a relatively sheltered spot near the far end of the range, the looming trees still casting long shadows across the land.

A makeshift table is set up on the front slope of the tank from muddy backpacks to allow for a simple place to play the card game that was paused earlier.

Turner manages to open his MRE without a struggle, his dexterity with the plastic packets almost looks like he's performing a magic trick. He grins as he pulls out a "beef stew" and hands the wrapper to Fitz, who immediately scrunches his nose in disdain. "Man, I swear, they make these things worse every year," he says, poking at the slightly soggy contents with his spoon.

Fitz, on the other hand, has gone with the good ol' "chicken chunks". He gives it a suspicious sniff, clearly deciding whether to risk it. "You ever think about how these were probably made by machines, and then a guy somewhere said, 'Yeah, that looks good, send it out'? Makes me wanna rethink everything."

I can't help but chuckle at that. "You mean the same guy who's probably wearing a white coat, forgetting to taste test *anything*?"

"Yeah, that's the one," Fitz responds, raising an eyebrow. "Dude's living the dream."

We sit there quietly for a moment, the only sounds being the distant hum of various other tank engines from the other crews, and the occasional clink of spoons against plastic. No one is in a hurry to finish eating. No one is really hungry, either. The MREs are a bitter reminder of what we're doing here—what we have to keep doing. There's no real rest for a tanker. Even when we aren't on duty, there's always something else—cleaning, prepping, waiting.

I look out over the range, my eyes tracing the now-empty stretch of dirt and grass. The craters from yesterday's shoot are still visible, although much of the chaos has been cleaned up. A few spent petals lay forgotten in the mud, discarded remnants of another round gone by. It feels almost absurdly quiet now, as if the land is holding its breath, waiting for something.

"Hey, Sergeant," Turner breaks the silence, his voice light but with a hint of concern. "You ever wonder if we're just... wasting our time with all this clean-up? I mean, it feels like we're just... running in circles, you know?"

I turn to face him, unsure if I'm ready for that question. But then I realize it isn't a question that needs an answer. It's just something that had to be said.

"I don't know, man," I say, taking a swig of my water, the coldness of it sinking into my chest. "Maybe we are. But it's what we do, right? Keeps us busy and out of trouble. On the other hand, you'd probably knock up every girl in the local town if you had down time."

Turner nods slowly, grinning. I can see in his eyes that he's daydreaming of all the things he'd do with more than 15 minutes of free time. But he doesn't push it. Instead, he gives me one of those half-smirks of his that's somehow both reassuring and mocking all at once.

"That's one way to look at it," he says with a shrug.

We fall into a comfortable silence again, each of us lost in our thoughts, but at least it's a familiar silence. A silence that says we've been through enough together to know when not to press. It's the kind of silence that feels like the pause between punches—waiting for something to break it, but knowing we're all just too tired to care what that something is.

I catch myself glancing back toward the treeline, where the remnants of my strange walk linger in my memory. What had I seen there? Or thought I saw? I don't want to get too caught up in it. It isn't the time. But I can't shake the feeling that something is waiting for me back there.

"Hey," Fitz says suddenly, while laying out his cold weather sleeping bag on the blowout panels, "at least tomorrow is only land navigation. Shouldn't be too hard. We've got the GPS and maps. It'll be a breeze."

That's enough to pull me out of my head and remind me that I'm doing what I love. A new mission. A new stretch of road ahead of us. My gaze shifts back to the range, and the eerie quiet that has settled over the landscape.

"Well, let's hope the next mission goes smoother than this one," Turner says, motioning out over the range. He's standing on the back deck laying out his own sleeping bag and somehow managing to stand in the cold wearing nothing but his Hello Kitty underwear.

"That did not go in our favor... We shot well, but... it was weird." I chuckle, trying to hide my amusement.

There's no response as we each quietly begin bedding down for the night, the weight of the day settling in our bones. The hard part now is getting enough rest before tomorrow.

Because tomorrow is land nav.

It's easily one of the most grueling events of the competition. Each crew is handed a list of coordinates scattered across 75 to 100 square miles of unforgiving terrain—rolling hills, dense woods, steep inclines, and muddy tracks that seem tailor-made to bog down a seventy-ton tank. The objective is deceptively simple: reach as many points as possible and punch a unique marker card to prove you were there.

It spans four full days, not just because of the distance, but because of the toll it takes—physically, mentally, mechanically. Strategy becomes everything. Some points are clustered close but buried in rough ground. Others are far apart and easier to reach—if you're willing to burn the fuel and risk running dry.

That's the balancing act: speed versus efficiency. Do you move fast and hit more points, risking breakdowns or getting stuck? Or play it safe, take fewer stops, and sacrifice quantity for consistency? And then there's the choice to rest. Stopping for the night gives your crew a breather and keeps everyone sharp, but every hour of sleep is an hour your rivals are moving. On the flip side, pushing through the night can win you ground—or burn your crew out completely.

It's not just a test of navigation. It's a test of judgment, resourcefulness, and how well your crew works under pressure. You're not just driving a tank—you're managing fuel, fatigue, terrain, time. Every decision is a gamble, and by the end of day two, only the smartest and most cohesive teams will have enough punches to stand a chance.

And for us? We'll need more than a smart plan. We'll need a little bit of luck.

Everyone finally completes the uncomfortable task of finding a place to sleep for the night on the tank or finding their place to bed down. The air temperature has already dropped significantly, a sharp chill creeping in as the light fades. Everyone is doing their best to settle in, trying to stay warm with what little they have. Field blankets, "woobies," are haphazardly thrown over shoulders, and sleeping bags are zipped up all the way to the chin, but the cold seems relentless, no matter how much you bundle up.

Vic slides into the driver's compartment, settling into his spot, the space a little too cramped to be comfortable, but at least it's warmer than outside. Fitz finds a space beside the turret, trying to get a little more distance from the damp ground. Turner lounges against the engine deck, trying to ignore the stiffening of his back after hours of movement and strain. I take my position on the turret, half out of habit, half out of necessity—always ready to react, even if it's in the dead of night.

The only sounds are the wind rustling through the trees and the distant hum of other crews settling in around the range. The night is calm and we all know it won't last. The cold isn't the worst of it, though. It's the constant unease, the feeling of being watched, the strange thoughts still swirling from earlier in the day. Everyone is trying not to think about it. But there's no way to ignore the weight of the unknown pressing in on us from every direction. We might have made it through the first two major events of the competition, but what about the next one? Or the one after that? No one says it, but we're all wondering the same thing. How long can we keep this up before we crack?

[CHAPTER SIX: TENSION ON THE FRONTLINES]

"Is known as Fiddlers' Green."

16 DECEMBER 1944

The voice cuts through the fog in my head before I even recognize it. A firm shake follows, jolting me upright.

"Sergeant, wake up."

My eyes snap open, and I'm met with the face of the Infantry Captain, his expression a mix of irritation and concern. His breath plumes in the cold morning air, and for a moment, I struggle to remember where I am, why I'm here.

I blink hard, trying to shake off the sluggish weight in my skull. My body aches like I've been hauling tank shells all night. My fingers are stiff, my uniform damp with cold sweat. I look around, desperate to orient myself.

The trees loom overhead, their bare branches clawing at the pale morning sky. Just a few yards behind, half-shrouded in the mist, sits the ruined Tiger tank. The same one from yesterday.

My breath catches.

Yesterday.

I remember stopping here. We'd pulled into the trees to check our bearings. The engine had cut out. But then, no, that's not right. That's not all that happened. We had been deeper in the forest. Miles in. The tank wouldn't move. But then it did. We tried to leave, again and again, only to end up back where we started. That endless, looping n ightmare.

But now... now we're back at the edge. Back near the Tiger.

"How...?" The word barely makes it past my lips. My throat is raw, my voice hoarse like I haven't spoken in days.

The Infantry Captain frowns. "That's what I'd like to know. Your tank's been sitting here all night. No lights, no movement. You were supposed to regroup with us yesterday evening after your run. What the hell happened?"

I swallow hard and glance around the inside of *Calculated Vengeance*. The rest of the crew is still inside, huddled against the cold. Fitz is half-slumped in the loader's seat, his helmet tilted forward, arms crossed tight over his chest. Harris stirs slightly in the gunner's seat but doesn't wake. Rich and Tommy sit peacefully sleeping in the hull.

I force myself to stand, my knees stiff and unwilling. My breath comes out shaky as I scan the ground. There aren't any tracks leading into the forest. We never moved.

I scan the area, trying to ground myself in reality, to find something, anything, that makes sense.

The knocked-out Tiger tank sits just behind, its hulking frame half-buried in frost and shadow. The jagged hole in its armor is still fresh, the blackened edges stark against the dull gray steel. Around it, the ground is pockmarked with deep craters, scars left behind when its ammunition cooked off in a violent chain reaction. I can still picture the fireball, the way the turret had lurched slightly as something inside detonated.

But that isn't what makes my breath hitch.

Scattered just beyond the wreck, barely visible in the morning haze, are the uniforms. German feldgrau, stiff with frost, motionless. Weapons lie among them, Kar98 rifles propped against trees, an MG42 on its bipod, belts of ammunition still neatly packed beside it. There are rations too, pristine as if they were left only hours ago, their waxed paper wrappings untouched by time. Everything looks hollow, abandoned mid-use. As if the men who once carried them simply… vanished. Or did they run? If they ran then why didn't they take their weapons or rations?

But there's something wrong—something that scratches at the back of my skull like a splinter I can't reach. There's no blood. No bodies. Just gear, laid out like a display. We lit up this treeline yesterday. I saw the tracers carve into the brush, heard the rounds slap into the area, the screams—real, human screams. But there's nothing here now. Not even drag marks or boot prints leading away. No blood in the dirt, no torn uniforms, no shattered helmets. Just the eerie stillness of an untouched crime scene. It doesn't make sense. If they died here, they should still be here. If they fled, they wouldn't have left everything behind. The forest doesn't look like it swallowed them—it looks like it never had them to begin with.

I shake the thought away and turn toward the huddled forms near my tank. The infantry. A few dozen or so of them, wrapped in greatcoats, stamping their feet against the cold. Some are sitting on their helmets, arms crossed, trying to conserve warmth. Their breath drifts in thin clouds, their eyes heavy with exhaustion.

The Infantry Captain sits on the side of the turret, arms tucked into his coat. "Hell of a show you put on yesterday," he says, his tone unreadable. "We were right behind you when you took out that Tiger. Watched the whole thing."

I glance at him, my mind still sluggish. I'm thankful the Captain witnessed the Tiger kill. It takes an officer witnessing the act for it to count as a confirmed kill for your tank crew's record.

"You hit it clean, right through the hull," he continues. "Didn't even have time to return fire. Then you hosed down the treeline, chewed through anything that might've been hiding in here. That was damn impressive."

The words feel distant, like they belong to someone else's memory. My hands flex involuntarily, the ghost of yesterday's battle still imprinted in my muscles. I remember firing. I remember the chaos. But I also remember something else, something that doesn't add up.

Because if we'd never left this spot, if we've been here all night...

Then where the hell had we been? Was it a dream?

A sharp crack cuts through the cold morning air. Then another. And another.

The area deep within the treeline ahead of us erupts with muzzle flashes, the distinct staccato of German rifles mixing with the deep, relentless chatter of an MG42. Dirt kicks up around the tank and infantry. Someone yells. Someone else screams.

The first man to go down is barely five feet in front of my tank. He's mid-step when the MG42's rounds tear into him, his body jerking as if yanked by invisible strings before he crumples into the mud. Another man beside him barely has time to react before a burst rips into his chest, sending him sprawling backward, his rifle slipping from numb fingers. A third soldier takes a hit to the shoulder, spinning violently before collapsing.

Shit.

I throw myself into the turret, gripping the rim as I drop myself inside. "Contact! Deep inside the treeline! A hundred yards out!"

Everyone explodes into motion.

Harris is already scrambling to his gunner's controls, his hands moving on instinct as he swings the turret toward the flashing muzzles in the trees.

"Loading HE!" Fitz barks, yanking open the ammo rack and dragging out a high-explosive round. He shoves it into the breach with practiced precision.

The breach slams shut. "Up!"

"Send it!"

The tank lurches with the recoil as Harris fires. The HE round streaks toward the muzzle flashes and a second later, the explosion rips through the forest, sending shattered wood and debris flying. The MG42 hesitates. But only for a moment.

The bow gun comes to life from Tommy's station, a steady stream of .30-caliber fire hammering into the trees, cutting down anything caught in its path. The gunner swings the turret's co-axial machine gun into position, squeezing the trigger, sending another wall of fire deeper in the treeline.

The Infantry Captain wastes no time. With a practiced motion, he scrambles up onto the back of the turret and grabs the .50 caliber mounted there. The massive weapon roars to life, deafening even over the chaos, its heavy rounds ripping into the woods. Each burst shakes the tank as spent casings rain down around us.

I don't think. I don't process. I just fight.

The cold morning is gone. The doubt, the confusion. Gone. There is only the battle, the enemy in the trees, and the instinct to survive.

The battle rages on in a deafening storm of fire and steel. The tank rocks back and forth with every shot, the thump of the main gun sending a shockwave through my chest, the rattle of the co-ax and bow gun filling every space in my skull. Every time the cannon fires, it's like the world stutters—vision blurs, ears ring, and for one fraction of a second, it feels like the earth itself reels from the impact. The smell of gunpowder mixes with the thick odor of oil and metal, coating the inside of the tank like a second skin. Shell casings clatter around our feet, hot brass pinging against the floor, the sound sharp and constant, like hail on a tin roof.

Outside, the woods are a blur of motion and muzzle flashes—infantry weaving between trees, tracers slicing the morning haze, and fire curling up from shattered tree trunks. The Germans are dug in deeper than we thought, and they're not letting go easily. Small arm rounds skip off our hull with a sickening clang, and every impact tightens something in my chest. I yell orders into the intercom, barely hearing my own voice over the chaos. The turret spins, groans, and locks onto another target. Harris is already squeezing off another shot. We are locked in a rhythm now—see, aim, fire—again and again, hammering the treeline like it owes us something.

"Another HE, coming up!" Fitz shouts over the chaos, shoving a fresh shell into the breach.

"Up!"

"Send it!"

Harris fires again, and another explosion tears through the treeline, swallowing muzzle flashes in a bloom of fire and splintered wood. The MG42's song of death stutters, then falls silent, but the rifle fire still comes in waves, relentless and desperate.

The infantry around us fights like hell. Some take cover behind the tank, bracing their weapons against its armor as they fire back. Others are pinned down, scrambling through the mud, trying to find an angle that won't get them cut down. I see another man take a hit. A single shot, clean through the throat. He drops his weapon and clutches at the wound, eyes wide with shock, falling backward as life drains from him.

I grit my teeth, forcing the anger down. No time. No room for that now.

The .50-cal barks overhead, the Captain keeping up a steady stream of fire, his jaw set like iron as he tracks movement in the trees. The enemy is still there, still fighting, but something feels different now. Their fire isn't as focused. It's sporadic, panicked. They're breaking.

Minutes stretch into eternity, the tank roaring back at the trees, the woods alive with muzzle flashes and the sharp reports of rifles and machine guns. And then, slowly, the gunfire thins.

The final German rifle cracks once, twice, then silence.

For a moment, the only sound is the ringing in my ears, the steam rising from the tank's barrel, the ragged breaths of my crew. My grip on the turret is so tight my knuckles ache. My heart slams against my ribs.

Harris draws in a sharp breath through his teeth, leaning in tighter to the sight. "I've got movement—figures in the treeline. They're running."

His voice cuts through with a brittle intensity, focused, but laced with something else underneath—disbelief.

I blink, trying to process. **Running**? Germans don't run. Not like that. Not in broad daylight, not when they think they've got the edge. Not unless something's got them scared.

I press the headset tighter against my ear. "Driver—forward. Let's go. We're chasing them down." My voice comes out flatter, colder than I mean it to, like it's already been stripped down to bone by the noise and pressure.

The tank lurches forward with a growl, treads chewing into the frozen earth. Branches snap beneath us, and the treeline ahead seems to shift—alive with the scattered shadows of fleeing shapes. I can't tell if they're Germans or something else, and part of me doesn't care. We're not letting them regroup.

Out of the corner of my eye, I catch the Infantry Captain still clutching the edge of the turret, his knuckles white. His face says it all—this isn't what he signed up for. Maybe he expected armor to hang back and cover him, not to charge headlong into the woods like a battering ram.

He mutters something under his breath I can't hear, then clambers down from the back of the tank with stiff, deliberate movements. I watch him retreat toward his men, jaw set and shoulders tight. He's decided he doesn't want to be part of whatever madness we're about to drive into.

Good. He'd only slow us down.

My jaw tightens until it aches, teeth grinding as my pulse throbs in my ears. They're *running*. I can't stop thinking about it—can't *accept* it. Not fighting. Not making a stand. Just scattering like cowards, slipping away into the woods with their tails tucked between their legs. No defiance. No price paid.

The rage rises, thick and hot, clawing its way up from the pit of my stomach. It doesn't matter that we've pushed them back. It doesn't matter that we hold the ground now. I want them *crushed*. I want to see them torn to pieces, burned out of the trees like the vermin they are.

They had the guts to ambush us—had the nerve to open up first, to butcher our men without warning. And now they just *run*? Like it's over? Like they don't owe something for what they've done?

No. Not this time. Not today.

"Quit running!" I roar over the grind of the engine shouting into the dense trees. "You'll just die tired!" My voice tears from my throat, hoarse and ragged, spit flying as I shout into the treeline. "Cowards! Stand and fight, damn you!"

The fury boils over, spilling past any sense of discipline or composure. I barely notice the bite of the cold wind as I lean out of the hatch, white-knuckled, gripping the rim like it's the only thing anchoring me. The tank lurches over roots and torn earth, chewing through undergrowth as we surge forward, and still I see them—figures, fleeting shapes between trees, barely more than shadows now.

They're ghosts. Slipping away. And it feels **wrong**. Like they shouldn't be allowed to disappear like this—shouldn't be allowed to just **leave**.

"They won't understand a damn word," I mutter to myself, breath fogging in the air—but it doesn't stop me. I cup my hands to my mouth and shout again, this time in broken, snarled German, words twisted by my fury and a poor accent: "*Hört auf zu rennen! Ihr werdet nur müde sterben!*"

Stop running! You'll just die tired!

But they don't stop.

They never even look back. Just flickers of motion between tree trunks, melting deeper into the forest like it's swallowing them whole. A sick feeling settles in my chest. I wanted to scare them, to punish them. But they're not scared. They're **gone**.

And I'm left shouting at shadows.

I slam my fist against the turret rim hard enough to sting, frustration crackling through every nerve. "*Feiglinge! Steht und kämpft!*" I shout, louder this time, the words ripping from my throat like an accusation hurled across the void. *Cowards! Stand and fight!* My voice now barked with sharper fury, my voice echoing off the trees like a curse.

But the forest gives nothing back.

No shouts. No answering fire. Just the whisper of wind twisting through skeletal branches, the crunch of ice breaking beneath the treads, and the distant creak of something shifting in the cold. The trees swallow my voice like they're used to devouring screams. That silence—it isn't peaceful. It's mocking.

My blood simmers hotter with each second. If they'd stayed and fought, at least there'd be something **honest** in that. But this retreat, this **vanishing**? It feels like theft. Like they're robbing me of something I **deserve**.

From his station, Harris breaks the stillness. "I see 'em!" he calls, voice tight through the intercom. "Shadows slipping through the trees—fast! Looks like they're breaking into two groups!"

"Which way?" I demand, twisting in my hatch to try and spot them myself.

"Both sides," Harris replies. "Splitting left and right. They're trying to lose us in the trees."

I slam my fist down again, the metal ringing out like a challenge. "Rich, keep us moving straight! We'll force 'em out into the open!"

"Copy," Rich answers from the driver's seat. His voice is steady, a calm core beneath the chaos. God bless him.

In the loader's position, Fitz is already one step ahead of me. "HE's up!" he shouts, slamming the breech closed with a satisfying clunk.

"Send it!" I bark.

The 76mm cannon kicks like a mule, rocking the whole tank back as Harris fires. The shell disappears into the forest with a crack, and a second later the underbrush explodes—flames, splinters, and a shockwave of dirt and bark erupt into the air. Smoke billows and mixes with the morning haze, rolling across the forest floor like it's alive.

Harris adjusts, already sighting in again. "Still moving!" he growls. "Damn, they're quick..."

Then, finally, the enemy answers. Small arms chatter back at us—sporadic, desperate bursts. A few rounds ping off our armor with faint metallic snaps, more warning than threat. They aren't fighting to win anymore. Just to **get away.**

"Come on, you bastards," I mutter, glaring into the trees, hand clenching around the rim of the hatch. "You wanted a fight? Then fight!"

But they don't. They never do.

Shadows dart through the fog like phantoms, impossible to pin down. Every time I think I've fixed on one, it's already gone, slipping behind a tree or vanishing in the folds of smoke. They move like they know the forest better than we ever could. Like they **belong** in it. We're intruders—no, **prey.**

The anger twists deeper in my gut, sharper now. They're not just running—they're mocking us by getting away.

The tank lumbers forward, the forest tightening around us. Branches scrape against the sides, brittle with frost, and the cold bleeds in through every seam. The treads clatter over churned-up mud and frozen roots, grinding deeper into terrain no tank has any business entering. But we follow, because I **refuse** to let them vanish.

The firefight behind us has dulled into silence, absorbed by the endless trees. All we hear now is the low growl of the engine and the occasional snap of a broken branch underfoot. It's like the forest is holding its breath.

Harris speaks again, voice low. "I don't see 'em anymore," he mutters. "They're gone."

My stomach sinks, but I don't let it show. I stay upright in the hatch, scanning the gray morning mist, daring those ghosts to reappear.

They don't.

And that emptiness, that unfinished feeling in the pit of my chest—that's worse than any firefight. Where had that rage come from? It isn't like me to just devolve into a fit of pure *rage*. It's like someone else was in my body. Like **something** was influencing my decision-making.

"Keep looking," I snap, gripping the hatch rim tight. My pulse is still pounding in my ears. My breath comes in short, angry bursts. They had been right there, running, scattering like rats in the underbrush. Now, nothing.

Fitz shifts uneasily in his seat. "Maybe they're settin' up an ambush?"

"Maybe," I admit. But something feels off. We've been chasing them hard, pressing them into the trees, keeping fire on them every step of the way. There should be something. Movement, a muzzle flash, a figure slipping between the trees. Instead, there's only the wind, bending the branches in slow, whispering waves.

The tank rolls on, past shattered stumps and churned-up earth where our shells had struck. Two hundred yards in now. No movement. No enemy. Just the trees standing silent, the cold pressing in on all sides.

I exhale, slow and controlled. "Rich, hold up."

The tank grumbles to a stop, steam rising from the exhaust into the frozen air. I scan the forest, eyes darting between the dark trunks, the skeletal branches reaching skyward.

Nothing.

Just the trees.

Just the wind.

The silence hangs thick in the frozen air, broken only by the steady idle of the engine. My grip tightens on the hatch rim, my breath is curling in the cold. We've chased them far enough. There's nothing left but empty woods and the ghost of a fight that had already moved on

I exhale sharply. "Rich, turn us around. We're heading back."

The tank groans as it pivots in place, treads grinding against the frostbitten earth. Harris lets out a frustrated sigh, pulling away from the gunsight. "Damn cowards," he mutters. "Ran instead of fighting. Pisses me off."

He isn't alone in that feeling. The chase had stirred something raw in me. A need to make them pay for what they did back there. But there's no sense charging blind into a fight we can't even see.

As we rumble back toward the treeline, the familiar sight of the American infantry comes into view. Their figures stand out against the snow-dusted ground, huddled together, tending to their wounded. And their dead.

The Infantry Captain spots us first, and begins storming towards the tank as soon as we roll up. His face is twisted with fury, his breath steaming in the cold air. He slaps a gloved hand against the side of the hull as if he means to shake the whole damn tank.

"What the hell was that?" he barks. "You let them get away! You had 'em running, and you just let 'em go!"

I bristle, my own frustration flaring white-hot. I pop the hatch, staring down at him with a scowl. "We pushed 'em as far as we could. They vanished into the trees. What do you want us to do? Chase ghosts?"

"I want you to do your damn job!" he spits. "I lost men today! Because your crew wasn't good enough to finish the damn fight!"

Something in me snaps. I shoot up straighter in the hatch, voice as cold as the air around us. "Not good enough? You think we didn't do our part? We put down that Tiger for you! We broke their line, kept 'em from overrunning your position, and gave you a fighting chance!

You'd have lost a hell of a lot more if it wasn't for us, so don't stand there and tell me we weren't good enough."

The Infantry Captain stares up at me, chest heaving, his hands clenched at his sides. He wants to argue, to spit back more rage, but the truth weighs heavier than his anger. His jaw tightens, and he looks away, back toward his men. Toward the bodies in the snow.

He doesn't say another word.

With a final glare, I drop back into the turret and slam the hatch shut. My hands are shaking, not from the cold, but from the fury still burning in my chest.

"Bastard," Harris mutters. "Like we didn't save his sorry ass."

I don't answer. I just let out a slow breath and lean back against the cold metal of the turret. Let him be mad. Let him blame us if it helps him sleep tonight.

But we know the truth. And that will have to be enough.

Finally, the Captain returns. He's calmer now as if he wasn't just yelling at me and accusing me of being the reason some of his men breathed their last today. His voice almost resembles control. "We're going to regroup," he said stiffly. "Call for field ambulances to come and take..."

He stops, the words catching in his throat. For a moment, the mask of command slips, and I see it. The raw grief behind his eyes. He can't even say it. Can't bring himself to admit that some of his men aren't getting back up.

He swallows hard and pushes forward. "First thing in the morning," he continues, voice harder now, "We're going to let you push into the forest and chase them down. Tank in front while the infantry hold fast behind. You'll have to settle this score yourself."

I feel my rage spark fresh. I turn back to him, fists clenching at my sides. "Are you kidding me?" I snap. "Alone? You just saw what happened! You're sending us in there blind without support? That's suicide! That's…"

"Enough." His voice is a blade cutting through my words.

He turns sharply, snapping his fingers at the nearby radioman. The soldier stiffens, and begins hurrying over with the heavy pack slung across his back. The Captain's hand hovers just above the receiver, his glare locking onto me like a predator sizing up its kill.

"You wanna keep arguing, Sergeant?" he growls. "Because I'll make one call to Battalion, to the Colonel, and have your entire damn crew court-martialed for disobeying orders and running in the face of the enemy."

My breath hitches in my throat. "That's not what happened, and you know it."

"I know what I saw," he spits. "And what I saw was a bunch of cowards turning tail and allowing the **enemy** to escape."

I can feel my pulse hammering in my skull, the sheer injustice of it making my hands shake. He isn't just angry, he hates us. Hates us enough to throw us to the wolves just to satisfy his grudge.

Harris mutters a curse under his breath, his hand twitching toward the hull like he wants to punch something. Tompson and Fitz are silent, but I can feel their eyes on me, waiting. Waiting for me to push back, to say something, to fix this.

But there is no fixing this.

I grind my teeth so hard my jaw aches. Every fiber of my being screams at me to keep fighting, to tell this bastard exactly what I think of him and his bullshit orders. But one word over that radio, and we're done. Stripped of our ranks. Shackled and sent home in disgrace. If they don't decide to throw us into the next meat grinder as punishment.

I force myself to swallow my fury.

"We'll be ready in the morning," I reply, my voice like stone.

The Infantry Captain smirks, satisfied, and drops his hand away from the radio. Without another word, he turns and begins walking off into the clump of his men.

I exhale slowly, my breath trembling as it leaves me. I feel Harris shift beside me. "This is bullshit," he mutters.

He isn't wrong.

And tomorrow, we'll likely be paying the price for it.

The Captain has barely taken a step away before he pauses, then turns just enough to glance back over his shoulder. There's something in his eyes. Something cold and cutting, like a predator toying with its prey. Something... almost unnatural.

"Oh, and one more thing..." His voice is calm, almost casual, but there is a weight behind it that made my gut twist. He lets the pause hang just long enough to make sure we're listening. Then, with a smirk that barely hides his contempt, he adds, "If, **when**, you run into contact tomorrow, you better be ready to handle it yourselves... I'm not sure my men will be... inclined to assist you."

The words settle over us like a death sentence. He isn't just sending us in ahead of the infantry. He's making damn sure our death warrant is signed in ink by the reaper himself.

I clench my fists at my sides, biting back the surge of rage that threatens to boil over. Harris mutters something under his breath, his hand tightening around the edge of the turret. Tompson and Fitz don't say a word, but I can feel the tension radiating off them like heat from an engine.

The Captain doesn't wait for a response. He just turns and walks away, his boots crunching against the frozen earth, leaving us standing there in the bitter cold with the weight of his words pressing down on us.

I exhale slowly, my breath visible in the night air. Tomorrow was already a suicide mission. Now, it's worse.

[CHAPTER SEVEN: DEAD ENGINES AND LIVING NIGHTMARES]

"Marching past, straight through to Hell."

17 December 2024

"See? This is why I said we should've taken the other path," Fitz grumbles, kicking a rock as he walks alongside the tank.

"Oh, shut the hell up, Fitz," Vic fires back from his spot in the driver's hatch, his head just poking up above the hatch ring. "Maybe if someone had been spotting instead of running his damn mouth, we wouldn't have almost ended up face-first in a ditch."

"You had **one** job, Vic! Drive in a straight line," Fitz snaps, waving his arms dramatically. "We're not even in combat, and you're already trying to get us killed."

"It wasn't that bad," Turner chimes in, swinging down from the side of the tank with a smirk. "We didn't even get stuck all the way."

"Yeah?" Vic spins toward him. "Then why the hell did we have to dig out the treads with the pioneer tools?"

I sigh, rubbing my temples as I listen to them bicker. "Alright ladies, enough. Look, the tank's fine, and **nobody** died. The only thing hurt here is Vic's pride."

Vic scoffs. "Damn right my pride's hurt. You think I wanna explain to the brass why the **only** American tank in this competition almost became a lawn ornament?"

"Just hope we get it out before the Germans show up to laugh at us," I mutter, shaking my head. "Now, are we done bitching, or do I need to get some crayons so you guys can **illustrate** your complaints?"

That earns a few chuckles, and finally, the tension starts to break. But as we gather around the tank, brushing off the mud and attempting to dig out some of the slick mud under the tracks, the weight of the exercise looms over us like a sack of bricks. We're supposed to be an elite crew and so far we've done nothing to prove that we're anything better than mediocre. Even this part of the competition, land navigation, isn't just about getting from point A to point B. It's about problem solving, resource management and crew management. And after nearly ditching our ride, we sure as hell have something to prove.

Vic throws the tank into reverse, the engine growling as the treads churn uselessly in the soft earth. The tank shudders but barely moves.

"Goddamn it," Vic mutters, shifting into neutral. "We're stuck deeper than I thought."

"Yeah, no shit," Turner deadpans, arms crossed.

"We need to give the treads something to grip." I say, looking around. I see some small bushes to my right and a small tree. I grab the axe and get to work.

We grab whatever we can, branches, loose rocks, even a small log, and jam them under the treads. Vic gives it another go. The tank lurches, tilts, and for a second, I think we might tip even further in. But then, with a metallic groan and a cloud of kicked-up mud, *Controlled Violence* finally drags herself free.

"About damn time," Turner grumbles, wiping his hands on his pants.

I pull out the map and check our position. What was supposed to be a smooth run has already turned into a mess. I trace our route with my finger, trying to gauge how much time we've lost.

"How bad?" Fitz asks, stepping up next to me.

I exhale sharply. "Bad. We're way behind schedule. If we keep following the planned route, we'll finish dead last."

"Great," Turner mutters. "Any bright ideas?"

Fitz looks up from the map and points ahead. "We could cut through there."

I follow his finger toward the treeline. The forest ahead of us is thick, dark, and completely off any paved paths. The rules don't explicitly say we **can't** take a shortcut, but there's a reason why most crews stick to the roads. Visibility would be shit, the terrain unpredictable. One wrong move, and we'd end up worse off than a simple ditch. But we could save a few hours rather than go around it.

"Are you sure about that?" I ask, raising an eyebrow.

Fitz shrugs. "It's a gamble. But unless you have a better plan, I say we go for it."

I glance back at the crew. Vic is still grumbling to himself, Turner looks amused by the whole thing.

"Alright," I say after a beat. "We're doing it."

Turner groans. "We're gonna die in there, aren't we?"

"Only if Vic finds another ditch." I smirk.

Vic flips me off. With a deep breath, I climb back up, feeling an uneasy weight settle in my gut as my gaze settles on the forest ahead.

We mount up and push forward, the tank rumbling over the uneven terrain, the treeline begins to loom closer. The forest ahead is thick, the kind that swallows light and sound, making it feel like a different world entirely. The closer we get, the more I feel that weight in my gut pressing down harder.

Then the radio crackles.

At first, it's just static. No big deal, probably some crew trying to transmit that's out of range. But then, faintly, through the distortion, I hear something.

"...Our... position is compromised... we **can't** *hold the line... artillery inbound... our medic was..."*

The voice is distant, garbled, like the transmission is bouncing off several mountaintops miles away..

"The hell was that?" Turner asks, leaning forward, brow furrowed.

Fitz taps the side of his headset. "I don't know, but that sure as hell didn't sound like normal English to me."

"It was plain English," I say slowly, adjusting the volume dial on my station's intercom box. The transmission is gone now, swallowed back into the static. "Probably some far-off crew having issues with their scenario. But that's not possible. There's no live-fire scenario today, and no other units outside the competition should be transmitting on our frequency."

The crew goes quiet. The tank keeps rolling, the trees creeping closer.

Then, another burst of static—this one sharper, angrier.

"Tiger! Tiger! Right stick, break off! Jesus Christ, where's our—"

The radio goes dead, swallowed by static once more. But just as I'm about to speak, a distant **boom** rolls through the air.

It's faint, almost muffled by the thick forest ahead, but it's there. A deep, percussive thud, the kind that settles into your chest like an aftershock.

I stare at the treeline, my grip on the map tightening. There wasn't supposed to be any live fire today. At least, there's not one on the schedule. And what was all of that about a Tiger?

"Tell me someone else heard that," I say, scanning the crew.

"Yeah," Fitz mutters. "And I don't like it."

I exhale, forcing the unease down. Up ahead, just off to the right, a perfect tank-sized opening in the treeline catches my eye. It's barely noticeable, almost swallowed by the undergrowth, but it's there, a natural path leading into the woods.

I tap the rim of the hatch. "Vic, take us in through that gap up ahead. Stay slow, watch for soft ground."

Vic hesitates for just a second before responding, "Copy that," and nudging the throttle forward.

Controlled Violence lurches ahead, leaving the open terrain behind as we slip into the shadow of the trees.

Nobody says a word.

Turner exhales through his nose. "So… Do we keep going?"

I glance back at the forest's edge, then back at the radio, fingers tightening around the map. Whatever that transmission earlier was, it wasn't normal. But normal or not, we're already committed.

"Yeah," I say, forcing my voice to stay steady. "We keep going."

We barely make it twenty feet into the trees when the engine sputters, then dies.

A thick, suffocating silence follows, broken only by the soft creak of the hull settling into the earth. For a moment, nobody speaks.

Then fury rises in my blood, for seemingly no reason. Double tapping the engine can cause extreme damage. Not only that but we were actively driving. Who knows what kind of damage the powerpack sustained. "Vic! Did you double-tap the engine?"

"I didn't touch a damn thing!" Vic snaps, already flipping switches and checking gauges. "Swear to God, she just… *quit*."

I slap the side of the hatch in frustration. "Bullshit! This thing doesn't just *quit*! You probably hit the engine shutoff button with your elbow or something stupid!"

Vic ignores me, cursing under his breath as he tries again. The ignition clicks, but the engine doesn't even attempt to turn over. No power, no response, *nothing*. I look around the inside of the turret and notice that none of the electronics are running. Everything is shut off as if we had parked the tank at the end of the day and shut everything down.

Fitz lets out a low whistle. "That's bad."

"Really, Sherlock? I never guessed," I mutter.

The electronics are down. Which means no comms, no fire control, *no radio*. If we have to slave-start it, basically a jump-start using another tank, then we're screwed. And without the radio, we've got no way to call for help.

Turner sighs. "Well… we *could* get out and start waving our arms around like idiots until another crew comes and rescues us."

Nobody laughs.

I finally decide to climb up onto the turret, needing to clear my head and get a better sense of where the hell we are. The cold air bites at my face the second I emerge. I stand slowly, boots planting firm on the steel as I rise above the tank. For a moment, I just breathe. In. Out. Trying to shake the tension that's been festering since we rolled into this cursed forest.

Then I look around.

And I freeze.

I remember clearly—we only drove in maybe twenty feet. Thirty at most. The treeline had still been visible behind us. I'm sure of it. But n ow?

There's nothing.

No edge. No break in the dense curtain of trees. Just endless forest in every direction, the trunks packed prison bars, their tops swallowed by mist. The sunlight is thin, washed-out, barely filtering through the canopy above. It feels later than it should be—later, or earlier, or not a time that exists on any clock I know. The shadows stretch long, bending and warping over the forest floor like something alive.

It makes no sense. None of this makes sense.

I turn in a slow circle, scanning for anything familiar, any landmark we passed. But all I see is the same. The same twisted trees. The same dim light. The same endless silence.

The forest swallowed us whole—and moved the walls.

I slide back into the hatch, unease curling tighter in my chest. "Something's wrong," I say aloud.

Turner glances up from his seat, brow furrowed. "You mean besides the tank dying for no reason and the radio being fried?"

"Yes," I say. "I mean... we were right by the edge. Now it's gone. It's like we're deeper than we should be. Way deeper."

Fitz leans forward, his eyes narrowing. "I thought we just drove in."

"We did," I say. "And now we're somewhere else."

There's a pause. That kind of pause where nobody wants to say what they're all thinking, because saying it might make it real.

Then I catch a glimpse of something in the mist.

Metal. Curved. Familiar.

The top of a Sherman turret.

And just like that, I know—we're not alone out here.

I glance over at Fitz, still watching the mist like it might suddenly part and give us answers.

"Hey," I say quietly. "You remember how far we drove into the tree-line?"

He doesn't answer right away. Just keeps staring ahead, brow furrowed like he's trying to force a memory into place.

After a beat, he shakes his head.

"I don't," he admits. "I don't remember driving into the treeline at all."

That catches me off-guard.

"What do you mean? We just talked about this less than five seconds ago. Did you already forget?" I ask, voice low.

Fitz hesitates again. "I remember the radio... There was something about a Tiger. Then a loud boom. Next thing I know, you're yelling, then asking where we are."

His voice goes tight near the end, like even saying it out loud makes it feel less real. Less safe.

I don't answer him. Because now I'm not sure I remember it clearly either.

And that's the part that scares me.

The quiet settles in again, heavier now. Outside the tank, the trees stretch out like dark sentinels. And somewhere beyond them... something moves.

It's slow. Distant. But undeniably there.

I glance at my watch.

4:45pm.

That can't be right. We had gotten unstuck from that ditch sometime around noon. It feels like we've been stuck here for minutes, not hours. The world is **off** in some deep, wrong way.

I decide that hiding in the tank won't do us any good, so I haul myself out of the vehicle and begin to start formulating a plan on how I'm going to get us out of here.

Then I see Fitz.

He's out of the tank, standing near the old Sherman.

At first, I think he's just stretching his legs, maybe trying to get a better view of the terrain. But then I realize—he's **talking**.

To no one.

He stands a few feet from the old wreck, nodding, gesturing slightly with one hand.

There's no one there.

"Fitz!" I shout, climbing out of the turret. "Fitz, what the hell are you doing?"

He doesn't flinch, just slowly turns as I approach. His face is pale, his eyes unfocused like he's trying to listen to something far away.

"They were **right here**," he says quietly. "I could hear them. See them, maybe. I don't know. It's like—like a dream. But not mine."

Fitz stands motionless in front of the Sherman tank, his head tilted slightly like he's listening to something I can't hear.

I step up beside him, eyes running along the old tank's weather-worn hull. The paint is long faded, but the outlines of its name—*Calculated Vengeance*—are still barely visible, ghosted along the side in flaking white letters. A quiet settles over us, broken only by the faint breeze threading through the trees.

Fitz doesn't look at me when he speaks.

"I think…" he starts, voice distant, "I think they're trying to tell me something."

I glance at him. "Who?"

He finally turns his head. "The crew. The guys that were in *that*." He nods toward the Sherman.

I look at him for a long second. "You seeing ghosts now, Fitz?"

He lets out a dry breath. "Not seeing. It's more like… I don't know. Like they're just *here*. Like the space around us is holding something it doesn't want to let go of." He rubs his temple, then gestures toward the Sherman. "I can't hear words exactly. Just… this *feeling*. Like they're desperate for us to understand something."

"What kind of something?"

Fitz shakes his head. "Something bad. I don't think they meant to do it—whatever it was. But it broke them. You can feel it… can't you?"

I look at the tank again. The gun is slightly elevated, none of the hatches are opened. There's no sign of a firefight around it. No shell impacts. Just a machine left behind in the middle of nowhere, as if its crew climbed out and never came back.

Fitz speaks again, quieter this time. "It's like they're warning us. Like they want us to know what happened… but I can't make sense of it. It's just noise."

Something cold coils in my chest.

Fitz takes a step closer to the Sherman, placing a hand lightly on its side. "I think they thought it was the Germans. That whatever got them… it looked like the enemy to them."

I don't say anything. Because I don't know what to say.

The metal under his hand groans slightly as the wind stirs through the trees. I take a half step back, uneasy.

He looks at me again, eyes wild.

"What if whatever happened to them… is about to happen to us?"

The wind shifts. Somewhere deeper in the forest, a branch snaps.

Not from the wind. Not from an animal.

From **weight**.

Something is out there.

And maybe the old crew was trying to warn us. Maybe they just didn't have the words.

Or maybe they screamed them for decades, and no one listened.

I turn back toward our own tank *Controlled Violence*.

It's still sitting where we left it, like the forest is trying to claim it one inch at a time. Turner's standing on the hull, arms crossed, eyes scanning the treetops. Vic leans against the front slope, chewing on a protein bar like it's the last meal he'll ever have.

I walk over from the Sherman and make my way over. "Anything?"

Turner shakes his head. "Nothing. Just… quiet."

I nod, wiping the sweat from the back of my neck. The air feels thicker now. It's breathing soup.

Then I glance at my watch. The time is now showing almost 6:30pm. The sun should be setting any minute now. Wait. Wasn't it just 4pm earlier? Where has the time gone?

I look up. The sky is barely visible only in faint patches through the trees. Pale light filtering through like the forest is **choosing** what it allows in. The light doesn't feel like daylight. It feels like a memory.

Fitz climbs back into our tank without saying a word.

I follow him.

Once on top, I find myself staring down at the map spread across the comms table. My eyes trace the edges of it—and I freeze.

This isn't **our** map.

The paper is old, creased and brittle. The markings are familiar but still not what we use anymore. Maybe fifty or so years ago, sure. My eyes land on a circle, drawn in red pencil, right over our current position.

Enemy Tank.

"What the hell..." I whisper. I don't remember picking this up. Don't remember seeing it at all.

Fitz leans over. "Is that... from **them**?"

I swallow. "Must be."

Vic turns in his seat. "Alright, what's the move?"

I hesitate, then point at a small, narrow trail marked on the map—the kind that wouldn't be visible from overhead. A gap in the forest.

"Take us through there."

Vic reaches for the starter panel.

Clicks. No engine.

He tries again. Nothing.

"Don't do this to me," he mutters, tapping the panel like that'll fix it.

Another click. Still nothing.

Turner smacks the side of the turret. "The battery's probably still dead."

No power. No comms. No way out.

The quiet settles in again, heavier now. Outside the tank, the trees stretch out like dark sentinels. And somewhere beyond them... something moves.

The forest is dead quiet now, soundless. Even the usual sounds—wind through the trees, distant rustling, birdsong—have vanished.

Turner is standing in an awkward position. Vic leans against the driver's hatch, his eyes half-open. I feel the weight of sleep hitting me. Something about the air feels... heavier.

The night presses in thick around the tank.

Mist curls around the chassis like fingers, licking the steel with slow, silent tendrils. Turner eventually passes out and Vic is dead asleep inside his cave. Fitz sits on the hull beside me, his legs dangling over the edge. We've barely spoken since earlier... I don't even know if I'd call it a day, since the Sherman. Something changed in him after that. It feels like minutes ago. Or was it hours ago? Hell, maybe something changed in all of us.

The forest is unnaturally still. Time has frozen to a stop.

No wind. No crickets. No distant sounds of movement—human or animal. Just nothing. The whole world is holding its breath.

Fitz suddenly stiffens beside me.

"You hear that?" he whispers.

I hold my breath and listen. At first, there's nothing.

Then I hear it too—harsh footfalls, crunching heavily over frost-hardened leaves.

Not loud. Not fast. Just deliberate. Controlled. Violent.

A patrol trying not to intimidate.

I raise a hand instinctively, signaling silence, even though no one else is talking. Fitz doesn't move. His head slowly turns toward the treeline.

That's when I see the first set of eyes.

Two pinpricks of dull amber light, hovering at about chest height just inside the brush. Not headlights. Not flashlights. They don't move like human lights. They don't glow—they gleam. Like reflection off a predator's eyes.

Another pair appears to the left.

Then a third—higher up.

"Flashlight," I mutter. "Now."

Fitz pulls the light from the loader's sponson and clicks it on.

Nothing.

He taps it. Shakes it. Hits the switch again.

Still nothing.

"Vic!" I call down into the turret. "Turner! Get up!"

A groggy voice from below. "Wha...?"

Fitz fumbles for another flashlight—nothing. I yank mine off my vest and try it. Dead. The batteries were full before the competition. I made sure of it.

"What the hell..." Fitz whispers, voice tight.

I glance back toward the trees—and the eyes are gone.

But now there's something else.

Movement. Slow. Purposeful. Several shapes—too dark to make out clearly, but darker than the darkness around them—emerge from the treeline. Silent. Upright. Not running. Not stumbling.

Stalking.

Vic's voice cuts through the hatch. "What's going on?!"

"Get the fuck up and button up! Now!"

Turner curses from below as I hear the starter grind. Nothing. I drop into the turret and shove Fitz in ahead of me.

"They're out there," I bark. "Something's out there."

Vic's head pops up from the driver's seat, his eyes wide. "What did you see?"

"I don't know. People. Shapes. Eyes."

"Eyes?" Turner echoes.

"Just lock down!"

Vic scrambles, hitting switches, then eventually pulling the hatch lever shut. I reach above me and slam the commander's hatch closed. The dull thud of metal-on-metal sounds heavier than usual. Finally, Fitz drops into the loader's seat and helps Turner yank the loader's hatch shut.

We sit in complete darkness.

"What the hell did you see?" Turner asks again, this time softer.

I take a breath. Try to collect my thoughts. Try to not sound insane.

"Something not human," I say. "I don't know how else to describe it. It's watching us."

Fitz nods, not looking at anyone. "They were circling."

I hear Vic murmur a quiet Spanish prayer in the driver's seat.

Outside, the tank groans as the wind—or something else—presses against it. We all flinch.

And then…

A tap.

Soft. Deliberate. Metal on metal.

On the hull. Just next to the driver's hatch.

Tap.

Pause.

Tap.

"Is that…?" Fitz doesn't finish.

Turner swallows hard, checking the turret power again. "Still dead. We've got no juice."

We sit still, eyes locked on each other, listening to the taps.

They move.

A slow drag of something hard across the hull. Like claws. Or metal fingers.

"We're going to die here," Vic mutters.

"No," I say. "Not like them."

Fitz looks up at me. "Like the Sherman crew?"

I nod slowly.

Outside, a thud. Louder. Something jumping onto the back deck.

The tank rocks slightly.

We all flinch.

"We're staying locked up until morning," I say. "I don't care what's out there."

"They can't get in, right?" Turner asks.

"No," I say hoping that whatever is out there can't, but I don't know this for a fact... It's just something I tell myself, and my crew.

Another tap. Three this time on the commander's hatch above me. I look up, heart pounding.

Then silence.

It stretches long. Unbearably long.

No one breathes.

Then—sounds.

Not footsteps.

Whispers.

Dozens of them. All around us. Just at the edge of hearing.

They're not in English. They're not in German.

They're not in any language I know.

They're... wrong.

My skin prickles as my brain tries to decipher them and fails.

"Do you hear that?" Fitz whispers.

I nod slowly. "They're talking."

"To us?" Turner asks.

I shake my head. "I don't think so."

"To each other."

The whispers rise, a swirling vortex of hushed chaos.

And then—

Nothing.

Gone.

All at once.

We sit in stillness, the sweat cooling on our skin despite the cold.

We don't speak again that night.

None of us sleep.

Not after what we saw.

Not after what we heard.

Outside, the forest waits.

Watching.

[CHAPTER EIGHT: STEEL AND SHADOWS]

"The Infantry are seen,"

17 December 1944

"My scouts reported movement roughly three hundred yards out." The Infantry Captain's jeep is parked next to our tank. A map is spread out across the hood of the smaller vehicle. The man's voice is calm as he gestures to a point on the map. I nod along like I know where he's pointing, but the truth is—I'm completely turned around. The past few days have been a blur of mud, blood, and chaos, and after what we saw in that cursed forest that we happen to still be on the edge of, I'd be lucky to tell you which direction is north. My internal compass is sh ot.

"Sergeant? Are you even listening to me?" His voice cuts through the fog in my brain like a slap, dragging me out of my thousand-yard stare.

"Yeah, something about people trying to kill us. Got it," I answer dryly, earning a few chuckles from the other NCOs standing in the loose semicircle around the map. Gallows humor is the only kind we have left.

Behind us, the radio in *Calculated Vengeance* starts crackling. I can't make out the words from here, but I spot Fitz hunched over the receiver, scribbling notes in that frantic, wide-eyed way he always does when trying to keep up. I'll have him fill me in later. Right now, I've got to pretend I care about this pep talk.

The Captain taps the map again. "German SS infantry company—estimated strength of eighty to one hundred men. Dug in ahead. We want your Sherman to push out far in front of the infantry and try to draw some fire in order to expose their positions *before* we even make a move. With luck, once the enemy sees armor, they'll think twice and break."

It's not the worst plan I've ever heard. But it's built on the hope that the enemy will be reasonable—and I've never met a reasonable Nazi. Especially not ones carrying *Panzerfausts*.

The Panzerfaust is the devil's weapon. A disposable, single-shot German anti-tank launcher that even a farmhand could use. It fires a shaped-charge warhead, compact and brutal, designed to tear through steel like tissue paper. Against our Sherman, especially from the sides or rear, it's devastating. The armor there is thin—almost too thin. A single hit can light the fuel, or cook off the ammo, either outcome turning a tank into an iron coffin before you can scream. It wasn't meant for long-range engagements. It was made for ambushes. For brutal, point-blank encounters—when enemy infantry is practically close enough to slap your hull.

That's why sending a tank in alone, unsupported, is a death sentence. Tanks may look invincible, but up close, we're slow, semi-blind, and vulnerable. We need infantry to keep the wolves at bay, and the infantry needs mobile firepower and cover.

I weigh the silence for a long moment before giving my answer. "We'll do it. But your crunchies stay close. I don't need some lunatic sticking a Panzerfaust into my side armor."

The Captain stiffens, just a little. Maybe I bruised his pride. But he reluctantly doesn't argue. He knows what we bring to the fight, just as I know what we lack. It's always a give-and-take between armor and infantry. They think we're arrogant brutes in a rolling fortress, and we think they're reckless speed bumps. Maybe we're both right. Maybe that's what makes it work.

For now, though, we've got a job to do. And when I have to drive this damn tank straight into the jaws of hell again, I just hope the infantry remembers to keep their rifles pointed outward—because I don't plan on dying in a steel box today.

The meeting wraps up with a few nods and half-hearted salutes. The Captain folds his map with a little more force than necessary and strides off toward his men, barking something about repositioning along the treeline. The other NCOs scatter, heading back to their platoons with that look in their eyes—part dread, part resignation. I watch them go for a moment, then turn and make my way toward *Calculated Vengeance*.

Fitz is still in the loader's hatch, hunched over the receiver with his helmet pushed back on his head and a pencil tucked behind his ear. His brow is furrowed like he's trying to solve an algebra problem with a gun to his head. When he sees me, he straightens and waves a few sheets of paper.

"Hey, Sergeant—got a bunch of stuff from Battalion while you were at your pow-wow."

I climb up onto the side of the tank and rest an arm on the turret. "Yeah? Anything useful, or is it the usual 'hurry up and wait' nonsense?"

He flips through his notes. "It's not nonsense, but it sure as hell ain't going to sit well with that Infantry Captain."

That gets my attention. "What do you mean?"

"They want us repositioned about half a mile *west* of here. Battalion's worried about reports of enemy heavy armor near the ridge on the other side of the forest. Says tanks are needed in reserve, not spearheading some dumb frontal push through the woods. We're supposed to hang back, dig in, and hold until further notice."

I stare at him, blinking slowly. "You're kidding."

"I wish I was. I double-checked the call signs and everything—it's legit. Came through just a few minutes ago."

I run a hand down my face. Of course. "So let me get this straight. The Captain wants us charging in front of his boys like a damn billboard for incoming fire, but Battalion wants us to sit tight and play sentry for armor that **might** be out there."

Fitz shrugs, helpless. "Yep. And neither of them seem aware, or care, that the other exists."

I let out a dry, humorless laugh. "Fantastic. Nothing like two chains of command pulling in opposite directions to make a guy feel safe."

He lowers his voice a bit. "So what do we do, Sarge? Follow the guy yelling at a map or the brass on the radio?"

I look out toward the treeline, where the infantry is already setting up. They're expecting us to roll forward any second. My stomach turns at the thought of driving headlong into a line of Panzerfausts just because some officer doesn't want to lose face.

"We follow **our** orders," I say finally. "From Battalion. If the Captain's got a problem with that, he can take it up with the damn Colonel. I'm not getting us all killed for someone else's bad plan."

Fitz nods and starts organizing his notes, already settling back into the rhythm. "Works for me. I didn't really feel like getting turned into charcoal today anyway."

"Yeah, me neither." I slap the side of the turret. "Let's get her warmed up and let the others know. We're not going anywhere until someone figures out who's actually in charge."

And with that, I'm already bracing for the next argument I'm going to have to win to keep my crew alive. I spot the Infantry Captain pacing near a cluster of his men, giving orders with exaggerated hand gestures like he's directing traffic in Times Square. I hop off the side of *Calculated Vengeance* and make a beeline for him, boots crunching in the frozen mud.

"Captain," I call out.

He turns, eyes narrowing like he already knows he's not going to like what I have to say. "Sergeant," he replies curtly, arms folded.

"We just got new orders from Battalion. Came through the tank radio while we were meeting. My tank is to hold position west of here—about half a mile back. Command wants us in reserve in case enemy armor shows up along the ridge."

The Captain's jaw tightens. "That's not what we discussed. I need your tank up front. You've seen the terrain—we need your firepower watching. If this turns into a firefight, my boys are gonna be in the shit."

I keep my voice even. "With all due respect, sir, I take my orders from Battalion. They've got the bigger picture. We've been told to hold back and cover from a distance. Charging out in front on the assumption the enemy **might** run isn't a good enough reason to disobey."

His face flushes. "Goddamn it, Sergeant, I don't care what some desk jockey a mile away says. I'm the one standing here looking at the terrain and counting my riflemen. If your tank sits back while we're advancing, you're screwing us."

"And if we push forward and get hit by a Panzerfaust, we're all dead before you can even react," I snap. "You want us to be bait. Battalion disagrees. So do I."

He steps closer, voice lowering, but the venom is still there. "You do what you want, Sergeant, but if you roll that tin can into trouble, don't expect my infantry to come running to save you. You'll be on your own."

I don't flinch. "Understood, sir. We're used to being on our own anyway."

He holds my gaze a second longer, then turns away sharply and storms off, barking fresh orders at a platoon like they're the ones who just picked a fight.

I stand there a moment, breathing through the burn in my chest, then turn back toward the tank. Fitz is watching from the hatch, eyebrows raised.

"How'd that go?" he asks.

I climb back up, shaking my head. "Exactly like you'd expect."

"Awesome," he mutters. "Nothing like teamwork on the Western Front."

I settle into the commander's seat, jaw clenched. "Let's just hope Battalion knows what the hell they're doing. Because the grunts sure don't."

Mentally, I'm still chewing on the Infantry Captain's parting words like a bad meal. Fitz is already back on the radio, trying to raise Battalion and report our predicament. We're lucky we can even reach them. The infantry's radios are short-range—smaller sets with less power. We've got a much stronger transmitter and a long whip antenna mounted on the turret, which gives us the range they don't have.

"All right, listen up," I call down into the turret. "Battalion wants us mobile. We're pulling back west and holding that ridge. Start preparing to move."

Fitz gives me a sharp nod from his seat beside the radio, Rich responds with a muffled "Copy," and Tommy looks relieved that we're moving from the front.

I turn to glance out over the rim of the hatch and spot the infantry beginning to move. A slow push, half crouched, weapons raised, disappearing deeper into the trees. The haze starts drifting through the branches. It feels wrong. Too eager. They don't know what's out there. Or maybe they just don't care anymore.

I let my eyes trail over the area around the tank as I mentally ran through our checklist—engine warm, tracks clear, gun traversable. Everything seemed fine. Except one thing.

"Harris!" I shout down toward the crew compartment. "Let's go! Gunner's seat isn't going to operate itself."

No response.

I lean in and peer farther down into the belly of the tank. "Harris, you deaf or just stupid today?"

"I'm here! I'm here" Harris barks back, voice sharp and more agitated than usual. "I can't find it."

"Find what?"

"My journal," he shoves aside a ration box and digs through his bag like it had just eaten his best friend. "It's not here. I always keep it tucked under the seat and it's **not here**."

I blink. "That's what's got you holding us up?"

"It's important, Sergeant Casey! You don't understand," Harris snaps, whipping around to check the side compartments. "It's not just notes. It's... it's everything. Thoughts, dreams, sketches, letters I never send. All of it. I've had it since Italy. It's been with me through everything. I don't go into combat without it."

I rubbed my temples. "Jesus, Harris, we're about to roll out and you're throwing a tantrum over a goddamn notebook."

"It's **not** just a notebook!"

"Alright, alright," comes Rich's voice from the driver's compartment, calm as ever. "Cool it. I think I see it."

We all turned to look as Rich leaned over from his seat and reached into the gunner's station. He holds up a worn black journal, its edges frayed and one corner taped where it had been torn.

"It's right here, sitting next to the gunner's seat."

Harris stares at Rich like he had just pulled a rabbit out of a hat. "That's **not** where I left it," he said, storming over and snatching it from Rich's hand. "I keep it **under** the seat. I always do."

"Must've slid out when we crossed that field yesterday," I offer, though I know full well the tank hadn't taken any jolts hard enough to dislodge something wedged under a seat. Still, better that than letting Harris spiral further.

"No," Harris mutters, hugging the book to his chest and glaring around like he expected someone to fess up. "Someone moved it."

I rolled my eyes and waved him toward the gunner's seat. "It was probably a turret gremlin, Harris."

Tommy pipes up nervously, "A what?"

"Turret gremlin. Little, the little bastards that live in tanks. Nasty suckers. They steal pens, hide your socks, misplace your gloves, and occasionally shift a journal to just the wrong spot to make you lose your mind."

Tommy is utterly dumbfounded, "You're kidding."

I shrugged. "Nope. We had one in my previous Sherman in '42. Bastard used to eat all my chocolate and hide my canteen. Swear to God."

Rich chuckles. "I lost a whole pack of smokes to one last week."

"I'm serious," I continue with a grin. "They sneak in when you're sleeping. Love tight spaces. Real bastards. Greasy fingers, always cold. They'll unbuckle your helmet strap just enough so it slides off right when you're climbing out. Saw one hide Harris' boot halfway across the compartment once."

Harris gives me a sideways look but finally drops into his seat, flipping open the journal to check its pages.

"They're especially attracted to sentimental objects, and love to inconvenience tank crews," I add. "So if you really care about something, make sure you tape it to the wall or hide it in your underwear. Otherwise, poof—it's theirs."

Fitz smirks. "Guess that explains where my flashlight went."

"Exactly," I said. "They don't **destroy** anything. They just move it. Just enough to screw with your head."

Harris mutters, "Well they better keep their grubby fingers off this."

I slap the side of the turret laughing, "There. He's back in the saddle. Rich, warm her up. Let's get moving before those grunts decide we're unreliable."

The engine coughs to life behind us with a low growl, the familiar rumble that always makes my chest buzz.

"My station checks out," Harris says, "We're good to go."

"Then let's move. Eyes sharp, safeties off, and Harris—hold onto that journal tight, or the gremlins might start a second draft without you."

He flips me off without looking up from the pages.

The tank rumbles beneath us, the vibrations steady and familiar as we roll across the muddy earth. The forest to our right stretches thick and unforgiving, like a wall of twisted black-green, broken only by the occasional flicker of movement—birds, maybe. Maybe not. The road is little more than a path now, a rough churn of tire ruts and frozen slush. *Calculated Vengeance* pushes forward without complaint, our tread chewing through the terrain. Somewhere deep in the forest is a line waiting to be crossed.

We just need to get out of here alive. And maybe, if we're lucky, we'll do it without the gremlins getting hold of anything else.

"Still no word from the grunts?" I ask into the intercom, watching the treeline.

Fitz replies from his perch by the radio, voice tight. "They checked in about ten minutes ago. Last word was they were moving into the dense stuff—said it looked quiet."

"It always looks quiet," Harris mutters through the intercom. "Until it doesn't."

We keep moving, the forest pressing closer with each passing second. It feels like it's creeping toward us, it's waiting for the moment we're distracted to reach out and drag us in.

Then it happens.

The gunfire cracks out sharp and sudden, echoing through the trees like firecrackers in a drum. First a few pops, then a full chorus—rifles, machine guns, maybe even a mortar thump. The depths of the forest explode with noise. The infantry is taking some heavy fire. We, however, are safe.

"All stop!" I bark.

The tank lurches as Rich throws it into neutral, the engine growling softly as we sit in the open. I press against the cupola, eyes scanning the treeline where the shots are coming from. I can't see anything—just flashes behind the trees, distant muzzle flares like tiny fireflies.

"Shit," Fitz breathes.

"That's the infantry," I say, more to myself than anyone else. "They're in it deep."

"Think they're getting torn up?" Harris asks, shifting slightly in his seat.

"I'd bet my stripes on it," I mutter. The fire isn't sporadic. It's disciplined, rhythmic. The kind of fighting that means people are dying.

We sit there for a beat longer, the crew waiting for me to say something. My mind races.

"Do we keep moving?" Rich finally asks. "Or... are we doing something about that?"

I glance toward the treeline again, then back toward the path ahead. Our original orders from Battalion still stand—fall back and wait for potential enemy armor, keeping pressure off the flank. The Infantry Captain's plan is in the dirt now, but we're still part of the larger push.

"They told us to fall back and wait," I say. "That's the job."

"But those guys in the trees," Fitz says quietly. "That's our infantry. They're getting chewed up."

"And they told us not to expect help from them if we got into trouble," Harris adds. "It kind of feels like karma if we leave them high and dry."

"Don't start throwing guilt around like that's going to sway me," I reply. "This isn't a morality contest. We do the job we're given, we follow orders."

"Yeah," Rich says slowly. "But we're also a tank crew, not a bunch of yes-men. We're human. If we hear our boys getting hit hard, maybe the job becomes figuring out how to help."

I clench my jaw, the sound of the firefight still rattling through the woods. It's growing louder and closer. More frantic. I hear someone scream—it's faint, muffled by the trees and engine, but I hear it all the same.

"We weren't sent here to babysit," I argue.

"But maybe we're the only thing that can make a difference right now," Fitz says. "They probably didn't expect to get hit *that* hard. Maybe they bit off too much."

I look out at the treeline again. That forest has a way of pulling people in and not letting them out. I've seen it firsthand. We all did. Still, if there's a chance we can break the pressure on the infantry, we might save lives. And if the line collapses, it'll roll back onto us anyway. Either we deal with this now, or we deal with it worse later.

"Goddammit," I mutter, thumping a gloved hand against the rim of the hatch.

I make my decision.

"Rich," I say into the intercom, "right stick. We're going back."

There's a beat of silence, then a soft, "Copy that," from Rich. The gears whine as he shifts us around. The tank groans and pivots slowly, tread grinding into the earth.

"Fitz," I continue, "try to get a hold of the infantry on the horn. See if they're still breathing, and if they need support."

"On it," he says, already tuning the dials.

I glance over to Harris, who's adjusting the elevation on the gun.

"You think we'll get close enough for clean shots?"

"If they're that deep, probably not without threading the needle. But if I see movement, I can work with it."

"Good. Keep your eyes up. Tommy, I want you to hose down anything that isn't a baseball-playing American."

We lurch into motion again, this time rolling towards the forest, to the sounds of combat. The tank is loud, heavy—there's no stealth here. But maybe that's the point. Maybe the sound of a Sherman rolling back toward them will give those infantry boys the morale boost they need to hold on just a little longer.

"Let's hope we're not too late," I say under my breath.

As we rumble toward the chaos, I grip the edge of the hatch and take one last glance toward the darkening sky. The sun's nearly gone now. Shadows stretch long across the ground, swallowed slowly by the approaching night. One way or another, we're headed into it.

We roll into the treeline like a fist through paper—branches snapping against the hull, pine needles brushing the turret, the tank grumbling in protest with each uneven bump. The sound of the firefight is no longer distant. It's right here, snapping through the trees around us like cracking bones.

"Eyes sharp," I say into the intercom. "We're in it now."

I catch glimpses of movement—American infantry taking cover behind trees and logs, their silhouettes ducking and firing through the underbrush. Tracer rounds arc through the fading daylight, streaks of red and white burning across the shadows. The smell of gunpowder hits me next, bitter and thick, curling into the tank through the open hatch.

"There!" Fitz shouts, pointing out a squad of our guys pinned behind a fallen tree not thirty yards ahead. "They're getting hammered!"

Harris doesn't wait. The turret swivels hard to the right, the gun lining up on a clump of brush where I just barely see muzzle flashes.

"HE loaded," Fitz calmly says.

"Send it."

The 76mm roars. The recoil shudders through the hull, and for a second, the forest seems to hold its breath. Then dirt and bodies explode from the brush—German soldiers flung into the air. Screams follow, then silence, then gunfire again, more desperate now.

"We got 'em good," Harris says.

The infantry we just saved scramble forward, pushing deeper into the trees. One of them gives a thumbs-up as he passes by the side of the tank.

"Fitz, let 'em know we're here to back them up," I say. "See if their officer's still breathing. And then throw another HE in the tube."

"Trying," he mutters, fiddling with the radio. "Signal's garbage in here. Might have to do this old-fashioned."

The tank keeps crawling forward, carving a path through the trees. Branches claw at the sides. I duck instinctively as a limb scrapes across the hatch, too close for comfort.

"God, this place is a nightmare," Rich mutters. "Can't see more than ten feet."

"That's the point," I reply. "Germans love it. Lets them get close enough to shove a Panzerfaust in your teeth."

We push forward another thirty yards, keeping close to the shifting line of American infantry. Harris picks off another German machine gun nest behind a root-cluster. A few stragglers try to run—Harris lets them. We're not here to waste rounds on ghosts or cowards.

Then I feel it.

It's not a sound, not exactly. More like pressure. Something in the back of my head goes tight. Like the air just got heavier. Fitz stiffens in his seat. Harris goes quiet. Even Rich's usual grumbling cuts off mid-breath.

"You guys feel that?" I ask slowly.

"Yeah," Harris says. "Yeah, I don't like it."

Something moves.

At first, I think it's the trees. But no—beyond the clearing, where the forest opens just enough to let in the dim gray light, something massive shifts in the distance. Maybe 200 meters out, near the edge of a ravine or some kind of slope. A shadow. Tall. Wide. Vague, but definitely real.

"What the hell..." Fitz murmurs.

"Is it enemy heavy armor?" Rich asks. "That could be a Panther that they were warning about."

"Panthers don't move like that. Whatever *that* is, it's much, much heavier." Harris says. "There's been talk of a King Tiger operating near here. Could be that."

My stomach tightens at the mention. The Königstiger—King Tiger. It's not just another tank. It's a damn monster. I've seen the intel sheets back at Battalion, heard the whispers from other crews. Eighty-eight-millimeter high-velocity gun that can tear through a Sherman from over a mile out. Frontal armor like a fortress. The thing's practically a bunker on treads.

"I thought they only had a handful of those," Rich says, almost like he's trying to comfort himself.

"Handful's all they need," I reply. "One of those things could stop an entire push cold."

We're quiet for a moment.

I'd like to believe it's not a King Tiger. That what we're seeing out there is just a figment, a trick of the fading light. But part of me knows better. If the Germans were going to dig in hard anywhere, it'd be here—deep in a cursed forest, where visibility is a joke and maneuvering is damn near impossible.

"Even if it is," Harris says, voice tight, "we've got no chance against it front-on."

"Then we don't take it head-on," I answer. "We stay smart. Stick with the infantry. Let it come to us if it wants a fight. The closer it is, the more effective our rounds will be."

I don't say the part we're all thinking: if it *is* a King Tiger and it sees us first, we won't even have time to yell before we're burning in hell.

Fitz swallows hard and goes back to watching the woods.

The shape doesn't roll or march—it glides, slow and deliberate, between the trunks. I can't make out a turret. Can't see wheels or treads. Just a massive silhouette that doesn't belong here.

"Could be fog messing with our eyes," I offer. "The mist plays tricks out here."

"It's not fog," Fitz whispers. "I see it too."

We all do.

I grab the binoculars and raise them, struggling to keep it in frame. The thing vanishes behind a copse of trees, reappearing a second later—but it's moved farther than it should've. It's not driving. It's floating.

"Still calling that a King Tiger, boss?" Harris asks, voice tight.

I hesitate.

"If it is," I say, "we're gonna find out fast."

Moments go by in silence but eventually it breaks, "Harris, keep your eyes on that thing. Loader, next round is HVAP. Rich, hold position here—we're not going in blind."

"Copy," Rich says. He sounds relieved.

I raise myself slightly in the hatch, calling out to a nearby infantry sergeant as he ducks behind a tree. "We've got eyes on possible enemy armor ahead! You've got anything heavier than a BAR, better get it pointed that way!"

He gives me a half-nod, then yells to his men. They begin repositioning, fanning toward our right flank.

The forest grows quieter now. Not peaceful. Just... tense. The fighting around us dies down, replaced by strained breathing and the occasional sharp rustle. Everyone feels it—the sense of something about to break.

I turn back toward the direction where the thing last moved.

Nothing.

Just shadows and mist and the kind of silence that doesn't exist in war.

"Still see it?" I ask.

"No," Harris says. "It's gone."

"It just vanished," Fitz adds. "Like smoke."

We sit there, the tank still idling. Somewhere deeper in the woods, a bird calls—sharp, wrong, echoing like a scream through the trees.

"Alright," I say finally, my voice low. "We stay alert, eyes wide. If it shows itself again, we light it up and figure out what the hell it is after it stops moving."

"And if it doesn't?" Fitz asks.

I glance at the sky—night's almost fully fallen now, the forest taking on that thick, drowning kind of darkness.

"Then we keep moving," I reply. "And we don't look back."

After what feels like a lifetime we decide it's time. *Calculated Vengeance* begins to slog deeper into the trees, the infantry fanning around us. We move as one, a bruised fist clawing forward through the dark. Somewhere in front of us, maybe real, maybe not, something watches.

And we go in anyway.

[CHAPTER NINE: SOULS AND STONES]

"Accompanied by Engineers,"

18 December 2024

The only sound is the occasional rustle of plastic as someone shifts their MRE pouch.

We sit in a loose circle on the tank's hull, our legs dangling over the side or drawn up close to our chests. The engine's been off for hours now, the armor cold beneath us. No one says a word. No one even tries. We're all here, we're all alive—but whatever passed for rest last night didn't touch a single one of us. I can see it in their faces. Pale, sunken, eyes red from staring too long at nothing. From listening too hard to things we couldn't see.

I chew, but it might as well be cardboard. Something with beef on the label. Or chicken. I don't remember what I grabbed, and it doesn't matter anyway. It all tastes the same once fear has taken the moisture out of your mouth.

Turner sits across from me, staring at the unopened cheese spread like it's going to explain something to him. Vic hasn't even touched his entrée, just peeled the seal off and then set it down beside his boot. Fitz is cradling a hot beverage bag like it's a lifeline, rocking it gently between his palms. I don't think he's even noticed the thing's been leaking from the bottom.

They're not talking because there's nothing to say that wouldn't sound insane. Because none of us want to be the first to try putting words to what last night was.

Because if we say it out loud, it becomes real.

The sounds started just after dusk—movement in the trees, soft but deliberate, circling. First just footsteps. Then branches cracking under something heavier than a person. Then... breathing. Long, labored, like a beast drawing air just outside the range of our headlights. The kind of sound that didn't echo right. It was close, but somehow far. Then the voices—half-whispers, half-static, crawling in over the comms. German, possibly? I'm not sure but they were clipped, wrong, like it wasn't being spoken *to* us so much as **through** us.

At some point the mist rolled in. Thick and clinging, like it had weight to it. It coiled around the hull and coated the vision blocks, seeping in through the smallest seams. And then the eyes. Just faint glows—red, yellow, green—low to the ground, shifting in and out of view. Every time we looked out, they were closer. Every time we blinked, they were gone.

We stayed sealed up inside, every man rigid at his station, sweating despite the cold, watching and waiting for something to make its move. Something we couldn't understand. Something that never did.

And then, just as the sky started to lighten—like flipping a switch—it all stopped. The mist thinned, the comms went quiet, and the birds began chirping like we were camped out in a national park. Like it had all been a bad dream.

I glance toward the Sherman, sitting just thirty yards away, half-sunk into the earth like it's waiting for orders that never came. The thing's a relic, but you wouldn't know it at a glance. Its hull is scarred with shrapnel pockmarks, the paint scorched and blistered in places, and yet somehow... it still looks ready. Like it could start up with a cough of diesel smoke and crawl back into the fight. The tracks are intact, the turret angled just slightly off-center, the gun barrel drooping like a weary arm. Ivy snakes up around the road wheels and clings to the lower hull, the only real clue that time has tried to bury it.

It doesn't look like it's been sitting there for seventy years. It looks like it rolled in under fire, parked to cover infantry, and then… was forgotten. Abandoned mid-mission. The hatches are all sealed, but I swear if one creaked open right now and a grimy, wide-eyed tanker popped out asking for a sitrep, I wouldn't even be surprised. It looks **that** untouched. That **present**. Like it never left the war. Or the war never left it. A machine frozen in its last command. A monument not to victory or loss, but to something unfinished. Something that never got the chance to end.

Fitz finally speaks, voice soft and hoarse. "Someone else saw it too, right?"

No one answers right away.

Turner clears his throat, a dry rasp. "If we didn't, I'm having one hell of a shared hallucination."

Vic lets out a weak chuckle, the kind that dies halfway out of his throat. "Well… at least we're all losing our minds together, right?" he says, forcing a grin that doesn't quite reach his eyes.

"It **was** staring back," Turner says. "I saw the eyes too."

I nod slowly. "They were circling us."

"Whatever it was… it didn't want in," Fitz says. He looks up at me. "Or maybe it couldn't get in. Maybe *Controlled Violence* is our only refuge."

I hate that he's right. Whatever was out there, it wanted us to **know** it was out there. And that was enough.

We fall quiet again. The kind of silence that presses in around the edges, threatening to collapse in. The birds chirp, the wind rustles leaves high in the canopy, and everything looks… normal. The kind of morning that belongs in a recruitment video, not a horror reel.

But I feel it. Still. A weight behind my ribs. A pressure that hasn't let up since the sun came up.

"Something happened out here," I say finally. "Something more than we can explain."

"Yeah," Turner says, flat. "No shit."

I glance at the Sherman again. That corpse has been here since probably some time in the '40s. The hull bears the same kind of markings I've seen a hundred times in museums, in old war films—except this one isn't behind glass or propped up on a concrete pad. It's real. Tangible. Scarred from combat and left behind like a ghost with no one to haunt.

What really gets me, though, is the bumper number stenciled on the front glacis plate. It's weathered, but legible enough. Same company. Same battalion. Same armored regiment as ours. Even the name stenciled on the side brings chills to my body.

That's… impossible. A coincidence, sure, but a damn strange one. *Calculated Vengeance*. It may not be the same name but it's the same initials.

Vic speaks again, barely above a whisper. "What if it's not just ghosts? What if it's the forest itself?"

That gets a few looks.

"I'm serious," he says, his voice gaining strength. "We've all felt it since we got here. Something is wrong with the air. With the **ground**. The fog, the radio weirdness, last night… It's like this place doesn't want us here."

Fitz shudders and hugs his knees tighter. "It wants us **gone**."

I take a deep breath. The air smells like pine and wet earth. Fresh. Normal.

"We're going to get the tank fixed today and get out of this place," I say finally. " But until the engine is up we stay alert, we stay together, and we don't let the forest mess with our heads."

None of them look reassured. But they nod anyway. What else can we do?

I look down at the plastic pouch in my hand. I can't remember if I've eaten any of it or not. I set it aside and slide down off the hull, boots thudding in the damp dirt.

The tank creaks as the others slowly follow, one by one. No jokes. No groans. Just the quiet shuffle of boots and the ever-present awareness that whatever came for us last night... may not be done.

After breakfast—or what passed for it—we finally muster enough energy to drag ourselves off the turret and start troubleshooting. The MRE trash gets stuffed back into the packs and thrown into the makeshift trashcan of the spare road wheel on the turret. The air is cold and still, and none of us says much. We're all trying to avoid looking at the Sherman again. Trying not to think about the eyes in the trees. The mist. The night.

Vic is the first to move with purpose, dropping down into the driver's hatch with the grim resignation of a man heading into a tomb. I follow him inside, slipping through the turret and hitting the master power switch on reflex. Nothing. No buzz. No clunk. Just dead silence.

"All right," I mutter. "Let's start from the top."

We begin the checklist. One by one. The way we were trained, the way we've done it a hundred times before. Only this time... something feels off. The tank's holding its breath.

First is the battery box. We pop it open, and Fitz helps Vic pull the cables and connections. Corrosion is there, but not enough to kill power outright. Still, we scrub the contacts, clean everything with our little survival brush set, then clamp it all back in place and try the switch again.

Nothing.

Next, the bitch plate. Vic pulls the cover with slow, tired movements, while I climb back up top to give him some distance to work. We check the starter, run leads to make sure it's getting power—nothing's burned out, nothing's loose. He taps the casing with a wrench for luck. Still nothing. He even speaks softly to it and asks nicely.

After that, it's fluids. Oil's full. Turboshaft's topped. No metal flakes, no discoloration. We look down deep in the engine bay and check over the harness lines—maybe something grounded out or fried? But again, everything **looks** fine. There's nothing obvious.

"Maybe it's the turret wiring," Turner suggests, already pulling panels off the gunner's side. We check the voltage to the GPS, the intercom system, and the sighting systems. I'm almost hoping we'll find a melted cable or a blown breaker, something that explains it all. Something **human**.

But there's nothing. Everything's intact. Everything looks like it should work.

And still, nothing does.

After about five hours of crawling over, under, and through every inch of *Controlled Violence*, we're no closer to an answer. Sweat's mixed with grime on all of us. Even Fitz stopped cracking nervous jokes somewhere around hour three.

Vic finally sits back on the sponson shelf, dropping his wrench with a clatter. "This thing's just... dead," he mutters, voice low. "It's not even acting broken. It's like it just gave up."

No one argues.

I glance toward the forest. The trees seem closer than before. Or maybe it's just the shadows playing tricks.

Either way, the tank isn't going anywhere. Not today.

Vic pops his head out from under the tinny sub turret hatch inside the tank, a smudge of grease streaked across his cheek and frustration etched into his face. "Maybe it's a turret gremlin," he says, only half-joking. "Little bastard probably crawled in last night and got cozy. Flipped a few breakers, unplugged some magic wire. You know, pissed off at us for not leaving snacks."

Fitz, slumped against the hull, groans. "Turret gremlins don't shut the whole tank down. They just mess with your socks, pens, or flip your dome light on at 3 a.m."

Turner doesn't even look up from where he's tracing a cable run. "Yeah, turret gremlins inconvenience you. This thing's doing a full mutiny."

Vic shrugs, trying to keep the usual grin on his face, but it doesn't quite reach his eyes. "Maybe it's a **really** motivated gremlin."

"No such thing," I mutter, rubbing my temples. "If it was a gremlin, we'd just be stuck with the radio playing country music in reverse or the loader's seat being mysteriously wet."

We sit in silence for a moment before I sigh, push off the hull, and say, "Screw it. The tank's embarrassed. That's my new theory."

And **that** is when the real idiocy begins.

Vic, returns to the sub turret access hatch in the middle of the fighting compartment half-curled under the turret floor panel, letting out a dry laugh. "Wouldn't even be the weirdest part of the week."

I rub at the back of my neck, exhausted and irritated. And then, because no one's said anything helpful in a while and the silence is starting to turn into something sharp.

Turner raises an eyebrow. "Excuse me?"

"The tank. Our **baby**. *Controlled Violence*." I chuckle and smack the top of the turret, "She's humiliated. We park her next to a seventy-year-old Sherman that's been to hell and back, and suddenly she throws a tantrum and refuses to start." I gesture vaguely at the hull like I'm explaining it to a classroom of cadets. "It's a pride thing. Doesn't want to be shown up by grandma."

Fitz actually lets out a weak chuckle. Vic peeks up at me with that tired grin of his, eyes bloodshot from hours of squinting at wires and connectors.

"So what, we pat her on the back and tell her she's still pretty?"

I snap my fingers and point at Vic. "Exactly. Here's the plan. We all turn around, no one looks at her, and Vic hop in the driver seat—you sweet-talk her a little. Let her know she's appreciated. Give her some compliments. Really pour it on. Then we go for a start!"

Fitz blinks. "Are we... actually doing this?"

"We've tried everything else. Why not shame and flattery?"

They all stare at me for a second.

Then, slowly, Turner turns his back to the tank, staring out to the dense forest around us. Fitz follows. I lean forward, tapping Vic on the shoulder. "Go on. Win her heart."

Vic climbs up into the driver's seat with the enthusiasm of a man about to perform a seance. He gives the dash a few loving pats. "Okay, baby girl. You're still the best, all right? No one's got treads like you. Not even that crusty old Sherman."

I cover my mouth to hide a grin. "Louder. She needs to hear it."

Vic obliges, still half-laughing. "You've got the smoothest ride, the most powerful engine... that turbine scream? Music. Pure, sexy music. You're a queen. A goddamn rolling goddess of war. That main gun is plenty big enough, don't you worry."

Fitz is practically shaking with suppressed laughter. Turner hasn't turned around, but I can see his shoulders twitching.

"Go ahead," I say, holding up a hand like I'm a conductor. "Try the start."

Vic shrugs and hits the switch.

The battery indicator lights up and the unmistakable sound of the computer systems booting up can be heard.

We all freeze.

There's a faint click, and then—**whoomph**. The turbine coughs once, sputters... and then the engine roars to life, that familiar banshee wail filling the crew compartment like the voice of an angry angel. The hull vibrates with power. The fans kick in. Everything **works**.

No one moves for a full two seconds.

Then Turner says, flatly, "Well. Shit."

"I..." Vic blinks at the panel, stunned. "I was *joking*. That wasn't a real thing I just did."

I smack the inside of the turret and whoop like we just won the Super Bowl. "*Controlled Violence*, you **diva**! You absolute **drama queen**!"

Fitz is grinning now, even if it's tired and a little rattled around the edges. "She just wanted a little love."

Turner shakes his head. "We are never speaking of this again."

But the engine's still screaming, warm and alive. The lights are on. Power's flowing. And for the first time in nearly a full day, something—**anything**—feels like it's going our way.

Even if it makes absolutely no damn sense.

We're all still a little stunned that the tank actually started.

The warm-up cycle hums in our ears like a victory song, and the vibrations through the hull feel like a familiar heartbeat. *Controlled Violence* is alive again—really alive—and for a moment, just a moment, things feel normal. I glance around at the crew. Fitz is grinning like he's just pulled off a magic trick. Turner slaps the back of his seat like he's patting a dog. Even Vic looks a little less ghost-struck.

We load in quickly, everyone eager to leave, slipping into our positions like we've done a hundred times before. I settle into the commander's seat, adjusting the headset and flicking through the startup checklist.

"All right, let's make sure she's not possessed," I mutter into the mic. "Crew, sound off."

"Driver up," Vic calls from below.

"Loader's good," Fitz adds. There's a metallic clang as he smacks the breech for emphasis.

"Gunner's up. Optics clean, turret motors responding," Turner says, already adjusting his sight.

I check the intercom and turret systems. All green. I watch the status lights blink to life one by one across the panel. Even the GPS—though hopelessly confused about where we are—flickers weakly in protest. Everything's operational. Everything but the radio.

Fitz reaches over and flicks through the channels again. Nothing but dead static and occasional feedback that sounds more like distant whispers than interference.

"No love from the radio," I mutter.

"Not even a 'welcome back' kiss," Turner quips. He sounds more like himself again. It's a relief.

"Radio's still busted," I confirm. "No big deal. We've been more isolated than this in training ops."

I stand up and take note of the surroundings. When I do I catch a glimpse of something between the trees—a thinning, a break in the underbrush that looks suspiciously like a path. Not a road, not a trail, just a narrow clearing cut unnaturally clean through the forest.

I tap the edge of my headset. "Vic, front-right quadrant. You see that break in the trees?"

"Yeah," he replies. "Looks like a dirt trail. Kinda narrow."

"Let's take a peek. Might lead somewhere we can pull off and try the long-range again."

"Roger that."

Controlled Violence lurches into motion with her familiar low groan. It feels good. The weight beneath us surges with power, steady and unyielding as Vic guides us toward the path. It's tight, the treads crunching over fallen branches and leaves, but we fit. Barely. And then the trees start to thin.

The path straightens.

"What the hell kind of trail is this?" Turner asks. "You seeing this?"

I am. At first, it looks like it was made for hikers or mountain bikers—dirt, compacted by use. But the further we follow it, the more unnatural it starts to feel. The ruts in the dirt begin forming into old depressions—paved stones, buried beneath time and moss. Cobblestones.

"Cobblestones?" Fitz says aloud, like the word itself is foreign.

"What kind of trail has cobblestones in the middle of a forest?" Turner says, eyes still on his sight.

I don't answer. Because I don't know.

The trees are wider apart now, almost as if trimmed back on purpose. Sunlight filters down through broken clouds and skeletal branches, dappling the tank in shifting golden-gray patterns. The path ahead curves gently to the left, and that's when I see it.

A church.

Old. Half-collapsed. The roof has caved in on one end, and the front bell tower leans precariously to one side. Most of the windows are shattered, jagged holes that look like open mouths caught mid-scream. The stonework is blackened in spots, as though burned long ago, and ivy coils up the crumbling masonry like it's trying to pull it all into the earth.

Sometimes there's a certain beauty to things that are dying, but it's impossible to describe. You have to see them for yourself.

"Stop here," I say.

But the tank doesn't stop.

"Vic?" I say, more firmly now. "Stop the tank."

There's a pause, then Vic responds, confusion layered thick in his voice.

"I... I haven't been driving since we hit the cobblestones."

"What?"

"I mean it. My hands are off the T-Bar."

I glance at the controls near my hatch. No overrides are active. The tank is moving, but no one is driving it.

A chill runs up my spine.

"You saying we're coasting?" Turner says, trying to laugh. "'Cause it feels like we're steering just fine."

"I'm telling you," Vic says. "Something's got the T-Bar. I'm not touching it."

The tank gently curves around a broken stone pillar and eases to a halt in the clearing beside the church. The moment we stop, the engine revs once—loud and sharp, like a final breath—then settles.

Then a familiar sound clicks through the cabin. The hiss of hydraulics. The soft whirr of the shutdown sequence.

"She's giving herself two," Vic says quietly. "I didn't hit anything. She's shutting down on her own."

For a moment, none of us move. The only sound is the tick of cooling metal and the soft chirp of birdsong overhead.

"Okay," Turner says. "This is officially weird."

I don't disagree.

I climb halfway out of my hatch and look around. The church looms beside us like a mausoleum. The cobblestone path ends right here, at its heavy wooden door, now half-rotted and hanging from one hinge. The roof has collapsed in and the widows have long since busted out.

Everything feels too quiet. Not peaceful—quiet. Like the kind of silence that comes before something terrible.

"Maybe she wanted to go to confession," Fitz offers weakly from below. "She has killed a lot of things."

No one laughs.

I swallow hard and glance around the tank. Our tank. *Controlled Violence* looks inert now, like she's exhaled all her anger and just wants to sleep. But I can't shake the feeling that she brought us here.

I don't know how.

I don't know why.

But I know one thing.

We didn't choose to drive down the road. We just wanted to get to the clearing to try the radios again.

The engine cuts out with a dying growl, leaving a silence that feels heavy, final. No one speaks for a long moment. We just sit there, each of us still in our positions, listening to the click and whine of the tank settling, systems powering down. The display screens go dark. The fans stop. The cabin is suddenly still and close, like the tank itself is holding its breath.

"Well," I mutter, unclipping my harness, "she brought us here. Might as well see why."

"Yeah," Turner says, not quite sarcastic, not quite serious. "I'm sure the *haunted* tank knows what's best. Aren't there like, a bazillion scary movies as to why you don't go into the destroyed church in the woods that your haunted vehicle brought you to?"

No one replies. We all start climbing out of the hatches, one by one. Cold air rushes in as everyone begins dismounting. Vic's the first out. He gives the tank a little pat as he climbs down, like he's thanking it or maybe warning it to behave.

Before I follow the others toward the church, I stop by my duffel bag lashed to the rear bustle. I unzip it, reach inside, and pull out my sidearm. A well-worn M17. It feels heavier than usual in my hands. I slide in a loaded mag, rack the slide, and holster it tight to my thigh. I'm not sure what I think we'll find inside that church, but I've learned better than to assume it'll be nothing. Whatever this place is, it's not normal.

We move toward the building slowly, boots crunching through frost-covered debris. The church looms over us—what's left of it, anyway. Stone walls cracked and crumbling, the roof caved in on the far end, a massive wooden door hanging crooked on rusted hinges. Despite the destruction, there's something undeniably sacred about it. Like the building refuses to fall all the way down. It just... endures.

Fitz steps carefully over a fallen beam. "I don't like this," he whispers.

"You liked the glowing eyes and growling in the dark?" Turner mutters.

"No," Fitz says. "But this is worse."

We step inside.

And the world changes.

The cold vanishes the instant we cross the threshold. The biting wind dies. The frost on our uniforms begins to melt as if the air itself rejects winter. It's warm in here—uncomfortably warm. Eighty degrees at least. My breath no longer fogs in front of me. The snow is gone. The ground inside is dry, dusty, and smooth, like this place hasn't known weather in decades.

I catch the scent next. Faint but distinct. Incense. Frankincense, maybe? Or myrrh? It clings to the air like a whisper, just strong enough to remind me of a funeral mass I went to as a kid. That same strange mix of peace and dread.

The church is long and narrow, lit only by thin shafts of sunlight piercing through holes in the shattered roof. The pews remain mostly intact, though many are broken or splintered, pushed off-kilter by time or impact. The altar stands at the far end, a slab of ancient stone bathed in that strange light. Dust dances above it like fireflies.

We walk down the center aisle together, boots echoing off old stone. Nobody talks.

There's something about this place that demands silence.

The altar is older than the church, I'm certain of it. Rough-hewn stone, too weathered for the surrounding structure. It's not part of the original building—the church must have been built around it. And carved into it, barely visible until we're close, are names.

Hundreds of them.

German names. French names. A few in Latin, maybe even older than that. They're engraved as if a machine did it. All uniform and perfectly spaced and sized.

I crouch down and run my fingers across a section. "You seeing this?"

"Yeah," Turner says, kneeling beside me. "What the hell is this? A memorial?"

Vic shrugs. "Maybe soldiers carved their names before battle?"

"But why the mix of names?" I ask. "These don't even look like the same nationality?"

"I don't know, man," Vic mutters. "Maybe it's a weird tourist trap."

"There's nothing out here for tourists," I say.

Fitz has wandered around behind the altar, he attempts to use his flashlight but, to no one's surprise, it doesn't work. He's quiet for a long time, too long. Then I hear his voice.

"Uh... Sergeant Carson?"

I look up. He sounds distant. Afraid.

"What is it?"

"You need to see this."

We all move at once, circling to the rear of the altar.

There, etched in a neat, orderly line are nine names. Fresh. Precise. The first five look like they have *some* weathering but not hundreds of years like the others...

Turner reads them aloud, slow and uncertain: "James Casey... Vince Harris... Richard Thompson... Anthony Fitzsimmons... Thomas Reynolds..."

He stops.

My heart has already begun to pound.

He continues.

"...Jack Carson... Ryan Turner... Victor Hayes... Aaron Fitzgerald."

The silence that follows is absolute. My blood runs cold despite the warmth.

We stare at the names like they're going to vanish if we blink.

"They're us," Vic says, almost inaudibly.

"And them," I murmur. My eyes scan the list again. "The World War II crew."

"No," Turner says. "No, this is bullshit. This is some sick prank. Somebody's fucking with us."

"In what universe would someone **know** the names of both our crew and a World War II tank crew?" I snap.

Vic's face is pale, his usual cheerful tone gone. "Maybe we're dreaming. Or dead."

"You feel dead?" I ask, voice hard.

He doesn't answer.

Fitz just keeps staring at the names. "Why would we be here?"

No one has an answer. I back away from the altar, feeling the air grow heavier, thicker. The incense seems stronger now, suffocating. My hand drifts to the pistol at my thigh. I look up at the pews and take in the sight. But this time, it looks different than when we first came in here.

It takes me a minute to realize what I'm seeing.

I glance at the pews again—not just the cracked wood and dust—but what's resting **on** them.

Uniforms. Each sitting in the pew as if the soldier wearing it had disappeared and simply draped their uniform on the pew as if they were simply undressing.

The first is so old it barely registers as clothing. Bronze, maybe iron—segments of what looks like a Roman lorica segmentata, arranged across a splintered bench. A faded red cloak draped behind it, its fabric dry and brittle as parchment. Next to it, on the next pew forward, something more intact: a chainmail hauberk under a tattered surcoat bearing a sun-faded heraldic crest. A knight's garb.

They keep going. Row after row. Each pew closer to the altar looks like it belongs to a different century.

The front third is occupied by Napoleonic uniforms in royal blue with gold braiding. Tall, absurdly stiff shako hats perched neatly on the edges of the benches.

Then farther up are khaki wool jackets, olive drab field shirts, and gray tunics. World War II-era uniforms, some American and some German. The American M1943 jackets are mixed in with German field-gray tunics, their insignia still visible: faded SS symbols, eagles stamped on the chest. Some of the German coats even carry the pink piping of Panzer troops—tankers. All of it laid out neatly, like offerings at a shrine.

And then...

I stop in my tracks. The frontmost pew is empty.

Because the altar isn't.

Four uniforms are folded neatly across the top of the stone, each spaced precisely, tanker boots at the base, completely unbroken and their straps wound tightly around them. Sticking out of the boots are gloves ready to be worn. Behind them are tops, pants and covers. OCP camouflage. Pressed so clean they look like they've never been worn. Like they just came out of the packaging. On each one was the regulation adhering "US ARMY" over where the heart goes, the opposite side has the name of the soldier and in the center of the chest is the rank. All of it is stitched sharp, bold, unmissable. Exactly where the names on our own uniforms sit.

CARSON

TURNER

HAYES

FITZGERALD

Our uniforms.

Our sizes.

Our patches. The division crest on the left arm. On the right it has the flag. It even has mine and Turner's deployment patch from our last combat deployment.

Even our blood types have a little patch above the division crest. This is only done in combat zones. In places like Iraq and Afghanistan.

It's almost like someone was waiting for us.

Like someone had **prepared**.

Turner stands upright, eyes scanning the ruined walls like he expects something to come crawling out. "I want to leave. I don't care where the tank brought us, this place isn't right."

Vic nods, swallowing. "Let's just... get back to the tank. Let's just go."

"Fine," I say, turning back toward the entrance. But I pause after a few steps and look over my shoulder, back at that slab of stone, at those names that shouldn't be there. The uniforms sitting atop the altar. The rows of uniforms from soldiers of wars gone past.

It's watching us. I can feel it. Not the building. Not the altar.

The **forest**.

Whatever's out there, it knows we're here.

And somehow, I think it brought us.

[CHAPTER TEN: A PATH RECLAIMED]

"Artillery and Marines;"

18 December 1944

The tank lurches forward, grinding over roots and churned-up soil as I brace myself against the commander's hatch. The forest continues to swallow us whole, trees clawing at the turret like they're trying to hold us back. I've lost sight of the infantry. Again. Not that we were ever really moving in-step longer than a few yards—they couldn't keep up with the pace we're pushing. But now, they're not just behind. They're g one.

"We're too far ahead," I mutter, mostly to myself.

"We're too close to stop now," Harris snaps from the gunner's seat. His voice is sharp, eager, like a man with something to prove. "That thing's out there, Casey. I saw it again, just past that ridge to the east."

"You sure it wasn't just another Panther?" Rich calls up from the driver's seat. "Or a trick of the trees? Whole damn forest is playing games with us."

"No," Harris says, firm. "This one's boxier. Bigger. Wide turret. Sloped like a King."

I suck in a slow breath. "Could be a King Tiger," I admit. "Could be."

Could also be we're seeing what we want to see. Or what the forest wants us to.

The hatch next to me clanks as Tommy pulls himself up beside me, binoculars slung around his neck. He's pale. Sweat glistens on his brow, even though it's freezing. The tension wormed its way into all of us.

"Nothing moving now though," he says, scanning the treeline to our left. "But there were tracks. I saw 'em when we crossed the creek and that abandoned willy jeep. Big ones. Fresh."

I nod slowly. We saw those tracks an hour back, and we've been pushing hard since. Seeing the abandoned jeep gave us hope that friendly units were nearby. It was probably abandoned after it got bogged down in the mud and the infantry accompanying it decided the juice wasn't worth the squeeze.

The forest's been closing in tighter the farther we go. The tall evergreens lean inward now, like old sentries whispering to each other about what we're doing here.

"Casey," Harris says again, quieter this time, "we don't get another shot like this. If it's a Tiger Two and it's moving alone—this could be our best chance."

It's a dangerous kind of confidence in his voice. Reckless. But it's not wrong.

"Alright," I say. "We keep on. No more chasing ghosts, though. If we don't spot hard armor within the next mile, we pull back and regroup with the infantry. I don't like being out here without a net."

A murmur of approval passes through the crew. The engine growls a little louder as Rich coaxes more speed out of her, and the Sherman barrels deeper into the gloom.

Ten minutes pass in tense silence, broken only by the creak of treads and the occasional snap of a branch against the hull. No birds. No wind. Just that low, oppressive hush.

We crest a shallow rise, and the landscape ahead opens up slightly—what looks like an old logging clearing. But something's off. The trees at the far end are shaped wrong. They don't move, even when the breeze should be catching them. They're too rigid, too dark, almost like shadows pretending to be trees.

I switch to the binoculars and sweep across the clearing.

Nothing.

Then, just for a heartbeat, I see it—movement in the treeline to the right. A flash of angular steel. The edge of a turret? Maybe. I call it in immediately.

"Possible contact—three o'clock, behind that dense patch of spruce."

Harris swings the turret and locks in. "Got it. Just a glimpse, but it's there. Wide gun mantle. That's no Panther."

"Rich, bring us slow and left. Keep her angled," I order. "Tommy, keep scanning. If it has friends, I want to know before it gets a shot off."

We edge forward into the clearing, every man holding his breath. The tension coils like wire inside the tank, wound so tight I can feel it in my chest.

But nothing happens.

"Still can't clearly see the son of a bitch," Harris growls. "If he's in there, he's real patient."

Or gone. Or not real at all.

A low mist begins to creep along the forest floor. That's new. We haven't seen fog since yesterday morning. It rolls in quick, slithering between the trees and rising around the tank like it's trying to pull us down.

"Fog's not right," Tommy says under his breath. "It's too fast. Might be smoke or gas."

I nod without taking my eyes off the treeline. "Feels wrong."

"I'm losing track of landmarks," Rich adds. "I swore we passed that downed pine already. That same V-shaped split in the trunk."

"We've been headed east," I reply. "Toward the creek and then north. That's what the map said. That's what we've been doing."

But even as I say it, I don't know if I believe it. My compass keeps flickering between northeast and southwest. Doesn't make sense.

Harris curses suddenly. "He's gone. If there was a tank out there, it's gone now."

I pound the hatch with my fist. "Pull us back. This isn't right. We're not engaging anything we can't see."

The tank turns around facing the way we came then stops moving.

Rich doesn't answer right away. Then, in a low voice, he says, "Uh, Casey… I think we've got a bigger problem."

"What do you mean?" I ask.

"I mean we're not where we're supposed to be. The trail we followed in? It's not behind us anymore. I—I don't see any tracks. No trail. Nothing."

"What are you talking about?" Harris says. "We came in through the clearing, we followed the trail—"

"There is no trail," Rich cuts him off. "Not anymore."

I look out again, and he's right. The clearing behind us is sealed. Trees packed tighter than they were before. Branches knit together like a barrier.

I slide the map from its pouch beside my seat and spread it out on my lap. I trace our path. It doesn't match what I'm seeing, though.

"Son of a bitch," I whisper. "We're not even close to where we thought we were."

Tommy glances down at me. "You think the forest's... moving?"

"No," I say, but my voice doesn't carry the certainty it should. "No. That's impossible."

The others fall silent. Even Harris doesn't argue. No one wants to be the one to say it out loud, but the thought is there, hanging heavy in the turret like smoke.

We're lost.

And not in the normal way.

Our best option is to return to the clearing and hopefully the reduced number of trees will allow a radio message to go out.

"Swing us back to the clearing," I tell Rich. "We'll get better radio reception there. Harris, let's look for that Tiger again. I don't want a surprise 88 in the face."

The tank makes another sharp U-turn and begins making its way towards the clearing.

The turret groans as Harris rotates it back toward the treeline. The fog still clings low to the ground, curling around the Sherman's hull. It feels like we're sitting in the eye of something. The forest watches us. Waits.

"I've got eyes on," Harris says a moment later. "Three o'clock —half-hidden behind that bend in the trees. Might be it."

I press my eye to the commander's sight. My heart skips.

There's something there. Angular. Low to the ground. Broad, sloping armor. It's not a full silhouette—some of it's masked by the fog and the trunk of a fat pine—but I see a massive road wheel, the squared-off edge of a turret, and the long, thick barrel of a gun.

King Tiger.

It's broadside to us.

And it's not moving. The most ideal target.

"Jesus," I mutter.

"Still think it's a Tiger II?" Harris says. He's too tense to sound smug.

"No. At least... not yet. Looks like it, but..." I study it a second longer. "It's off."

"How?"

"Can't tell. Just... it's still. Too still."

I grab the throat mic. "Fitz, AP round, now."

There's a clatter as Fitz slams a new round into the breach. "Loaded!"

The tank crawls to a stop to give Harris the best chance at hitting the target as possible.

"Range?" I ask Harris.

"Two hundred, two-fifty max."

Close. Damn close.

I don't like it. But I can't pass on this.

It's right there. It's real enough.

"Harris, when you've got it centered—take the shot."

Harris steadies his grip on the elevation handwheel. The seconds stretch. The forest around us holds its breath.

Then—

"On the way."

The 76mm cannon roars, rocking the tank. The shell screams across the clearing and punches clean through the side of the Tiger.

Only—it doesn't.

There's no spark. No explosion. No flash of metal, no ricochet. No shattered track, no plume of fire.

The shell just—passes through.

Like it wasn't there at all.

It impacts a tree on the other side of the target and then impacts the dirt further on.

Silence.

"What the hell?" Fitz says.

Harris lifts his face from the sight, eyes wide. "It—it didn't hit. I mean—it **did**, but it went **through**. Like it was... I don't know. Like it wasn't solid."

"You hit dead center?" I ask, disbelief crowding into my voice.

"Dead. Center. Like the tiger from the other day."

I press my eye back to the optic. The tank is still there. Still perfectly broadside. Still unmoving.

But now—now I see it.

It's not right.

The lines are **too** clean. The shadows don't fall the way they should because there are no shadows. And the longer I stare at it, the more it looks less like a tank and more like a **drawing** of a tank, something sketched from memory and stretched out across fog and trees like a curtain.

Like a child's cardboard cutout hung on wires in the forest.

"What the hell is that thing?" Tommy whispers from beside me.

"Looks like a King Tiger," I say, low. "Acts like a ghost."

Harris keeps his eye on the scope. "Want me to fire again?"

I don't answer right away. I'm trying to reason it out. There **was** something here—we followed the tracks, we saw glimpses of movement. But this—this thing in the trees—it's not what we tracked.

It's a shape. A lure.

I feel the hair rise on the back of my neck.

"No," I say finally. "Hold fire. Pull us back, Rich. I want us out of this clearing."

Rich doesn't answer.

"Rich?"

"I... Casey, I think we've been here before."

"What?"

"I swear. Look at that hill just past the enemy tank. The one with the stones on it. I saw that exact ridge half an hour ago. We circled."

"We haven't turned."

"I **know**," Rich says. "That's what's wrong."

I open the hatch, despite the cold, and stand up into the chill air. The forest stares back at me. The tank—if that's what it is—sits across the clearing, unmoving. Fog snakes along its outline, and I swear I see it flicker.

Just for a second.

Flicker like a film reel catching a bad splice.

"Fitz," I say. "Take a look."

He climbs up beside me. Lifts the binoculars. Freezes.

"That's... that's not metal. Casey, I can see trees *through* it."

My stomach knots.

A trick. A trap.

We came out here chasing a beast and found a shadow.

I drop back into the hatch. "We're done here. Back us off. Slowly."

"Copy," Rich mutters, gears grinding as he eases us into reverse.

The turret stays locked on the silhouette as we backtrack. Harris doesn't say anything. None of us do. We keep our eyes on the thing, half-expecting it to vanish—or worse, *move*.

But it doesn't.

It just sits there, frozen.

It *wants* to be watched.

We pull back into the trees and the clearing vanishes behind us, swallowed by the mist and the dark.

I exhale, slow and quiet, like I'm afraid the forest will hear.

"Still think we're chasing a Tiger?" Tommy asks.

"No," I say, voice low. "Now I think the forest is chasing us."

We've been driving for the better part of an hour now. It feels longer. The light's dimming—not quite dusk, but the forest makes it hard to tell where the sun is, or if it's even still out.

The map on my lap might as well be a crossword puzzle. Useless. I've flipped it sideways, upside down, refolded it twice. Doesn't matter. Nothing matches. The landmarks are wrong. The trails don't line up. We've passed the same tree twice without ever turning around.

"How far are we from the front line, Rich?" I ask.

"Should be ten, maybe fifteen minutes to the infantry's last known position," he says, but there's no conviction in it. "If this is still the same damn trail."

"We've been following this path for too long to still be behind our own guys," Harris mutters. "They'd be dug in by now. Smoking cigarettes. Eating chow. Not invisible."

"I don't like this," Fitz says. He's hunched low beside the loader's seat, arms crossed like he's trying to make himself smaller. "We should've found somebody by now."

I don't respond. I don't want to admit I'm thinking the same thing. That maybe we're not just lost—we're *misplaced*. Dislodged.

Then the rumble under the treads changes.

It's subtle at first, a shift in texture, but even inside the tank I feel it: a difference in the road. I lean out of the hatch and squint down at the ground as we roll forward.

Cobblestone.

The dirt and gravel have given way to a rough, uneven road of old stones, worn smooth at the center by centuries of use. They're laid in a distinct, deliberate pattern, the mortar between them cracked with age. Moss grows along the edges.

"Rich, you seeing this?" I ask.

He nods without looking back. "This isn't on any damn map."

No way it's Wehrmacht engineering. This road's too old. Too **ancient**.

"It's Roman," Tommy says suddenly from below, binoculars resting in his lap. "Looks like the kind of thing they used to lay down in the old empire days."

"How the hell do you know that?" Harris asks.

"Read a lot," he shrugs. "History was kinda my thing before all this."

I file that away and scan ahead again. The cobblestone trail bends slightly to the left as it dips into a hollow between two thick trees. Mist coils at the edges. Then I see movement.

"Hold," I bark, rapping the hatch. Rich slows us to a crawl then stops.

"What do you see?" Harris asks.

I lift the binoculars.

Figures. Half a dozen, maybe more. Men on the trail, crouched or kneeling. Tools in their hands. Pickaxes, shovels. They're digging. Or working.

They're in uniform, but it's not like anything I've ever seen before.

No helmets. Shakos—those tall, old-world hats. Long coats, deep blue with red piping. Some kind of brass buttons glinting even in the low light.

And what looks like muskets.

"What the **hell** am I looking at?" I mutter.

Harris traverses the turret to the men working, using the sight to get a magnified view. "They Germans?"

"They're **something**."

"Maybe it's some weird SS unit doing sabotage," Fitz offers. "Like, sappers. Laying mines or something."

He's grasping. But it's all we've got.

"They're working on the road," I say, watching the way the figures move—smooth, efficient. Too calm. "If they're laying mines we need to stop them. Harris, get on the co-ax. We're not running any risks here."

I hop out of the turret and take my place behind the .50 cal that sits adjacent to the commander's hatch.

"Fitz, ready a HE round just in case."

"Loaded."

I double-check through the binoculars one last time.

Still there.

Still working.

Still wrong.

"Fire."

The machine guns come alive—familiar clunks and rattles as they're loaded, locked, lined up. The co-ax opens up in a crackling burst. Tommy even opens up with the bow machine gun as the .50 thunders its loud thump under my hands. Tracer rounds streak down the road, dancing like fireflies in a straight line toward the figures.

They don't flinch.

Not one of them turns.

Then—

The bullets hit the stones and **bounce**. Clinking and skipping like stones on a lake.

No impact. No blood. No reaction.

It's like shooting at a film reel. The figures keep working, oblivious. Or maybe not oblivious—maybe **unreachable**.

"What the **hell**?" Harris says. "I aimed dead on."

"They didn't even notice," Tommy mutters. "They didn't **hear** it."

"Again," I snap.

Another burst. Three machine guns. Spent shells rattle off the hull. The tracers rip across the path and glance off the stones just before they should have struck flesh.

The workers are still digging. Still moving in perfect rhythm. The sound of their picks and shovels carries through the trees—**clink, scrape, clink**. Soft. Measured. Timeless.

"They're not real," I say aloud, trying to convince myself.

"What are they, then?" Fitz asks, eyes wide.

I shake my head. "Shadows. Echoes."

Fitz leans close. "Casey, the road—look at it now."

I swing the binoculars down.

The cobblestone is darker ahead. Wetter. Almost red. Like something's soaked it.

And the workers—they're fading.

Not vanishing—**thinning**. Losing color. Losing shape.

One by one they go translucent. I can see the trees **through** them. The forest beyond. And then, like smoke in the wind, they're gone.

Gone.

The path ahead is empty.

Nothing but fog curling over the wet stones.

Everyone is quiet.

Only the engine hums beneath us.

Fitz whispers, "We're not supposed to be here."

And for the first time since I took command of this tank, I don't have anything to say. I don't know what to do.

I don't give it more than ten seconds. Whatever that was—whoever they were—I want **no** part of it.

"Rich," I say, louder than I need to. "Left turn. Ninety degrees. We're done with this road."

There's a pause. "Roger," he says, and the Sherman's treads groan as he swings the tank off the cobblestone and back onto the rough, mossy ground beside it. The tank tilts slightly as we leave the trail, climbing over a tree root thick as a thigh. A few low branches scrape the turret, but I'd rather take our chances through the woods than stay on that cursed road.

"You think those were German ghosts or **our** ghosts?" Harris says after a minute. His voice is low, trying to sound like a joke, but it lands hollow.

"No such thing as ghosts." I feign confidence.

We roll forward, carving our own trail now. There's no sign of where we came from, and the mist seems to thicken with every yard. The trees aren't thinning. If anything, they're drawing in tighter, as if they want to shut us in. The light begins to fade. Our concept of time has long since disappeared.

I check the map again out of habit. Worthless.

"Tommy," I say. "Keep your eyes on the right. I don't want to miss a trail if we cross one."

He nods from below, face pale, knuckles white on the grips of the bow machine gun.

For a while, no one says anything.

Then Fitz speaks.

But it's not what he says—it's **how** he says it.

"That wasn't the worst of it," he mutters, voice flat.

I glance down the turret and catch a glimpse of him near the loader's seat. He's not looking at anyone. Just staring ahead at the back wall of the turret like it's a window to something none of us can see.

"What?" I ask.

He blinks slowly. Doesn't answer.

"Fitz," I say again, sharper this time. "Speak up."

He turns his head toward me, slow and stiff, like it takes effort. His eyes are glassy. "They were building a grave."

The words hang there, heavier than the smoke of a HE round.

Harris turns. "What the hell are you talking about?"

"They weren't laying mines," Fitz says. "They were digging a trench. Long. Wide. Deep. Big enough to fit all of us."

I feel a chill crawl across my spine like an insect with too many legs.

I didn't see a trench. Just the figures. Just the motion.

But I can't say he's wrong. I can't say **anything** for a few seconds.

"How would you know that?" I finally ask.

He just looks back at me. Doesn't blink.

"They looked at me."

"The hell they did," Harris snaps. "They didn't look at **anyone**. They weren't even solid."

"They looked at me," Fitz says again, voice as lifeless as a shell casing. "They **nodded**. Like they'd been expecting us."

I couch into the turret, straining to get a better look at him. "Hey," I say, softer now after taking off my throat mic, "Fitz. You feeling alright?"

He gives a half-shrug and looks away.

Tommy shifts in his seat. "Something's wrong with him."

"No kidding," Harris says. "Kid's talking like he got dosed with gas."

"It wasn't gas," Fitz mutters. "You'd smell gas."

"I didn't say it **was** gas—"

"Quiet," I snap. "Both of you."

Fitz closes his eyes and leans his head back against the cold steel. He's sweating, but his skin looks pale. Too pale.

I rap twice on the hull. "Rich, hold up."

The Sherman grinds to a halt, idling. I drop down into the hull.

Fitz barely moves.

"Can you stand?" I ask.

He nods slowly. "Yeah. I just... I'm tired."

"You've done this job for a little over a year," Harris says. "You've never been tired."

Fitz finally looks at me again, and there's something in his eyes now. Not fear—**resignation**. Like a man who already knows the punch is coming and doesn't plan to duck.

"They called me," he says.

It takes me a second. "Who did?"

He doesn't answer.

"You're not making sense, Fitz."

"The ones from the trench. From the road. They called me by name. I heard it."

"That's impossible," Tommy mutters, barely audible.

"I think we should go back," Fitz says.

Harris laughs bitterly. "Back to **what**? The ghost workers? The tiger that wasn't real? The fog that eats our brains?"

Fitz shrugs. "At least we know where we are back there."

"No," I say, my voice firm now. "No one's going back. That road is **done**. If we're gonna die, it's not gonna be on cobblestone laid by the dead."

"Why do you assume we're dying?" Fitz asks.

That silences everyone again.

I look hard at him. "We're literally fighting Germans in Germany."

He gives me a faint, tired smile. "We're not supposed to be here. You said it yourself."

"I meant in this stupid forest not the war," I snap.

"You meant **wrong**," he replies. "Like we stepped into something that doesn't want us to leave."

Rich's voice crackles over the intercom. "Casey. We're not turning. Not really. We're still going straight."

"What?"

"The tank. I've been holding left, but it's not turning. It's—hell—I don't even know. It's just driving."

I climb back up and poke my head out of the hatch. The forest looks the same in every direction—mossy trunks, low mist, skeletal branches. But he's right. The tank isn't cutting a straight left the way it ought to. We're continuing on, gently, subtly, like someone else has the tillers.

"You feel that?" Harris asks beside me. "Like we're being **drawn**."

I nod, just once.

This isn't a trail. It's a **road**. And we're along for the ride.

I drop back down, the air inside suddenly thicker than it was five minutes ago. Fitz is looking sicker than ever.

We can't turn the tank.

Rich **tries** but he simply can't.

Every few seconds he mutters a curse word, kicking at the tiller bars like a man trying to stir a rock. The Sherman doesn't respond. It keeps rolling. Same speed. Same direction. A gentle, unnatural ease like the machine is coasting downhill—even when the ground's flat.

"I'm not in control anymore," he says finally. "I haven't been for the last twenty minutes."

I don't know what to say to that. I just stare at the controls, watch his feet, his hands. He's doing everything right. The tank just isn't listening.

"You trying to scare us?" Harris mutters from the turret. "This your idea of a joke?"

Rich looks up, face white under the grime. "You think I'd joke about this?"

Harris opens his mouth but says nothing.

The forest isn't thinning. If anything, the trees lean in more now, pressing like a crowd trying to see what we'll do. There's no sound outside but the low growl of the tank and the occasional scrape of branches on armor. Not even birds. Not even wind.

Then the cobblestone returns.

It slides beneath us like a whisper. One moment it's moss and dirt, the next it's carefully laid stones, old and dark and damp with mist. Same path. Same road from before. The one we *left*.

Except now we're back on it, and none of us made that choice.

Tommy peeks his head out the bow gunner's position and mutters something I can't quite catch.

"How long have we been driving?" I ask.

Rich glances at his watch. Taps it. "No idea. I think my watch stopped. Maybe an hour? Maybe five?"

Fitz hasn't said a word. He's curled in the loader's seat again, arms wrapped around his chest like he's cold. His lips move, but he's not talking to *us*.

He's talking to *something else*.

I don't ask what. I don't want to know what.

We pass the place where we opened fire on the ghosts, though there's no sign anything ever happened. No churned stone. No shell casings. No blood. Just empty road and thin fog.

The tank keeps moving.

Eventually, through the haze, something massive begins to rise.

A chapel.

It looms beside us like a mausoleum. The cobblestone path ends right here, at its heavy wooden door—half-rotted and hanging from one hinge. The stonework is stained with moss and soot, and the roof's collapsed inward like a lung caved in under pressure. Every window's shattered, jagged glass lining the sills like crooked teeth.

We don't stop ourselves.

The tank **stops**.

Engine off.

No clunk, no sputter—just silence. Like something threw a switch. Like it decided this was where we needed to be.

I swallow, hard. "Everyone out. Get some air."

No one argues.

We climb out slow, one by one. My boots hit the cobblestone and I suck in a breath through my nose. It's cold, sharp, *clean*. Not like the inside of the tank, where the air had turned sticky and thick.

Fitz had been sweating buckets. Harris was getting snappier by the minute. Tommy's hands wouldn't stop shaking. Even I'd felt dizzy and confused, like I'd been drinking radiator fluid. It lifts almost instantly.

That's when I remember.

"The exhaust leak," I say out loud, almost laughing.

Harris turns to me. "What?"

"Carbon monoxide. Rich said something about it last a few weeks ago. We thought it was minor. Guess it wasn't."

"You think that's what all this was?"

"I don't know," I admit. "But it explains the headaches. The halluci-nations. The weird feelings."

Rich rubs his eyes. "Jesus. We were getting poisoned."

Tommy leans against the side of the tank and takes deep, grateful gulps of air. "So that was all in our heads? The ghost workers? The tiger?"

I hesitate. "I'm sure most of it. Maybe."

I don't say the other half of what I'm thinking: **hallucination or not, we're still lost, and the tank still drove itself.**

Fitz coughs behind me. I turn—

—but he's not there.

I scan the area. No movement. Just the ruined church, the tank, the road behind us. No Fitz.

"Where's Fitz?" I ask.

Harris looks up. "Thought he was right behind me."

"Tommy?" I ask.

He shakes his head, panic already creeping into his voice. "He was climbing out when I did."

"Fitz!" I call out, stepping around the rear of the Sherman. "Fitz, sound off!"

No answer.

The fog's thicker again, curling like smoke along the stone and dirt. I jog to the front of the tank, eyes sweeping the church, the treeline, the road behind us.

Nothing.

"Fitz!" I shout again, louder this time. "Get your ass back here!"

Still no reply.

"Shit," Rich mutters. "Maybe he went to puke or something? Behind a tree?"

"He wasn't right," Harris says, quieter now. "He's been off since the road. Since he said those things."

Tommy swallows hard. "You think... he went in?"

We all look at the church. A small amount of what looks like candle-light escapes the busted-out window next to the entrance.

I don't want to go in.

Every part of me screams not to.

But I'm not leaving Fitz behind. Not now. Not ever.

I turn to the others. "Grab your weapons. Stay close. We're going to rescue our loader."

[CHAPTER ELEVEN: ECHOES OF THE FORGOTTEN]

"For none but shades of Cavalrymen"

19 DECEMBER 2024

We don't talk on the walk back.

Not a word. Not about the altar. Not about the names. Not about the impossible warmth in that shattered chapel or the way the light bent around the walls like it didn't belong in this world. We don't talk about how long we were inside. It felt like minutes—maybe—but when we step back into the snow-covered fog-drenched forest, the sky has changed. The sun's no longer visible behind the gray ceiling, but it's darker. Heavier. Like hours passed while we were there. Like we missed time.

Vic swears we were only gone twenty, maybe thirty minutes. But my body's internal clock says it's been six hours.

No one argues.

Even the forest's gone quiet. Too tranquil. The birds, the wind—whatever life used to hum beneath the trees—has gone still. We walk single-file, automatic, like men returning from the dead. I'm first. Fitz last. Our boots crunch over gravel, then soft moss, then back to loose dirt as the tank comes into view again, black and hulking in the gloom. It feels wrong now. Like we left something behind in that church... or brought something back.

Fitz is the first to speak. "I'm starving," he says, voice brittle. "You think there's any K-rats left?"

We all stop.

Turn toward him.

"What did you just say?" Turner asks, slow, like the words might bite.

Fitz shrugs, avoiding our eyes. "K-rations. You know, the little boxes. Crackers, chocolate, meat spread. They usually come with a cig and—"

"We don't use K-rations, Fitz," I say carefully. "Not since the Korean War."

He blinks. "What? No, I meant MREs. Yeah. MREs. Must've just—" He cuts himself off and looks down, ashamed. "Sorry. I'm just tired."

We all are. But it's not just fatigue. There's a shadow over us now. Like something clung to our backs when we left that church. A weight. The light's gone from Fitz's eyes, and I can see it mirrored in Turner and Vic. That cold, hollow look like someone reached inside and scraped out the part of you that believes in morning.

We climb back into the tank like ghosts entering their own tomb.

Surprisingly when I hit the master power button the electronics begin slowly coming to life. It takes a moment for the systems to warm up. The interior's still heavy with the scent of sweat and oil, but it's also different now. There's a thickness to the air. A metallic taste at the back of my throat. Nobody says much as we run checks. Nobody has the energy.

Turner sits in the gunner's seat, staring through the sights and making sure they work but not tracking anything. Vic leans forward at the driver's station, hands on the controls but not moving them. Fitz curls up against the loader's seat, arms around his knees like a scared kid trying to make himself small. I watch them all from my spot in the commander's seat, hands resting on the edge of the hatch.

Something is unraveling inside us.

No—between us.

And I don't know how to stop it.

The radio crackles.

Not loud. Just a whisper of static. We all jump a little. I glance at Turner, who twists a dial on his internal comms box and presses his CVC to his ear.

"Say again?" he asks. "You're coming through broken."

The radio spits back half a sentence in a voice that sounds—wrong. Clipped syllables. An accent I can't place. Or maybe too many at once.

"What's... position... Do you.... help... coordinates unknown..."

Another burst of static. Then silence.

I reach over and kill the volume. "Nobody responds to anything unless I say so. Got it? We don't need whatever is out there trying to kill us coming to our exact grid."

Turner nods. So does Fitz. Vic just keeps staring ahead.

We sit in that quiet for what might be minutes. Might be hours. The forest's light never changes. Just that eternal twilight smeared across everything. And the mist—Jesus, the mist—presses in like the walls of a coffin.

We're low on food. Lower on water. The engine's got power again, but the terrain has us boxed in. We still haven't seen or heard from the NATO crews we were supposed to be competing with. It's like the entire world went silent while we were inside that church.

After what seems like a long time, I speak. "We need to move. Pick a direction and go."

No one argues. Not even Vic.

But something's shifted in Fitz. He keeps glancing over his shoulder, toward one treeline. Then the other. Then back again.

I don't like the way his fingers twitch.

After a while, he speaks up again, voice barely louder than a breath. "There's someone out there."

Turner gives him a sharp look. "What are you talking about?"

"I saw them." He won't meet our eyes. "When we came back from the church. I saw someone walking next to us through the trees. Just out of reach. I thought it was a trick at first, but... they were keeping pace."

I stare at him for a long moment. "Why didn't you say anything?"

"Because I don't know what I saw," he snaps, then instantly recoils. "I mean—I didn't want to say something dumb. I figured I was just... seeing things."

"You are," Turner mutters. "We all are."

I don't correct him. Because he might be right. Or he might be wrong. Either way, saying it out loud won't change what's happening to us.

"Get us moving. We're not staying still."

Vic blinks like he's coming out of a dream and starts the engine. The tank rumbles to life beneath us, a beast shaking itself awake.

As we roll forward through the mist, the trees peel back just enough for a narrow path to appear. It feels familiar. But everything does out here. The same branches. The same fog. The same constant sense of being watched.

I glance back toward the chapel, but it's gone now. Just trees where it stood. As if it was never really there.

And I think—we left something in there. Or maybe it followed us out.

We'd been driving for what feels like another hour—maybe two—but the landscape hasn't changed. Still the same pale trees, same soft turns, same muted colorless sky bleeding through the canopy. I'm convinced there's no escaping this forest. It should only be a few miles wide and a few miles longer. But somehow we can't escape.

The tank rumbles steadily beneath us, and Vic swears he's following a slope back toward where we came from, but it all looks the same. And even if we **did** find our way back, what would we be going back **to**? A ghost chapel and a stone path that shouldn't exist?

I pull my map case open again anyway, spreading the laminated grid across my knees. We were on this section before, near the junction of sectors 45 and 72. At least... we were supposed to be.

"Fitz," I say, glancing back toward him. He's still hunched beside the loader's rack, one boot tapping a twitchy rhythm on the steel floor.

"Fitz," I say, rapping my knuckle against the folded map on my lap, "grab the GPS and give me our grid. I want to get us plotted out of this... place."

He blinks, like the question's a little too big for the moment. "Uh... yeah. One sec." He crawls forward and grabs the handheld GPS from its clamp above his station, tapping at the scratched screen.

The thing's been glitchy since we entered the forest—drifting signals, weird latency—but it's still our best shot. I watch him squint at it, trying to get a fix.

"I've got coordinates," Fitz says slowly. "Grid reference... three-zero Uniform..." He rattles off the rest of the numbers.

I frown. "Wait. Say that again? It says thirty-*two* Tango here on the map."

Fitz checks the screen and repeats, "Three-zero Uniform. Same numbers."

I glance down at the map and feel my stomach drop. That grid square doesn't even exist on our chart. "That… doesn't make sense."

"Why?" Turner asks, raising an eyebrow. "Wrong zone?"

"Absolutely, *32 Tango* is the map section we are in. *30 Uniform* is several hundred miles south and to the east or something like that."

"Could it be a map scale thing?" Vic suggests. "Old overlay, maybe?"

"No." I shake my head. "Even if the scale was off, something would line up. The grid you just gave—" I point at a spot of empty space about two feet away from the map showing where the grid he gave me would be on the map if it extended that far, "—it's hundreds of miles away."

Fitz frowns and looks down at the unit again. "It's got a full signal. Says it's accurate within one meter."

"Then either the GPS is broken, or reality is."

"Weird numbers," Turner mutters. "Feel like something out of a dream. Or like… scrambled coordinates. Like someone—or something—doesn't want us to know where we are."

I glance at the digits again.

19201, 12151

For a split second, I try to make sense of them—not as coordinates, but as something else.

Almost rhythmic.

Almost… deliberate.

"You think it means something?" Fitz asks quietly, like he can read my thoughts.

"No. Maybe." I say. "And that's exactly why it's bothering me."

The wind rustles through the trees outside, but it sounds like it's breathing instead. The forest doesn't care that the numbers are wrong—it already knows exactly where we are.

And wherever that is... it sure as hell isn't on my map.

I slowly close the map. "I give up. We're off the board," I say quietly.

Fitz shifts uncomfortably. "What does that mean?"

"It means," Turner says before I can answer, "we're not where we **think** we are. Or maybe we **never** were. And for once in his life Sergeant Carson doesn't know what to do."

Nobody says anything after that.

The engine hums. The fog presses in tighter. The trees whisper things we can't hear.

And above us, the sky keeps turning, slow and gray and uncaring.

I return to my normal standing position. Half in the turret and half out as we continue to punch though the forest trying to find a way to pop out.

I stare at the numbers Fitz gave me, heart thudding harder with each passing second.

30U 19201 12151

They don't make sense. They're nowhere on the map. I run my finger along the quadrant grid again, more slowly this time. Still nothing. These coordinates don't exist. Not in Belgium, not in Germany. Hell, not even in the Atlantic. Just... blank space.

"What the hell is this?" I murmur.

Fitz looks like he's not feeling right. He's perched halfway out of the turret, elbows resting on the rim like he's watching for something in the trees. His eyes scan lazily, unfocused. Like someone waiting for a b us.

I lean over the map spread across the back of the .50 cal mount in front of me, eyes narrowing at the numbers again.

19201 12151

It buzzes at the edge of my memory, something just out of reach. I squint, trying to trace the thread. Then, like a switch flipping, it clicks.

Middle school. Seventh grade. Mr. Nellis's math class. We used to pass notes back and forth, dumb little jokes and doodles, but some-times—when we didn't want anyone else to know what we were saying—we used a dumb cipher. A=1, B=2, and so on.

I grab the stub of a pencil and write the numbers out along the bottom of the map.

19 20 1 —
12 15 19 20 —

S. T. A.

L. O. S.

It may not be complete but the message is clear. Stay lost.

My pulse freezes. I don't say a word. I just stare at the letters like they're going to catch fire. I glance at Fitz again, still slack in the turret hatch. The breeze ruffles his collar, and I notice his face is pale. Waxen, almost.

Stay lost.

It's a warning. Or a command.

I don't know which would be worse.

My hand trembles slightly as I fold the map shut. I shove it back into the side compartment. No one else needs to see this. We're already fraying at the seams. Another thread pulled and we'll unravel for good.

"Coordinates check out?" Turner asks from the gunner's seat, not even looking up.

"Yeah, I just had to triangulate. We'll head west and swing north. Try to meet the ammunition pad from the live fire."

No one questions it. I think they're too tired to care.

I climb back into the commander's seat and close the hatch halfway, just enough to lean on it. My ears are still ringing from the silence of the church. My mind's not much better. There's a buzz behind everything now. A kind of static that never quite goes away. It's not just fatigue. It's something in the air. Like the forest has a frequency of its own and we're all starting to tune in.

The tank growls as Vic coaxes it to life.

That's when Fitz speaks.

"Some things are best left unsaid," he murmurs.

I blink. My stomach drops.

I glance back.

He's still in the same position, half in, half out, eyes fixed on the treeline like he didn't say anything at all.

"What?"

He doesn't answer.

"Fitz," I say, sharper now. "What did you say?"

He looks down at me, but there's something wrong in his eyes. Like a curtain has been pulled shut behind them. "I didn't say anything, Sarge."

I stare at him for a second too long.

He returns to scanning the trees, calm as can be.

Did he really say it? Did I imagine it?

"Hey, Fitz," I press. "You feel okay?"

He shrugs. "Little hungry. Little cold. But yeah."

The same chill prickles up my spine that I felt in the chapel. Like someone has walked over my grave—but this time, I think it's wearing my name tag.

I call out to Vic. "How's she handling?"

He exhales slowly, both hands on the controls. "Like she wants to drive herself again. Feels stiff. Like the steering's a suggestion."

"Engine's stable?"

"For now."

Turner shifts. "We don't have the fuel to go far on a wild goose chase. We need to find a clearing. The signal's not going to punch through this much foliage."

"I know."

But I don't. I don't know anything. Not where we are. Not how long we were gone inside the church. Not why Fitz said what he said—or if he even said it at all.

I just know the forest doesn't want us here. Or maybe it does, and that's worse.

I glance at the map one last time. It's still folded beside me, the coordinates burned into my mind.

32T 19201 12151

Stay Lost.

It isn't just a cipher. It's a message. And someone—or something—wanted us to hear it.

We roll into a clearing not long after. The mist is thinner here—sunlight breaks through the branches in hazy shafts, illuminating the wet ground and the churned-up earth beneath our treads. For the first time in what feels like days, we can see more than twenty feet in any direction.

"This might be our best shot at getting a signal out," I say, leaning forward and pressing myself up against the hatch ring.

Turner nods. "If anything can punch through, it'll be here. Elevation looks a little better, too."

I glance back down at Vic. "Kill the engine."

Vic hesitates for half a breath, then switches it off. The Abrams winds down into stillness—no rumble, no vibration—just the chirp of birds, the rustle of unseen wind through leaves, and the quiet hiss of coolant ticking in the hot engine.

Silence. A real, solid one.

It doesn't feel comforting. It feels hushed.

Fitz groans softly. I look up and see him still half-perched out of the turret. He's gone pale again—sweat sheens on his cheeks despite the chill.

"Alright," I say, unlocking my hatch. "Out. All of you. Fresh air."

Turner raises a brow. "What, now?"

"Now," I say firmly. "Fitz looks like hell. And I'm not letting whatever happened to him back in that church happen again."

They don't argue. I climb out and feel the air hit my face like a slap—cold, sharp, cleaner than the recycled staleness inside the tank.

Fitz moves sluggishly as he climbs out. He stumbles when he hits the ground, catching himself on the tread. His face is pinched and distant, like he's halfway through a fever dream.

I walk a few paces forward, stretching my legs, trying to shake the tension from my spine. My eyes fall on something just past the tall grass, partially obscured by vines and underbrush.

I freeze.

It's there again. The Sherman.

Same busted track. Same faint white star faded on the flank. Same scorched, open hatch.

"…No way," I breathe.

Turner sees it next. "Oh, **come** on."

Vic lets out a strained noise. "That's not possible."

"We left that thing behind," Turner growls. "We **left** it."

"It's the same tank," Vic says hollowly. "Same rust. Same broken tread. Same everything."

Fitz doesn't say anything.

I step forward slowly, pulse kicking up behind my ears. "Maybe there's more than one. Could be a replica. Something—"

"It's **not** a replica," Turner snaps, turning to me and pointing to the side. *Calculated Vengeance* is painted across the hull. "It's the **same** tank. Same damn scratches on the side. Same busted .50 mount. It's **exactly** the same."

The forest doesn't move, but the air feels tighter, like it's pressing in around us. Even the breeze seems to hesitate.

"You think it **followed** us?" Vic says, eyes wide.

"That doesn't make sense," I mutter. "We were inside the church. Then we were moving for at least twenty minutes. No way we circled back." I forget that a tank can't just move on its own. Not without a driver. But then again... our tank drove us to the church.

"You sure?" Turner says. "Because I'm starting to think this goddamn forest doesn't play by normal rules."

The words spark something sharp in me, and I snap back without thinking.

"Oh, now you're the expert?"

Turner steps toward me, jaw tight. "You're the one barking orders like you know what's happening, and guess what? You don't. You haven't had a clue since we crossed into this place."

Vic raises his voice, nervous and angry. "Don't yell at him! He's trying to keep us alive!"

"Doing a **great** job," Turner sneers. "We've got a tank that drives itself, a map that doesn't match the terrain, and a commander that wants us dead!"

I round on him. "You think **I** want this? You think I planned this out? What the hell do you expect me to do, Turner? Pull a rabbit out of my Kevlar and wish us back home?"

Turner closes the last few feet between us, fists clenched.

"You wanna talk about plans? What was the plan in the church, huh? Sit around while ghost nuns wrote our names in blood? Maybe we can *pray* our way back!"

"Shut up!" Vic barks, voice cracking. "***Both*** of you!"

We all freeze.

There's a second of dead silence.

And that's when we notice it. We were angry. Fighting. Turner and I, we're close. We don't have beef with each other. Is the forest turning us against each other? That's when I realized what Vic was trying to point out.

Fitz is gone.

I turn back toward the tank. He's not by the tanks. Not on top. Not behind us. The turret's empty.

"Fitz?" I call. Nothing.

"Fitz!" Turner shouts, already jogging a few steps toward the treeline.

"Goddammit," I mutter, panic building in my throat.

We all start moving, circling the tank, checking the brush. My boots sink slightly in the wet grass. The forest feels suddenly bigger—like it's *watching* us, amused.

No footprints. No trail. Just... gone.

"He was just here," Vic mutters. "He was *just* here."

"We didn't hear anything," Turner says, scanning the underbrush. "No twigs, no rustle. No sound at all."

I swallow hard. "Fan out. Keep eyes on each other. Don't go far."

We move as one, sweeping out just enough to scan the perimeter. I can't stop the knot forming in my gut. One second we're arguing, the next, our youngest crew member is gone without a trace.

"Fitz!" I call again, louder this time.

No response.

Just the rustle of trees, and the damn mist curling in like it's trying to hide something.

The clearing doesn't feel open anymore. It feels like a trap.

Turner stops, slowly raising a hand. "Sergeant…"

"What?"

He points.

At the treeline, just past the Sherman's burned-out hull, something shifts.

A shape.

A silhouette.

And then it's gone.

We run toward it without thinking.

But Fitz isn't there.

We spend the better part of an hour combing the clearing and the edge of the woods. The sun, if it's still up there, offers no guidance. The mist hasn't lifted—it just swirls and thickens, curling tighter around us like a shroud. Every shadow looks like him. Every sound might be his voice. But it never is.

Turner circles back toward the edge of the clearing and kicks a tree in frustration. "He wouldn't just vanish."

Vic's pacing again, muttering, "He was sick. He was right there. Right **there**. How did we miss him?"

No one has answers. The fog presses in from all sides, muffling the sounds of the forest, muting our footsteps. There's something unnatural about it—not just thick, but heavy. Like it's watching. Listening.

Eventually, we regroup near the Abrams. The four of us are quiet now. There's a weight on all our shoulders, like we've been carrying cinderblocks in our rucks.

"I don't like this," Vic says, hugging his arms. "Something's wrong with this whole place."

Something has **been** wrong. Since the moment we crossed into this forest. And now Fitz is gone, and it feels permanent in a way none of us want to admit.

I scan the trees one last time. "Let's check the tank. Maybe he circled back while we were searching."

Turner scoffs. "Yeah, maybe he slipped by all three of us like some kind of damn ninja."

"Just look," I say. "Please."

We round the Abrams. That's when I see it.

Not by **our** tank.

By the Sherman.

Fitz.

He's standing still, one hand resting on the rusted WWII hulk like it's an old friend. His back's to us. His body is too rigid, too symmetrical. Like a mannequin that forgot it was supposed to move like a human.

For a moment, none of us breathe.

Then he turns.

It's Fitz. And it isn't.

Same jawline. Same eyes. Same height. But he's... skinnier, sharper, somehow. Hollow, like something had been scooped out of him and never put back. His cheeks are sunken, his eyes ringed with the kind of exhaustion that doesn't come from one bad night—it's the wear of years of horrors endured without rest. Dirt clings to his skin like it's part of him now, packed into every crease and shadow of his face. There's a bruise on his temple, dried blood at the corner of his mouth. He looks like he's been through hell and then kept going.

His uniform is tattered—olive drab, not our camo pattern. The cut is old, worn, stained dark with mud and time. The patches are gone, torn or maybe never there to begin with. No name. No flag. Nothing that says he belongs to any modern army we recognize. And yet, standing there in front of the old Sherman, there's no denying it—this is Fitz. Not our Fitz, but Fitz all the same.

My stomach churns.

He looks at me first.

"Hey, Sergeant Casey, got a spare lighter? Mine's out," he says with a familiar smile, like we've just come back from leave.

I blink. "What?"

He turns to Vic. "Glad you're back too, Rich. I missed your humor."

Vic stumbles backward like he's been slapped. "No. No, don't use that... that's not my name."

Then he glances at Turner.

"Ready for some cards, Harris? I've been practicing for *decades*."

Turner's mouth opens but no words come out.

I look between them. We're all very confused.

And then I remember.

The names on the altar. The nine names. Our four, and *their* five.

James Casey. Vince Harris. Richard Thompson. Anthony Fitzsimmons.

Our Fitz isn't just missing.

He's been *replaced*.

"I don't understand," I say. "Who are you?"

The Fitz-thing tilts his head. "What do you mean Sarge?. I'm me, Fitz."

"No, *you're not*," Turner growls. "You're not our loader."

A beat of silence. Then:

"Of course I am. I'm Anthony Fitizsimmons," he says softly, then smirks. "I'm Fitz. Just not the one you brought in with you."

I step forward. "Where is he? Where's *our* Fitz?"

The figure looks at the ground beside the Sherman with a smirk so dumb it makes me want to punch him. "He's close by. But he's not ready to come back yet. He's a little busy *remembering*."

"What the hell does that mean?" Vic snaps.

The figure's eyes linger on mine. "Speaking of remembering... I'm glad you remembered your names," he says, voice tinged with something like pride. "Most don't. Some do, in time. But some require... reminding."

The fog wraps tighter around us. I swear I hear whispering in the trees—our voices, but wrong. Echoing with static and age.

I glance at the others. Turner's knuckles are white on his side arms grip. Vic looks like he's going to vomit.

"What is this place?" I ask, voice barely above a whisper.

The thing that wears Fitz's face doesn't answer.

Instead, he turns back to the Sherman, brushing his hand across the corroded hatch like it's a shrine. Reverent. Almost loving.

Then he glances back over his shoulder.

"We'll be waiting. Let us know when you're ready to *fight*... to *die*."

And just like that, he's gone.

The fog folds in on itself, the mist shifting like a stage curtain, and the figure vanishes with it. One blink, and the spot he stood is empty.

No footprints.

No sound.

Just the Sherman tank sitting there, like it has for eighty years, rusted and quiet.

Waiting.

We stand in silence, the three of us. Hearts pounding. Minds spinning. Trying to piece it together.

"That... that wasn't him," Vic says finally.

Turner shakes his head, voice hollow. "I don't know what the hell that was."

I don't speak.

I can still hear the way he said it.

"Sergeant Casey."

Like it was **me**.

Like he was **my soldier**.

And suddenly, the memory hits—our names. Not just etched into the altar. Burned into this place. Like it's trying to rebuild something from our echoes.

Calculated Vengeance isn't just a tank.

It's a mirror.

A warning.

A cycle.

I kneel slowly and press my hand into the cold earth. It feels older than time. Older than this war or the last. I think of all the souls that came through here. All the men who never left.

And how many versions of us are still walking around in this fog.

Waiting to be found.

Or **forgotten**.

I rise and look at the Sherman one last time.

We don't speak.

But I think we all understand.

[CHAPTER TWELVE: WHAT REMAINS OF STATIC AND SILENCE]

"Dismount at Fiddlers' Green."

19 December 1944

We arm up in silence, but it doesn't stay that way for long.

Tommy slams the loader's hatch shut harder than necessary after pulling out one of the grease guns. "Great. Just perfect," he mutters. "Lose one guy and suddenly we're playing scavenger hunt in a god-damn haunted graveyard."

"You think I wanted this?" Harris snaps, yanking his .45 from its holster like it wronged him. "I didn't tell Fitz to go ghost-hunting in a church that doesn't appear on any map."

"You sure didn't stop him, either," Tommy fires back. "You were too busy pretending none of this is happening."

"That's rich coming from you," Harris growls. "You've been jumping at shadows since we hit the forest line."

"Alright, enough." My voice cuts through the morning air like a knife, but even I can feel the edge wobbling. "We're not doing this. We don't tear each other up. Not now."

But I can tell the words aren't landing right. There's something festering underneath all of us. A heat that's not from exertion or fear, but something more primal. Like the forest itself is trying to rub us raw, pushing us to turn against each other. On the other side of the coin, we've been fighting for weeks without rest. It might just be exhaustion. At this point, I can't tell which is which.

Rich doesn't even look up from checking the other grease gun's magazine. "We shouldn't split up," he says quietly. "Not out here. Not anymore."

I nod, grateful for his grounding tone. "We won't. We stay together."

"And if he's not in the church?" Harris asks, already halfway to a scowl. "Then what? We keep wandering till we all end up like him?"

"You don't know what's wrong with him," Tommy mutters.

"What the hell is that supposed to mean?" Harris turns on him, shoving his shoulder.

"Nothing," Tommy says too quickly. "Just—he looked off. You saw it."

"He's been through hell. We all have. Doesn't mean we start pointing fingers and calling people monsters."

"I didn't say that—"

"You're thinking it."

"Shut up," I bark, sharper than I mean to. Both of them flinch. So do I. I close my eyes for a moment and breathe in slowly. Even that's hard to do here. The air's too still. Too thick. "Everyone grab extra ammo. We find Fitz. That's all we do. We don't argue. We don't panic. We find him and then leave."

I sling my Garand over my shoulder and step off the tank, boots crunching on the half-dried mud below. The others follow. Tommy's dragging his feet like he's walking toward a firing squad. Rich looks wired, jittery. Harris keeps glancing into the trees like something's watching him.

Maybe something is.

The path to the church feels longer than it looks. Thankfully, the fog's starting to lift, just barely. Thin beams of weak light cut through it, giving the world a washed-out, dreamlike pallor. It should be comforting. It isn't. Everything looks like it's been bleached by fear.

Tommy's breathing is too loud. I hear it over the leaves and twigs crunching underfoot. "If he's hurt," he says, not looking at anyone, "I swear to God I'll kill him. Put him out of his misery."

"You hear yourself right now?" Rich asks. "That doesn't even make sense."

"He ran off. He left us."

"He was sick," I remind them. "We all were. Probably still are. Monoxide leak, remember? Could explain everything."

"No, it can't," Harris says. "Not all of it. Not the ghosts on the road. Not that tank looking like it got dragged out of a nightmare. You saw it, Casey. You saw all of it."

I stay quiet. I don't have an answer that makes any of this less insane.

"Maybe we're already dead," Tommy says under his breath. "Maybe we're the ghosts now."

"Oh, screw off with that," Harris growls.

"Think about it," he continues. "What if we died back there? Back when we fell asleep because of the monoxide. And now we're just stuck here."

"Cut the crap."

"I'm serious! What if this is punishment? What if—"

"Private Thompson!" I snap, spinning around. He stops mid-sentence. "You're not helping. You want to fall apart, do it after we find Fitz. Not before."

He nods, chastised, but I see it in his eyes—he's hanging by threads. We all are.

We move in silence for a while after that. The church waits for us, half-swallowed by fog and shadow. It hasn't moved, but it feels... closer. Like it leaned in while we weren't looking.

The door's busted and crooked on its hinge. One of the windows is shattered completely, like something—or someone—smashed their way in.

Rich shoulders past us and leads the way. "Let's just get this over with," he mutters.

Inside, the air's warmer. Like someone lit a fire that never went out, but there's no smoke, no crackling flames—just a dry, suffocating heat that seems to press down on our lungs. The kind that makes you sweat behind your ears and itch beneath your collar, even though you're standing still.

The scent hits next. It's faint but unmistakable—incense, aged and bitter, like what you'd smell walking past an old church back home. It doesn't belong here. There's no altar boy swinging a thurible, no priest chanting in Latin. Just us, standing in this hollowed-out skeleton of a chapel, weapons clutched with white knuckles, as if they actually might protect us from whatever the hell is watching.

And it *feels* like we're being watched.

The roof's half gone, the rafters split and jagged like broken ribs. Sunlight cuts through the open beams in pale streaks, lighting up the dust floating through the air like embers. The stained-glass windows—what's left of them—are shattered, shards of color scattered across the stone floor like confetti after a wedding. One pane still clings to the frame behind the altar, a weather-worn image of a saint I don't recognize, the face smeared dark with soot or age or both.

The altar is still there. Solid stone, cracked at the corners but standing tall in the center of it all. The inscriptions carved into its face are old, deeper than the surrounding erosion. The letters are Latin—I can make out enough from my school days to recognize it's not gibberish. A prayer maybe. Or a list. But there's something off about them. Some of the letters look fresher than the others, like they've been retraced recently.

It doesn't feel **evil**, exactly. Just... wrong.

I feel a chill crawl down my spine anyway, despite the heat. Something about this place presses in on you, makes your skin crawl and your thoughts drift in directions you don't want them to go. This church wasn't on the map. It wasn't supposed to be here.

"Fitz?" I call out, my voice echoing more than it should in a place so ruined. It bounces off the walls and disappears into the dust.

Nothing answers.

We move cautiously through the pews, which are surprisingly intact—at least in shape, if not stability. A few have collapsed in on themselves, and others are so rotted they creak if you so much as look at them. The wood's dry and splintered, ancient despite the war having only just torn through here.

Rich takes the left side, sweeping his grease gun between the rows. Tommy lingers closer to the door, one eye always watching the outside. Harris heads straight down the center aisle, toward the altar. I don't know what I expect him to find—Fitz curled up behind a pew, maybe. Knocked out. Or praying.

But he's not here.

He's not **anywhere.**

Harris slows as he nears the altar, then stops, eyes climbing the cracked stone surface like he's reading something none of us can see. He tilts his head, brow furrowing.

"You see this?" he mutters. "The writing?"

"Yeah," I say. "Latin probably. Maybe German. Nothing to worry about."

"Yeah, but… it's weird, right? Some of it looks new."

"Someone could've passed through here. Chaplain. Locals. Who knows."

He doesn't look convinced. Neither am I.

Harris stops in the middle of the aisle and cranes his neck back, looking toward the collapsed roof. "I don't like this," he whispers. "This place—it feels…"

He trails off, just shakes his head and rubs at the back of his neck like something's crawling beneath his skin.

"We keep looking," I say, keeping my voice calm. In control. Like I'm not just barely holding it together. "Back out and circle the perimeter. Check the treeline. Maybe he didn't make it this far after all."

"Maybe he was never here," Tommy says, his voice low but sharp.

I turn toward him. "What's that supposed to mean?"

"I just…" He hesitates. "I didn't see tracks on the way in. No footprints. No fresh ones anyway. It's like we're chasing a ghost."

"Watch it," Harris mutters.

"I'm serious! We all *felt* like he came here, but what if we just told ourselves that?"

"That doesn't make sense," Rich says. "He's gotta be somewhere."

"Exactly," I cut in. "And until we find him, no more guessing games. We stay together. Stay sharp."

They grumble but follow. I'm not sure if they're afraid of disobeying orders or of being alone, even for a second. The church settles behind us like a weight pressing between our shoulder blades. I glance back at it once before we step outside. The dust hasn't moved. The stained glass is still broken. The altar still stands.

But I can't shake the feeling that it's watching us leave.

Something's wrong with the forest.

With this church.

With us.

With **everything**.

Outside, the trees sway gently in the breeze—like nothing's wrong. Like the world hasn't tilted sideways on us. The sun's dropped lower, shadows stretching long across the mossy earth. Everything looks... quieter now. Calmer. Even the air feels thinner, cleaner.

We spread out in a loose line, rifles in hand, circling the church's perimeter like we're patrolling a bombed-out farmhouse in France. I keep my eyes on the treeline, but there's no movement—just pine and fog and the occasional low chirp of a bird. First one we've heard all day.

After a few minutes, something starts to shift between us.

Our breaths come easier. The pressure behind my eyes fades. That low throb in my skull—the one I hadn't even realized was there—is gone. The tension that's been wrapped around us since Fitz vanished seems to unravel thread by thread.

Harris is the first to speak. He glances toward Tommy, then clears his throat. "Hey. Reynolds."

Tommy looks up, surprised.

"I was outta line earlier," Harris says. "When I snapped at you back by the tank. I—look, you were probably right. About the monoxide."

Tommy blinks. "Uh... thanks."

"We were all breathing it in for hours," Harris adds, like he's trying to justify the way we'd all been at each other's throats. "Could've fried anyone's brain a little."

"Yeah," Rich mutters. "Makes sense."

Tommy shrugs one shoulder. "Water under the bridge."

Harris nods, and for once, there's no sarcasm behind it. Just a kind of quiet fatigue.

It's strange—how fast we all seem to settle down once we're outside the vehicle for a while. Like someone turned down the volume in our heads. Even the forest seems less hostile. Less like it's leaning in, listening.

We don't find any tracks, but we keep walking, circling around the back of the chapel. That's when I spot him.

"Fitz?" I call.

He's sitting on the ground with his back against a low hillock, legs splayed out like he just plopped there and forgot to get back up. He lifts a hand, slow and casual, like we're not even the ones he expected.

We rush toward him. I crouch in front of him while the others fan out around.

He doesn't look hurt. Just tired. Pale and a little shaky, sure—but more alert than I expected. His helmet's gone, hair a tangled mess, and there's a leaf stuck to the side of his cheek like he'd been lying down at some point. Next to him is a spot where he's clearly vomited multiple times.

"You alright?" I ask.

Fitz nods slowly. "Yeah. I think I just... needed some air."

"You scared the hell out of us," Harris mutters.

"I didn't mean to," Fitz says. "I—" He squints at me. "You wouldn't happen to have an MRE, would you?"

We all stare at him.

"A what?" Rich says.

"MRE," Fitz says again. "Meal, ready to eat."

I blink. "You mean a K-ration?"

"No, I—" Fitz pauses. His brow furrows, like he's trying to remember something important but it keeps slipping away. "Yeah. K-ration. That's what I meant." He rubs his temple. "I think I'm just... not okay right now."

"Or maybe you *hit* your head," Harris mutters. "Talkin' like that."

But no one presses him. We're just glad he's alive.

It's only then I notice what he's leaning next to.

There's a cannon that's tucked halfway into the undergrowth behind the church, like someone tried to stash it out of sight centuries ago. The wheels are spoked wood, the barrel polished to a gleaming brass that somehow hasn't tarnished even a little. It looks old world, antique. But it's spotless. Not a speck of rust or grime.

Tommy's the first to point it out. "How the hell has that thing not aged?"

"It's gotta be a replica," Harris offers.

"Out here?" Rich says. "In the middle of nowhere?"

"Maybe the church used it as decoration."

We all stare at it for a moment longer, unease creeping back in around the edges. But none of us wants to touch it. Or talk about it. There's something about the shine on the brass—too perfect, too unnatural.

It's not just the cannon.

As I look closer, I notice five trunks—wooden, brass-hinged, and propped open in a perfect line like someone laid them out just minutes before we arrived. Inside each one is a full uniform: crisp, clean, and folded with military precision. Not our uniforms. Not American. These are older—brighter blues, faded reds, even white trim on one. Some of the coats shimmer slightly in the afternoon light, like they'd been pressed and polished this morning.

Matching hats sit atop each pile. Cartridge sacks rest on top like someone's about to shoulder them. Each trunk has a musket leaned carefully against it—long-barreled, flintlock, polished to a shine. The barrels gleam. The wood stocks are smooth, oiled, not a single crack or splinter.

I take an unconscious step forward before I even realize it. The others do too, each of us drawn without thinking.

There's something ceremonial about the way it's all arranged. Like we stumbled onto some forgotten changing room for soldiers of another time—like someone left it for us. Or *to* us.

Even the cannon accessories are there—ramrods, powder horns, worm tools, all leaned neatly along the cannon's rear wheel as if awaiting hands that already know how to use them. There's no rust. No wear. No mold or musty smell. Just clean oak, polished brass, and sharp iron.

It looks like an invitation.

A calling.

None of us speak for a long moment. My eyes drift to the far-left trunk. Something about it catches me. The way the hat's angled. The way the jacket's sleeves rest over the folded belt. It's… familiar.

I swallow hard.

It looks like **my** size.

Like it's **mine**.

I can't explain it—there's no logic to the thought. But I know it. Somewhere deep, behind the ribs. That left trunk is for me. And I'm supposed to step into that coat. I'm supposed to pick up that musket.

And never take it off.

I shudder and pull my gaze away. Fitz stirs behind us, rubbing his eyes.

"We need to move," I say, louder than necessary. "We need to get him back to the tank."

The others nod quickly, too quickly. Like they've just broken out of the same spell.

We don't talk about the trunks. We don't even look back at them.

But as I help Fitz to his feet and we start walking, I can feel that trunk—**my** trunk—watching me. Waiting.

And for the life of me, I can't shake the feeling that if I'd taken one more step… I wouldn't have come back.

"Let's just get him back to the tank," I say.

We help Fitz up. He moves slow, a little unsteady, but he insists he's fine. Still, I keep a hand on his shoulder as we guide him back through the trees. The cannon disappears behind us as soon as we're out of sight, swallowed by the brush like it was never there at all.

As we walk, Harris claps Fitz gently on the back. "You had us lookin' under every damn rock."

"I wasn't tryin' to disappear," Fitz says. "I remember walking... and then I just felt like I had to sit down."

Rich frowns. "Did you see anyone? Or hear anything?"

"No," Fitz says, shaking his head. "Just... thoughts. Like my own memories that weren't my own. But I think I'm alright now."

None of us know what to say to that. Not really.

When we reach the tank, we settle him on top of the turret and pass around a canteen. Fitz takes a long drink, then exhales like he's just come out of a fever dream. The rest of us post up on the turret and hull, keeping watch.

"Alright," I say, stretching my back after several moments of silence. I hop down from the turret to the hull. "Let's get Fitz something to eat."

"I'll check the stowage," Harris grunts, sliding off beside me. "We should still have a crate of K-rats left."

Tommy follows, rummaging through the canvas packs near the rear of the hull while Thompson climbs back inside the turret to double-check the rack behind the loader's seat.

"You know," Tommy mutters, "if I ever meet the guy who designed our storage layout, I'm gonna sock him in the mouth. Everything's always buried under everything else."

"It's a tank, not a kitchen," Harris snaps. "Stop whining."

Thompson's voice echoes from inside the turret: "Hey, did we move the cans from the left sponson?"

Harris frowns. "No. They should be in there."

I lean into the turret and check myself. Empty. No crate. Just a pair of empty canteens and a roll of bandages half unraveling across the deck.

"Maybe they slid during movement?" I offer.

"Maybe the turret gremlins got 'em," Tommy jokes from inside.

Harris snorts. "Well tell your gremlins that they better cough up some Spam and crackers or I'm eating my boots."

Tommy chuckles, a soft laugh that spreads between us like warmth. Even Fitz cracks a grin when he leans back out of the hatch.

"Imagine the gremlins having a full meal in there," he says. "Sitting cross-legged behind the breech, sipping coffee like—'Sorry boys, requisitioned this ration for the war effort.'"

That gets us laughing harder. For a brief moment, it feels like old times. Like France. Or even training stateside. Jokes and bullshit and bellyaching.

Then the laughter fades.

Because we realize none of us has found the crate.

Harris opens the driver's side tool compartment. Nothing.

I rip through the canvas duffel in the commander's rack. Bandages, spare oil rags, half a bar of soap. No food.

Thompson climbs back inside and checks beneath the gunner's seat. Empty.

Tommy kicks at the snow-dusted dirt with the heel of his boot. "Wait. We **had** them. Yesterday. I made coffee with one of the packets. I saw the crate. I **packed** it."

"It's gone," I mutter. "All of it."

A long silence follows.

No one speaks. Just the whisper of wind and the low groan of pine trees.

Then Harris says what we're all thinking: "We didn't eat it. No way we went through an entire crate in twenty-four hours. Unless we've been out here longer than that."

"Maybe someone moved it?" Thompson offers, but even he sounds uncertain.

I shake my head. "No one's touched it."

I look back toward the turret. Toward the empty racks. The bare shelves.

And I feel something I haven't felt since our first firefight.

A deep, gnawing unease.

Something's wrong. And it's not just the missing food.

It's **everything**.

We sit in silence for a long while.

The wind moves through the trees with a kind of purpose—soft, but insistent. The rustle of branches and leaves feels almost like whispers now. Not words. Just shapes of them. Half-thoughts. A murmur you can't quite ignore.

Fitz dozes lightly inside the tank, still pale but breathing evenly. Tommy checks his pulse every so often, like he's worried it might vanish if he stops. Harris and I lean on opposite sides of the hull, boots resting on the cold metal tread, weapons slack in our hands.

Rich's the first to break the silence.

"You ever think maybe we didn't kill any Germans back there? When we were helping the infantry during the ambush."

I blink. Look over at him. "What are you talking about?"

He shrugs, eyes distant. "Just... what if they weren't Germans? What if they weren't **anything**?"

Harris groans softly. "Jesus, not this again."

"No, listen," Rich says. "Think about it. We found what was left of 'em, sure. Blasted them out of their own skin with HE. Split people in half with MG fire. There wasn't anything **human** left. And the way they moved—the way they charged us—"

"They were Krauts," Harris snaps. "They ambushed us. We won. End of story."

"No insignias," I murmur.

Harris turns to me. "What?"

"There were no insignias," I say. "No unit insignia. No helmet markings. Their gear was stripped, like it'd been buried and dug back up. And remember how they came at us? No formation. No cover. Just a straight sprint into the guns like they didn't care."

Harris scoffs, but I can see the crack in his expression. He remembers. We all do.

"Could've been fanatics," he mutters. "Could've been... green."

"They didn't scream," Tommy says. "They didn't even flinch when we opened up. No one does that."

None of us respond. The breeze picks up again. Somewhere behind us, the trees shift and groan like old wood under pressure.

I glance down at my tank, suddenly unsure if it's ever actually done what I believed it did.

Then the radio clicks to life.

We all freeze.

The radio's receiver buzzes with static—low and crackling like a vinyl record left spinning. The kind of static that should come with a voice, but doesn't. Then, from the crackling box, a faint sound emerges.

"*...to anyone who can hear this...*"

We jerk upright. Harris scrambles into the tank to adjust the receiver. "Say again—this is Able Seven, repeat your last, over."

More static.

Then, clearer this time: "*...you're not alone out there...*"

We stare at each other, pulse hammering.

"This is Sergeant Casey with 4th Armored," I say, stepping to the hatch. "Requesting location and status. Over."

"*...don't stay on the road...*"

The voice is almost unrecognizable. It's male, American. But it's old. Worn. Like it's coming through from a different decade. And it's terrified.

Harris flips the channel knob. "This isn't one of ours," he whispers. "It's not even on the same frequency."

"*...it starts at night... It will have you by morning...*"

There's a long burst of static.

Then silence.

Tommy looks like he's about to be sick. "Did he say *it* comes?"

We all heard it. That word. Not **they**. **It**.

"What the hell's *it*?" Harris snaps, but he's pale now too.

We sit with it for a while. The question hangs in the air, cold and heavy.

"...*This is Able Seven, requesting support... anyone out there? Please advise... over.*"

Silence.

"*...please... leave...*"

A whisper now. The last transmission. Then the radio cuts out entirely with a dry **pop**.

Gone.

No clicks. No static. Just gone.

Harris slowly turns the knob. Nothing. Every channel dead. Every frequency flatlined.

I take a deep breath and climb into the tank past Fitz, who stirs at the motion. I grab the map and flashlight from the side compartment, lay it out over the ammo rack. My fingers trace the lines, the ridges, the known checkpoints.

"I think we need to call it in," I say finally. "We're cut off. Something's wrong out here. And we're running out of time."

Harris looks at me like I've lost my mind. "And say what? That we got jumped by ghost soldiers and the woods are whispering? They'll think we went shell-shocked."

"I don't care," I say. "We need to try. If we sit on our hands any longer, we're going to end up like those voices—just static in the trees."

No one argues.

As soon as Fitz looks steady enough to sit up on his own, I give the order. "Mount up. We're moving."

No one argues. Not after what we saw—those trunks, that cannon, those fresh uniforms that didn't belong to any of us but still felt like they did. I catch myself looking back more than once as we gather our gear. The trunks remain just as we **packed** them... No, as we **left** them. Open, like invitations. Waiting.

Tommy climbs in first, helping Fitz up and into the hull like a kid being tucked into bed. Rich slides into the driver's seat, twisting a ragged scarf tighter around his neck. Harris gives the church one last long look before settling into the gunner's position, jaw tight, eyes distant.

I climb in last. The turret hatch clanks shut behind me like the sound of a coffin lid falling closed. I'm not risking my life sitting half out of the tank like I normally do. If something is coming to kill me it's going to have to make it through our steel first.

"Let's get the hell out of here," I mutter.

Rich turns the starter. The engine sputters, chokes, then grudgingly rumbles to life, like something old and angry that should have been left sleeping. The tank jerks forward, treads snapping frozen earth and grinding over stubborn patches of snow.

We crawl out of the churchyard and into the trees, where the forest leans in—watching, waiting. The branches claw at the turret with wooden fingers, not brushing but **grasping**, as if trying to drag us back. It doesn't want us gone. It wants us **dead**. And somewhere deep in the rot of my mind, a voice whispers what I can no longer ignore: the forest knows me. And it hates me. And I think—no, I **know**—whatever it is that's coming for me. For my crew. It's **personal**.

I glance through the rear vision blocks and see the church one last time—its stone walls crumbling, roof caved in, altar just barely visible through the doorway. The cannon sits just outside like a monument to a war no one remembers. Or one we were never supposed to forget.

The tank shudders as Rich threads us through a narrow gap in the trees. We don't talk. Even Fitz stays quiet, his breathing shallow, his eyes half-lidded as he leans against the hull like someone too tired to dream.

It's maybe five minutes of slow crawling through the woods before we hear it—the engine sputtering.

Then choking.

Then dying.

The tank rolls forward another ten feet on sheer momentum before the tracks stop and the hull settles with a groan.

Rich curses softly. "Outta gas."

"You're sure?" I ask.

"I'm sure," he says, checking the gauge. "We ran the last of it dry when we had it running most of the night and trying to get out of that place."

I consider that for a second. I'm too scared to open the hatch. I could go for the fresh air as the dull headache begins to creep in but I'm not about to risk my head getting shot off.

We're in a clearing.

Open. Round. A wide patch of bare earth and brittle winter grass carved like a crater into the trees. The overcast sky hangs low overhead, and for the first time since we entered this damn forest, I can see all the way to the treetops.

I breathe in. The air is thick. Heavy. Filled with poison. But the potential for death outside the steel confines of our coffin is too great for me to risk. The pressure, that weight we've all been feeling pressing in on our skulls, seems just a little more oppressive.

"This might be the best damn place we're gonna get a signal out," I say.

Harris pokes his into my cupola and begins looking out the vision blocks. He has yet to learn what the term 'personal space' is. "Hell of a coincidence, huh?"

I nod slowly. "Yeah. Hell of a thing."

"Coincidence or not," Rich says, "we're not going anywhere else."

"Exactly," I say, thumbing the latch on the long-range set. The old radio crackles in my hands, louder than usual but still in working order.

It's now or never.

I key the transmitter one more time.

"This is Sergeant James Casey, 3rd Armored Division, Charlie Company. Sherman tank, callsign *Calculated Vengeance*. We're requesting immediate support or recovery. We are out of fuel, short on rations, and have one man that's too ill to fight. Grid reference unknown. We are stationary in a clearing approximately five klicks northeast of last known friendly infantry position. I say again: stationary, out of fuel, requesting immediate assistance..."

I release the button. Nothing.

We wait.

Five seconds. Ten. A full minute. Even after what feels like eternity, the radio doesn't answer.

[CHAPTER THIRTEEN: THROUGH THE HATCH OF TIME]

"No Trooper ever gets to Hell"

20 December 2024

The forest is quiet this morning. Still, like it's holding its breath.

A pale grey light filters through the trees. It's hard to tell how long we've been here. Days maybe? The sun never seems to rise all the way in this place. The mist just shifts color, cycling through shades of confusion.

Surely the other crews from the competition have noticed that we haven't returned from the land navigation exercise. That is if that much time has elapsed. I'm not even sure what day it is.

We're gathered around the tank, not speaking at first. Nobody wants to bring it up. Not the names on the altar. Not the church. And especially not Fitz.

Finally, Turner breaks the silence.

"So… is he done 'remembering' or what?"

Vic shoots him a sharp look, but it's not angry. More like he's afraid of the answer. "Don't say it like that."

Turner shrugs, but his voice is quieter now. "Just saying. Last night was... not normal. He looked at us like he knew who we were. Like we were the ghosts."

Vic rubs his hands on his thighs, scrubbing away dirt only he can see. "I don't think he's lost. I think he's stuck. Like—like he's in both places at once."

"That's comforting," Turner mutters.

I look toward the WWII tank—*Calculated Vengeance*, pristine looking and barely swallowed by the moss and earth. The mist clings tighter around it than anywhere else, as if the forest is trying to pull it back in. But the hatch is cracked open now. Not like we left it.

"He's not out here," I say. "Not really. So maybe we check in there."

"The Sherman?" Vic asks.

I nod. "Yeah. If this place really wants him, that's where it'd keep him."

No one argues. We gear up slowly, almost ritualistically. We have no idea what we could encounter and none of us is taking any chances. Weapons slung, boots laced, gloves pulled on ready for a fight. The chill hasn't left us. Maybe it never will.

We cross the distance to the old tank in silence.

The closer we get, the more I feel it in my chest—that sense of weight, like a rope around my ribs being pulled tight. My breath comes short, but I push forward. We need to know.

 The Sherman shouldn't be here. Not like this.

Its hull is scarred with the jagged aftermath of combat. There's deep gouges and blast marks, but the metal itself looks too intact. Clearly they weren't knocked out by another tank or an anti-tank weapon. Somehow, it's only just parked here from the last firefight. The paint should be rusted off and flaking, but the faint marking and stenciling still clings to the side, stubborn and sharp around the edges.

The bumper number, **23**, is the worst part. Its number matches ours exactly. Because of course it does.

There's no rust. No moss. No decay. Just the faint, acrid sting of spent propellant hanging in the air, from when the cannon fired seemingly minutes ago. The hull gives off a strange warmth, from having the engine running for hours.

The commander's hatch sits just barely ajar, cracked open enough to leak a thin line of light from the shadows within.

Vic climbs on top of the turret from instinct. He pauses at the lip of the commander's hatch, one hand on the cool metal.

I hesitate. Something about the thing feels **wrong**. Not just old. Not just out of place. Like it's waiting.

But I climb up anyway.

We throw open the hatch and get hit in the face with light from a flashlight. It takes a second for my eyes to adjust.

Inside, the Sherman smells like oil, mildew, and something else—like old paper, dust sealed behind glass. It's cramped, smaller than our Abrams, and somehow feels even tighter with the past pressed into every surface.

And there, in the loader's spot, is Fitz.

He's sitting cross-legged on the floor, back against the wall, staring at something just above eye level.

Photographs. Dozens of them.

Pinned to the inside of the tank with rusted tacks and old tape. Black and white, most of them. Faded faces stare out: young men in uniform, arms slung over shoulders, dirty and smiling as if they don't know what's coming for them. Letters are folded beneath some, notes scrawled on the backs in looping cursive.

One by one, we climb into the tank, each of us settling into our assigned position without thinking. It's instinctual—automatic, we've done it a thousand times before

"Where the hell did these come from?" Turner murmurs.

Fitz doesn't look at us. Doesn't blink.

"I think I know them," he murmurs, fingers grazing the edge of the photo like it might crumble if he presses too hard.

His eyes fix on the man in the center. A young, grimy, helmet tilted back just enough to catch the light. The resemblance is... uncanny. His fingers hover over the man in the photo's mouth, where a crooked tension pulls the lips tight. Not quite a smile. Not quite a grimace. The same twitch he gets when he's trying not to lose it.

The others crowding behind, half in shadow, faces streaked with soot and sweat, are a dream half-remembered. My stomach turns. One of them has Turner's cocky, arrogant grin. Another wears Vic's haunted eyes and diligent hands.

Fitz doesn't say anything else. Just stares. Breathing shallow. Like something's shaking loose inside him, and he's afraid of what it is.

Vic crouches beside him. "Fitz. You alright?"

He turns his head slowly. His eyes focus on me, but I'm not sure he's really looking at me.

"*We* were here. Before... us, I guess. I don't know anymore."

He points to one of the black-and-white photos. It shows five men standing in front of the Sherman, grinning. One of them—dead center—has the same jawline as Fitz. The resemblance is close enough to make my stomach turn.

"That's Fitzsimmons," Fitz says, tapping the photo gently. "He's me. I think. Or I was him."

Nobody knows what to say.

"Fitz," I finally say. "How long have you been in here?"

He shrugs. "A while. A minute. A year. I don't know."

"Why here?"

He looks around like he's seeing the place for the first time. "It felt safe."

Vic puts a hand on Fitz's shoulder, grounding him. "You found it, man. We're here now. Let's get you out of this ghost trap."

But Fitz doesn't move. His eyes drift to another photo, this one water-damaged but still visible. The soldiers in it wear different uniforms—French, maybe. Napoleonic era? One leans against a cannon. The brass is untarnished.

"They left things behind," Fitz whispers. "But it never lets them go. Just keeps them. Like trophies."

A chill runs through the tank.

I glance back through the open hatch. The sun is finally starting to break through the clouds, casting pale light across the treetops, but the forest beyond feels distant now—blurred, like it's been pushed further from reality. This rusted shell feels sealed off, preserved in its own timeline, and stepping inside feels less like exploration and more like a violation. Like something out there knows we're here now.

Inside, the outside light begins filtering down through the open turret hatch and casts long slashes of gold and white across the interior. It's tight—more cramped than I expected—and the air has this heavy, metallic tang. Not like rust. More like cordite and grease. Burnt oil. The ghosts of a firefight that should've happened generations ago.

It doesn't feel abandoned. And as crazy as it sounds. It feels like home.

Everything is where it **should** be. Spent shell casings litter the floor, some still rocking gently as if they were disturbed seconds ago. The turret basket has that same greasy feel I remember from the Abrams. The way the metal rubs raw against your gloves after a long mission. There's a scuffed tin can wedged under the gunner's seat, just like Turner keeps under his.

I blink. My hand grips the edge of the breech without thinking, bracing exactly where I always when trying to reposition. Muscle memory is guiding me—only this isn't my tank.

But everything about it feels **lived in**. Not like a relic. Like something we just stepped out of for a smoke break.

The powder smell clings to my tongue, bitter and sharp. And underneath it, something else: the cold, metallic scent of fear. I've smelled it before.

Hell, I've **shot** it before.

There's still a live shell clamped in the breech. Rounds sit snug in the ready racks, not a speck of dust on them. Spent casings litter the floor in every direction, so many I can't shift my weight without them crunching under my boots. The paint on the labels isn't even scratched. The .50 and .30 cal machine guns are mounted and fully belted, the ammo links stretched out like someone was still laying down suppressing fire when time froze. The canvas bags that would normally catch the brass are overflowing. Thousands, maybe. It's a miracle no one slipped and cracked their skull.

There are scorch marks on the walls. Scabs of melted paint where hot brass casings must've lit something up inside. The ventilation fans are scorched black. One of the side panels is punched in but not broken.

But the strangest part is the **heat**. It shouldn't be warm in here—not this warm. It's been sitting untouched for decades, out in the forest with no maintenance, no power, no crew. The weather should've taken it back. But the air feels like a furnace was running just yesterday. Sweat beads on my neck and trails down my back.

Vic runs his fingers along the driver's side tray, where someone had carved initials—*J.V.*—into the steel. His hand comes away clean. Not dusty. Not corroded. Just warm.

"What the hell is this?" Turner mutters. He's crouched near the gunner's seat, poking through a pile of live .30 cal belts. "This looks fresh. This **all** looks fresh. You telling me someone's been keeping this up for eighty years?"

"No one's keeping this up," I say quietly. "That's the problem."

Fitz hasn't said a word since we climbed inside. He's still staring at the wall of pinned photographs—black-and-white shots of young men in uniform. Some smiling. Some not. There's a map beneath them, torn at the edges, marked with pencil lines and what looks like coffee stains. Or blood. Hard to say. The whole thing feels like a shrine.

I perch on the edge of my seat and scan the interior.

"Jesus," I whisper. "They must've gone through hell in here."

Vic nods slowly. "They didn't give up, though. Look at this. Still ready to fight. Even at the end."

Turner shifts behind me. "Or they **never** stopped."

There's a silence that follows that line. Heavy. Not just thoughtful—**dreadful**. Because we all feel it. There's a weight in the air, a tension that doesn't belong to us. Like something's **watching**. Waiting.

I look down at the floor again, at the brass and the shell fragments, and I swear I can still smell gunpowder. Not faint, either. Sharp. Like the last round was fired minutes ago.

This place is a tomb. But it doesn't feel like a dead one.

Fitz finally speaks, voice low and distant. "They held out for as long as they could."

I glance at him. "You mean the tank crew?"

He nods slowly, fingers still touching the photos. "They knew what was coming."

"What was coming?" Turner asks, more sharply than he means to.

Fitz doesn't answer. He just keeps looking at the faces in the picture. And I can't tell if he's recognizing them... or **remembering** them.

I lean back and close my eyes for a second. There's something about the rhythm of this place that messes with your sense of time. I can feel the thrum of the forest outside—wind catching the trees, birdsong rising. But in here? It's like being underwater. Every sound is dulled. Every movement feels too slow or too fast.

"We need to get out of here," I say finally.

No one disagrees. Even Fitz doesn't argue. He just pulls away from the photos, lets his hand drop, and follows us back up to the hatch.

But as I climb out last, I can't help but glance back one more time.

The brass still gleams on the floor.

And for a split second, I could swear I hear a voice whisper something from the gunner's seat.

Just one word.

"*Again.*"

I blink, and it's gone.

We quietly and instinctively gather at the front of the tank. Not **our** tank. Or is it **our** tank? I don't even know anymore.

Fitz is quiet at first, still sitting on the front hull with his knees pulled up and the faded photo still clutched in his hand. He keeps rubbing a thumb over the faces—over his own face, or the man who could've been his twin. The rest of us stand in silence. No one says it, but we're all afraid that if we speak too loud, we'll shatter him completely.

Finally, Fitz speaks.

"They stopped here," he whispers. "This tank. This crew. They stopped here."

He doesn't look at any of us. His voice is distant, like he's remembering a dream—or a nightmare. "They were on a mission. Protecting some infantry. Then they found a serious target. A King Tiger, I think. They'd been fighting for a while, and when they finally found it... it wasn't a Tiger... It was something else."

He swallows, and his hand trembles a little on the edge of the driver's hatch ring.

"Before all of it, though, their previous assistant driver was killed. Then they got a new guy before the previous guy's blood even dried. They seemed optimistic. Not about Tommy—well, maybe a little about Tommy. He was new, eager. But they were excited because they'd just bagged a Tiger. Full penetration through the turret ring. One shot. Turner got the angle just right. It was a good kill."

Everyone shivers when he uses the name *Turner* and not that of the *Calculated Vengance's* gunner. Maybe we are the WW2 crew. None of us speak. We don't need to. We can see it on his face, the way it's all flooding in at once—details no nineteen-year-old modern loader should know. Words that don't belong to him.

"But then they got hit. Ambush. Sides of the road lit up—infantry with Panzerfausts. MG42s pinning them down from the trees. They returned fire. *Turner* laid it down hard—two belts through the co-ax and a handful HE in under thirty seconds. Casey yelling for smoke. Rich backing the tank up over brush so thick they thought they were gonna get hung up on a stump. But they made it. They fought their way out."

He takes a shaky breath. His voice is rough now. "Then they parked here. Right here. They thought it was over."

A long silence stretches out. Fitz blinks rapidly, then rubs his face with one hand, the photo crumpling slightly in his other.

"But it wasn't," he says finally, barely audible. "Something else happened here. Something worse. But I—I can't... I can't remember it all. It's like it's right there, but if I look too hard, it hurts."

He rocks forward slightly, hunched and small. Vic shifts beside him, like he's about to say something, but stops himself. We all know this is Fitz's moment. We're just here to witness it. To listen to it.

Fitz reaches slowly into his jacket. His hands fumble for a moment before he pulls something free: a beat-up, dark green notebook. The edges are frayed, the cover scuffed and stained with old oil, maybe blood.

He holds it like it's something sacred. Then hands it to me.

"It's Harris's journal," he says. "The gunner. *Calculated Vengeance's* crew. But... look at the handwriting."

I flip it open carefully, past the first few pages of blocky, aggressive writing. And then I see it. My stomach twists.

It's Turner's handwriting.

Same slant. Same tight spacing. Same habit of not crossing t's unless he's paying attention.

"This is your writing," I mutter, looking up at Turner.

Turner stares, eyes narrowed. "I've never seen that before."

"But it's yours. I've seen you fill out our logbooks and gunner's book. Same little curl on the capital G. Same flat-bottomed s's."

Turner takes the journal and flips through it with a scowl. But I can see the tension in his jaw, the way his eyes move just a little too fast over the lines, like he's trying not to absorb it. Vic leans over his shoulder, eyes wide.

"This doesn't make sense," Vic murmurs. "How would—?"

"It doesn't," Turner cuts in. "It's not mine. It just... looks like mine."

Fitz leans back, his head resting against the metal wall. His breathing's steadier now, but there's a look in his eyes—distant, lost—that I've never seen before.

"I think this happened before," he says. "All of it. Not just to them. I think we've been here before. Not in this tank. But like... in this **place**. This moment. Like we're playing out something that already happened. Again and again."

The words hang there, heavy. None of us speak. Outside, the morning mist is beginning to rise, curling through the trees like smoke. The silence feels enormous.

Turner slowly closes the journal and sets it on the engine cover beside him. He doesn't say anything, but his leg is bouncing—a nervous tic I've only seen during firefights.

I look around the outside of the Sherman again. I take it in and remember everything that's happened in the last... I don't even know how long. The photo. The names carved into the altar back in the church. The trench coats and muskets, clean and waiting, just outside.

Wait. I don't remember there being any muskets and trench coats waiting outside.

Something about this place has soaked through time like water through cloth.

We aren't the first.

And if we don't get out of here soon... we won't be the last.

We're still standing around the Sherman when the first burst of static hits.

It crackles out of nowhere—sharp and alive, like a match struck too close to your ear. We all flinch. Turner jerks his head toward the sound, eyes narrowing.

"Did anyone touch the comms?"

"No," I say, already pushing off the Sherman's wall and moving toward **our** tank. "That wasn't us."

The static intensifies—not random white noise, but pulsing, rhythmic, like something just outside the range of speech.

Then a voice breaks through.

At first, it's just a faint mumble. Then clearer. Clipped. Measured. American, but the kind of radio voice you'd expect from a black-and-white war doc. But it sounds **exactly** like my voice.

"This is Sergeant James Casey, 3rd Armored Division, Charlie Company. Sherman tank, callsign Calculated Vengeance...*"*

I freeze mid-step. My stomach flips like I've been gut-punched. Fitz stops breathing.

"We're requesting immediate support or recovery. We are out of fuel, short on rations, and have one man that's too ill to fight…"

The others are scrambling to climb on top of the Abrams now. I'm already sprinting back toward *Controlled Violence*, heart hammering in my chest.

"Grid reference unknown. We are stationary in a clearing approximately five klicks northeast of last known friendly infantry position. Repeat: stationary, out of fuel, requesting immediate assistance…"

I scramble up the hull, slipping on the dew-slick steel, and hurl myself at the commander's hatch. No finesse. Just panic and muscle. I dive headfirst, half-falling inside. My shoulder slams the hatch ring, my boot catches the rim, but I don't stop. I tumble into my seat because the whole damn forest is chasing me, heart pounding loud enough to drown out the static still echoing in my ears.

This can't be happening.

Not again.

Vic is already in the driver's hole, flipping switches. Turner appears beside me a second later and leans into the radio set. The ancient transmission continues, looping again, the same urgent voice from another lifetime.

"This is Sergeant James Casey, 3rd Armored Division…"

"It's the same name," Turner breathes. "From the journal. From the church wall."

"Same tank," Vic says. "*Calculated Vengeance*. That's them."

We all look at Fitz, who's still standing on the turret outside, one hand on the .50 cal mount like he's not sure if he wants to come back inside.

He does, finally. Drops in silently and sits on the loader's seat like his bones are made of glass.

I reach for the transmitter. My hand hesitates. "You're sure no one's screwing with us? Could be the other crews pulling a prank. Running old recordings through the net."

"No way," Turner says. "No one else has access to that kind of file. Not this deep into the forest. And not with this kind of interference."

He's right. The whole week has been nothing but dead air. Every time we tried to raise someone—anyone, the TOC, even local air support—we got jack shit. Just silence and static.

Until now.

"Try hailing them," I say.

Turner flips the switch, dials the frequency manually. "This is *Controlled Violence* actual, requesting contact with Sergeant Casey, call-sign *Calculated Vengeance*. Over."

Nothing. Just the same loop.

"...one man too ill to fight. Grid reference unknown..."

He tries again. And again. Same result.

I glance at Fitz, who still hasn't said a word.

"You okay?"

He looks up slowly. His eyes are red, raw with memories. But there's something else there too—recognition. Familiarity. Grief.

"I remember that call," he says quietly. "I was sitting right next to him. Casey. When he keyed the mic."

His voice trails off while he's waking up from someone else's dream.

"You're saying this... isn't just a recording," Turner mutters.

"I don't think it is," Fitz says. "I think it's them. *Us*. Somewhere out there."

Vic looks toward the trees outside the hatch. "But that would mean…"

"Yeah," I cut in before he can finish. "That would mean a whole lot of things."

Like time doesn't work right out here.

Like we're not just trapped in a forest—we're caught in something older, something that **remembers**. Maybe something that *feeds*.

I take the transmitter and press it to my mouth, but I don't say anything yet. The words feel heavier now. Like they matter more than they should.

Turner shifts uncomfortably. "They said they're five klicks northeast of their last known position. That could be anywhere."

"Unless it's **this** position," Vic says.

We all look around.

It makes a kind of awful sense. If they parked here, if they called for help **here**, then maybe the reason we were able to send a transmission from this exact spot earlier wasn't coincidence. Maybe this patch of land doesn't just give signals—it traps them. Holds them.

And plays them back.

I finally speak into the mic. "This is Staff Sergeant Carson, *Controlled Violence* actual. I read you, *Calculated Vengeance*. We copy. Say again, do you read **us**? Over."

No reply. Just the same grim message, looping like a memory too painful to let go of.

Turner looks at me. "What if they're still out there?"

"They are," Fitz whispers. "They just don't know they're already gone."

We sit in the tank, listening to the past speak its last breath, again and again.

Outside, the trees don't move. There's no wind, no birdsong. Just the whisper of history repeating itself through the static.

And for the first time since we entered this cursed forest, I start to wonder if help is even possible.

Or if we're just next in line.

Fitz breaks the silence first.

His voice is low and tentative, but it cuts through the haze of looping radio chatter like a knife. "There might be something in the gunner's logbook."

We all look at him.

"What?" I ask.

"The Sherman," he says, nodding toward the open hatch, the ancient tank still looming just beyond the Abrams like a ghost on our doorstep. "If Harris was anything like Turner, he kept a record. Every round fired. Every engagement. Every time they got into it."

Turner folds his arms. "Yeah. I **did**. Or well, **do**. More or less."

Fitz looks at him with something that's not quite a smile. "Exactly. I think Harris did too. And if we find it, we might finally get a clean look at what happened."

I hesitate. Part of me doesn't want to know. Not really. But we've come too far to stop now. We've heard their voices. Seen the inside of their home. I'd be lying if I said I'm not haunted by the idea that we're living inside their unfinished story.

"Alright," I say. "Let's find it."

The four of us climb out of *Controlled Violence* and make our way back to the Sherman. The morning mist is starting to lift, thin beams of light cutting through the trees and glinting off the tank's rusted curves like gold leaf. The forest is still silent, but it's not peaceful. It's expectant.

We duck inside again, one by one, the metal groaning beneath our boots. There's a new layer of unease now that we've heard Casey's voice. My voice.

Turner slides into the old gunner's seat like it's his own, fingers brushing over the worn metal and cracked leather. He instinctively opens a rusted compartment under the seat, grunts, and pulls something free.

A logbook.

Bound in olive drab canvas, stained with grease and oil. And blood. It's unmistakable. The lower corner is soaked dark, dried into the pages like a thumbprint from the dead.

He hands it to Fitz.

"Your idea," he says. "You do the honors."

Fitz hesitates. Then opens the book.

For a moment, it's just the sound of pages turning. Then he begins to read, slowly, aloud, his voice trembling but steady.

"Entry one... '*Tank prepped and rearmed after Ormstadt engagement. New assistant driver assigned. PFC Tommy Reynolds.*' Tommy. They liked him."

He flips a few pages.

"Next entry..."

His thumb traces the top of the next page.

"'Engaged enemy armor. Tiger I. Gunner reports solid AP hit, knocked out at 800 yards. Ammunition detonation. Muzzle flash from rear position. Spun and engaged three MG nests with co-ax and HE. Crew reports multiple infantry KIA.'"

He clears his throat. "'Damage to hull. No casualties.'" He huffs a quiet, shaky laugh and mutters, almost without thinking, "Nice shot, Harris."

Turner raises an eyebrow. "You mean me?"

Fitz's smile fades as he nods, slowly. "Yeah. Guess I wasn't dreaming that damn Tiger during the live fire. Knew it felt real."

Turner leans over and tries to deflect the conversation. "That's textbook. Standard sweep and assault."

Fitz nods, but his fingers keep shaking.

"Next few entries... more of the same. Spot, engage, clear. All in fast succession. Then this..."

He pauses, brows furrowing.

"'Engaged heavy armor at extreme close range. Suspected King Tiger. Fired one AP. Missed. No return fire.'"

I lean in. "One round?"

"That's what it says."

"Odd," Vic mutters. "Why no follow-up if they missed?"

Fitz flips the page—and something changes.

His voice drops. Slows.

"Next entry... pages later. Different handwriting. Same hand, but... messier. Rushed."

We gather tighter around him as he reads on.

"'Ambush in clearing. Heavy fire from all directions. Nighttime. Couldn't see the muzzle flashes. Fired everything we had. Coax and bow ran dry. .50 jammed. Casey yelling to hold. Thompson reloading main gun. Harris injured. Casey took over gun. Fired everything—HE, AP, smoke, didn't matter. Just kept firing. Took hits. Whole thing shaking. Couldn't tell if it was from us or them. Didn't stop.'"

The logbook is smudged with what looks like a palm print. Right over the middle of the entry. Like someone tried to close the book too fast, or maybe—

"I think that's blood," Turner says quietly, echoing my thoughts.

Fitz continues.

"'Crew status: unknown. Think Tommy was killed. Rich screaming, don't know if from pain or fear. Casey lost radio. Tried to get it back up, but lines were down. No contact. No response. Out of fuel. Almost out of ammo. Parked here.'"

He turns the page, but it's blank.

The next one too. And the next.

Turner exhales. "That's it?"

Fitz looks down at the last scrawl of ink. "Looks like it."

"But who were they fighting?" Vic asks. "No mention of armor. No callouts for German units. No actual hits recorded against them."

"No idea," Fitz mutters. "They weren't labeling anything by the end. Just... firing. Surviving."

I take the book gently from his hands, thumbing through the last few written pages. The handwriting is a mess—jagged, uneven, some letters skipped like the writer's hand was trembling too hard to keep up.

And there's no enemy name. Not one. Just: *ambush, fire, dark, don't stop firing, he won't shut up, screaming, out of time.*

Turner's face is pale. "That's not battlefield reporting. That's panic."

We sit inside in silence, surrounded by the aftermath of someone else's nightmare. Spent shells still litter the floor. Live rounds in the ready rack glint in the dim morning light. Everything looks exactly as it did when they finally stopped shooting—because there was no one left to shoot. Or maybe nothing left to fight.

"If they ran out of gas why didn't they just ditch the tank and make it back to friendly lines?" Turner asks quietly.

"Because they didn't think they could."

Fitz's voice hangs in the turret like smoke—thin, lingering, bitter. No one says anything for a long while.

The radio behind us crackles again, but it's meaningless now. Just static. Like breath through clenched teeth.

"Fitz," I say quietly. "Hand me the transmitter."

He blinks, like I've just asked for a cigarette from a ghost. "That's not gonna work," he mutters, voice low, distant. "We both know that."

"I'm asking anyway."

He hesitates, then passes it to me without another word. The moment the cold metal touches my hand, something shifts in the air—like the pressure drops or the sound of the forest outside dulls down to a low, wet hum.

I key the mic. Expect nothing.

Instead, the static hiccups—then sharpens.

I blink. "This is *Controlled Violence*, Abrams main battle tank, four crew, position unknown. Responding to earlier transmission—Calcul—uh, *Calculated Vengeance*. Say again, *Calculated Vengeance*, this is *Controlled Violence*. Do you copy?"

The others are still. Fitz has gone pale. Turner's just staring at the transmitter like it's leaking smoke.

Nothing for a heartbeat. Two.

Then—

"*...Copy. Send it for Calculated Vengance.*"

A man's voice. Rough. Tired. Real. I'm too afraid to respond.

"*This is Sergeant James Casey, Charlie Company. Sherman tank,* Calculated Vengeance. *Go ahead,* Controlled Violence."

I stare down at the mic in my hand like it just turned to gold. "We received your earlier transmission. Wanted to know—what happened to you? Why are you out here?"

Silence.

Then: "*We followed what we thought was a King Tiger. Slipped through the lines... It wasn't like the others.*"

His voice drifts in and out like an old cassette. "*...Fast. Wrong silhouette. Couldn't get a read on it. But it moved like it wanted to be seen. Drew us deep into the forest.*"

I glance at Fitz. He's barely breathing.

Casey continues: "*Got eyes on it near some kind of chapel. Just... sitting there. Like it was waiting. We took the shot. AP right through it.*"

His voice falters. "*Didn't do a damn thing. Just went right through like a bullet through a sheet.*"

He doesn't elaborate, but I can feel the weight of it. A tank round not doing anything isn't just strange—it's impossible.

"We parked near that church," he goes on. *"Started to realize things weren't right. Everything was... off. The trees didn't look the same anymore. Our compass spun. The map didn't match."*

A beat of dead air. Then:

"We ran out of fuel the next morning. That's when they came."

My grip tightens on the transmitter. "Who?"

He's quiet for a long time. When he finally speaks, it's with something close to shame.

"I didn't know. We couldn't see them all the way. They came in fast, hard. Lotta movement, but not much shape. We hit them with small arms first. Then heavier stuff. We fought back. Fought like hell. Burned through everything we had. I was not about to let my crew get killed. Get **taken**.*"*

There's a rustle on the other end. Like someone shifting, uneasy.

"We got all of them," Casey says. *"Every last one."*

He doesn't sound proud. Just... hollow.

Turner mouths the words: ***all of them?***

I don't ask who ***they*** were. Neither does anyone else.

Because we already know.

I clear my throat. "Are you still in the tank?"

Another long pause.

"No."

The air inside the Sherman suddenly feels thinner. The hair on my arms lifts.

"But we're close," Casey adds.

That's worse somehow.

"What do you want us to do?" I ask.

Another beat.

"Stay put. Keep your crew close. Watch the trees. Protect your crew at all costs."

Static crackles in like a wave breaking. I press the button again.

"Casey?"

Nothing.

"Casey, come in."

The mic hisses—then dies.

No more voice. No more ghost.

Just silence. And the soft, patient noise of the forest exhaling through the vents.

I lower the transmitter slowly. No one says a word.

Fitz leans forward, his voice barely audible. "He never said who they were."

Turner nods, brows drawn. "Doesn't have to. Sounds like the same thing that's stalking us."

Vic's eyes flick toward the hatch. "Why didn't he describe them?"

Fitz's jaw clenches. "Because he couldn't."

I look at him. He's staring at the floor, but his voice is steady now. Grounded.

"Or because he **didn't want** to. Because saying it out loud makes it real. Because if he admits what they were..." He trails off, swallows. "He would be severely punished and ostracized for using this much ammunition shooting at ghosts and demons."

We all freeze.

Turner exhales slowly. "Jesus. Just kind of how we had so much dumb stuff happen to us from the others in the competition after they found out we saw the jeep. They thought we went crazy like they must have been."

"It was dark. They were scared. Something was moving through the trees. The lines were messed up." Fitz looks up at us, eyes glassy. "They thought it was the enemy. But maybe..."

He doesn't have to finish. The idea clicks into place, sharp and sickening.

Whatever Casey and his crew fought—whatever they **killed**—may have been just as lost and terrified as they were.

Or maybe it wasn't.

Maybe the forest wanted them to believe that.

And maybe it wants the same from us.

The tank creaks around us. Metal settling into memory. Outside, the birds are quiet again. Like they're waiting for something.

The transmitter sits limp in my hand. No more voice. No more lifeline.

Just us. And the silence that follows.

Fitz whispers, "It's happening again, isn't it?"

I look at him.

And I don't lie.

"Yeah. I think so."

[CHAPTER FOURTEEN: WHERE IT SHOULD HAVE ENDED]

"Ere he's emptied his canteen;"

20 December 1944

The light comes slow through the periscope slits. Just a pale gray glow at first, pushing back against the black. No sun yet. Just haze and silhouettes. But it's enough to let me know we've survived the night.

Nobody speaks.

There's a faint, constant hum in my ears that might be real or might just be in my head. At this point I can't tell anymore. My tongue feels dry and leathery. My fingers are trembling slightly even when I'm not moving them. Harris is slumped in the gunner's seat, hands still hovering near the traverse handles, like he's been frozen there. Rich's breathing is shallow behind the driver's controls, he doesn't even try to move. I'm not sure he **can**. Fitz is tucked against the loader's sidewall, knees drawn up, arms cradling his helmet like it's some kind of talisman.

Tommy is the only one who slept. Maybe an hour. Maybe less. He's curled against the floor like a kicked dog.

Nobody wants to be the first to speak. Words would make it real.

We stayed sealed inside after the engine sputtered out sometime around sunset. Kept the hatches shut, even though it was getting harder to breathe. The air's been stale since before dawn, thick with sweat, cordite, and rust. I've had a headache pounding behind my eyes for hours now. There's a strange warmth in my chest that won't go away—like I'm not getting enough air, no matter how deep I breathe. I've convinced myself we're okay, that it's just nerves. But I catch Harris wiping sweat from his lip, and Tommy coughed hard enough earlier that I thought he'd pass out.

We haven't said it out loud, but none of us trust what's outside.

Last night, there were **eyes**. Red ones. Dozens of them. At first, I thought it was just the reflection of moonlight on frost. But they moved. They **watched**. They crept around us like wolves circling a wounded elk. Too low and too fast to be men. Too many. Fitz swore he saw one get up on its hind legs.

We didn't open fire. Thought about it. Hell, we damn near did. But I couldn't justify wasting the ammo when we couldn't even tell if we were hallucinating. We haven't slept. We haven't eaten. We've been trapped in a steel box full of ghosts and shadows, with no fuel, no hope of reinforcement, and no idea if anyone even remembers we're out here.

The morning fog is rising. It clings to the trees in wisps, thin and deceptive. The way it curls around the hull makes me feel like the tank's being swallowed whole by the forest.

I finally speak. "We need air."

Harris grunts but doesn't move.

"I mean it," I say again. "We're cooking in our own breath. We either open something, or we pass out."

Tommy groans and starts shifting in his seat. His hands fumble for the hatch lever.

"Wait." Rich speaks up, voice hoarse, barely audible. "What if they're still out there?"

I look around. Four pairs of eyes on me. No one's in command right now, not really. They're just hoping I make a call they can live with.

"Nothing's moved in hours," I say, more confidently than I feel. "They'd have come by now. If there was anything real, they'd have attacked already. Whatever we saw... it's gone."

That last part is a lie. I don't believe it. But I need **them** to.

Tommy cracks the hatch an inch. Cold air blasts in, sharp enough to make us all flinch. It smells like frost, wet pine, and metal. But nothing else.

I lean toward the opening and inhale deeply. It helps. Slightly.

Fitz crawls up beside me, blinking at the pale daylight. "Jesus," he mutters. "It's morning already?"

I nod. "We made it through."

He doesn't look convinced.

I look through the vision blocks and scan the perimeter, too scared to pop my own hatch. Nothing. Just frost-touched earth, twisted roots, skeletal trees. Our tracks still lead in from the way we came, now mostly filled with mud and slush. There's no movement. No sound.

No red eyes.

Still, the forest doesn't feel **right**. It's that same dead quiet we've stumbled into before and by now, it should feel routine, but it never does. Not just the lack of birds or squirrels, but the kind of stillness that feels like the whole forest got emptied out, either scared off or eaten. The kind of quiet that doesn't just **sit**—it waits.

My breath fogs in the air, and I watch it dissipate.

Behind me, Harris calls, "We gonna try to move?"

"Move where?" Thompson answers, coughing again. "We're out of fuel, remember?"

"We could hoof it," Reynolds offers weakly.

"To **what**? No grid, no radio, no infantry." Harris snorts. "Yeah, good luck finding your way out of a cursed forest."

I cut them off. "We're not doing anything until we all get our heads clear. We're not thinking straight. We're all,,," I pause. I want to say **sick**, but it feels wrong. "...tired. We open the hatches. Cool down. We eat, drink. We take ten. Then we talk."

No one argues.

We open the hatches. Slowly. Warily. One by one, the lids creak open, letting in cold air and filtered gray light, breaking the seal on what may have become our tomb. The forest breathes in and out, slow and steady. Can we even deny it any more? It's watching us through the mi st.

Fitz climbs out and perches near the .50. Tommy leans against the open assistant driver's hatch, sipping from a dented canteen. Harris just rubs at his eyes, like the fog's gotten into his skull.

Fitz doesn't move much, but at least he's sitting upright, attempting to pull open a ration box with trembling fingers.

For a second, it feels like the worst might be behind us.

Then we hear it.

Voices. Faint and distant, dragged in on the mist.

I hold up a hand without thinking—an instinct, not a command—and we all go still, straining to hear.

The voices are hushed. Low. Tense. Male. A few of them, at least three. Maybe more. Talking in short bursts. Too far to make out words, but close enough that they sound like they're right on the edge of the treeline. Just beyond the visibility line.

Rich ducks down without a word, pulling his hatch closed. Tommy follows, slamming his shut so hard it makes me flinch. Fitz practically dives into the vehicle then pulls his hatch shut immediately.

I scramble back inside and pull mine closed, a hollow metallic **thunk** sealing us in again. The inside of the tank feels darker than before, like the light got shut out along with the air.

"Did you hear that?" Fitz whispers, voice cracking.

"Everyone heard it," I mutter, checking the periscope.

Shapes move out there. Vague. Shadowy. Tall, but not towering. Some upright. Some hunched. They flicker in and out of the fog, phantoms that are there one moment, and gone the next.

"I think it's Krauts," Rich whispers, eyes wide. "Could be a scout team."

"No way," Thompson says, but it's not convincing. "No German patrol's gonna be this far up, not without armor support."

"You think they need it?" Reynolds hisses. "They've got the forest on their side!"

"**Shut up**," I snap.

The tank falls silent again, save for our breathing. I try to focus through the periscope, wiping condensation off the lens with my sleeve. The shapes are still there. Moving slowly. Cautiously. A sweep pattern. There's enough to be slightly more than a platoon.

"Could be Americans," Harris says quietly, but I can hear the doubt in his voice.

"Then why the hell are they coming *at* us?" Thompson says.

"Maybe they're scared," Fitz answers. "Same as us."

The voices fade in and out, drifting closer, then further. A hiss of consonants, a guttural edge. I squint, trying to make sense of the tone. The cadence feels... off. Almost like it's being **mimicked**.

"It doesn't sound like English," I say finally. "Could be German."

"Shit," Rich breathes.

I take a long breath and force my voice steady. "Check the MGs. Fitz—get an HE round in the breech. Quietly."

Fitz doesn't question it. He just moves. Calm. Focused. A man returning to familiar territory.

I hear the muffled **clack-clack** as he works the loader's controls. The shell slides into the chamber with its normal ease. Harris pulls the box feed for the co-ax and checks the feed tray. Tommy, shaking off his exhaustion, double-checks the bow gun.

We're back in the battle rhythm now. Not panicking. Just moving like a crew's supposed to move. Like we're about to punch our way through the enemy lines again. And for a moment—just a second—it feels like w e **might** be okay.

But I can't shake it. That sound. The way the voices ebb and twist. The shapes that don't walk quite right. Like they're trying too hard to **be** something else.

"Eyes up," I murmur. "No one opens fire unless I say so."

The fog presses in against the periscopes, curling like smoke over the glass.

I hear Fitz chamber the HE round with a dull **click**.

"We got thirty seconds before they're on top of us," he says.

"No ID yet," I reply. "Hold."

I grip the turret ring, sweat slicking my palms despite the cold. The longer I stare, the more wrong it feels. The forest isn't just quiet—it's *waiting*. Like it knows something we don't. Like it's playing us.

"Should we... say something?" Rich whispers. "Call out, I mean. In English. Let them know we're here?"

"Not until we know what we're dealing with."

"What if they're friendly?"

I hesitate. Because if they **are** friendly, then they're being real goddamn stupid about approaching an idle Sherman with guns hot. No signals. No shouts. Just creeping closer with fog cover like ghosts in boots.

"We wait," I say. "Another few seconds. If they get close enough to see us and don't call out... we assume they're not friendly."

Fitz doesn't say anything, but I can feel his eyes on me. Wide. Scared. Trusting.

I can't let him down.

But God help me—I don't know if we're about to be attacked or if we're aiming at our own boys.

I pull open the side satchel next to my seat and fish out three grenades, handing them down to Rich without a word. He takes them like they're hot, like just touching them might set something off. Then I dig around until I find the spare 1911 mags and pass those too.

"Just in case it gets personal," I mutter.

Rich nods, jaw tight. He doesn't like it—but he understands.

The fog outside thickens, clinging to the periscopes like breath on glass. But I can still see the shapes. They're coming closer now. More defined. More... human.

But still not **right**.

Then a voice cuts through the fog.

Loud. Sharp. **Challenging**.

We all flinch.

It echoes out over the woods, bouncing strangely in the mist, warping around the metal skin of the Sherman. The words are muffled—garbled. Like a throat full of gravel, shouting through cotton.

"**What the hell did he just say**?" Harris snaps, eyes jumping to me.

I don't answer. I can't. Because I don't know.

It was English. I **think**.

But not a greeting. Not a warning shot. Something demanding. Something we were supposed to answer.

Another voice joins the first—also shouting. Also unintelligible. Harsher this time. Angry.

And then—

"I **see** it!" Tommy hisses. "On his collar. **SS marks. Skull and crossbones.** Clear as day!"

"Are you **sure**?" I ask, turning from the periscope.

His face is pale. Bloodless. Eyes wide and shining in the half-light. "Yes. Yes, Sergeant. Goddamn SS. Right there. I saw it."

"You **think** you saw it," Harris growls.

"I know what I saw!"

"Bullshit," Harris fires back. "You're seeing ghosts!"

"They're not ghosts!" Tommy barks. "They're real, and they're right fucking there!"

I cut in, voice low but sharp. "Tommy. Look at me."

He doesn't move at first, but then he glances away from the periscope, eyes wide and wet with fear.

"You're telling me you saw SS runes and a skull and crossbones. That's what you saw?"

"Yes, Sergeant. Clear as goddamn day."

I lean closer, my voice dropping even more. "You better be a hundred percent. Because if that's SS out there, that's no joke. They don't take prisoners. They don't play games. They'll carve us up slow just to hear us scream."

Tommy swallows hard.

"We're not just talking about a firefight. We're talking about a fight to the death. You *sure* that's what you saw?"

He hesitates for half a second—but in this moment, it feels like a full breath between life and death.

"I'm sure."

Harris shows a rage that I've never seen from him, "Fucking *bullshit*—"

"Enough!" I shout, snapping my head toward Harris before the next argument can spark. "This ends now."

The turret goes silent again. Just the low hum of tension and the distant crunch of boots in snow-draped mud. The shapes are spreading out now. Forming a loose semicircle around the tank. At least two dozen of them. Maybe more. I can't tell.

They haven't fired.

But they also haven't backed off.

My brain claws through every possibility. American platoon? Then where's the recognition signal? Why whisper like ghosts and yell like devils? Why not identify themselves clearly? If it *is* the enemy, why haven't they opened fire? Why creep toward a sitting tank with so much caution?

Unless they **know** we're watching.

Unless they're waiting to see if we blink first.

I look at each of my men. My **crew**. Fitz has the next HE round ready. Harris is by the controls, one hand on the firing mechanism, the other clenched into a fist. Tommy has the bow gun zeroed in on the movement. Rich's got his .45 drawn and his eyes locked onto the periscope, like he can shoot through it if he stares hard enough.

And I think about what happens if I guess wrong.

If I **don't** act.

If I let them get too close.

If they pull Panzerfausts, or satchel charges, or something worse.

If they breach the tank.

If they **kill** my boys. My men.

I lean in toward the mic and speak low. Steady.

"If they were friendly, they'd have identified themselves by now."

No one disagrees.

Not out loud.

"Tommy," I say. "Keep the .30 trained. Harris—if they cross the ditch line, you put one into the dirt in front of them. Not at them. ***Near*** them. A warning."

He gives a small nod.

"If they ignore that... we go hot."

"Jesus," Rich whispers. "We're really doing this."

"I'll do everything I can to protect this crew," I say. "No matter what. That's my job. That's ***always*** been my job."

Another voice cuts through the fog—closer now.

Still shouting. Still expecting something from us.

Still no signal. Still no ID.

I grit my teeth.

"Death before dismount."

The crew responds without hesitation.

"Death before dismount," Harris echoes.

"Death before dismount," Rich and Tommy repeat, one after the other.

Even Fitz, barely above a whisper: "Death before dismount."

The words don't make us brave. They don't make us safe.

But they make us ***ready***.

And in this place, that's all we have left.

The shapes keep coming.

"They're still coming," Rich says. "They're gonna be right on us in seconds."

I make my choice.

"Tommy," I say. "You're up. Remember the challenge? Do it by the book. If they're friendly, they'll answer."

Tommy hesitates only a moment before moving. He pulls the hatch lever. It screeches, reluctant and rusty from the night. He shoves it open with one arm, the other gripping a 1911. A grenade dangles from his left hand by the pin ring. He lifts himself halfway out, fog curling around him like smoke from a fire.

"Thund—!"

The crack of the rifle cuts through the forest like a whip.

Tommy jerks.

His body sags, folding in half as though his strings were cut. The pistol clatters from his hand. The grenade hits the floor of the tank with a hollow thud. Blood sprays across the front seat and down onto Rich's boots. Tommy tumbles backward into the assistant driver's seat, mouth open, one eye half-lidded. He's dead before he hits the st eel.

For one frozen moment, the tank is dead silent.

Then I erupt.

"They all die today," I snarl, voice pure acid. ***They all fucking die today.***"

"On 'em!" Harris screams.

The tank explodes to life.

Rich lunges over Tommy's body and rips open the bow MG, cranking the charging handle like a madman. I slam a gloved fist against the ready rack. "Send HE, now!" I roar.

"On the way!" Harris' foot slams into the switch on the floor shooting the main gun.

The whole Sherman jerks as the main gun hammers backward. A blast of smoke and dust kicks out from the barrel, and I barely register the round screaming into the trees before the loader is already slamming the next one home.

Harris roars over the gunner's controls, sweeping left and right with the .30 cal, ripping into the approaching shadows. The figures jerk, stumble, vanish behind trees—but we don't stop. No one stops. There's no second-guessing, no hesitation.

It's a slaughter.

I'm screaming orders, barely audible over the barrage. "Keep her singing!"

More shapes flicker in the fog, some dropping to the ground, others diving for cover, but the ones closest—closest to Tommy—are hit first. Bodies drop. The fog swallows them, hides them from view, but we keep shooting.

I don't care who they are anymore.

They shot my soldier.

They didn't say the right words. Didn't try hard enough to be understood. Didn't do anything except keep coming, shouting in the morning light, and now Tommy is gone.

Rage drives every action. It drowns the fear, silences the doubt, overrides every whisper of reason in my brain. There's no room for anything else.

Just death.

And fire.

And vengeance.

There's an undeniable grenade explosion at the front of the tank. It's close enough that we feel the blast inside but are still completely unharmed. It's going to take more than one grenade to take us out.

The .30 cal is now in Rich's hands and barking to life, the staccato rhythm of it deafening in the close steel confines of the Sherman. The barrel starts to glow red within seconds, casing after casing bouncing off the floor and his boots. He doesn't stop. Doesn't even blink. He leans into it, eyes wild, teeth clenched, face twisted in a snarl as he cuts through the shapes outside.

I swing the turret with a shove of the commander's handle, lining up on a group of them just breaking through the fog. "Harris—on!" I shout.

"Already there!" he snaps, and the co-ax machine gun joins the chorus, twin streams of firepower chewing into the mist. The tracers rip through the haze like a stitched red scream, lighting up broken silhouettes, bodies folding like paper in the woods. Screams echo, but they're distant—faint and scattered, torn away by gunfire and fear.

"Loader—HE!" I bark.

"Up!" Fitz shouts, shoving the first high-explosive round into the breach.

"Fire!"

The whole tank rocks as Harris stomps the trigger, the cannon roaring like thunder. Dirt and snow erupt from where the shell lands, throwing a group of shadows skyward in pieces. The smoke from the explosion washes over us, glowing faint orange in the rising dawn.

"HE!" I shout again, already rotating.

Fitz slams another shell in with trembling hands. "Up!"

"Fire!"

Another explosion, closer this time. The fog shudders with the impact, and bodies hit the ground with sickening thuds.

"Another!" I bark.

Fitz is already loading—faster now, fingers bleeding from catching on the lip of the shell box, knuckles raw from the edges. He grunts, winces, but keeps going. The tank rocks again with the violence of the main gun.

"Smoke!" Harris calls. "Obscure the right flank!"

"Loader, smoke—now!" I snap.

"Up!"

"Fire!"

The round thumps from the barrel, landing with a hiss and a billow of thick white smoke that eats the edge of the trees. For a moment, it blinds us too, but we don't stop. Can't stop.

"Keep tearing them apart," I snarl. "I want the whole goddamn forest burning."

Rich doesn't say a word. He expertly reloads then just keeps firing. His barrel is red-hot now, smoking from the heat. The metal is nearly glowing. He doesn't let up. He howls between bursts—a raw, unhinged sound. I don't think he even hears himself.

Harris calls out targets between co-ax bursts. "Left flank! treeline! Moving!"

I shift the turret, just enough. "Loader—HE!"

"Up!"

"Fire!"

The explosion sends limbs and debris skyward. A helmet cartwheels end over end, smoking. It lands near the tank and rolls until it stops at the hull. Empty.

There's no hesitation anymore. No doubt. The fury takes over—pure, boiling rage. Tommy's blood is still hot on the seat. Still wet on Rich's uniform. We kill. That's all that matters now.

"They all die today," I growl. "Every last one. Light them up!"

Harris's co-ax seizes up due to overheating requiring Harris to clear the jam.

"Loader—HE!" my voice is becoming horace from the shouting. The fighting. The smoke.

"Up!"

"Fire!"

The shell lands hard, dust and fire washing over the rocks. Something rolls out from behind them. It doesn't move.

Grenades explode outside, shaking the hull. One slams against the rear deck and goes off with a violent thud that rattles every bolt in the turret.

"They're trying to get close!" Rich shouts. "Bastards are trying to breach us!"

"They won't!" I snap. "Kill them before they get the chance!"

The co-ax goes quiet—barrel smoking, done for now. Harris doesn't stop. He yanks the hatch open, tosses a grenade of his own outside. We hear it hit the dirt, roll once.

Boom.

Another scream. Something gurgling. Something crawling.

"More right!" Rich barks. "I see more!"

His bow gun erupts again, chewing a line through the smoke. The smell of burned metal, gunpowder, and blood fills the tank. The air is thick, humid from the heat and sweat, almost hard to breathe. Fitz coughs—he's not stopping either. Just loading, loading, loading.

We are gods in a steel beast, and we are wrath.

"Bring up another HE!" I yell.

Fitz does. "Up!"

"Fire!"

The shell lands short but hits a tree—splinters rain through the air, sharp and deadly. I see a figure stumble through the blast, missing most of his arm.

Rich mows him down with a roar. "You fuckers think you can take us?" he screams. "Try it! Come on!"

The fog is thinner now—burned away by muzzle flashes and smoke grenades—but the shapes still twitch out there. Some trying to flee. Some crawling. Some still coming, unbelievably. Suicidally.

"Let's end it!" I snarl. "One more—straight center!"

Fitz throws in the last HE. "Up!"

I aim between two shattered trees, where a few remaining silhouettes duck and move.

"Fire!"

The shot tears through them like a hammer of God. Dirt rains down on the tank roof, ash and blood mixed in it.

Then... silence.

For the first time in what feels like hours, the Sherman is quiet.

No gunfire. No shouting. No shell casings clattering across the floor. Just the low groan of cooling metal and the faint hiss of the smoke launcher still venting something chemical into the air.

My ears ring. A high, needling whine that makes it hard to think. Makes it feel like everything around me is underwater. I glance at Harris. He's still gripping the co-ax's handles, knuckles bleeding from smacking them against everything in the turret during the fight. Rich hasn't moved from the bow gun, his cheek resting on the receiver like he's passed out there. Fitz leans against the loader's seat, breathing hard, forearms resting on his knees, chest rising and falling with sharp, staccato jerks.

We don't speak.

There's nothing to say.

Outside, the fog seems to dissipate.

It doesn't swirl like before. Doesn't twist in those unnatural ways. It hangs still—like the forest is holding its breath. Like it saw what we just did and doesn't dare move. As if it fears us now.

I slowly sit back in my seat, muscles sore and tight, the heat from the turret making it feel like we've been baking alive. Sweat beads on my brow and stings my eyes. I blink it away and look toward the assistant driver's seat.

Tommy's still there.

Head bowed. Blood soaking through the collar of his jacket, seeping into the seat cushion beneath him. His face is calm now, like he fell asleep mid-thought. There's a pink mist dried along the ceiling above him, and flecks of bone on the rim of the vision port. But all I can focus on is his expression.

He looks peaceful.

"Tommy..." Fitz murmurs, voice hoarse.

We all turn toward him.

He doesn't finish the thought. Just lowers his head again, pressing his palms against his eyes, blocking out the world.

I look back at Tommy. There's a lump in my throat I can't swallow. Something sharp, stuck there. This kid had a quiet voice and a quicker smile than he let on. He used to hum to himself while refueling the tank. Always made the worst instant coffee I've ever tasted. And now he's gone. Just like that. Shot before he even had the chance to speak.

I don't know how long we sit like that. Minutes? Hours? The seconds stretch thin.

The fog begins to shift.

It lifts slowly, as if peeling back a veil. Rays of sunlight stab down through the trees, catching on the steam still rising from the scorched earth outside. The shadows pull away, no longer pressing in like they did before. They retreat behind the trees, higher up the hills, as if the forest itself is recoiling.

I push open the commander's hatch.

The cold air hits my face hard, sharp and clean. I climb up, blinking into the light, the sudden brightness jarring after so long inside the steel box. My boots clunk against the turret as I stand fully upright. The others follow. One by one, hatches open, heads emerge.

No one says anything.

The forest is still. Not even birdsong. Just the soft hiss of smoke and the distant creak of broken branches settling.

We climb down.

The dirt is churned into mud from the shockwaves. Bootprints everywhere. Theirs. The dead are scattered across the clearing like broken toys—limbs at impossible angles, faces frozen mid-scream, uniforms torn and burned. I see one tangled in the roots of a tree, his leg missing, helmet askew.

Another lies facedown in the mud, half of his torso gone.

A few still smolder.

Fitz turns and vomits behind a tree. Harris walks in silence, one hand resting lightly on his sidearm. Rich is staring at the bodies like he's waiting for one to move, for one to twitch and prove this isn't real.

But it is.

I move toward Tommy's side of the tank, to where he fell. There's a dark stain that trails down the hull from the assistant driver's hatch, thick and congealed. His blood. I crouch down and reach out, touch it with two fingers.

Still warm.

"He didn't deserve this," Fitz whispers behind me.

"No," I say. "He didn't."

"He was just... trying to do the right thing."

I nod. What else is there to say? He followed orders. He showed courage. He died before he could finish a single word. That's what this place does. It doesn't just kill you—it swallows you before you even know you're in its mouth.

"Do we say something?" Rich asks. His voice is quiet. Barely above the wind.

I look around. There's no chaplain here. No graves. No ceremony. Just trees and fog and the endless hush of the forest pressing down on us.

I take a breath.

"We'll remember him. That's what we do. When we get out of here, we make damn sure the world knows what he did. That he stood tall in the end. That he wasn't afraid."

Fitz nods slowly.

Harris mutters, "He had balls. More than most."

We stand there for another long moment.

Then I turn away from the tank and walk forward.

The smoke is thinner now. The whole battlefield sprawls out ahead of us—if you can even call it that. It's a massacre. Craters from our HE rounds, tree trunks sheared in half, debris everywhere. Rifles, helmets, packs. Bodies.

But it's when I step over one of them that something strange crawls up my spine.

I crouch down.

The uniform is torn to hell. Burned, stained, twisted. But I don't see the SS insignia Tommy swore he saw. I don't even see a German uniform. No gray wool. No skull-and-bones. Nothing like that.

I roll the body gently, careful not to look at the ruined face.

Dog tags clink together at the man's neck.

And then I freeze.

I don't breathe.

Behind me, Harris asks, "What is it?"

I don't answer.

Not yet.

Because as I rise and look around—really look—I start to see the details I missed before. The faded patches. The combat boots. The gear pouches. The helmets. The webbing. The faces.

They're not German.

They're not SS.

I open my mouth, but the words don't come.

Because that's when we realize— They were Americans.

[CHAPTER FIFTEEN: THE WAR THAT'S REAL]

"And so rides back to drink again"

The Abrams hums like a dying animal. The engine is running because frankly, we're all cold and the engine is the best heat generator we have.

Power flickers through the systems in sick pulses—lights dimming, the turret groaning as if trying to move underwater. Eventually the engine cuts off... Again. I'm not even surprised anymore when the engine decides to give up. We've been running on fumes for too long. Fumes, fear, and the stubborn kind of hope that turns to madness when you hold onto it too tight.

The green glow from the instrument panel bathes us in ghost-light. It makes the grime on our faces look like blood. Makes the tank feel like a tomb.

We're out of MREs. Out of water. Out of ideas.

Fitz is in the loader's seat, knees drawn to his chest, helmet off, hair sweat-matted and sticking up in all directions. He's not even pretending to rest anymore—just staring into the floor waiting for the cold metal to open up and tell him a way out.

"They're whispering again," he mutters.

I don't look at him. "No one's whispering."

"Yes they are." His voice is small. "Same voices as before. Same rhythm. Like… like a sermon. I can't make out the words but they're there. Under the engine. Under the tank."

"There is no engine," Turner says, quiet, steady. "Power's unreliable. Systems barely even run."

That gets a flicker of eye contact between the three of us. Fitz looks like he's about to start crying. Turner doesn't blink. And Vic… Vic's on his knees in the driver's hatch, hands trembling as he checks the cable lines again, even though he's checked them five times already.

"I think the battery's done," he says, but it doesn't sound like a diagnosis. It sounds like a confession.

I slide down into the commander's seat. The cushions are damp with condensation. I feel it soaking through my pants. Everything in here is slick, cold, and close.

"You can't hear them?" Fitz asks me again. "You really can't?"

I shake my head. "Seems like it's only you."

He doesn't seem reassured. "I think they want us to follow."

"To what?"

"I don't know," he whispers. "But it's important. They said it's important."

I don't answer. I rub at the bridge of my nose instead, trying to push back the ache forming behind my eyes. My stomach is twisting in on itself. I haven't eaten in nearly two days. Drank the last of my water yesterday morning. If I'm hallucinating, it'll be hard to tell.

Outside, the forest is dead quiet. No wind. No birds. Not even the mechanical creak of trees swaying. Just stillness and the thick, heavy presence of being watched.

We're not built for this. Tanks are supposed to move, to punch, to crush and dominate. We're not supposed to wait. Not like this. Not in a goddamn coffin of steel, starving and sick, while the forest plays games with our minds.

Turner finally moves. He shifts his weight forward and sets his rifle across his knees. Still doesn't look at me.

"You should tell us what we're doing," he says.

"What do you think we're doing?"

"Waiting to die."

The words hit harder than I expect. Fitz flinches. Vic stops fumbling with the cables. The silence that follows isn't awkward—it's surrender.

"I'm not planning on dying in this goddamn forest," I say.

Turner shrugs. "Planning don't mean shit in a place like this."

I press the heel of my hand against the side panel, feeling the shudder of the hull. "We wait for the sun to rise. Then we figure out our bearings, retrace to the last checkpoint, maybe even get the radio working."

"You tried the radio already," Vic says without turning around.

"Yeah, didn't say I had a good plan. Just the only one we've got."

Fitz shivers. "It's not gonna let us leave."

"What?"

"The forest," he whispers. "It knows we're here now. It's... watching."

"I swear to God," Turner growls, standing up. "If you don't stop talking about the goddamn forest like it's alive—"

"Then what's been happening to us?" Fitz snaps back. "Huh? You think all of this is just coincidence? That we just **happened** to get stuck here, that the WWII tank we found just **happens** to have a crew with our same damn structure and names? That their damn loader just **happens** to be named Fitz too? We saw our own names carved into that church altar. We saw the photos in that tank. This is more than bad luck."

Turner squares off with him, knuckles whitening around the rifle grip. "Or maybe you've just gone soft in the head."

"Enough," I bark. It comes out harsher than I mean it to, but I don't take it back. "Both of you sit the hell down."

Neither of them move at first. Then Turner slumps back into his seat. Fitz turns away, shoulders tight, jaw clenched.

Vic finally speaks. "I don't think we're making it out."

That kills the room.

He says it so plainly. No anger. No drama. Just like he's been thinking about it for a while and finally couldn't keep it in.

I look at him, this soft-spoken kid from Boise who's always been solid, steady, the one we didn't have to worry about. And now even **he** sounds hollow.

"What makes you say that?" I ask.

He doesn't look back. "Because we were never supposed to be here in the first place. And because nothing we do makes a difference. We fix the tank—it breaks again. We move—it brings us right back. The world out there isn't moving forward. It's folding in."

"You don't know that."

"Don't I?" he says. "Feels like we've been in this same loop for days. Same trees. Same air. Same goddamn silence."

Fitz wipes his face with a trembling hand. "Maybe we died already."

"Stop," I say.

"No, really," he goes on. "Maybe we didn't make it out of that ditch. Maybe the tank burned. Maybe this is what comes after."

"No," I repeat, louder now. "We're not dead. We're not cursed. We're not ghosts. We're a U.S. tank crew and we're going to get the hell out of here."

They look at me like I've grown a second head.

But I **need** to say it. I need to believe it. Because if I don't, they won't. And if **they** don't, we're finished.

The power flickers again. Lights dim. A slow, warning groan ripples through the turret as the battery strains under the weight of being alive.

We sit in silence for a long while.

Breathing. Watching. Listening.

And that's when I hear it—low and distant. Not a whisper. Not voices.

Something heavier.

A sound echoing through the trees like thunder on treads. Like a great, grinding engine. Not our tank.

Something bigger.

Something coming.

The noise hasn't stopped.

It fades and returns, ebbing and flowing—low, distant, mechanical. Metal grinding, something massive turning over in the deep. It echoes through the trees, too faint to pin down, but strong enough to raise every hair on my arms.

Vic hits the driver's display with force out of pure frustration. "You hear that? Tell me that's not an engine."

Turner's head jerks left, then right, like he's trying to track a ghost. "No... no, it's just the hills messing with us. Echoes. Acoustic illusions." His voice doesn't sound convincing.

Fitz swallows hard, his grin twitching at the corners. "Or maybe it's a Tiger... y'know... crawling back out of the grave."

No one laughs.

I realize I'm holding my breath. My head feels thick, like I'm underwater, and the sound just keeps ebbing and surging, never close enough to see, never far enough to ignore.

"I'm too damn tired to argue," I say, my voice lower than I mean it to be. "We move on foot."

They look at me like I've slapped them.

"We're not abandoning the tank," Turner says, half-rising.

"We're not," I reply. "But we can't sit in it waiting for the power to die and for whatever that is to find us. We're not helping anyone if we rot in there. I need to know what's out there. I need to know if we've got a chance. We get out of this hellscape, get our heads screwed back on, and then we come back for our chariot."

Turner hesitates. Vic says nothing. Fitz just nods like he was waiting for this moment all along.

We pack light. Rifles, radios that probably won't work, flashlights, and what little gear we still trust. I mark what I think is the tank's position with a red X on our map and stick it in my bag.

Feels wrong to leave it, but it also feels like the first right thing we've done in days.

We head into the woods in a staggered line.

The fog clings to the trees like old webbing. It moves in slow, lazy coils, brushing around our boots and rifles. It's not dense enough to hide in—but it's enough to feel like something could be hiding **us**.

No birds. No wind. Just boots on moss and the creak of gear.

I lead, rifle raised, every breath shallow. Turner's at the rear, his gaze flicking side to side. Vic walks like his bones hurt. Fitz keeps looking over his shoulder at something the rest of us can't see.

The deeper we go, the stranger the woods feel. Trees twist slightly inward, their crooked fingers inching ever closer to grasping our tank. The ground is soft, but not natural—torn up and filled in; a broad, fresh grave for us to pass over.

Then we hear it again.

The sound.

Not ahead. Not behind.

Everywhere.

Rumbling. Grating. An engine, not quite real. It doesn't sound like our tank. Doesn't sound **modern** at all.

I stop in my tracks, raising a fist. The crew halts behind me.

We listen.

It's gone again.

Fitz leans in close. "Did you hear it that time? Closer. It was **closer**."

Turner exhales sharply. "Could be a tank from the competition. Maybe they're looking for us."

"No one would send a tank this deep without radio," Vic mutters.

"I don't think it's real," Fitz says. "I think it's an echo."

Turner scoffs, but doesn't argue.

I motion for us to keep moving.

It takes another twenty minutes before we find it.

There's a clearing near the edge of a thin treeline—grass half-dead, sun barely cutting through the fog. The air here smells different. Older. Stale like the inside of a sealed attic.

In the center of the clearing is a shallow crater.

Not recent. Erosion has dulled most of the sharp edges. Moss creeps along the rim. Whatever made it—shell, mine, bomb—it happened a lifetime ago.

At the bottom, half-buried in dried leaves, is a helmet.

I slide down into the crater before anyone can stop me.

The helmet is a World War II issue. Cracked open along the crown. Rusted nearly through. But it's what's *carved* inside that stops my heart.

JAMES CASEY

I crouch, running gloved fingers along the letters. They're uneven, scratched in with a knife or nail. It's not decoration. It's identity.

Turner slides in beside me, keeping his distance. "You look like you've seen a ghost."

"Yeah," I say. "That was the commander. The one in the Sherman."

The one in the photos. The one whose story we've been chasing without even knowing.

Vic's voice comes from above us. "You see that? Along the rim."

I look where he's pointing and only then notice them—bones, pale and splintered, littering the edges of the crater. Shattered femurs, ribs half-buried in the dirt, some are fragments too small to name. There's no sign of a firefight—no casings, no scorch marks, no impact craters. Just... bones. Like something dumped them here.

"They're not all from one body," Vic says, still standing back. "Too many."

I crouch, my stomach tightening. "Could've been a mine," I offer.

Fitz shakes his head. "A mine would have been deeper. Plus, if they had been practicing proper spacing, it wouldn't have killed them all. Maybe a bomb?"

I glance around at the untouched trees. "Bomb would've leveled half this clearing."

We all fall quiet. The air feels heavier.

"Doesn't matter **what** killed them," I say finally, the words tasting like metal. "What matters is **who** did."

Fitz's eyes meet mine, and we both know the answer before he says it. "It's whatever's been hunting us."

I see them then—four dog tags laid out by a rock, someone meant to remember them but never got the chance. I pick each one up slowly. The names are familiar.

Vince Harris
Richard Thompson
Anthony Fitzsimmons
James Casey

Turner kneels, mouth drawn tight. "Jesus. This is them."

Fitz steps back, eyes fixed on the crater like it might swallow him too. His voice is quiet, almost unsure. "Well... I guess that answers the question we've been dancing around." He swallows, glancing at the tags. "They didn't make it out. Just like we thought..."

No one responds.

There's a photo, too—tucked in a rusted ammo tin that somehow stayed dry. I pull it out carefully, wiping the dirt from the surface.

It's a little girl, maybe five or six, in a swing. Smiling. Behind her is a house with a porch and two chairs. There's a woman's handwriting on the back. I don't have any children. Never had the opportunity but somehow I feel as if this little girl is **mine**.

"For when you come home. – Marlene"

I don't say anything.

But I feel the picture burn against my palm like it knows exactly how long it waited to be found.

We sit in the crater for a long time.

No one talks.

There's something about the bones—their stillness. The finality of them. We've seen bodies before. But this feels different.

This is an ending.

Vic finally speaks. "They died right here. All of them. I don't know how, or why, but... this was it."

Turner crouches near the helmet. "I think they were trying to get away from something. Or maybe they thought this was a safe spot."

"Didn't work, obviously," Fitz's voice lacks just enough emotion to reflect how we are all feeling about this entire situation.

I run a hand down my face. I'm too tired to think clearly. The tank's behind us. That sound—whatever it is—is still moving. And this place... this place **wants** to be remembered. Wants to be **seen**.

"Grab what's useful," I tell them. "Dog tags. Any gear. We'll come back for the rest if we can and give them a proper burial."

Fitz pockets the photo, almost reverently. Turner gathers the tags. Vic sets the helmet on the edge of the crater like a marker, brushing dirt off its dome.

And for a moment, none of us move.

I feel the weight of history hanging in the fog. The memory of men who fought and bled and *failed* to make it home. The echo of something older than all of us, buried deep in the roots of this cursed place.

Fitz stands near the edge of the crater, rifle cradled against his chest, eyes locked on the old helmet as if it might move on its own. He hasn't said a word in a while. Not since we found the photo. Not since we found the dog tags laid out like a funeral offering.

He speaks up finally, his voice small, almost careful.

"Do you think he made it?"

I don't look up.

"Who?" I ask, though I know exactly who he means.

"*You*... I mean *us*... I mean the crew of the Sherman."

I stay quiet.

I don't want to say it.

Turner answers instead, his tone flat. "He didn't make it out. None of them did." He holds up the dog tags and gives them a little jingle.

Fitz doesn't respond right away. Just keeps staring. I can't tell if he's disappointed or just finally letting the truth settle in.

I kneel again, picking up the helmet one last time. The inside is crusted with rust and time. It's fragile now—like if I squeezed too hard, it would collapse in my hands. I turn it over once, twice, then carefully place it back where we found it.

"Now we know how the story ended," I say.

Vic's crouched a few feet away, arms on his knees, face pale beneath the grime and stubble. He's been the quietest of all of us since we left the tank. Watching everything. Taking it in like he's expecting something else to drop out of the fog.

He mutters something under his breath. I don't catch it.

"What?" I ask.

He looks up at me, the tremble in his jaw barely hidden. "I said, **that's gonna be us**."

Nobody moves.

"Vic—" I start.

But he cuts me off. Louder this time.

"We're not getting out of here."

The words hang in the air. Not shouted. Not panicked. Just **said**. The words were waiting for someone to speak them into existence.

Turner looks away, jaw clenched.

Fitz swallows and says, "Come on, don't say that."

But he doesn't sound convinced either.

I shift my weight, trying to stand taller even though every part of me aches. "We don't know that."

"We don't **not** know it either," Vic says. "Food's gone. Water's gone. Power's shot. Radios are dead. No one's found us. We've been stuck in this forest for—what, two days now? Three? And it's not just the fog. This place doesn't work like it should."

"No shit," Turner mutters. "But giving up isn't a plan."

"I'm not giving up," Vic says. "I'm being realistic."

"Realism gets you killed in combat, good training keeps you alive," I snap.

He opens his mouth, then shuts it. He's smart enough not to press the point, but I can see it—clear as day—in his expression.

He's already halfway there.

They all are.

Even me.

Fitz's eyes bounce between the three of us like he's waiting for a fight to break out.

I look back to the bones in the crater. Those tags. That photo.

Casey's crew probably thought they were going to make it too.

Probably told themselves it was just another mission. That they'd get out. That help was on the way.

But help never came.

And now they're bones under a tree with no one left to mourn them.

"This forest," Vic says suddenly. "It's like it **knows** what we're thinking. Like it waits for us to feel it. The moment we start to believe we're dead... it makes sure of it."

"You're not helping," I say sharply.

He shrugs. "I'm not trying to."

Turner steps forward, between us. "Jack," he says carefully and quietly. "What's the next move? We just keep walking until something shoots at us?"

"No," I say. "We head back to the tank. We think. We regroup. Reconnect power and see if it'll start again."

"And if it doesn't?"

"Then we figure something else out. Walk out if we have to."

He doesn't look satisfied. Neither does anyone else.

I exhale slowly, glancing back toward the line of trees. Fog hangs just a little higher now—almost like it's lifted its skirt to peek at us.

"None of this is in the tank platoon manual," I say.

"No shit, it would be really funny if they had a chapter called 'What to do if you find yourself being chased by demons that are probably going to kill you in a haunted forest'," Turner says again, and this time there's almost a smile behind it.

I look at Vic, then Fitz. "We're not dead. Not yet. Until then, we keep moving like we have a purpose. Like someone *is* coming to help us. And if they're not, then we'll find our own way out."

Vic's lips press into a thin line. "You don't believe that."

"I believe we're still breathing," I say. "That's all that matters."

We leave the crater behind in silence.

But something follows us.

Not footsteps.

Not movement.

Just a feeling.

Like the trees are listening now.

The deeper we go, the more I feel it—just behind my shoulder, just beyond sight. Not something watching with eyes, but with intent. The forest isn't angry.

It's ***expectant***.

The walk back is quiet.

Not just between us—but *around* us.

Even the forest seems to hush. No wind. No birds. Not even the faint rustle of branches we've grown used to. Something's watching, holding its breath.

The fog has thinned just enough to see farther than we could earlier. Trees stretch tall and thin above us, like skeletal arms, their limbs laced with a thousand threads of fading mist. I keep my eyes on the path—or what counts as one out here. There's no trail, no markers, just instinct and an unspoken understanding that we *have* to get back.

No one speaks.

But when we see the tanks, the silence breaks.

Controlled Violence sits like a monument in the clearing ahead, metal dull under the low-hanging sky. And beside her—tilted, half-eaten by vines and dirt—is the Sherman again, that decaying ghost of a machine that carried its crew into this same forest eighty years ago.

Fitz spots it first.

"There," he breathes. "We made it."

Relief flutters in my chest, small and fragile. I glance back—half-expecting something to leap from the trees behind us. But there's only mist.

We pick up the pace, boots crunching on damp earth. We're maybe fifty meters out when everything changes.

It starts as a tremble.

So faint it feels like a memory—like something you *almost* imagined. A vibration in the soles of my boots. A hum in the pit of my stomach.

Then it deepens.

Low. Deep. Wrong.

A sound that doesn't belong to any engine I've ever known.

Not thunder. Not artillery.

It's heavier.

It **moves**.

The forest groans.

A tree somewhere in the distance snaps in half like dry kindling. The crack echoes for miles.

We all stop.

Fitz presses a hand to his ear like he's trying to block it out. Vic's already looking over his shoulder. Turner shifts beside me, rifle half-raised.

"What the hell is that?" he whispers.

I don't answer. I don't know how.

It keeps going. Bark tearing. Branches breaking. A massive, deliberate shifting of weight—like a building uprooting itself and learning to walk.

It fades for a moment, almost like it's leaving.

Then it circles back.

Still far—but closer now.

Fitz mutters, "I don't want to see it again."

That does it. Officially creeped out.

"Back to the tank," I say, voice low. "Now."

We break into a sprint.

Branches claw at our gear. Vines snag at our ankles. The forest is finally fighting back to keep us here. But we don't stop.

The sound chases us—not just footsteps but **treads**. That deep, mechanical grind of something huge plowing through earth and stone. The kind of sound that belongs to one thing and one thing only.

A tank.

Someone laughs—maybe Fitz, maybe Vic—as hope breaks through the fear. "It's rescue! It's them! They're here!"

I want to believe it.

We all do.

We clear the treeline in a rush. The Abrams looms ahead, familiar and beautiful. We scramble up the hull like drowning men clawing onto a lifeboat.

Fitz nearly slips—Turner catches his arm and hauls him up.

Vic collapses beside the turret, panting, eyes scanning the trees.

Laughter bursts out again, wild and disbelieving. "They found us!" Fitz yells. "I told you we weren't alone!"

I don't smile, but my grip on my sidearm loosens just slightly.

Until I hear it.

A sound like no diesel engine I've ever known.

It roars behind the trees—louder now.

Metal groaning under ancient weight. Exhaust screaming through a throat too old to be alive.

And then—

We see it.

Just a glimpse.

A break in the fog, barely there.

But enough.

A silhouette.

Massive.

Sloped armor. Long barrel. Treads wider than a truck. Its shape is unmistakable—like a monster in a story you don't dare say aloud.

A King Tiger.

But **wrong**.

It shimmers at the edges, blackened and distorted, its form flickering like an old reel of film burning in the projector. Its markings are half-gone. Its hull is scorched in places, melted in others.

But it moves.

Alive.

And it's **charging**.

Straight at us.

Every instinct in my body screams. I draw my pistol, knowing it won't do a damn thing, but needing it in my hand anyway.

Turner stares, frozen, mouth open.

Fitz drops to his knees, repeating, "No, no, no, no-"

Vic fumbles for his rifle, eyes wide with something past fear.

I hear myself whisper.

"Oh god."

The ghost of the King Tiger barrels forward—engine howling, tracks tearing through root and soil like paper.

The forest doesn't move.

It **parts**.

It fears what follows it.

It's **coming to us**.

It doesn't move like a dream.

It moves like death.

That ghost-Tiger snarls out of the fog, its monstrous weight crushing everything in its path. I can see its bow. Its turret. Its gaping gun—black and long like a goddamned executioner's blade.

But my brain—our brains—don't catch up.

We **stare**.

It's not possible. Not now. Not here.

It's an echo. A fever dream. A vision conjured by this cursed forest.

It **has to be**.

And then—

Ratatatata.

The Tiger opens fire with the co-axial MG42 next to its main gun. The tank is as real as life—spitting ancient fury in a high, stuttering rhythm. A heartbeat of hate.

Another burst—this one from the bow-mounted MG42, lower-pitched, chewing through trees as it walks its fire across the clearing.

But it's not **aiming** at us, not at first. It's just firing. Spraying the ground, the trees, the empty air—as if trying to sweep away the ghosts.

I don't move.

None of us do.

We're still on top of the Abrams, weapons half-lowered, eyes locked on something our minds won't accept.

It's not real. It's not **real**.

The muzzle flashes cast pale stutters of light in the fog—half-revealing the beast with every flicker. Its front glacis is blasted and blackened, its tracks caked in blood-colored mud.

Turner is the first to say it out loud. Quiet. Shaking. "It's not real. It can't be."

Fitz presses his hands to his ears, rocking slightly. "It's not shooting at us. It's not- it's not even **here**."

The noise tears through the clearing. That ripping, rattling growl of old steel spitting lead. It's deafening. Insane.

But we just... stand there.

Until the bullets begin to hit.

Not us.

Not flesh.

But **steel**.

CLANG.

A round strikes the Abrams—deflected, harmless.

But real.

CLANG-CLANG.

Another skitters off the turret armor.

Then another.

A storm of ricochets—a swarm of angry hornets.

Turner flinches. Fitz screams.

Vic dives first—no hesitation—vanishing into the driver's hatch like a rat fleeing a cat.

Then Turner.

Then Fitz, scrambling, barely avoiding a fall.

I stay frozen for half a second longer.

The tank is real.

The bullets are real.

The **enemy** is real.

"Move!" I snap out of it, and throw myself into the commander's hatch.

And that's when the Tiger fires its main gun.

Boom.

The forest **rips** open.

A sound so loud it's more pressure than noise. It hits a hammer to the chest.

The shell screams overhead—too fast to see, but we **feel** it, a streak of hellfire slicing the air—

—and then an explosion behind us. Thunder and dirt. A tree snaps like a twig and crashes down with a splintering groan.

Debris rains down across the Abrams.

I slam the hatch shut, heart jackhammering in my ribs.

It's real. This is real. This is a fight. This is war.

Inside, it's chaos.

Fitz is scrambling to get the breach clear. Vic is already at his station. Turner is breathing hard, almost hyperventilating, muttering, "That wasn't real, that wasn't real, that wasn't real—"

"It's real now," I bark. "Button up the hatches! We are engaging. This is a warning order!"

The tank **responds**.

I don't mean Vic gets it going.

I mean **she** does.

Controlled Violence hums to life with zero hesitation.

No stutters.

No flickers.

Power floods through the systems. Lights stabilize. Turret control clicks back online.

As if she knows.

As if she's been waiting.

"Give me a crew report." My voice is calm and practiced. This is when training takes over, and everything after is natural.

The tank's engine revs and the breach falls open as if answering my crew report.

"Driver ready, tank in drive."

Fitz slams a round into the breech. "Sabot loaded!"

"Gunner ready, sabot indexed. Target Identified. Range 150 meters."

"Target the Tiger," I order. "Line of fire, open with main. Hose with co-ax for any bailers."

Turner steadies himself behind the sights. No more shaking.

Just quiet now.

Focused.

The tank's screens come alive. Fog dances in the lens. Then—movement. That hulking ghost form in the haze, crawling forward again, slow and deliberate.

It hasn't seen us rearm.

It doesn't know what's coming.

I settle into my command seat.

"Fire and adjust."

"On the way!"

The gun kicks.

BOOM.

It's less a sound and more a violent *event*—a seismic punch from inside our guts that shakes the tank down to the tread blocks. The entire hull lurches as the sabot round screams downrange at nearly a mile per second.

There's no time to think. No time to feel anything except the surge of smoke and steam filling the turret, choking the air like breath from a furnace. The pressure blast makes my ears ring, rattling in my skull.

Outside, the fog *explodes*.

Steam whips off the gun tube. Smoke from the propellant mixes with the damp forest air, forming a swirling wall of gray. The world beyond the gun vanishes in that instant. Visibility: zero.

"Can't confirm effect on target," Turner grits out, already switching back to co-ax, fingers moving by reflex.

"Suppress the target zone," I say. "Let it know we're still breathing."

BRRRRRRRT.

The co-ax comes alive, rattling out short bursts into the whiteout ahead of us. Spent casings clang off the loader's station like hail.

Turner adjusts angle. Fires again. Another controlled burst.

BRRT. Pause. ***BRRT***.

Then silence.

No return fire.

No movement.

We wait.

The smoke begins to settle, rolling across the field like retreating waves.

For a few seconds, we're all holding our breath.

The fog clears just enough to show shapes again—shadowed outlines of trees, burned bark, scorched earth.

And—

Nothing.

No Tiger.

No wreck.

No burning hulk.

Just a tree behind where the Tiger had stood. Its trunk is cracked. One limb glows faintly, blackened and catching slow flame—resin bubbling from the impact burst. A soft hiss as sap meets heat.

But there's no enemy.

"Where the hell is it?" Fitz asks, his voice thin, like it's squeezing through the silence.

Turner's still behind the sights, eyes narrowed. "I had it lazed. I know I did. We didn't miss."

"You didn't," I say. "It was there. I saw it. We all did."

Vic murmurs, not turning around, "Then where'd it go?"

No one answers.

I climb partway up the hatch, flipping open the commander's hatch to scan the area. My eyes sweep back and forth, stabilizers humming faintly.

Nothing.

No tracks.

No smoke.

No Tiger.

Just a clearing torn up by the blast—and the eerie quiet settling in behind it, heavier than before.

"Scan again," I say, low. "Turner, recheck the horizon."

He cycles through the views. Thermal, day sights, low-light.

Still nothing.

It didn't flee.

It didn't explode.

It didn't *move*.

It just—

Isn't.

Turner sits back from the scope and lets out a slow breath. "That thing took a sabot round to the chest. If it was real, it should be confetti right now."

Fitz is staring at the loader's panel, like the controls will offer an explanation. "We didn't miss. We couldn't have. I saw the muzzle flash. I *heard* it firing at us."

"You think it wasn't real?" Vic asks, finally turning in his seat. He looks paler than normal. Sweat glistens on his temples. "Then what the hell were the bullets?"

"We felt them," Fitz says. "The ricochets. The shell that hit behind us..."

"They were real." Turner's voice is flat. Unnerved. "The tank was real."

"But now it's not."

I stare out the hatch again, trying to make sense of it. The clearing looks like a battleground, fresh from a modern war—torn earth, fire, and that gnawing hum of ozone from the static still lingering in the air. You don't get that from hallucinations.

You don't *hallucinate recoil*.

You don't imagine *shell impact*.

And you sure as hell don't load and fire sabot on instinct unless there's a damn target.

But there's nothing there now.

Nothing but silence.

"Sergeant?" Fitz's voice is small. "What do we do?"

I close the hatch slowly.

The tank creaks as the engine cools again, the faint tick of metal settling in the quiet like a dying clock.

"We prep another round," I say. "And we wait."

Because the one thing I'm sure of, as the fog starts creeping back toward us like a living thing—

—is that it's not over.

Not even close.

Maybe we imagined it.

That thought worms its way into my head as I settle back into the commander's seat. My fingers tighten around the control handle and I feel the sweat between the gloves and the rubberized surface.

Maybe it was some kind of shared delusion. A hysteria brought on by stress, hunger, exhaustion. Maybe the isolation, the forest, the madness of everything has finally cracked us. Maybe—

"Sargent?"

It's Fitz. His voice is unsteady. Almost hollow.

I glance back and catch him staring at me. Not blinking. Not moving. Just **looking** at me like I'm something he doesn't recognize.

He's pale, mouth slightly open. His hands hang limp over his knees like he's forgotten he has fingers.

"What?" I ask, more sharply than I meant to.

He doesn't answer. Just lifts a hand and points. "Your chest."

I follow his gaze downward.

My breath stops.

There—center mass, just below my collar—three distinct impacts on my vest. The carrier's nylon was shredded, the ceramic plate spider-webbed, and it just saved my life. My chest throbbed like a mule had kicked me, but no blood. No holes

The plates caught them.

Three rounds.

Direct hits.

I lean forward, stunned. I press a hand to the damage. It **hurts**. A deep, heavy ache, like someone slammed a hammer into my chest.

"Jesus…" I whisper.

Turner turns in his seat, seeing the look on Fitz's face. "What's going on?"

Fitz answers for me. "He got hit."

"What?"

"Three shots. Right in the chest."

Turner leans over and sees the vest. He lets out a breath, low and rattled. "You didn't feel that?"

"I didn't feel **anything**." My voice is barely audible now. "I thought—I didn't even think we were—"

Real.

None of this was supposed to be real.

I sit back hard against the hatch wall, the tank suddenly feeling like a coffin. The pain blooms now—delayed, cruel. The shock wearing off. My body registering the trauma that should've taken me out.

I close my eyes, breathing slow, trying not to shake.

The Tiger was real.

It fired on us.

I was **shot**.

And if I had been standing just an inch higher—if I hadn't been inside the hatch, partially covered—those rounds would've punched clean through.

Turner speaks, quietly. "Still think it was a ghost?"

"I don't know what the hell it was," I mutter. "But it wasn't in our heads."

Vic says nothing. He's staring at the control panel, fingers unmoving.

Fitz finally leans back, rubbing his face with both hands like he's trying to wake up from a nightmare that refuses to end.

"Why did it stop?" he asks. "Why didn't it finish us?"

No one answers.

The tank creaks again.

I look down at my vest one more time, and I realize the weight in my chest has nothing to do with the impacts. It's fear. A new kind. The kind that makes you doubt every rule of reality you thought was carved in stone.

I was hit.

And I didn't even feel it.

We all saw that thing.

And now it's gone.

I sit there, the tank groaning around me, fog seeping in through the viewport edges, and think: we are **so *far* beyond** anything we were trained for.

[CHAPTER SIXTEEN: THE FOURTH OPTION]

"With friends at Fiddlers' Green."

20 December 1944

We line the bodies up in silence.

No one speaks. No one needs to. The air is thick with it—shame, grief, something heavier than all our gear combined. We move slowly, carefully, deliberately. Like the dead will wake if we do this wrong.

Forty-two of them. Maybe more in the trees, but these are the ones we can find. Their limbs are tangled like they fell mid-run. A few still have rifles clenched in white-knuckled fists. Most are already stiff, faces frozen in shock or pain or something in between. One of them is the captain we'd met earlier—still has the map tucked into his vest, soaked through with blood.

I look at his dog tags. **James T. Smith**. He refused to learn my name, assuming we'd never make it out of this alive. I guess he was right.

Rich tries to help at first. He lifts a boot, then lets it fall. He turns away, stumbles to a tree, and retches into the roots. I don't blame him.

We lay the dog tags gently on their chests. I don't know why. Maybe it's just something to do with our hands. Maybe it's penance. Fitz is pale and shaking, muttering prayers under his breath, not loud enough to make out the words. Harris doesn't say anything at all.

Tommy's at the end of the line. His eyes are closed. That's the only kindness the bullet gave him. One round. Right through the head. Just like that. He probably didn't even know he had died by the time he slumped back in his seat.

I kneel beside him. His hands are empty.

"He didn't fire," I say aloud, more to the forest than to anyone else. "He never even fired."

Harris stands a few feet away, chewing the inside of his cheek. "They saw a guy pop out of a tank with a weapon and panicked," he says, flat. "Same thing we would've done."

"No," I whisper. "Same thing we *did*."

That hangs in the air like smoke.

We don't talk about it, but we all know. The echoes of the shot still live behind our ears. The way Tommy's body folded. The way I screamed the moment it happened—too late to stop it. Too late to make it matter.

Rich wipes his mouth, turns back toward us with red-rimmed eyes. "They were Americans," he says, voice cracking. "I saw one of their patches. I refused to believe it. I heard that they had Germans pretending to be Americans."

Harris nods. "Probably had the same problem we did. Couldn't tell friend from foe. You see a tank that doesn't answer the passphrase and someone jumps out with a gun..."

"You shoot," I finish, the words like ash in my mouth.

Fitz kneels beside Tommy, placing his hand on his chest like it might start beating again. "He was a kid," he mutters. "Just a damn kid."

So were we. Every single one of us.

I look up. The forest is a still-life painting; even the birds seem to be silent in reverence for what happened. Too still. Not even the birds dare break this silence. The fog's retreated, but it left something worse behind—clarity. We see the wreckage we've made now. There's no hiding from it. No pretending.

"Do we bury them?" Fitz asks.

I shake my head. "No time. No way to do it proper."

Rich stares at the line of bodies. "Then we mark them. Leave something behind so someone knows we didn't just leave them here."

Harris grunts. "Someone. Or something." I shoot him a look, but he shrugs and says, "You think we're alone out here?"

"No," I admit. "But I'm still hoping whatever else is out here has better target identification than we do."

That gets a bitter chuckle from Rich. Fitz doesn't laugh.

We use sticks and helmets to mark the spot—crude, but clear. Harris scratches something into a mess kit lid with his knife: *American dead. Mis ID. No intent.* It's not enough, but it's all we have. We wedge it into the dirt at the head of the line like a gravestone.

When we're done, I linger a little longer beside Tommy. I want to say something, but nothing comes out. He doesn't need words. He needs time we can't give him.

"I'm sorry," I whisper anyway.

Before we move, I glance back down the line one more time. Eleven bodies. American uniforms. Our own.

"Write it in the log," I tell Harris quietly.

He raises an eyebrow. "You sure?"

"They deserve something. Even if it's just ink and paper."

He nods slowly, pulling the battered logbook from his side pouch. The metal cover's scuffed, corners bent. He flips past coordinates, ammunition counts, gunner tallies—days when this war made more sense. He kneels down beside the tank tread, balancing the book on one knee, pencil poised.

"What do you want me to put?"

I think for a long moment. Then: "Engaged unit in low-visibility conditions. Heavy contact. Close quarters. No survivors. Forest interfered with identification."

He gives me a look—flat, unreadable—but writes it down anyway. No mention of friendly fire. No mention of Tommy. Just enough truth to pass, just enough to bury it.

When he's done, he closes the book, tucking it under the corner of a helmet left by the bodies. "If someone finds them," he says, "maybe they'll know they weren't just forgotten."

Maybe.

We pack up after that, not because we're ready, but because we have to be. There's still something in this forest, something that brought us here, and I don't think it's done with us yet.

As we walk away, I feel it watching.

Something old.

Something patient.

Something that knows the weight of guilt—and feeds on it.

We walk.

We've been walking for hours, maybe longer. The forest doesn't give us light, or time, or direction. The map's useless now, and the compass spins like it's drunk. The sky—what little we see of it through the tangled canopy—is just a smear of gray, smudged like charcoal against wet paper.

Rich is silent. Still pale from earlier, but steady. He hasn't said a word since we left the bodies behind. I think he's afraid that if he opens his mouth, he'll start screaming and never stop.

Harris keeps the .45 drawn. He walks rear guard, muttering every now and then under his breath. Mostly curses. Sometimes names. Once, I hear him whisper to Tommy, and I pretend I don't.

We pass a tree with a gash along its bark, clean and sharp like it was struck by a blade. I could swear we passed it an hour ago. Or maybe I dreamed it. Or maybe it's dreaming us.

No one says it out loud, but we all feel it.

We're not getting out.

Not because we can't. But because the forest won't let us.

"We should've stayed with the tank," Rich says, voice hoarse. "At least we had cover there. Steel between us and... whatever this is."

"And what?" Harris snaps. "Wait for the Krauts to hunt us? Wait for more 'unknowns' to wander in so we can put another round through someone's kid brother?"

"That's not what I meant."

"No?" Harris stops walking, turns. "Then what *do* you mean?"

"Enough," I say, my voice low but firm. "We keep moving. Keep it together."

Rich nods, eyes down. Harris wipes at his face and turns back, jaw tight.

We walk again.

The woods grow thicker the deeper we go, like the forest is folding in on itself. Branches arch overhead in ways that don't seem natural—ready to knit closed behind us. We pass a clearing that smells like blood, even though there's nothing there. No corpses. No animals. Just the scent of rot, and something worse: the gnaw of guilt.

Harris pauses again. "I think we're walking in circles."

"We're not," I say automatically, though I'm not sure anymore. My boots are soaked through. My legs ache. My rifle's beginning to feel like it's carved from stone.

Rich points up. "That tree. The one with the broken limb. We passed it earlier. I remember it."

I stop and stare at it.

It's true. We have passed it. We *are* walking in circles.

"We're being punished," Rich says. His voice is quiet. Almost reverent.

Harris laughs bitterly. "By trees?"

"By *something*. This place. You feel it. We all do. This isn't just a forest anymore."

No one disagrees.

Hours pass. Maybe longer.

The cold starts to dig into our bones. Not the kind you shake off with movement—this is colder. Deeper. It feels personal.

We start seeing things. Just on the edge of vision. Shadows between trees. Figures just barely not there. We start hearing things. The crunch of footsteps just out of sync with ours. Once I hear a voice whisper *James*, and I whip around, weapon raised—but there's nothing.

Nothing we can *see*.

The path narrows into a gulley, the roots underfoot slick and coiled, the veins of a grotesque organism. Rich stumbles. Harris helps him up without a word.

"We should've died already," Harris mutters. "When that Tiger hit us a month ago. When we crossed that damn minefield a week ago. When that ambush happened that got Jameson killed. But we didn't. You know why?"

"Why?" I ask, already regretting it.

"Because we're not done yet. Because this goddamn forest has plans."

"Plans?" Rich echoes.

"We did something," Harris says. "We killed our own. You saw their uniforms. You saw Tommy. You think this place lets that kind of thing g o?"

He looks at me then. Like I'm supposed to answer for all of it.

Maybe I am.

But the weight in my chest says otherwise. I tighten my grip on my rifle. "We keep moving."

At some point, the fog returns. It slinks between the trees, chasing our hope away from the ground up. It clings to our boots and chokes the sound out of the air. The woods fall silent again—not the peace of quiet, but the heavy hush of something holding its breath.

I glance at Rich. His eyes are wide, darting.

"Maybe we're already dead," he says. "Maybe this is it. Hell's not fire. It's this. Guilt and trees."

"You're not dead, Private," I say. "You're still walking."

"But are *you*?" he asks.

I don't answer.

Eventually, we come to a stone outcropping we swear we haven't seen before, and yet—it looks like someone's been here. There are old bootprints. A rusted tin of rations. An empty ammo belt.

None of it is ours.

Harris crouches down beside a half-rotted stump. "This stump's burned through," he says. "Cut at an angle. That's a tank shell if I've ever seen one."

"How long ago?" I ask.

He shakes his head. "Could've been yesterday. Could've been decades. Feels like both."

I kneel beside it. Something's carved into the bark of the stump. Faint. Eroded. But I can still make it out.

CASEY.

My breath catches.

I didn't put that there.

But it's my name.

"We're not leaving, are we?" Rich asks.

I rise slowly. "We're going to try."

"Even if we're the last ones left?" he asks.

I look at him. Harris. The trees.

Something watches from behind the fog. Close. Closer than it's ever been. Maybe it's been here the whole time.

"Especially if we're the last ones left," I say.

Because if we give up now, then the forest wins.

And maybe we deserve to be punished.

But not like this.

Never like this.

We don't stop until we reach a clearing—a clearing with fresh snow and the tracks of small animals. It's beautiful. We've stopped pretending we'll find better. Even though this is the most calming clearing that we've seen this whole time, throughout this whole war, the trees still crowd close, watching. Breathing. Judging.

Harris drops his pack with a grunt and slumps to the ground. Rich sinks beside him, arms wrapped tight around his knees. I stay standing. My legs ache, but I need the ground to feel like it's still under me. Like gravity hasn't betrayed us too.

"We can't keep doing this," Rich mutters with a thousand-yard stare. "Wandering. Pretending like there's a point. We need to pick a direction—*any* direction—and just go."

"Pick a direction?" Harris scoffs. "You think we'll magically walk out of here and into Allied lines with no food, no water, and a guilt-slick trail behind us?"

"It's better than dying out here!" Rich snaps, louder than I've ever heard him. "We're soldiers, Harris. If we find the front, if we get to the Allies, they might—"

"***They'll shoot us***," Harris cuts in, voice low and sharp. "We killed friendlies. We killed a goddamn Captain. You think they'll shake our hands and thank us for our service?"

Rich fires back quickly, but there's no strength in it. "We didn't know. It was dark. It was snowing. You saw him raise his rifle—"

"I saw ***Tommy's head receive a hole***." Harris lurches to his feet now, face flushed, breath steaming in the cold. "That's what I saw."

Rich recoils like he's been struck. The silence that follows is thick enough to choke on.

I close my eyes. My hands are trembling again.

"We didn't mean to," Rich says quietly. "We were scared. Alone. You think they won't understand that?"

"No," Harris says. "Because we don't even understand it. Not really. Not enough to explain it, not in a way that matters."

"We tell them it was foggy," Rich tries again. "That they didn't signal. That we thought we were under attack."

"We tell them," Harris growls, "and they string us up as an example. ***Look what happens when you lose your head. When you shoot your own.***"

He sits again, slower this time, like the anger drained out and left his bones brittle.

I still haven't spoken.

Because they're both right.

And they're both wrong.

"Then what?" Rich asks after a long while. "What are we supposed to do? Just keep walking until we starve? Let the forest... *have* us?"

"We could hide," I say. "Bury our tags. Try to disappear. Go north, maybe. Wait for the end of the war."

Harris shakes his head. "Have you ever heard what the SS does to their own deserters they catch in the trees, let alone those of their enemy?"

We don't answer.

Because we have.

"I've seen what they did to a Polish partisan," Harris mutters. "Left her hanging from a light pole. Alive. Just high enough so the crows wouldn't have to stoop."

"Jesus," Rich whispers.

"No. Not Jesus. Jesus couldn't help. *Men* did that." Harris looks at me now, eyes sunken, unreadable. "You want that for us? If we hide and the wrong patrol finds us?"

I feel old. So damn old. Like the days between yesterday and today have piled on like decades.

I look at my crew. What's left of them.

A kid with a ghost behind his eyes.

A man running from what he saw in a single flash of gunfire.

A boy trying to hold it together with silence.

So we sit. Not because it's safe here—it isn't—but because we've run out of places to go.

Harris drops to the dirt with a grunt and pulls his knees to his chest. Rich lowers himself more slowly, glancing around as if he's afraid and as if the forest might bite if he shows weakness. Fitz lingers near the edge of the clearing, his silhouette thin and twitching in the half-light.

I stay standing. My legs hurt, but it feels wrong to sit. Like I'd be giving up some last sliver of control. Or worse—acknowledging we've already lost it.

None of us speaks for a long time.

"I keep thinking we'll hit the edge soon," Rich says eventually, his voice dull. "If memory serves me right, there's a road just past the next rise. A farmhouse. Hell, I'd settle for a damn scarecrow. *Something* that doesn't smell like rot or sounds like teeth clicking in the dark."

"You think there's an edge?" Harris mutters. "You think this place has boundaries?"

Rich doesn't answer.

"No," Harris goes on, shaking his head. "There's no edge. No fence. We're not in a forest anymore. We're in a trap shaped like one."

He drags his hand through his hair, then presses the heel of his palm into his eye socket like he's trying to shove the memories back inside.

"I say we keep moving," Rich offers, desperate now. "If we make it back to Allied lines, maybe... maybe there's a chance—"

"There's not. We've been over this." Harris doesn't even look up.

Rich frowns. "We're not deserters. We stayed. We fought. We—"

"We *shot an American captain in the head and proceeded to use the main gun and co-ax on the rest of his men*, Rich."

Silence.

"You think the Army's gonna pin a medal on that?" Harris asks, voice low. "Or even listen long enough for us to explain?"

"We didn't know," Rich whispers. "It was dark. He didn't respond. Tommy came out with a weapon—"

"He came out because *I told him to*," I say, finally. My voice comes out like gravel.

That shuts them both up.

Fitz still hasn't turned around. He's watching the trees. Or maybe he's watching **something** in them.

"I gave the order," I say. "I told him to pop the hatch. Told him to give the challenge."

I can still hear his voice.

Then the shot. Then the way he folded. How Harris screamed. How I yelled *return fire*, like that could undo what had already happened.

Rich looks down. Harris stares at the dirt.

"I didn't know who they were," I say. "I didn't know if they were lost. Or scared. Or just... **human**. But we didn't wait long enough to find out."

"You think the brass will forgive that?" Harris asks. "Think they'll say, *War's hell, boys,* and let us off with a slap on the wrist?"

Rich's lips move like he wants to answer, but nothing comes out.

"They'll court-martial us," Harris continues. "Maybe worse. They'll want to make an example of someone. And it'll be us."

"We could hide," Rich says, quieter now. "Deep enough, long enough... the war ends eventually, right? Then we find a boat, change names. We vanish."

"They'll find us," Harris says. "You know how they handle cowards in this war? No trials. Just a shovel and a bullet."

"So what then?" Rich snaps. "We just sit here and wait to die?"

He stands now, pacing in a tight circle, voice rising. "You want to throw yourselves at the Krauts? See how long we last against a patrol? Against a tank? What the hell do you want me to say?"

"You're not thinking straight," Harris says flatly.

"***None of us are!***" Rich shouts. "We're lost in a forest that isn't a forest, where the trees breathe and the paths circle back and our dead kid's body is goddamn *gone*. You want straight thinking? That died with Tommy!"

Fitz turns around, slowly.

His face is pale. Dirty. His eyes look too big for his head in the dusk.

"We don't have to wait," he says.

"What?" Rich asks.

"There's another option."

I already know what he means. I see it in the way he looks at me. Not with challenge, not with fear—but with resignation. Like he's been walking with the weight of it in his pocket this whole time, and only now is he ready to show us.

He unclips the grenade from his belt.

Doesn't raise it. Doesn't move like he's going to pull the pin.

Just holds it.

Harris stares at it like it's started ticking.

"You're serious," he says. "You'd rather—what, ***end it all*** here, than risk a bullet from a friend or a rope from an officer?"

Fitz shrugs. "I don't want to die scared. Not in this place.It'd be fast."

"You're all out of your minds," Rich mutters, backing away. "We just need a little more time. A few more miles. We'll find something."

"We've found **nothing**," Harris says. "For days. Just snow and silence and guilt. And maybe that's the point."

I reach out and gently lower Fitz's hand. The grenade stays in his grip, but the tension eases a little.

"I'm not ready," I say.

None of us are.

Not yet.

We sit again, slowly this time. The cold seeps in. A branch cracks far off through the trees.

I listen to it.

To the quiet.

To the weight of what we've done.

To the thing in the woods that **knows**.

Fitz doesn't look away from the grenade in his hand.

"The fourth option. It's our only liberation. We can go out together. We won't let them or **it** take us."

He shifts the grenade into his other hand, fingers curling around the body, thumb settling on the safety lever. The pin's ring catches a glint of soft light as he hooks a finger through it—steady, deliberate.

[CHAPTER SEVENTEEN: A CURSE FROM MARS]

"And when man and horse go down,"

20 December 2024

It's green inside the tank. That kind of ghost-light cast from the dim dome lights—meant to preserve night vision, but it only seems to bleach the life out of everything.

No one sleeps.

Fitz is curled up against the turret wall, shaking. His rifle clutched like a lifeline, eyes wide and bloodshot. His foot keeps tapping the floor, rhythmic and erratic, like a tell in a game of cards he doesn't know he's playing.

Vic's down in the driver's hole, hunched forward like a caged animal. His legs are twitching, one heel bouncing against the foot pedal even though the tank is off. Every so often, he mutters something under his breath—too labored to make out. His hands, usually calm and steady, are trembling over the dash. He's not even pretending to check the controls anymore. His behavior reminds me how alone the driver is in the Abrams. Completely separated from the rest of the crew.

If we ever needed to get to Vic, we'd have to turn the turret completely around, raise the ammo basket and push open the swing gate and **then** we could get to him through a small opening.

Turner sits by the breach, arms crossed, jaw clenched so hard I swear I can hear the grind of teeth. He's got that look—like he's waiting for a camera crew to pop out of the ammo door and hand him a reality show contract: *Snapped: Combat Edition*. His rifle's on his lap. Not idle. Not relaxed. Ready.

And me? I'm in the commander's seat, pretending to be in control. Pretending this thing we're inside is still a tank and not just a very expensive coffin.

It smells like sweat and rust and bad body odor in here. There's no food left. We gave up tearing open the last MRE packet yesterday. Was it yesterday? I don't even know how long it's been since we ran out.

Now we sip condensation from the armor seams when we can find it. Little beads of moisture that form like dew on the inside plates, tasteless and warm, but it keeps the headaches at bay. Barely.

After the **excitement** of our run-in with the Tiger we've decided it's best to lock ourselves inside *Controlled Violence* and hope we can come up with a better plan... or maybe get rescued. Our logic is simple. If we are inside the tank, whatever in this forest is trying to kill us can't seem to get in through the armor.

The silence is the worst part. Not the kind that means peace—but the kind that hums with tension. The kind that wraps around your neck and dares you to speak.

I try anyway.

"We need a plan," I say. My voice cracks from the dryness in my throat. "We can't stay buttoned up forever."

No one responds. Not even an eye shift.

"Whatever that was—it's gone. Or hiding. Either way, we need to figure out our next move."

Still nothing.

My hand closes around the grip beside the seat. I try again.

"Fitz," I say. "You holding together?"

He blinks. A slow, delayed motion like the question had to swim through molasses to reach him. Then he nods. Or maybe his head just rocks on instinct.

"I'm fine," he whispers. Very clearly not 'fine'.

I call out to Vic. "Anything on the power? We've still got a reserve charge, right?"

He doesn't speak at first. But after some time he does, his voice is barely audible. "I might be able to go for a start but if we can't get her started on the first try... we might be dead in the water."

"Turner, how's the teeth on our baby looking?"

Turner slowly shifts. "We've got maybe two sabot, one HEAT, a few belts of 7.62 and a few mags of 5.56 and pistol," he mutters. "After that, we're fighting ghosts with bad language."

"Better make 'em count," I say.

He doesn't answer. Just stares back at the sealed breech like it holds all the answers if he looks hard enough.

I take a breath. The air's stale and metallic. Makes my teeth ache.

"I know last night was—hell, I don't even have the word. But we're still here. That means something."

Fitz's tapping stops.

Turner's brow twitches.

"I don't think we're supposed to be," Vic says, breaking the silence.

My stomach knots.

"What?"

"I don't think we're supposed to be here," he repeats, slow and flat. "I think the forest made a mistake. We were supposed to die back there."

Turner snorts. A bitter, humorless sound. "Yeah, well. I guess death's got a schedule to keep."

"No," Vic says, shaking his head. "I'm serious. That thing—it wasn't attacking like it wanted to win. It was hunting. It had us. We were dead. And then—poof."

"It missed us... mostly," I groan, rubbing my ribs. My plate carrier took the three rounds like a champ, but I still feel like I got run over by a truck. "Pretty sure this counts as a 'service-connected injury'. If the VA ever decides to agree with me, that is. They probably wouldn't be convinced we had to fight a ghost tank in a haunted forest. Speaking of ghost tank—Fitz, stick your head out of the hatch and see if it's still there."

"It's not," Fitz says. "It *left*. I saw it turn. It backed off."

Turner sits up straighter. "You saying it let us live? How generous."

"Here's what I think," Vic whispers, "we weren't supposed to see the end of their story. Things got worse the first time we saw *Calculated Vengeance*. The forest is probably trying to cover up what it did. That it killed the crew."

No one talks for a long time after that.

The Abrams creaks. The armor groans like something ancient shifting in its sleep. Every pop of metal sounds like footsteps just outside.

"We're not dead," I say finally, more for myself than them. "That means we've still got a say in what happens next."

Turner's lip curls, like he wants to argue. But he doesn't. Not out loud.

Fitz wipes his mouth with the sleeve of his dirty uniform. "I keep hearing whispers when I close my eyes."

"Yeah," I murmur. "Me too."

A beat.

"I heard my mom last night," he says. "She died two years ago. Pancreatic cancer."

The tank is quiet.

"I never told you guys that, did I?"

"No," Turner says.

Fitz nods, slow. "She said it wasn't over yet. That we had to finish what **they** started."

I feel a chill slide down my spine despite the stifling heat.

"They?" I ask.

Fitz just shrugs.

We sit there. Four shadows huddled in a steel beast, waiting for a world that doesn't make sense anymore to decide if we keep going or fade like the rest.

Eventually, I lean forward and tap the edge of the turret. "We'll give it another hour. Then we check power, check comms, and make a call. If there's a way out of this place, we'll find it."

No one argues.

But no one agrees either.

The tank creaks again.

And somewhere outside, beyond the armor, the forest listens.

The forest outside looks clearer now. The fog that had clung to the trees like cobwebs is gone. But the stillness it left behind is worse. I know the fog will be back. It always comes back in massive unrelenting waves.

Out of the vision blocks, the trees are stiff, unmoving. No wind. No birdsong. No rustling of leaves. Just the green glow of the tank's interior behind us and the pale, motionless woods ahead.

"I hate this more," Vic mutters from the driver's hole. "The quiet."

I nod without meaning to. "Same."

It feels wrong. Like the forest is holding its breath.

Fitz shifts again. He hasn't put down his rifle once. He hasn't even set it across his lap—he's holding it like he expects to use it any second.

"I saw something last night, at least I think it was last night," he says, and it's the kind of sentence you don't want to hear in a place like this.

He's speaking to the floor at first, voice barely above a whisper. "I was dozing off, trying to get some sleep—I don't even know what time it was—and I looked through the CITV. Just scanning, you know? Couldn't sleep."

No one interrupts him.

"And I saw... me. Or what looked like me."

I look up from my lap, slowly.

Fitz is still staring down, eyes distant.

"Standing next to the Sherman. Just... standing there. Different uniform. Same face. Hands at my sides like I was waiting for something. Watching the tank."

His fingers tighten on the rifle. "I didn't imagine it. I know I didn't. He looked at me. Like he knew I was watching."

Turner glances over, mouth pressed into a hard line. He doesn't mock it. Doesn't scoff. That says more than any words would. I can tell Turner wants to tell Fitz about our run-in with the **other** Fitz. Turner seems to come to the same conclusion I do. If we tell our Fitz about the other Fitz, it might just shatter his mind.

"I blinked," Fitz continues, "and he was gone."

The silence creeps back in.

Vic swallows. His voice is hoarse, like he's been holding something in too long. "I heard the engine running last night."

That gets everyone's attention.

"I didn't say anything," he says, "because I thought maybe one of you was trying to charge the system, or maybe I imagined it. But it was real. The whole hull was humming. I could feel it in my feet."

Turner turns toward him slowly.

"I checked the dash," Vic says. "Nothing lit. No ignition. And none of you were moving. You were all asleep. But I swear—" He hesitates, eyes darting to me. "I swear it—**she**—was running. Just for a second. Like she wanted to go somewhere."

Fitz makes a low, nervous sound in his throat.

I open my mouth to respond, but Turner beats me to it.

"I saw someone in your seat when I woke up, Sergeant."

His voice is flat. Not accusing. Not emotional.

Just factual.

"I came to," he says, "looked up, and someone was sitting in the commander's chair. Not moving. Just watching the screens. It clearly didn't look like you… It didn't look like anyone."

He doesn't blink. Doesn't look away.

"I thought it was you. Until I realized you were snoring in your favorite spot two feet from me."

I feel a cold pressure settle on my chest.

Turner leans back, arms crossed again. "Didn't say anything at the time. Figured maybe I'd dreamed it. But now?"

He leaves the thought unfinished. Doesn't need to say it.

I force a breath in through my nose. "Alright," I say, trying to keep my voice steady. "Let's just slow down. We've all been through a hell of a few days. Minimal food. Barely any sleep. We're all seeing things. That's what this place does."

No one argues.

But no one agrees either.

"Fitz," I say, "you didn't see yourself. You saw something that looked like you. Probably a reflection, or a trick of the light. Your mind filling in the blanks."

He doesn't respond. Just hugs the rifle tighter.

"Vic," I go on, "the engine doesn't start without someone pushing the button in your station. You'd know that better than any of us. So maybe you felt a vibration or something, but it wasn't the powertrain."

Vic's jaw flexes, but he nods. Reluctantly.

I turn to Turner last. "And no one was in my seat."

"You sure?" he asks, quiet.

"Yes."

But my voice cracks halfway through, and that's the part that betrays me.

Because I'm **not** sure. Not anymore.

And Turner knows it.

I feel it—like a shadow pressed up against the back of my skull. The sense that something's watching us from just outside the armor. Not curious. Not aggressive. Just... waiting.

And deep down, I think we all feel it.

Something changed.

We should've died when that King Tiger fired. We should've died when Vic sent us flying in the ditch before we ever entered this forest. We should've never even shown up to this competition.

We *are* going to die. But I'll be damned if I don't do everything in my power to prevent that.

Whatever the answer is, it's out there. Waiting.

And our tank— *Controlled Violence*—it feels like it's waiting too.

Like it knows it's going to be needed again.

I lean back in the commander's chair, running a hand down my face.

We're running out of time.

And worse—we're running out of reason.

I can't sit still anymore.

Every second in this tank is a reminder that we've lost control—over the mission, over the situation, maybe over reality itself. And if I don't do something, I'll lose control too.

"Alright," I say, louder than I mean to. My voice bounces off the turret walls and draws the others' attention. "We're going through the tank. Full systems check. By the book. Prep it for startup."

Vic looks up from the driver's hole like I slapped him. Turner's eyes narrow slightly, gauging me. Fitz doesn't even blink—he's already halfway to standing.

"Thought we were shut down," Turner mutters. "Stuck here. Forest won't let us leave, right?"

"Maybe not," I say. "But it hasn't stopped us from trying. Every time we gave it power, we got farther. Maybe this time we get *out*."

I catch my reflection in the periscope glass. I don't look convinced. But I say it anyway.

"Back to routine. Get moving."

Vic grunts and slides back into his station. Turner shifts toward the gunner's controls, flipping switches like he's on autopilot. Fitz opens the loader's hatch without a word and hoists himself out. The air outside still looks frozen, the trees brittle and lifeless—but he doesn't hesitate. He swings down, boots crunching into the fresh snow that's accumulated on the cold back deck. There's the unmistakable sound of grunting as he pulls the bitch plate out of place so he can check fluids.

For a moment, it almost feels normal.

The hum of a crew working through startup protocols.

The whisper of boots on armor.

The thump of hatches and clicks of latches.

But it's all surface. Underneath, we're frayed and unraveling.

I sink into the commander's chair and begin my own checks—comms panels, override relays, GPS system that still refuses to show anything but a random location on the globe and a date that hasn't been accurate since we crossed the treeline.

And that's when I see it.

A faint scratch on the metal panel next to my right hand.

It's low—where my hand brushes sometimes during gunnery.

I lean closer, brushing grime away with my thumb. The light is dim, but I can still make it out.

Jack M. Carson.

It's scratched in shallow, almost delicate lines. Like someone took their time.

And it's *old*. Rusted out inside.

There's no flake to the metal. No shine from a fresh scratch. It's dulled, worn by years of vibration and grime. Faded like it's been here longer than I've owned this uniform.

I freeze, blood draining from my arms.

I didn't do this.

I know I didn't.

There's no way I could've missed it all these weeks. I'd have seen it. *Felt* it.

I glance around the turret. No one's watching me. Vic is muttering to himself up front, flipping breakers. Turner is tracking power connections. Fitz is still outside, running his hands across the engine access points.

No one saw me do it. Because I didn't.

But it's here.

And it's in the ***exact same spot*** that Casey's name was scratched into the Sherman.

Same style. Same size. Same pressure.

I reach out, fingers hovering over the carved letters. My own name, like an echo. Or a prediction.

Or a memory I haven't lived yet.

I should call it out. Ask the crew if they're messing with me. If this is some horrible joke.

But I don't.

Because deep down, I know what they'll say.

They'll say the same thing I would: **It was always there.**

The longer I stare at it, the less real the rest of the tank feels. The glowing green screens. The smell of oil. The taste of metal sweat.

It all blurs into background static, like I'm sitting in a replica of my life built just well enough to fool me when I'm tired.

And I'm so damn tired.

I close my eyes for a moment, grounding myself on the solid pressure of the armor beneath me.

This is real.

That's what I tell myself.

This is real. This is now.

But the scratch is still there when I open my eyes.

And the worst part is—I can feel that it belongs. Like it's always belonged. Like I've **been** here before, and every step I take is just retracing someone else's path.

I don't remember carving it.

But some part of me remembers being the man who did.

Footsteps crunch outside. Fitz climbs back up, face pale and drawn.

"Fluids are good," he says, breathing hard. "Everything's clean. Levels are fine." He hesitates, then adds, "Didn't expect that."

"Good," I say, clearing my throat. "We'll finish the sequence and try ignition. Maybe this time—"

But I trail off. Because he's still staring at me.

Not quite at me—at my seat.

His eyes flick to the scratch and widen just slightly.

He doesn't say anything.

And that silence says everything.

"Vic, go for a start and be nice," I say, my voice low but firm, laced with all the hope I have left. Maybe more hope than I should still have. I need this to go well. I need something—*anything*—to work like it's supposed to.

"Clear!" Vic calls out automatically, his voice echoing through the hull. The ritual of it is comforting. Familiar. Like muscle memory trying to pretend we're still in a world that makes sense.

Then, softer, almost tenderly, he leans forward and whispers to the dashboard, "Come on, sweetheart. Start for me."

His hand twists the ignition.

The engine coughs once—sharp and rough, like it's been holding its breath for hours.

Then again, louder, grating metal against metal as it strains.

A third time, it sputters and chokes and finally roars to life.

For a second, I think she's got it.

But the roar falters—like it's being dragged backward—and the sound winds down in a tired, whimpering groan. A long exhale, almost human in how defeated it sounds. And then... nothing. The forest is fighting her as much as it's fighting us.

Just silence.

She gives up.

Just as exhausted as we are in this place.

No alarms, no clunks of warning systems, just the absence of motion. The absence of **will**.

I close my eyes and let my forehead rest against the cool metal wall beside me. That sound—of her trying and failing—hits harder than I thought it would. Hurts more than it should. It feels personal.

The last time she ran smooth, it was during the fight with the Tiger.

That **thing** came for us, and I called the crew to combat. She lit up instantly on her own, like a match struck in the dark. No hesitation. No delay. It was like she knew what was coming, like she wanted to fight beside us.

She responded like one of us.

And we trusted her for it. Maybe even loved her for it.

I open my eyes and glance around at the rest of the crew. No one says anything. No one blames Vic. It's not his fault. We all heard her try.

I wonder if she's holding back now. If she knows something we don't.

Maybe she's **saving** her energy. Like a runner at the beginning of a marathon.

Maybe, in some impossible way, she's waiting. Conserving power for what's coming next. For the next thing that's going to try and kill us.

Because something always does.

And she always knows.

We sit in that silence for a long time. The kind that bends time around it, makes minutes stretch like hours. No one wants to say it, but we all know—we're running out of options. If the tank doesn't **want** to start, we can't move. And if we can't move, we're going to die out here. Whether it's from dehydration, starvation, or whatever the hell else this forest is hiding.

I glance at the radio panel. It's an ugly thought. The last card in the deck. I've been putting it off since the beginning—since everything went to hell. We all have. Because if the radio works, then someone might hear us. And if **someone** hears us, they might come for us. I've been putting it off because admitting defeat in this tiny forest is that last thing I want to tell the other crews.

Still, I know what has to be done.

"We try the radio," I say.

Turner looks up from his seat, his eyes bloodshot and unreadable. "Seriously?"

"We try it," I repeat. "Just to see if anyone's still out there. Anyone from the competition. Hell, even one of the organizers. Someone might be trying to get through to us. Maybe they've been trying this whole time."

Vic shifts in the driver's hole like he's shrinking into himself. "Or maybe we're just opening the door to more of... **this**."

I can't argue with that. But doing nothing means dying for sure. At least trying gives us a sliver of control—however small.

I reach for the handset. It's warm in my hand, sticky with the residue of dozens of sweaty grips. My thumb hesitates over the transmit switch. I exhale through my nose, then key up.

"This is *Controlled Violence*, call sign Eagle Team. Broadcasting in the blind. Requesting immediate assistance or location of nearest friendly unit. I say again, this is Eagle Team—anyone copy?"

Static.

I try again. A different frequency.

"This is Eagle Team, active participant in the international competition. We are lost in the Hürtgen Forest and require immediate assistance. Any unit receiving, please respond."

More static.

Turner watches me without blinking, arms crossed tightly across his chest. Fitz is curled up in the loader's seat, gripping his rifle like it might disappear if he lets go. Vic has his knees pulled up, hugging them, like he's trying to vanish.

I try a third frequency. Then a fourth.

Each time, nothing but the hollow sound of the world forgetting we exist.

Then—just as I'm about to key down again—the speaker crackles.

It's not a response. It's a *pulse*. Like someone breathing into the radio.

Everyone freezes.

More static—then something *moves* beneath it. Like a whisper clawing its way up from a cave bottom.

A voice.

Soft. Strained.

Wrong.

"C... Controlled... Violence..."

I feel my guts twist. It's English. But not *quite*. It's laced with an accent I can't place from just two words. The words are chewed on, spit out, dragged across a tongue that doesn't fully understand them. The cadence is wrong. The syllables stretched too far. It's the kind of accent you hear in documentaries about people who haven't been alive for eighty years.

It pauses, then crackles again.

"We are... looking... for you..."

The hair on my arms stands straight up. The voice sounds like it's smiling.

Fitz lets out a small whimper.

Another burst of static. Then, a different voice:

"Where... are... they? Are... they... alive?"

After that, laughter. Dry. Grotesque. The throat it's coming from isn't even flesh.

I reach for the radio switch to talk back. I need to tell them we are alive and well and if they want another round, we're here. We're waiting.

"We are comi—"

Turner reaches over, slams his hand down, and **shuts it off**.

The tank goes dead quiet.

For a second.

But the voice doesn't stop.

A flood of words from various voices keep coming from it—*from the radio that's no longer powered.*

It echoes—not from the speakers, not from outside—but from **inside our heads**.

Like the forest isn't just listening.

It's speaking **through us**.

Fitz starts crying.

Not loud, not wailing. Just the quiet, broken sobbing of a kid who finally understands he's not going home.

Vic starts rocking slightly. "I want out. I want out. I want out..."

"Vic," I say, but he doesn't hear me.

"I want out. I want out. I want out."

Turner has his fists clenched so tight his knuckles are bone white. He wants to smack Vic. That much I know. But there's no easy way to get to him.

I sit there with the handset still in my hand, not even sure how long I've been holding it. The cold metal feels like it's dug into my palm. The skin's raw. Maybe bleeding. I don't check.

I don't move.

Because something about that voice felt... familiar.

Not the sound. But the *intent*.

It wasn't searching.

It wasn't asking.

It was **hunting**.

The tank is finally silent again. Each of us is locked in our own private hell.

Then—faint at first—there's a flicker.

Vic stops rocking. Fitz looks up.

Out past the front glacis, through the periscope, a dim yellow glow pulses through the treeline. Then another. Two lights like lanterns swaying in a breeze that doesn't exist.

"They're back," Turner mutters. "It's the Tiger."

I stand, lean forward toward the sight. It's not searchlights. It doesn't look like headlights either. Not modern, not LED or IR. These lights glow soft, old, like the filament bulbs from a half-century ago—dull yellow or amber, like kerosene.

Fitz grips his rifle tighter. "Could be a reenactor crew or something? A lost group?"

"Reenactors don't carry live ammo," Turner snaps.

The glow swells for a second. A figure walks through it—between the lights, he's stepping through time itself.

Even at this distance, we can see the stagger in his gait. One leg dragging. The other crunching with purpose. A rifle slung over his shoulder. Helmet crooked on his head. Jacket flapping in a breeze we can't feel.

He's World War II, no doubt about it. The cut of the uniform. Steel pot. Canvas gear. Every detail screams **American infantry, late-war**.

But his skin is too pale. Like paper. Like ash.

He stops just at the edge of the treeline. Still backlit by the flickering yellow glow. The flames—or headlights, or whatever they are—cast long shadows around him, but none from him.

He turns toward us.

None of us move. No one breathes.

Even from this far out, I feel it. Like he's *seeing* me.

Not looking.

Seeing.

Fitz breaks the silence with a whisper: "Do we shoot?"

Nobody answers.

The figure tilts his head, slow, unnatural. Like a puppet rediscovering its strings.

Then, he turns and walks again. Deeper into the woods. Right into the dark between the trees.

Vic shudders, pressing his back into the hull like it can absorb him. "We're not getting out of here. We're not supposed to. The tank—it's cursed. All of it. Steel and oil and blood."

"Shut up," Turner mutters, but there's no real anger in it. Just fear.

Vic continues anyway, eyes wide like he's reading something the rest of us can't see. "It wants us. This place. It wants the tank. It wants us *inside* it. You don't get it. The only way it lets you go is if you're dead."

Turner throws up his hands. "So what, we just sit here until it comes back with that damn Tiger and finishes the job?"

Vic points at the hatch. "I'm not dying in here. Not in this coffin."

Turner doesn't look at him. "I'm not leaving anyone behind."

Vic stares at him. "I'm not asking you to. I'm telling you—we get out now, or we die in this damn shell."

My heart pounds like a drum. They're both looking at me now. Waiting. Asking me to decide whether we live or die. Whether we run—or hunker down and make our final stand.

I turn back toward the radio. It's cold again. Dead.

The tank is our world. It's all we've ever had. It's shielded us from IEDs and RPGs, storms and bullets, the worst things men can throw at each other. But now? Now it feels like a trap. Like a steel lung we can't breathe in anymore.

But I know what happens if we step outside. I've seen it. The forest doesn't play by the rules. It bends them. Breaks them. Eats people whole. That figure out there? That wasn't a man. That was a warning.

I remember the Sherman crew. Their pictures. Their names. Their e nd.

"I'll make the call," I whisper. "If we step out of this tank, we're exposed. We're nothing. Just four guys in a cursed wood. Outgunned. Outnumbered. Alone."

Turner doesn't flinch. "But maybe we live. Maybe if we get out now, we're not part of... whatever **this** is."

Vic looks like he wants to believe that.

I stare down at the command console. My fingers brush the name scratched into the steel: **CARSON**.

Not fresh.

Old. Worn. Like it's always been there.

I don't remember carving it.

And I **never** will.

That settles it.

I take a breath, steady my voice, and say the words that seal our fate.

"Death before dismount."

They don't argue.

Turner gives a slow nod. "Ride it out, then."

Fitz wipes his nose, sniffling. "Just like the Sherman guys."

Vic doesn't move. Just closes his eyes.

I grab the intercom handset again. "Everyone to battle stations. Lock hatches. Check ammo. Load sabot. We fight."

And in that moment, the tank responds. She comes alive.

The power whines up.

The optics flash.

The turret hums.

No one touched the controls. It's like she **knows**.

Outside, the forest grows still.

The lights are gone.

But the pressure—***the weight***—settles around us like a hand closing into a fist.

And I know the next chapter's already written in steel and smoke.

[CHAPTER EIGHTEEN: DESIGNATE TANK, TARGET IDENTIFIED]

"Just empty your canteen, and go to Fiddlers' Green."

20 December 2024

"This is Eagle team… We are… requesting help. Over," I key out over the net, my voice sounding thin and small over the static hoping that our final plea will be heard. I pause, waiting. Hoping. Nothing.

The only sound is the low hum of the forest and the scream of our engine. No birds. No wind. Just that constant, low vibration, like the woods themselves are holding their breath.

As if on cue, the mist curls around the tank. A shroud, thick and unmoving, clinging to every surface. It seeps through the trees, over the barrel, through the periscopes. It's thicker now than it's been since we rolled into this goddamned forest. So thick it's hard to tell where the trees end and the sky begins—if the sky still exists at all.

It's almost as if the *Fog of War* itself has found a battlefield. It's come down from the place humans weren't meant to touch and draped its bloodstained curtain over us. And now that we're under it, we can't remember what was real before and what wasn't. Not clearly anyway. The sounds, the smells, even each other—it's all starting to slip. We know it's daylight, or at least it should be, but not enough light pierces this fog to tell what time it is. Everything is gray. Washed-out. Like the color's been drained from the world.

None of it matters. The fog is so thick we might as well be blind. Every shape that emerges from it is a potential enemy. A potential *entity*. Every rustle might be a search party coming to rescue us. Every tree could be a demon in disguise. I swear I've seen men standing just off the trail, unmoving, staring—only for them to vanish when I look again. We're all seeing things now. But the line between paranoia and truth has vanished like the trail behind us.

The fog is no longer just a condition of the air—it's a condition of the mind. We're suffocating inside it. Not just from the haze outside the tank, but from the pressure building inside. We've lost direction, lost communication, lost the thread of what the hell we're even doing out here. And worst of all, we've started to lose trust in our own senses.

Something is coming for us. That much we know.

But beyond that, the line between imagination and reality is gone.

We couldn't sure if the next shape that moved through the mist wore a German uniform—or just something that looked like one. We probably couldn't even tell if it's a rescue party, or the Sherman crew returned from the grave for one last game of cards.

And maybe worst of all, we wouldn't be able to tell if it was a friend... or the demon itself, waiting to claim our souls for trespassing in its godless home.

The forest twisted those lines, and they don't mean anything anymore.

Soon, something will step into our sights. And we'll fire. Not because we know what we're shooting at, but because we don't.

Because the fog demands it.

And that's the part that scares me most.

I glance to our left. Through the mist, I can just make out the silhouette of *Calculated Vengeance*. What's left of her at least.

They never stood a chance.

They were soldiers. Just like us. Sure, we aren't fighting in a war, but they wore the same flag we do. They weren't killed by the enemy. Not really. Whatever happened to them... it was something else entirely. Something far worse.

They were exhausted, confused, cornered. Worn down by constant fighting, fear and the ever-looming hand of the reaper. That was until something **broke** inside them. And I can feel that same crack forming in us now.

We thought this was a competition. A NATO exercise. A test of skill and endurance.

But this forest... it's not part of the test. It's something else. A trap. A wound that never healed. A graveyard with teeth.

I think back over the last few days. The visions in the trees, the voices that didn't belong to anyone still breathing, transmissions from radios that should've been silent. Things no one could explain. Things we don't talk about anymore, because to talk about them is to admit they're real.

And if they're real... then we're already dead.

The radio tries to crackle to life but static fades back into silence.

I lower the radio handset and let my head rest against the cold interior of the turret. For a few moments, I just breathe. In and out. The metal smells like oil and rust and sweat. It's the smell of every day we've been out here.

In front of me I hear Turner stirring from his poor attempt at slumber in the gunner's station.

"You ready for this?" I ask without looking up.

"Not really," he mutters, voice low, hollow. "I think I can hear... *it*."

I don't ask what. We all hear things out here now. It's just part of the air. It's part of the *fog*.

The glow returns.

Dim at first, like before—flickering gently through the trees. Twin orbs of yellowish light bobbing low, drifting closer.

Turner's eyes glue themselves to his sight. He's gripping the side of the gunner's station like it's the only thing keeping him from floating away.

"Hey, Sergeant," he says quietly, voice barely carrying over the hum of the optics. "You think... you think those could be friendly?"

I don't answer at first. Just watch the lights, trying to count how far apart they are. Too narrow for a Humvee. Too wide for a tank. Too slow for anything with a diesel.

Turner clears his throat. "I mean, it could be a vehicle. Or one of the other teams. Maybe they figured out we broke down. Maybe they've been looking for us. I need certainty."

I look at him. His eyes won't leave the light, but his voice is shaking. There's something behind it—something deeper than just hope.

"Ryan..." I start.

He finally looks over at me. His face is drawn tight, pale in the green glow of the systems panel.

"I just don't wanna be wrong... Not like last time... Not again," he says. "I don't want to light something up thinking it's the enemy and then... find out later I killed a friendly."

It hits me like a sucker punch.

That's what this is. It's not hope.

It's guilt.

He's not scared of dying. He's scared of making the same mistake he almost made in the past. Of opening fire and realizing too late that he was looking at someone who came to help.

I take a slow breath, let it settle into my lungs, and say the only thing I can.

"There's zero chance those are friendly." It's the lie that I've been telling myself since we entered this forsaken forest. "Look at what we've already been through. Plus, I even have holes in my plate carrier."

He flinches.

"I mean it," I go on, gentler now. "Whatever's out there... it's not here to help. It's not even real, not the way we are. You saw that **thing** through the trees. You heard the damn radio saying it was coming for us. Looking for us. This forest isn't giving us rescue convoys. It's giving us tests. Lies. It wants us to doubt. It wants us to **die**."

Turner closes his eyes. His jaw clenches like he's chewing something bitter.

"But if it's **not** real," he says slowly, "why do I still feel like it knows my name?"

I don't answer.

Because I've felt the same thing.

Instead, I rest a hand on his shoulder. Solid. Grounding. The best I can offer.

"I don't know what the hell's coming," I tell him. "But if you pull that trigger when I say so, I'll carry the weight with you. That's a promise."

He nods once, just enough to show he hears me.

The lights in the forest don't get closer.

But they don't fade, either.

He lets out a breath and leans back against the turret wall. "I've been thinking about it. A lot."

I don't have to ask what *it* is. I know exactly what he's remembering.

That day was just a few years ago, but it feels like a lifetime. Turner came within a heartbeat of pulling the trigger on what he thought was a hostile.

It wasn't.

It was a friendly tank. An allied partner operating significantly out of position, about a mile away during our major combat operation in the province. Turner was green back then—too young, too raw to be a gunner. His vehicle ID skills were still rough edges waiting to be sharpened.

One wrong call. One slip of the finger.

And everything would have changed.

We'd be telling a different story now. Or maybe we wouldn't be telling any story at all. He would have been busy making big rocks into small rocks.

That near-mistake burned into Turner's soul, a scar he carries every day. But it also forged him. Made him the sharpest, most unflinching tank gunner I've ever seen. Because from that moment on, he never took a shot without absolute certainty.

"You stopped," I say, gently. "You asked for confirmation."

Turner doesn't respond at first. He just sits there, hunched slightly forward, eyes tracing the distant glow filtering through the trees. Finally, he speaks, voice low and brittle.

"Because you said something."

He turns to look at me, jaw set.

"If you hadn't—"

"But I did," I cut in, quietly. "And you listened."

He nods, but there's no relief in it. His eyes are still haunted, still running through all the ways it could've gone wrong.

"That crew in the Sherman..." he says slowly, like it's been weighing on him for a while. "They didn't have anyone to pull them back. No one to second-guess. I keep wondering if the forest got them... or if they made a mistake they couldn't come back from and decided that the consequences would be too much. It was a different time then."

His voice lowers to a whisper.

"If they fired first—on someone who wasn't the enemy—how do you live with that?"

I don't have an answer.

The air in the tank is thick. The hum of the systems. It's the only sound for a while. Turner leans his head back against the turret wall, eyes drifting toward the ceiling.

"They didn't have *you*," he says, just above a breath. "They didn't have someone to stop them. Or someone to save them."

I want to believe that matters. That we're different. That we've held the line—if only barely. But deep down, something cold coils in my gu t.

Because I don't know if we've been spared a mistake… or if we're standing on the edge of one.

I look away. My throat tightens at that. I don't want to be the guy they rely on to keep the nightmares at bay. I'm not sure I can do it anymore.

"They didn't have **us**," I say after a long pause. "We're still here. Still together. That's something."

Turner nods, but the guilt never leaves his face.

"We're not them," I say, as firmly as I can manage. "We're not done yet."

Outside, the forest closes in, setting the stage for the third and seemingly final act.

I open my hatch a crack, just enough to feel the cold air on my face. The forest is still blanketed in fog, thick and unmoving. It's holding its breath. I glance toward the *Calculated Vengeance*. The wreckage is half-sunk in shadow, a ghost of what it once was.

They never stood a chance.

We're not doing much better.

I glance down, meaning to check our map again. But the one in my hands… isn't ours.

It's old. The paper is yellowed and brittle, edges curled like dried leaves. The ink is faded, but legible. The markings are **handwritten**.

And right there, circled in a rough pencil stroke, is what I think is our *exact location*. Next to it:▯
"*Enemy tank – 12/20/2024.*"

Enemy tank.

I freeze.

This isn't possible. I don't remember taking this. We never found a map inside *Calculated Vengeance*, and even if we had—why would I keep it?

I run my thumb over the words like that'll make sense of them. But it doesn't.

I glance back at the map—still in my hands. The ghostly old paper stares back at me like it's waiting for something.

The light starts dimming further as if the forest itself is drawing the sun down ahead of schedule.

The quiet settles in again, heavier now. Outside the tank, the trees stretch out their dark sentinels. And somewhere beyond them, beyond the two glowing orbs... something moves.

It's slow. Distant. But undeniably there.

The sky is still choked in that same dull gray haze it was when we crawled out of our lame attempt at slumber. The sun never even broke through the mist. The light never changed. The shadows haven't moved. I would swear it's still early morning.

I shove the hatch fully open and stick my upper body out, needing fresh air—or at least whatever passes for it in this place. The wind has a sickly chill to it, and the trees seem... closer than they were an hour ago. Like the forest is breathing around us, slow and steady and ***inhaling***.

That's when I see Fitz.

He's not where I left him. He had just been sitting in the turret with Turner and I. Hadn't he?

He's standing maybe thirty feet away, by the *Calculated Vengeance* wreck. At first, I think he's just pacing, restless, trying to clear his head. But then I notice the way his head tilts slightly, as if listening intently. His lips are moving. He's speaking in low, measured tones.

And there's no one around him.

"Fitz?" I call out yelling over the roar of the engine.

No answer.

I swing myself down from the turret and cross the muddy ground toward him, boots crunching over half-frozen leaves. "Fitz, who are you talking to?"

He turns to me slowly, like I've just pulled him out of some deep trance. His face is pale and hollow-eyed, skin drawn tight over his cheekbones. I notice the sidearm he holds in his hands, knuckles white.

"Woah there, buddy, let's talk about this first." I freeze in my tracks.

"They were right here," he says softly. "The crew. From *Calculated Vengeance*."

"What are you talking about?"

"I—I can see them," he says. "Not like ghosts, not glowing or anything like that. They look... normal. Muddy. Tired. One of them is leaning against the tank, smoking a cigarette. Another is complaining about his socks being wet. The last one is shouting, but I can't understand him." He pauses, eyes drifting back to the old war relic. "They look so **human**. Like they're... stuck here. Like us."

My throat goes dry. "Fitz. Are you sure it isn't a dream? Hallucination?"

He shakes his head, almost violently. "No. I **hear** them. I feel it. One of them is pointing toward the woods. He's saying something about

'Enemy Tank' and 'Enemy Tank'. But we're not at war. I have no idea what he's talking about."

I feel the words land in my gut like a punch.

Enemy tank.

I glance back at our tank, then over toward the Sherman, then out at the trees.The woods are trying to choke out what little light remains.

Fitz keeps talking, his voice now shaking, he drops to the ground and leans his back up to the hull of the Sherman, "What if they are **warning** us? What if they see whatever's out there and are warning us that it's coming and the only term they can use is *Enemy Tank*?"

I kneel down beside him, trying to keep my voice calm. "You think that's what got them? The forest?"

He doesn't answer at first. Just stares off into the woods, the whites of his eyes wide and glassy. "I don't know. But it felt like they want me to see. Like they are **trying** to warn us. And maybe they don't have the words for it."

A long silence passes between us.

I look back at the Sherman. The old steel carcass looms in the gloom, half-swallowed by the earth. A coffin with a turret.

"They couldn't be saved... Those that did at least *try* to save them paid the ultimate price," Fitz mutters. "And whatever's out here... I don't think it wants to be understood. I think it just **wants**."

"Are you saying someone tried to save them? They were being rescued?" My voice trembles.

Before Fitz can respond, something in the woods snaps.

Both of us freeze.

It gets close this time. Not just a branch in the distance—this was near. Too heavy to be human. Too slow to be wind.

The trees groan.

 The forest watches.

 And I suddenly know, deep in my bones, that we're being hunted.

After what feels like hours, the engine sputters once, then goes still—like a held breath finally released. Our tank reminds us, in her own way, that she's more than just steel and circuits. She has her own instincts. And maybe she knows when it's safest not to move.

We brace for the worst.

We wait for the sound of treads, for the shriek of metal, for another whisper over the radio.

But nothing comes.

Just silence.

No screams. No gunfire. No voice from the dark.

Only the sound of frost settling over armor, and the slow, endless creak of the trees.

And that's almost worse.

The trees groan. The forest watches.

My chest tightens. It's no longer a tank competition. This is true combat.

"Back to Controlled Violence," I whisper. "Make her REDCON One, battle-carry sabot. Either we die here, or *it* dies here. Death before dismount."

Fitz doesn't argue. He bolts. His boots crunch over the frozen ground, loud as rifle cracks. I'm right behind him, pulse hammering in my ears.

Something heavy shifts in the darkness—too slow for wind, too deliberate for an animal. A low creak follows us, branches bowing as if the woods itself is reaching.

We dive for the hull, scrambling up the glacis and dropping into steel safety. The hatch slams, cutting off the forest's breath.

The radio hisses and pops like it's breathing, then the voice returns. It's thick, wet and full of static. There's a heavy accent that doesn't belong to the English language. It's thick with German.

"We are... *coming*... for you."

Five words. No context, no origin, no call sign.

Just a warning.

Or a promise.

Vic's fingers hover over the driver's controls, frozen in place. Turner's jaw clenches, his hand moving instinctively to the grip of his gunner's control handles. Fitz has gone dead quiet. No jokes, no one-liners. Just wide eyes fixed on the radio, like it might bite.

I don't blame them.

Everything about this feels wrong.

At first, I think it's just the treeline shifting as the light dies. But I see it—no, I *feel* it first. The rumble beneath the earth. The groaning of roots. The thudding beat of something impossibly heavy and fast. The dying light behind the treeline is nearly gone now, swallowed by the horizon and the canopy above. What little remains only sharpens the silhouettes ahead of us, deepens the black between the trunks.

But something's coming.

Something massive. Something impossible.

The last threads of daylight slowly unravel behind the trees, and whatever faint glow still bleeds through the gray winter sky is swallowed whole by a shape—wide, heavy, and crawling toward us like gravity made flesh. It's not just big. It's **real**. It has weight. Presence. It displaces the forest like it doesn't care what was here before.

Is it a tank?

My throat tightens. The King Tiger. The one from yesterday. The one that tried to kill us.

Maybe it's back to finish the job.

Or maybe it never left.

Or maybe—it's not even a machine. Maybe it's the forest, dressed up in steel and warpaint. Maybe it's **death**, wearing the shape of something we once understood, something we used to command.

Fog thickens as it approaches, swallowing details, warping lines. I can't make out the shape. The model. The era. Just its presence—dark and deliberate and **wrong**. There's the loud roar of the engine growl. The clanking of tread clatter. The thudding echo of something coming straight at us like it's hunting.

"Is that—?" Fitz starts to whisper, but I raise a hand.

We all see it.

Two faint lights burn low in the fog. Barely a yard off the ground. They flicker in the haze like animal eyes—hungry and unblinking.

Predator lights.

Not rescue.

Not salvation.

Turner murmurs, "It's back..."

And no one corrects him.

No one says, **That might be help**. Because none of us believe in help anymore. Not here. Not in this place. Not after everything we've seen.

If this were a friendly tank—if this was something from our reality, from our time—we'd be hearing comms. Callsigns. Voices.

Instead, there's only silence. Cold and waiting.

My hands are numb. Not from the temperature.

From dread.

It's coming straight at us.

And I think—I *feel*—the forest is finally ready to collect.

If it was a Leopard, it would make sense that the Sherman crew would call it an 'Enemy Tank,' not realizing that we've won the war decades ago. But it could also be the thing that killed them.

I don't know what it is.

And honestly, I don't care anymore.

Because it's coming straight for us.

And I won't let it take my crew.

We're not just a tank crew anymore. We're survivors of something bigger than war.

Something older.

The forest already claimed the lives of one crew and likely those of many other soldiers that had been pulled into this awful forest while on a wartrail. It dragged them down into the mud and buried them beneath time and terror.

Not us. Not today.

I slap the side of the turret and shout, "Vic, get that engine turned over now. I don't care how. Slam your boots together, make a deal with the devil. I don't give a shit. We are **not** dying here."

Vic's already scrambling, panic replaced by adrenaline. Fitz drops down into the loader's seat, hands shaking.

They're scared.

I'm scared.

But I'll burn this fucking forest down before I let it have them.

Let whatever's coming try.

Let the ghosts, the echoes, the demons, whatever this place is hiding come at me.

I'm ready.

The crew is ready. We will fight here. We will die here.

The radio crackles again, louder this time—like it's forcing itself to be heard through a wall of static and time.

"Wir sehen euch."

I freeze.

The voice... It sounds familiar.

No, no, no. That's not possible. There's no way any other other crews heard our plea for help earlier today. That's the forest again, playing its sick little games. Mimicking voices, stealing names, twisting memories. It can sound like anyone. Like **him**.

Vogel.

But it **can't** be Vogel. He's never coming for us. The voice is a fragment of the past we stumbled into. A ghost of a ghost. It's just like Fitz. just like how that wasn't **our** Fitz, this isn't **our** Vogel.

"Wir kommen... für euch."

I grip the edge of the hatch so tightly my knuckles ache.

Vic's cursing under his breath, coaxing the engine like it's an animal on its last breath.

"C'mon, c'mon..." he mutters, fingers dancing across switches.

And then—

A low groan.

A sputter.

The unmistakable roar of life.

The engine finally turns. It's an unmistakable whine bringing a small amount of joy to my body.

We all flinch at the sudden vibration rattling through the hull, but it's the most real sound I've heard in days. Turner grabs the gunner's handles and the turret springs to life. The tank wants blood. It needs blood. And it doesn't care **who** or **what** it comes from.

"Give me a crew report." My voice cuts through the thick silence. Steady, sharp, a tether to control. Every instinct screams to run, but this is where training takes over.

The tank's engine growls in response, the breach drops open as the tank **herself** responds to my orders.

"Driver ready. Tank in drive."

Fitz pulls on his gloves, his hands trembling. His eyes flicker with raw panic. This isn't just another drill and, thankfully for him, he's never been this close to hell before.

"Sabot loaded."

We're not leaving. Not now. Not ever.

The trees outside shift in a slow, unnatural rhythm, something alive breathing just beyond reason. Shadows twist, and that shape—impossible, terrible—slips through the darkness, closing faster than it should.

I don't know what it is.

I don't want to know.

This tank is everything. Our fortress, our coffin, our last goddamn hope.

And whatever hunts us...

They'll have to get through me first.

"Designate tank." My voice is instinctual.

"Identified enemy entity. Range: 600." Turner's calm cracks ever so slightly, a tremor beneath the words.

"Up!" Fitz pulls up the arming handle, hands shaking so badly it might as well be his last.

Through Turner's sights, I see it. A hulking shape moving with purpose through the trees. Its angular shape gleams like armor under the dim light. Two bright, unblinking lights of predator's eyes, cold and unyielding.

All I feel is ice crawling down my spine. If this was truly a rescue, they'd have called over the radio by now. Told us they were coming, that they were searching for us. They'd have made themselves known.

The only message we ever got, the only call that reached us, was the forest itself. That damnable demon living in this hellhole, snarling through the radio, reminding us how unwelcome we are. Telling us to make peace with our God, because this was our reckoning.

Come to us.

Let us show you what we're made of.

No fear. No terror. Only combat.

"Fire and adjust."

Fiddler's Green

Halfway down the trail to Hell,

In a shady meadow green

Are the Souls of all dead Troopers camped,

Near a good old-time canteen.

And this eternal resting place

Is known as Fiddlers' Green.

Marching past, straight through to Hell

The Infantry are seen.

Accompanied by the Engineers,

Artillery and Marines,

For none but the shades of Cavalrymen

Dismount at Fiddlers' Green.

Though some go curving down the trail

To seek a warmer scene.

No Trooper ever gets to Hell

Ere he's emptied his canteen.

And so rides back to drink again

With friends at Fiddlers' Green.

And so when man and horse go down

Beneath a saber keen,

Or in a roaring charge of fierce melee

You stop a bullet clean,

And the hostiles come to get your scalp,

Just empty your canteen,

And put your pistol to your head

And go to Fiddlers' Green.

[ANNEX IV: DECLASSIFIED GLOSSARY OF TERMS]

General Military Terms

ARTICLES OF WAR – *The legal framework for discipline and punishment in the U.S. Army during WWII. Cited when threatening punishment for mishandling classified information*

Battalion – *A military unit typically consisting of 300–1,000 soldiers. Tank battalions were usually made up of three or more companies.*

Brass – *Slang for high-ranking officers. Used when soldiers are frustrated by conflicting orders between field officers and "the brass" back at headquarters*

Call Sign – *Radio identifier assigned to a specific unit, vehicle, or person (e.g., "Team Eagle" or "Controlled Violence").*

Chain of Command – *The structured order of authority in military units.*

Court-Martial – *A military trial. Threatened for those who disobey orders to remain silent about classified incidents*

Designation – *An official label or call sign given to a tank for identification, such as Controlled Violence or Calculated Vengeance.*

Field Orders / Orders from Battalion – *Directives given by higher headquarters (Battalion or above).*

K-Rations / MREs – *Field meals. K-rations were the WWII standard, while MREs ("Meals Ready to Eat") are the modern replacement. The mix-up between the two reflects the supernatural bleed between past and present*

NATO – *North Atlantic Treaty Organization; multinational defense alliance formed in 1949.*

OPORD *(Operations Order)* – *Formal directive issued by a commanding officer, outlining mission, tasks, and execution details.*

Punitive Measures – *Harsh disciplinary actions threatened under military law for leaks or disobedience*

Restricted / Classified – *Levels of security classification; information not cleared for public release.*

SACEUR – *Supreme Allied Commander Europe; the senior military commander of NATO forces in Europe.*

Sarn't – *Slang for "Sergeant," used informally between enlisted soldiers*

Static / Dead Air – *Silence or white noise over a radio, often terrifying for crews reliant on communication in battle*

Tank & Crew Terms

Assistant Driver / Bow Gunner – *Position in WWII Shermans. Operated a forward-facing .30 caliber machine gun and assisted with driving tasks. Eliminated in modern tanks due to crew reductions.*

Breech – *The rear part of the main gun where ammunition is loaded. The loader inserts the round into the breech and closes the breechblock; firing is impossible until the breech is fully sealed. Breech malfunctions are dangerous, as a misfire or cook-off can occur if a round is stuck.*

CITV *(Commander's Independent Thermal Viewer) – A panoramic sight mounted on Abrams tanks, allowing the commander to search for and designate targets independently of the gunner. A key advantage in "hunter-killer" operations, where the commander can spot targets while the gunner is still engaging another.*

Cupola *– The Tank Commander's hatch, often fitted with periscopes, vision blocks, and a mounted machine gun.*

Driver *– Controls the tank's movement and positioning. In both Sherman and Abrams tanks, the driver is seated in the hull at the front.*

Gunner *– Crew member responsible for aiming and firing the main gun and co-axial machine gun under the TC's orders. Uses fire control systems to engage targets.*

Hull *– The main body of the tank. Houses the driver, engine, and some ammunition storage.*

Leopard 2 *– German-designed main battle tank, first introduced in the 1970s. Known for reliability, firepower, and modular design. Widely adopted by NATO nations.*

Leopard 2A7 *– Modernized variant of the Leopard 2, optimized for urban and asymmetric warfare. Features upgraded armor, electronics, and crew protection. Part of a long line of variants (2A4, 2A5, 2A6, etc.), each with incremental improvements. The Leopard 2 family represents multiple "flavors" of the same tank design, tailored to the needs of different armies.*

Loader *– Responsible for loading ammunition into the main gun. Calls out round type ("Sabot Up!" / "HE Up!") and ensures the breech is safely closed before firing.*

M1A2 SEP V3 Abrams *– Current U.S. main battle tank (MBT), heavily upgraded with advanced armor, targeting systems, and electronics. The SEP V3 (System Enhancement Package, Version 3) includes improved protection, fuel efficiency, and digital systems, making it one of the most advanced tanks in service worldwide. Armed with a 120mm smoothbore cannon.*

M4A3E8 "Easy Eight" Sherman – *Late-war U.S. medium tank, introduced in 1944. The "Easy Eight" was an improved Sherman variant with wider tracks, better suspension (HVSS – Horizontal Volute Spring Suspension), and a more powerful 76mm gun. It offered improved mobility and firepower compared to earlier Shermans, though it still struggled against German heavy armor like Tigers and Panthers.*

Tank Commander (TC) – *Crew leader. Responsible for tactical decisions, issuing fire commands, and maintaining situational awareness. In combat, the TC coordinates all crew actions.*

Tracks – *Continuous tread system that distributes the tank's weight, allowing movement over rough or soft terrain. Vulnerable to mines and anti-tank weapons.*

Turret – *The rotating armored section of the tank housing the commander, gunner, loader, and the main gun. Provides 360° fire coverage.*

Weapons & Ammunition

.50 Cal (M2 Browning / "Ma Deuce") – *Heavy machine gun often mounted on the commander's cupola. Powerful, effective against vehicles, infantry, and light armor.*

AP (Armor-Piercing) – *Ammunition designed to penetrate armor plating. In WWII Shermans, often insufficient against German heavy tanks.*

APC (Armor-Piercing, Capped) – *WWII anti-armor round with a hardened tip, designed to defeat sloped armor.*

Browning .30 – *Standard U.S. medium machine gun of WWII; mounted on Sherman tanks in hull and co-axial positions.*

Canister – *Modern anti-personnel tank round. Essentially a giant shotgun blast of hundreds of tungsten balls for close-range use against infantry.*

Coax – *Coaxial machine gun mounted alongside the main gun; fired by the gunner. Sherman: .30 caliber Browning. Abrams: 7.62mm M240.*

Cook Off – *When stored ammunition ignites from heat or fire without being deliberately fired, often catastrophic.*

HE (High Explosive) – *Ammunition designed for blast and fragmentation; used against infantry, buildings, and unarmored targets.*

HEAT (High-Explosive Anti-Tank) – *Ammunition that uses a shaped charge to burn through armor with a jet of molten metal. Effective even at long ranges, though less accurate at extreme distances.*

HVAP (High Velocity Armor Piercing) – *WWII experimental tungsten-core ammunition, rare but effective against German Panthers and Tigers.*

Main Gun – *Primary cannon of the tank. Sherman (WWII): 75mm or 76mm gun. Abrams (modern): 120mm smoothbore cannon capable of firing advanced anti-armor rounds.*

Ready Rack – *Designated ammo storage inside the tank for rounds prepped for immediate use. In Shermans, dangerously close to the crew compartment. In Abrams, insulated for improved safety.*

Sabot (APFSDS – Armor-Piercing, Fin-Stabilized, Discarding Sabot) – *Modern tank ammunition. A long, dart-like penetrator is encased in a lightweight "sabot" (sheath). When fired, the sabot peels away, allowing the penetrator to fly at extreme velocity and punch through armor.*

Sabot Petals – *In tank terminology, "sabot" refers to a lightweight carrier or shroud that surrounds a smaller-caliber, high-density projectile, such as a kinetic energy penetrator, allowing it to be fired from a larger-caliber gun barrel. The sabot fills the gun barrel, ensuring the propellant gases exert pressure evenly on the projectile, which enables higher muzzle velocity. Once the round exits the barrel, the sabot separates from the penetrator, which continues toward the target at high speed.*

Slang & Tanker Phrases

Belly Armor – *Underside of the tank, considered one of its weakest points.*

Buttoned Up – *Operating with all hatches closed; crew is sealed inside for protection, but visibility and airflow are limited.*

Death Before Dismount – *Tanker motto expressing fierce loyalty to their vehicle and mission; the idea that a tanker would rather fight and die in their machine than abandon it.*

Fiddler's Green – *A mythical resting place in cavalry lore, described as a paradisiacal tavern where soldiers who fall in battle gather to drink, dance, and rest forever. Tankers, inheriting cavalry traditions, often recite or reference The Cavalryman's Poem, which describes Fiddler's Green. In this book, each chapter opens with a line from that poem, reinforcing its symbolic weight.*

Hull Down – *Tactical position where only the turret is exposed to enemy fire; hull remains hidden behind cover.*

On the Way! – *Gunner's call immediately before firing the main gun.*

Redcon-1 – *Full combat readiness: crew in position, all systems operational, weapons loaded.*

Sabot Up! / HE Up! – *Loader's confirmation of which type of ammunition has been loaded (armor-piercing sabot or high-explosive).*

Tanker Boots – *Post–WWII evolution of combat footwear for armored crews. Instead of laces (which could snap, freeze, or snag inside a vehicle), tanker boots use leather straps and buckles. They became a distinctive and practical symbol of the tanker community.*

Traverse – *Rotating the turret left or right.*

Unbuttoned – *Operating with hatches open; improves visibility but exposes crew to enemy fire and weather.*

Up! – *Loader's call to confirm a round is loaded into the main gun.*

WWII-Specific Terms

Ardennes Offensive (Battle of the Bulge) – *German counteroffensive launched in December 1944 through the Ardennes; caught Allied forces off guard in bitter winter conditions.*

Bazooka – *Portable U.S. rocket launcher used against tanks and fortifications.*

Bogie / Suspension Bogie – *Part of Sherman suspension system; easily damaged in rough terrain or by enemy fire.*

Hürtgen Forest Offensive – *Dense, tangled woodland on the German–Belgian border. Fighting there in late 1944 was among the bloodiest U.S. battles of the war, marked by attrition, cold, and poor visibility.*

Pak 88 (Eighty-Eight) – *German 8.8 cm Flak gun, one of the most feared and effective anti-tank/anti-aircraft weapons of the war.*

Panzer – *German word for "armor"; used to describe tanks and their crews.*

Panzerfaust – *The Panzerfaust was a family of single-shot, man-portable, disposable anti-tank weapons developed by Nazi Germany during World War II. The name translates literally to "tank fist" or "armor fist" in German, symbolizing its purpose as a weapon designed to destroy armored vehicles. It was one of the first disposable anti-tank weapons, consisting of a pre-loaded, recoilless launch tube that fired a high-explosive anti-tank warhead.*

Pink Piping – *Uniform trim identifying Panzer Corps troops on German uniforms.*

SS Symbols – *Insignia of the Schutzstaffel, Nazi paramilitary forces.*

Tiger / Panther – *German heavy and medium tanks respectively; heavily armored and greatly feared by Allied tank crews.*

Wehrmacht Eagles – *German military emblem worn on uniforms.*

Willy Pete (WP) – *White Phosphorus; used in artillery and tank shells for smoke screening and incendiary effects. In WWII it was common slang among U.S. troops.*

[AUTHOR: DECLASSIFIED SERVICE RECORD]

FILE NO.: [REDACTED]-**BROCKINGTON**
CLASSIFICATION: DECLASSIFIED

NAME: BROCKINGTON, DANIEL N.⬚
DOB: [REDACTED]
POB: [REDACTED]

US ARMY ENLISTED SERVICE RECORD

Date of Initial Enlistment: 06/2018

Branch: U.S. Army

MOS: 19K – M1A2 Abrams Armor Crew Member

Positional Qualifications:

Driver – 04/2019

Loader – 04/2019

Gunner – 10/2019

Deployment: South Korea, Camp Humphreys (06/2019 – 02/2020)

Exit From Active Duty: 12/2021

US NAVY OFFICIAL MILITARY PROFILE SHEET

Branch: U.S. Navy Reserve

Rate: Intelligence Specialist

Enlistment Date: 03/2022

Periods of Active Duty: 03/2023-10/2023

Current Status: Active Drilling Reservist

CURRENT OPERATIONS (CIVILIAN ASSIGNMENT)

Unit: Joint Chiefs of Staff – J7 – Joint Exercises Division

Role: Instructor Controller / Forces Planner (Ground)

Primary Duties:

Produces OPFOR Campaign Plans and Briefs in support of joint training events.

Operates models and simulations (AWSIM, JCATS, JSAF, JTLS, JLOD) to replicate friendly and adversary ground forces.

Develops M&S systems plans and provides training to operators.

Advises on adversary tactics, techniques, and procedures to ensure realistic joint training environments.

AUXILIARY DUTIES / HOBBIES

Historical Interpreter, **American Revolution Museum at Yorktown**.

Conducts live demonstrations of musket and artillery drills.

Educates visitors on daily life in recreated 18th-century encampments.

Fiction writer with focus on the psychological, historical, and paranormal costs of war.

Author of *Fire and Adjust.* Current writing project is [REDACTED]

Multilingual capability: English (native), Swedish (proficient), Norwegian (conversational); maintains strong interest in language acquisition.

FINAL KEY POINTS

Continues to serve in uniform today.

Civilian expertise in armored warfare simulations and adversary tactics.

Married; caretaker of three dogs, one cat, and six ducks.

Maintains early-to-bed discipline, a habit forged by years of service

Believes that steel, stories, and battlefields carry ghosts.

Recommendation: Subject demonstrates persistence, loyalty, and a steady hand. Proceed with trust—but remain alert.

THE ARMOR SCHOOL
Leach
1-81 Armor
Headquarter
4322   7148 2nd
Battalion Comm
LTC Bradley S.
Command Sergea
CSM Brandon M.

TRIBALE
U.S. ARMY
COMPAN
2 MTB 112 AR
CAPT McGOOD
COMMANDER

www.ingramcontent.com/pod-product-compliance
Lightning Source LLC
Chambersburg PA
CBHW021435310726
48971CB00005B/1373